Stacey Fidler lives in a small village in Cambridgeshire. Originally from Kent, she was born in Margate but grew up in Ramsgate where she visits often. Married to Chris she has two sons who are her world. Adam who is twenty-one and Todd who is thirteen years old mean everything to her.

In September 2009 she was diagnosed with breast cancer and had to have chemotherapy and radio therapy.

She has been given the all clear!

ELIZABETH OAKENDALE

Stacey Fidler

ELIZABETH OAKENDALE

Vanguard Press

VANGUARD PAPERBACK

© Copyright 2010
Stacey Fidler

A CIP catalogue record for this title is
available from the British Library.

ISBN 978 184386 659 6

*Vanguard Press is an imprint of
Pegasus Elliot MacKenzie Publishers Ltd.*
www.pegasuspublishers.com

First Published in 2010

**Vanguard Press
Sheraton House Castle Park
Cambridge England**

Printed & Bound in Great Britain

CHAPTER ONE

Newcastle, 1840

It was a very cold winter's morning as Mary and her twin sister Beth arrived for their first day at work.

They had both been given jobs as maids.

As they walked towards the large house their feet crunched in the crisp snow, their noses and cheeks were red and they could hardly feel their fingers through the cold.

They both entered at the lower part of the house and the butler escorted them to the kitchen where they were given their duties for the day.

Beth was told to start by washing dishes, whilst Mary had to make tea for the master and his wife.

As Mary took the tray up the stairs towards the master's drawing room she became extremely nervous; she then knocked at the door and waited for a reply.

"Enter," said the master in a stern voice.

"Good morning, sir," said Mary as she entered the room.

She put down the tray on the table and poured out the tea, but she was so nervous she was shaking.

Although Mary and Beth were twins they were completely different from one another; Mary had dark hair and blue eyes, whilst Beth had red hair and green eyes. Mary was the quieter of the two whilst her sister Beth would often speak her mind.

Once Mary had delivered the master his tea she made her way back down to the kitchen where she was then told to polish the silver, whilst her sister peeled vegetables for lunch.

A short time later the bell rang for Mary to collect the master's used tea tray, so she left what she was doing and made her way back up to the drawing room. But as Mary picked up the tray she tripped, spilling what tea was left in the pot and this made the master furious.

"Clear that mess up at once, you stupid girl," he shouted.

Mary feeling rather embarrassed cleaned the tea up as quickly as possible, holding her head down as the tears filled her eyes. She then went back downstairs to finish off polishing the silver and then she had to clean out the fire grates, which was not a very pleasant job.

As the girls were kept very busy for most of the morning the time went rather quickly and it did not take long before lunchtime had arrived. Once again it was Mary who had to take the master his lunch and she was absolutely dreading facing him, after making such a fool of herself earlier that day. As she entered the room she could feel herself getting more and more nervous and what made things worse was that the master was rather hostile towards her.

"Pick your feet up this time, girl, as I do not want anymore accidents," he shouted.

"Yes, sir, sorry, sir," replied Mary in a softly spoken voice.

As she put the meal on the table another gentleman standing in the room looked at her and gave her a smile. His name was William, he was the master's son. Mary then left the room but as she left she heard a voice call to her.

"Excuse me, miss," he said.

Mary looked around and standing in the hallway was William.

"My father is rather scary isn't he?" he told her.

"Oh no, sir, it was my fault. I was a bit clumsy," replied Mary.

"Well I think you are doing an excellent job," said William.

"Thank you, sir" she replied.

Mary then went back downstairs to wash up the pots and pans and to finish other chores that she was given and by the end of the day both girls were extremely exhausted.

That evening the two girls walked home together to the small house that they shared with their parents in Newcastle. When they arrived home they were tired, cold and very hungry and they stood by the log fire to get warm whilst their mother prepared their dinner. After they had eaten they told their parents how their day had gone, but Mary felt quite disappointed in herself as she spoke about the accident that she had had that day and she certainly was not looking forward to going back there again the next day.

After a while had past the girls were looking and feeling extremely tired and were told to go to bed as they had an early start again the next morning, but Mary could not sleep very well as she was worrying about what the next day would bring. But lucky for her the next day went very well and she did not make any more mistakes.

As Mary scrubbed the doorstep she saw William again.

"Good afternoon," he said with a smile.

"Good afternoon, sir," she replied.

"I'm William. What is your name?" he asked.

"My name is Mary, sir," she told him.

"Is my father in a better mood with you today?" asked William.

"Yes thank you, sir," replied Mary.

"Good, he can be such an old grump at times," said William.

Mary did not answer she just gave a slight smile.

"I had better be going now but I hope to see you again soon," William told her.

As William walked away Mary smiled to herself; she thought how charming he was, unlike his father whom she thought was quite rude.

Nearing the end of the day Mary was asked to take some sandwiches up to the master as he had guests and as she entered the room the master made her feel extremely small in front of everyone.

"This is my new maid," he told his guests. "She is doing a rather good job when she isn't spilling tea everywhere."

With that everyone started to laugh and Mary could feel herself going red in her face with embarrassment.

"I think she has now learned from her mistakes, after all I gave her a jolly good talking to," said the master. "You may now be excused," he told her.

Mary left the room trembling with nerves and feeling as low as she could possibly feel and she could still hear him laughing about her from outside the door. So in temper Mary put her tongue out at him, not that he could see her because the door was now closed, but it made her feel a whole lot better.

"That's not very nice," said a voice.

Mary looked around and walking along the hallway was the master's son William.

"Sorry, sir," said Mary as she bowed her head in shame.

"That's alright, Mary, I've wanted to do that to him for years," he told her laughing.

Mary smiled back at William even though she was still feeling slightly embarrassed at being caught out.

Over the next few weeks Mary started to really enjoy her work and she enjoyed it even more when she did not have to see the master of the house. Mary and her sister Beth were given one afternoon off a week which they had to take on separate days, so they did not get much time to see each other, unless of course it was the time they spent working together.

One day on Mary's afternoon off she bumped into William as she walked home from work.

"Good afternoon, Mary. Are you going anywhere nice?" he asked.

"No, sir, I'm just on my way home," she replied.

"I'll walk with you. If that's alright by you?" said William.

"Yes that would be lovely," she told him.

As William walked Mary home they talked about any and everything and he joked with her about silly things which made her laugh and over the next few months they both became very good friends and often met up when it was Mary's afternoon off. But then one day something was about to change all of that, Mary was called in front of the master. As she entered the room Mary could instantly see that the master was not at all happy.

"How are you enjoying your work?" he asked.

"Yes I enjoy myself very much, sir," she replied.

"You have not got any problems at all?" asked the master.

"No, sir, everything is just fine, thank you, sir," replied Mary.

"Well you might not have any problems, young lady, but I have a big problem with you. I have been watching you very closely and you are becoming too friendly with my son William," he shouted.

"I'm sorry, sir," said Mary.

"Sorry is not good enough. You will not associate with my son anymore otherwise I will have no choice but to dismiss you from your duty here. Is that understood?" shouted the master.

"Yes, sir," replied Mary.

"Good, now get back to work," he told her.

Mary left the room in tears and when she arrived back inside the kitchen the cook noticed how upset she was, so she walked towards her to see what was wrong. Mary explained everything to her, from how friendly she and William had become, to why the master had put a stop to their friendship.

"Well, my dear, you are the maid and he is the master's son. You must know your place and stay right away from him," said the cook.

"But William is my friend," explained Mary.

"Friend or no friend you must stay away from him or you will be out of a job," said the cook.

Mary dried her tears and continued with the rest of her chores, but she was still feeling extremely upset and could not understand why the master was being so cruel to her.

The next day as Mary arrived at the house with her sister Beth she heard a voice call out her name; it was William.

"Hello, Mary," he said.

"Good morning, sir," she replied back.

She then quickly ran down the steps to the lower part of the house.

"Mary, wait. What's the rush?" he asked.

"Sir, I must not speak with you," said Mary. "It is the request of your father."

"What? My father has requested that you do not speak with me?" asked William.

"Yes, sir, he said that I will be dismissed if he sees us talking together again," replied Mary.

"It is your afternoon off today, isn't it?" asked William.

"Yes, sir," she replied.

"I will speak with you later then," he told her.

"But, sir," said Mary.

"No buts, I will speak with you later," said William.

He walked away looking rather angry, so Mary made her way into the house.

Later that afternoon Mary walked home alone, but she had only been home a short while when William knocked at the door.

"What are you doing here, sir?" she asked.

"I had to see you, Mary, and as I could not talk at my house I thought that I would come here to see you," he told her.

"But your father has forbidden me to speak to you," said Mary.

"Yes I realise that, but I want to see you and if it means that I have to come here without my father knowing then I shall have to do that," said William.

Mary had become very fond of William and she thought that his father was being very unreasonable for stopping them speaking to one another, so she agreed that William could come to her house to see her and after that day they met in secret once a week.

THREE MONTHS LATER

"Bye, Mum, don't forget I won't be home this afternoon as I have got to help cook the food for the master and his wife's anniversary party this evening," said Mary.

"Alright, dear, I'll see you both tonight," she told her daughters.

Everyone was busy rushing around trying to get everything just right for the master's anniversary party. But two of the staff had not arrived for work as they had influenza, which meant Mary not only had to work on her afternoon off, but she also had to help wait on the guests that evening as well.

As the big night arrived Mary gave out drinks to all the guests and she tried hard not to spill any of them as she knew she had to make a good impression for the master's special night.

"Hello, Mary," said William.

"Good evening, sir, I hope you have a lovely evening," Mary told him.

"I am already having a lovely evening because you are here," said William.

"Excuse me, sir I had better go and get some more drinks," said Mary.

"You are not blushing are you?" asked William.

"Stop it, sir, you will get me into a lot of trouble if your father catches you talking with me," said Mary.

William just laughed so Mary walked away from him even though she would have loved to have stood and spoken with him, but she knew the master would be angry if he saw them together.

As the evening went on things seemed to go very well; everyone was dancing and enjoying themselves and then the master gave a speech. He thanked all the guests that had made his night really special and of course his wife whom had been loyal to him over the years. Then William asked if he could also make a speech. He stood up in front of everyone and wished his parents well and everyone applauded as he made a toast to them both. Then William paused for a few seconds as he looked around the room.

"Get on with it, William, we haven't got all night," shouted his father.

"I would just like to make an announcement, Father," said William nervously. "I would really like it if you gave your blessing to the woman I want to marry."

"What on earth is going on, William? I never realised you had met a young lady," said his father.

"Yes I have and she is standing over there. Come here, Mary," William told her.

Mary stood as stiff as a board not knowing what to do next.

"Mary, come over here," said William once more.

Mary slowly walked towards William and she could see the anger on her master's face.

"What is the meaning of this?" shouted the master.

"I want to marry Mary," replied William.

"Over my dead body," said the master.

"I will marry Mary with or without your blessing," William told him.

Everyone gasped and looked shocked as William brought shame upon his family, but William could not see what he was doing wrong; all he wanted to do was be with the woman that he loved.

"I warned you to stay away from my son and you deliberately disobeyed me. Now get out, you are no longer wanted here," the master told Mary.

Mary turned and started to walk out of the room with everyone looking at her rather disgustingly.

"Mary, wait," shouted William. "If she goes then so do I," he told his father.

"If you walk out with that maid then you are no son of mine," said the master.

"Just as you wish," said William.

He then took Mary's arm and walked out of the room in front of everyone and out of his father's life for good.

"Are you sure about this, William?" asked Mary.

"I've never been more certain about anything ever before," replied William.

"But what about your inheritance?" said Mary.

"I don't need anything as long as I have you. That's if you'll have me, of course," said William.

"Yes, yes, of course I will," she told him.

Mary and William went back to Mary's parent's house where they stayed for the next few months until they eventually married. It was only a small wedding and only Mary's family attended and a few close friends, but that did not bother either of them as long as they had each other, which they did and Mary was now known as Mrs William Oakendale.

"Mary, I have something to show you," said William.

"What is it?" she asked.

"Come outside and you'll see," William told her.

Mary followed William outside and waiting for her was a horse and carriage.

"Get in. We're going on our honeymoon," said William.

"But we cannot afford this," said Mary.

"Yes we can. I had some savings which I have used so we can go to Yorkshire for a while," he told her.

Mary's face lit up and she hugged William all excitedly.

"I've never been on holiday before; in fact I have never been out of Newcastle," said Mary.

"Then what are we waiting for? Come on, let's get going," said William.

When they arrived in Yorkshire they were overwhelmed by the beautiful sight of the countryside and after being there for a week or so they did not want to leave.

"Maybe if I can find work here we might be able to stay on here more permanently," said William.

"Yes, I would really like that," Mary told him.

William still had a small amount of savings left but he knew that it would not last much longer, so he had no choice but to look for work if they were to stay on in Yorkshire. So he started asking around at different places but for a while he was unsuccessful, until eventually someone directed him to a large house that was looking for farmhands. The house belonged to a couple called Mr and Mrs Lockwood. They were very friendly and offered William work straight away and they even offered Mary work as a maid.

The Lockwoods had two young sons: Joseph who was the eldest and Ernest, who was only two years old. Mary often watched them play outside and hoped one day soon she would also have children of her own.

After living in Yorkshire for a few years Mary gave birth to her first son John; a year later she had another son William. She took her children to work with her as she needed to keep her job at the Lockwoods and when her eldest son John was three years old Mary had her third child, a daughter whom they named Elizabeth. Elizabeth was the image of her mother, with dark hair and big blue eyes and her parents doted on her, being that she was the youngest and the only daughter they had.

It was extremely difficult for Mary trying to raise three children and keep a job going as well, but she managed to do just fine and she even found time to make and sell jam to some of the locals in the area.

"Come on, children, let's get you into bed as it is getting late," said Mary.

"You sit down. I will put the children to bed," said William.

"I can't sit down, I still have cakes to bake for the fair tomorrow," said Mary.

"I am sure you can leave that until the morning, after all you have not got work at the Lockwoods' tomorrow," said William.

"Well I suppose I could leave them until the morning," said Mary.

"There is no supposing about it. Now go and sit down because you look exhausted," said William.

William took the children up to bed and tucked them in and by the time he came back downstairs a few minutes later Mary was fast asleep in the chair.

"Work, work, work, that's all you do, you'll wear yourself out," said William to himself.

He then covered Mary with a blanket and kissed her on her forehead, but she was so tired she did not even notice.

As the next few years passed things started to get a lot easier for Mary; the children were getting older and did not have to be watched all the time and they could play outside on warmer days whilst Mary did her chores at work.

The children would often stand and watch as the Lockwoods' two sons Joseph and Ernest went riding on their horses and when William and Mary had time off from work they would often take their children to the little stream, where they would sit for hours watching the ducks and swans. The children often fed bread to the ducks and swans and then they would run and scream as they got chased by them when they got too close and this made Mary and William laugh. They often had picnics up by the little stream as it was such a nice quiet place to just sit and relax and as they walked home they collected acorns, as they liked to throw them to see who could throw the furthest. Elizabeth being the youngest could never quite compete against her brothers; she would try hard to throw an acorn but they always beat her and she would get quite cross as they teased her.

"Play nicely, children," William told them.

But the boys would still tease poor Elizabeth.

When the boys were old enough William would take them to work on the farm with him, whilst Elizabeth being the youngest would still go to work with her mother at the Lockwoods' house. But the Lockwoods were very kind to Elizabeth; they would often give her books to read as William and Mary could not afford to buy any for their children and Elizabeth would spend hours learning how to read.

On Elizabeth's seventh birthday the Lockwoods gave her some oil paints. She was absolutely thrilled with them and could not wait to start learning how to paint. She was not very good at first but the more she practised the better she became. On the evening of Elizabeth's birthday she waited up for her father to return home from work and as he opened the door Elizabeth ran towards him all excitedly.

"Look, Father, I have some paintings to show you," she said looking pleased with herself.

"Well aren't they something," said William.

"Mr and Mrs Lockwood gave me some oil paints for my birthday. Aren't they kind?" said Elizabeth.

"Yes they are. You are a very lucky girl," William told her.

"Come on, Elizabeth, it's past your bedtime," called her mother.

"Oh do I have to go to bed yet?" asked Elizabeth.

"Yes you do," replied Mary.

Elizabeth then kissed her parents goodnight and reluctantly walked upstairs to bed.

"Elizabeth was so excited with her paintings, I just had to let her stay up a bit later to show you what she had done," said Mary.

"Yes she seemed very pleased with them, it was really nice of the Lockwoods to give her such a nice gift," said William.

That evening William and Mary sat down together and spoke about how their lives had changed so much and how lucky they were to have each other and three lovely children.

"Do you think you would change anything in your life if you could?" asked Mary.

William thought for a few minutes before he answered.

"Yes, actually, I would change one thing," he told her.

"What would that be?" asked Mary.

"I would change the fact that I did not run off with you sooner," replied William with a smile.

"You soppy old goat," she said as she kissed him.

CHAPTER TWO

One day whilst at the Lockwoods' Mary heard William calling her name, so she quickly came running out from the house.

"Quick, quick, get Elizabeth and come with me," said William.

Mary ran back into the house to get Elizabeth and as she came back outside William asked her to follow him. They walked up to the nearby stables and there on the stable floor was a foal that had just been born.

"Oh isn't he beautiful," said Mary.

The children had never seen a foal before; even the Lockwoods' two sons came inside the stable to have a look at their new addition.

"He's a bit wobbly," said John, the eldest son of William and Mary.

"Yes he is," said Elizabeth giggling.

They all stood watching as the foal tried to stand up and then it fell back down again.

"He's alright isn't he?" asked Elizabeth looking rather worried.

"Yes of course he is," replied Mary.

"What is his name?" asked William, the youngest son of William and Mary.

"I'm going to call him Admiral, as my parents said that I could have the next horse that is born," said Ernest Lockwood.

"Aren't you lucky to have your very own horse," said William Jr.

"Yes I am. But you can come and see him whenever you want," he told the children.

"Come on now, let's leave Admiral to have a little rest now," said Mary.

"Oh can't we stay a little bit longer?" asked Elizabeth.

"No because he needs to get some sleep now," replied Mary.

They all left Admiral in peace and went back to work again and Elizabeth sat down to do some reading, but she could not concentrate very well as all she kept thinking about was Admiral.

"Do you think Admiral is alright, Mother?" she asked.

"Yes, he will be fine, after all he has got his mother with him," replied Mary.

"When can I see him again?" asked Elizabeth.

"Maybe tomorrow," replied Mary.

"But that is ages away," cried Elizabeth.

Mary just looked at her daughter and smiled and then continued with her work.

At the end of the day when Mary had finished her work she called to Elizabeth to take her home, but Elizabeth did not answer. So she called again and again but still Elizabeth did not answer. Mary then left the house to see if Elizabeth was playing outside, but she was not anywhere to be seen. So she quickly went back inside the house and searched all of the rooms just in case Elizabeth was hiding somewhere, as she had done many times before.

"Elizabeth, where are you?" called Mary.

But there was still no answer and by this time Mary was beginning to panic. She then decided to go and find William to see if he had seen Elizabeth, but he had been busy working and had not seen his daughter.

"But where can she be then?" shouted Mary.

William and his sons left the work that they were doing to help look for Elizabeth and after a short time had passed William called to Mary to let her know he had found her. Mary came running towards William with a look of relief on her face.

"Where is she?" she asked.

"Take a look in there," said William.

Mary looked and there lying on the stable floor next to Admiral was Elizabeth; she was all curled up and fast asleep. William and Mary looked at each other and smiled, then Mary gently woke Elizabeth up to take her home.

Every day after that Elizabeth would go and visit Admiral and she would spend hours with him, just stroking him and talking to him.

One day whilst Elizabeth was at the stable with Admiral Ernest came inside.

"You here again?" he asked Elizabeth.

"Yes, I can't keep away he is so gorgeous," replied Elizabeth.

"Yes, he is," said Ernest.

"I wish I had my own horse," Elizabeth told him.

"You never know, maybe one day you will," said Ernest.

"No, that will never happen," she replied.

"I'm going for a ride on him in a minute, you can watch if you like," said Ernest.

"Yes, alright, I will," said Elizabeth.

Elizabeth had really grown to love horses and she used to love watching Ernest and his brother Joseph racing each other. She used to stand there watching and just imagine herself riding her very own horse.

One morning as Elizabeth walked up to the stables she could hear the sound of horses neighing and then she saw smoke coming out from the stables and realised that they were on fire. Elizabeth quickly ran back to the house to tell her mother.

"Come quickly, I think the stables are on fire," she shouted.

Mary left what she was doing and quickly ran out of the house and up towards the stables; she then called to William and her two sons to warn them. William came running across as fast as he could and he pulled open the stable doors and the horses came running out, all except Admiral.

"Where is Admiral?" screamed Elizabeth.

The smoke was too thick and billowing to see him, so Elizabeth not thinking ran into the stable to rescue him.

"Elizabeth, no!" screamed her mother Mary.

But it was too late, Elizabeth was already inside the burning stable, so her father William ran in after her but he could hardly see with all the black smoke.

"Look," shouted John. "There is Admiral," he said as he came running out.

"But where are William and Elizabeth? They haven't come out yet," screamed Mary.

Mary and her two sons were shouting and screaming for them to come out, and then John decided to go and find them. But by now Mary was hysterical. Not only was her husband in the burning stables but two of her children as well.

After a few minutes had passed which seemed more like hours, William came running out from the stables with Elizabeth in his arms; he laid her on the floor and thankfully she was not hurt, just dirty through the smoke.

"Where is John?" shouted Mary.

"I thought he was with you," said William.

"No, he went into the stables to look for you and Elizabeth," Mary told him.

William rushed back towards the stables but was beaten back by the flames; by this time the Lockwoods and their sons had also arrived to help.

"Quick hurry, William," shouted Mary.

The Lockwood sons realised that the fire was just too out of control to save John, so they grabbed hold of William to stop him from trying to get back inside. All they could do was watch as the stables burnt to the ground.

Mary stood screaming as she fell to the ground in despair; she felt as if her whole world had fallen apart within a matter of minutes.

"My baby, my baby," she cried.

But there was nothing anyone could have done to have saved John; the stables were literally burnt to the ground like torn pieces of paper.

Mrs Lockwood took the children inside the house whilst Mr Lockwood arranged for a carriage to take them all home.

"Come inside and have a brandy," said Mr Lockwood. "Your carriage will be here shortly to take you home," he told them.

Mary was shaking and screaming still whilst William stayed silent; he was too shocked to say anything and in another room the children were sitting hugging each other, sobbing their hearts out.

"I am so terribly sorry this has happened and I would like you to know that you can have as much time off from work as you need, with pay of course," said Mr Lockwood.

"Thank you," said William.

When they arrived home the children went upstairs to their rooms, whilst William put a blanket around Mary to keep her warm as she was still in shock.

"Why did this have to happen? Why?" repeated Mary.

"I don't know," replied William, trying to be strong.

He then knelt down on the floor in front of Mary and put his arms around her, but as she sobbed more and more it was too hard for William to control his feelings and he also broke down in tears. Elizabeth who was upstairs could hear her parents crying so she came downstairs.

"It's my fault that John is dead. Isn't it?" said Elizabeth.

"No it was a terrible accident," William told her. "Don't ever blame yourself."

"But he only went into the stable to help us. If I hadn't of gone in there none of this would have happened," said Elizabeth.

"It could have quite easily have been you when you tried to save Admiral," said William.

"But it wasn't, it was John. Wasn't it?" said Elizabeth.

"Yes, I know, so you should think yourself lucky you are still here," he told her. "Now let's get you tucked up in bed."

Elizabeth lay awake all night just thinking about her brother John; she felt as though she had caused his death and felt sick with guilt.

The next morning whilst everyone was downstairs talking about John, Elizabeth just sat alone in her room; she was absolutely devastated and did not want to face anyone.

Later that day Mr Lockwood paid them a visit; he told them that the fire had been started deliberately as there was a strong smell of petrol from what was left of the stable.

"But who would do such a thing?" asked William.

"That, my friend, remains a mystery because I do not know of anyone that has a grudge against me or my family," replied Mr Lockwood.

"Well I just hope they catch whoever did this before I get my hands on them," said William.

"Yes I can quite understand how you feel," said Mr Lockwood.

"Would you like a cup of tea whilst you are here?" asked Mary.

"No thank you, I do not want to impose upon you, but there is something that I would like to ask you both," said Mr Lockwood. "I know it's not my place but I would like to pay all the expenses for the funeral costs. Only I do feel rather guilty about John's death, being that it happened whilst he was on my premises," said Mr Lockwood.

"You do not have to feel guilty about anything; it could have happened to anyone," William told him.

"Nevertheless, I still feel that I would like to help," said Mr Lockwood.

"That is most thoughtful of you, thank you," said Mary.

"You do not have to thank me, it's the least I can do," said Mr Lockwood. "I will make all the necessary arrangements."

William Jr sat on the chair just listening to Mr Lockwood and his parents talking; he could not take everything in that had happened to his brother and he just sat in silence. William had been extremely close to his brother; they did everything together and William was going to miss him terribly.

"If there is anything else I can do for you both you only have to ask," said Mr Lockwood.

"Thank you but you have done more than enough for us already," said William.

"How are the children coping?" asked Mr Lockwood.

"Well William is very quiet which is understandable, but Elizabeth won't even come out of her room as she is blaming herself for John's death," replied William.

"Just give them a bit of time, after all it's been quite a shock for them losing someone so close," Mr Lockwood told them.

"Yes, it's a shock to us all," replied William.

The next few days did not get any better for the Oakendales; William Jr was still very quiet, Elizabeth still stayed alone in her room and Mary sobbed bitterly most of the time. The only person that was trying to hold things together was William; he was trying to be strong for everyone, but deep inside of him was a terrible pain of loss.

On the day of the funeral William and Mary stood arm in arm at the graveside; it was a very emotional time for everyone and many people attended to pay their respects to John.

"Father, why did God take John away from us? After all he was a good person," asked Elizabeth as she walked with her father.

"When family or friends are taken from us either from sickness or accidents everyone asks the same question, but nobody knows the answer," replied William.

Everyone went back to the house and had a drink to toast the life of John, but William Jr sat outside alone thinking about his brother.

Later that evening William called to his children to come outside with him; he then told them to look up at the stars. He then pointed to the brightest star that he could see in the sky and told them it was John watching over them. The children's faces lit up as they now felt that John was still with them; all they had to do was look up into the sky and there he was and this made a whole lot of difference to how they coped with the death of their brother.

As the next few weeks passed William and Mary decided it was now time for them to return to work, but it was quite upsetting for them as they first walked into the grounds of the Lockwoods'. As they walked towards the house they looked over towards the stable where John had tragically died and they noticed that the stables were already starting to be rebuilt. Mr and Mrs Lockwood came out from their house to welcome William and Mary back and they were asked to join them for a cup of tea.

"How are you both feeling now?" asked Mr Lockwood.

"It's been a very tough few weeks, sir, but we are coping well; it is the children we are more worried about. They are still very quiet and hardly talk about John anymore," said William.

"Yes, they are very quiet still," said Mary.

"Well maybe I can cheer them up later as I have some pigs being brought here this afternoon and I was hoping that you and William could make a pen for them before they arrive," said Mr Lockwood.

"Yes alright, I'll go and tell William as soon as I have finished drinking my tea," said William.

Whilst William and his son built the pigpen Elizabeth sat quietly in the garden painting a picture with her oil paints.

When the pigs finally arrived the children started to get excited.

"Look, William," Elizabeth called to her brother. "There is a mother and a father pig."

But as she said that following behind were two piglets. William and his father put the pigs inside the pen that they had built earlier.

"Can we name them?" asked Elizabeth.

"Yes, I suppose so," replied her father.

"I'll name the mother and father, you can name the piglets," said William.

"Alright, I'm going to call them Teeny and Tiny," said Elizabeth smiling.

"I think I'll call the other two Percy and Petal," said William.

Elizabeth and William watched as the pigs ran around the pen and rolled around in the mud. Then Mr Lockwood came outside to see them.

"Would you like to feed them?" he asked the children.

"Yes please," they replied.

Mr Lockwood gave the children some food for the pigs, but he warned them to be careful not to get dirty. William Jr opened the gate of the pen and the children went inside and started to feed the pigs and they both giggled as they watched the pigs snuffle down the food and grunt as they ate. Then William suddenly realized that the gate had not been shut properly.

"Quick, Elizabeth shut the gate," he told her, as she was the nearest.

Elizabeth ran to shut the gate before the pigs had time to get out, but as she ran she slipped and went face down in the mud. William had seen what had happened so he quickly ran and shut the gate and then helped Elizabeth up. But as he helped his sister up, he could not stop laughing because she was covered in mud. Mr Lockwood had seen what had happened through his window and he came outside and started to laugh as well.

"Oh, Elizabeth, you had better go and find your mother; she will have to take you home and get you cleaned up," he told her.

Elizabeth waited outside the house whilst her brother went and found their mother; he then explained to her what had happened and she followed him outside. When Mary saw the state of her daughter she also burst out laughing.

"It's not funny, I stink," said Elizabeth.

But that made Mary laugh even more. She then took her daughter home to get washed and changed and then she walked back with Elizabeth to the Lockwoods' house to finish her chores.

Elizabeth could not wait to get back to the pigpen again, but her mother told her to be more careful this time. As the children played and laughed at the pigs, Mr Lockwood was watching them through the window and he smiled to himself as he was pleased to see the children smiling once more.

A few days later Mr Lockwood asked William how the children were coping without John and William told him that they were fine when they were at work as they had things to occupy them, but they seemed to go very quiet whilst at home, as it was then they seemed to miss John the most.

"Umm, maybe I can help," said Mr Lockwood.

"What do you mean?" asked William.

"Just leave it to me and I'll see what I can do," he told William.

William just looked puzzled as he did not have a clue as to what Mr Lockwood was talking about.

Later that evening there was a knock at the door, so William got up and answered it. It was Mr Lockwood.

"Hello, sir. What are you doing here?" asked William.

"Could I come in for a few minutes?" he asked.

"Yes, of course, please do," replied William.

Mr Lockwood walked into the house and looked straight at Elizabeth and William.

"Is this the house where William and Elizabeth Oakendale live?" he asked the children.

"Yes, you know it is," giggled Elizabeth.

"Then I guess this belongs to you," said Mr Lockwood, as he pulled out a black puppy from inside of his coat.

"Oh look, a puppy," shouted Elizabeth.

"You can have him on two conditions; one that you take him for walks and the other is if your parents do not object," said Mr Lockwood.

"We will take him for walks," said the children. "Please can we keep him?" they begged their parents.

"I guess we have another mouth to feed then," said William smiling.

"Oh thank you," said Elizabeth as she hugged her father.

"It's not me you should be thanking," he told her.

"Thank you, Mr Lockwood," said Elizabeth.

"Yes, thank you very much," said William.

"You just make sure you look after him," Mr Lockwood told them.

"We will," they shouted.

As William saw Mr Lockwood to the door he thanked him again.

"Maybe having a puppy around will make a lot of difference to the children," said Mr Lockwood.

"Yes, I think you might be right," said William.

"Oh I almost forgot, here are some apples for the children from my wife," said Mr Lockwood.

"Thank you," said William.

After Mr Lockwood had left William walked back into the room and he could see such a difference in the children as they played with their new puppy.

"Here is an apple each for you both from Mrs Lockwood, but you'll have to go and wash your hands first," William told them.

The children did as they were asked then they both sat down to eat their apples, but the puppy kept jumping up at them, so William gave him a piece of his apple.

"Look, he likes this," said William.

"Yes, I expect he does, but do not give him too much as you might give him a stomach ache," said Mary.

William then ate most of his apple and gave the core to the puppy.

"Look, he might like the apple but he certainly doesn't like the pips; he's spat them out," said William.

"That's what we could call him," said Elizabeth.

"What?" asked William?

"Pip, of course, silly," replied Elizabeth.

"Yes, I like that," said William.

"Well I think it's about time you two got ready for bed and let Pip get some sleep, poor little thing looks worn out," said Mary.

When the children went upstairs Pip tried to follow them and this made the children laugh.

"No, Pip, your place is down here," Mary told him.

She then put a blanket on the floor for him to lie on. William and Mary sat together watching Pip as he rolled around and found his way about the house and before they went to bed they took him out into the garden, but being as he was so small they could hardly see him in the dark.

Mary was up quite early the next morning as Pip had kept her awake most of the night whimpering, so she decided she might as well go into work a bit earlier with her husband.

When Mary arrived at work everything was quiet, so she assumed the Lockwoods were still in bed. But then she heard a strange moaning noise, so she walked out into the hallway to see what it was and lying at the bottom of the stairs was Mr Lockwood. He had a bad cut on his head and was bleeding and he kept asking for his wife.

"Lie still, Mr Lockwood, I am just going to get William so that he can help you up on to a chair," Mary told him.

Mary ran out of the house as fast as she could and called to William to come straight away. William ran back with her to the house and saw Mr Lockwood lying injured on the floor.

"What has happened?" he asked.

"I don't know. I think he has fallen downstairs," replied Mary.

William lifted Mr Lockwood up on to a chair and he bathed his head which was cut quite bad.

"My wife, you have got to help my wife," said Mr Lockwood.

William and Mary just looked at each other. Realising that this was no accident Mary stayed with Mr Lockwood whilst William searched for his wife.

Mrs Lockwood was eventually found tied up with her two sons in the library.

"It was the McClean brothers," she kept saying.

The McClean brothers had broken into the Lockwoods' house in the early hours of the morning, but had been disturbed by Mr Lockwood. But before he could do anything he was hit over the head knocking him down the stairs. They then tied up Mrs Lockwood with her sons to stop her from reporting the break-in, which gave them enough time to get away.

"It was them that started the stable fire," said Mrs Lockwood.

"How do you know that?" asked William.

"I heard one of the brothers talking; he said that my husband should have given him a job when he asked for one, then none of this would have happened.

Mrs Lockwood and her sons Ernest and Joseph were not hurt in any way, but were quite shaken by their ordeal.

Once the police were called it was not long before a massive search was on to find the McClean brothers. Mrs Lockwood looked over her house accompanied by the police to see if any valuables had been taken and it was then that she noticed some silver was missing and also Mr Lockwood's rifle. Mrs Lockwood warned the police that they were armed and she was extremely worried about what they would do next. The police left the Lockwoods' house soon after taking statements and the search was on to find the brothers.

A few hours later the brothers were eventually found in a nearby barn, but they had a family held hostage in the barn with them. Armed police surrounded the barn and the brothers were told to come out with their arms up. After about an hour the hostages started to come out one by one, and then the eldest brother appeared to come out.

But the youngest brother started to fire shots at the police, so they had no choice but to shoot back and they shot the eldest brother, killing him instantly. Within seconds of that happening the youngest brother ran out of the barn and fired shots at the police again, but he was also shot dead. Hearing the news that the McClean brothers were dead the local people started to cheer; they had always had a bad reputation and caused a lot of trouble wherever they went. When the Lockwoods heard the news that the brothers were dead they were quite relieved that it was all over and they could now get back to normal with their lives.

As a reward for William and Mary's kindness in helping the Lockwoods they gave them a pouch of money. William tried hard to refuse the money as he only did what anyone would have done under those circumstances, but the Lockwoods persuaded them to take it. So they decided to use the money to travel back to Newcastle to visit Mary's parents, as she had not seen them or her sister since just after she married William, and Mary's parents had never even met their grandchildren.

CHAPTER THREE

"Hurry up, children, the carriage is here," their mother told them.

"I'm just coming, I'm trying to get hold of Pip," said Elizabeth.

"You get in the carriage whilst I get the dog," said her father.

Once they were all inside the carriage they set off on their long journey back to Newcastle.

"It's a long way isn't it?" said Elizabeth a while later.

"Yes it is. But we have still got a long way to go yet," her mother told her.

"In a little while we will stop to stretch our legs and then Pip can have a run around as well," said William.

"But I'm bored," said Elizabeth.

"How can you be bored? Just take a look at that beautiful countryside," said Mary.

Elizabeth just raised her eyebrows then leaned on her brother William and fell asleep.

When they did finally arrive in Newcastle Mary's father had the shock of his life when he opened the door and saw his daughter Mary standing there.

"Well, well. Look who it is," he told his wife.

Mary's mother came out from the kitchen to see who was at the door and she burst into tears when she saw Mary.

"Oh my goodness me. Come in, come in," she told them.

"You must be tired out," said Mary's father.

"Yes and thirsty," replied William.

"I'll make us all a pot of tea," said Mary's mother.

"Whom may I ask are this handsome pair?" asked Mary's father as he looked at his grandchildren for the first time.

"I'm Elizabeth," she replied.

"And I'm William," he told his grandfather.

"Good looking and polite, they must take after me," said Mary's father smiling.

William and Mary laughed then Mary started to look around the room, recognizing things she had not seen for many years. Not a lot had changed in the house since Mary had moved away, but a lot of other things had changed. For instance, Mary's twin sister Beth was now married and had two children of her own and William was told the dreadful news that both his parents had since passed away. William was quite upset to hear the news about his mother's death, but as for his father he still had not forgiven him for the way he had treated Mary in the past.

"Your father passed away first and within a few months your mother went. I do not think she could live without him," said Mary's mother.

"How my mother could have loved a miserable old beggar like that I'll never know," said William.

"Oh, William, you shouldn't speak about your father like that," said Mary's mother.

"Well it's true," replied William.

"But you should never speak ill of the dead," Mary's mother told him.

Mary then started to speak to her parents about her son John and how he died tragically in the stable fire.

"That must have been terrible for you all," said Mary's mother.

"Yes, it was. It's taken us along time to get over it," said William.

"It's such a shame we did not get to meet him," said Mary's father.

"Yes, I know he would have loved to have been here today," said Mary.

"Grandma, do you know I like painting pictures with oil paints?" said Elizabeth.

"Do you really? You must be very talented," her grandmother told her.

"I was not very good when I first started painting, but now I can paint very well," said Elizabeth looking pleased with herself.

"You have two beautiful children. You must be extremely proud of them," said Mary's father.

"Yes we are," replied William.

"And who is this?" asked Mary's father as he looked down at their dog.

"Oh that's Pip, he was given to us by Mr Lockwood," replied Elizabeth.

"Mr and Mrs Lockwood are the people we work for, but they are more like friends than our employers," William told them.

"I'm so pleased everything has turned out so good for you all. After all, it must have been quite hard for you, William, giving up everything to be with my daughter," said Mary's mother.

"Money does not mean anything to me. As long as I have the love from my family I am happy," said William.

"You chose a good one there, Mary," her father told her.

"Yes I did," she replied.

"Mother, I'm tired," said William.

"Come with me, I'll show you upstairs," said Mary's mother.

But as Mary's mother got up from her chair she quickly held her leg as if in pain.

"Are you alright, Mother?" asked Mary.

"Yes, I'll be fine in a moment," she replied.

Mary looked at her father as if to ask what's wrong with her mother.

"I'm afraid your mother has got arthritis in her knees," said Mary's father.

"Oh that's awful. Is it very painful?" asked Mary.

"It can be sometimes," she replied. "But you know me, it will take more than this to stop me from getting around."

Once the children were in bed, the adults all sat down and chatted for hours about everything that had happened in their lives over the past years.

"Wait until Beth knows you are here, she will be so thrilled," said Mary's mother.

"Yes, hopefully we will see her tomorrow," said Mary.

"Well she usually calls in here first thing in the morning and she will have the shock of her life tomorrow when she sees you," said Mary's mother.

"Oh it's so good to see you both," Mary told her parents.

"Well it's been quite a while. Hasn't it?" said her father.

"Yes it has, it's been too long," replied Mary.

The next morning Mary got up early and cooked breakfast for everyone; she thought that maybe her mother deserved a rest, especially now that she had found out that she was suffering from arthritis.

"Ummm, something smells good," said Mary's father.

"He doesn't say that about my cooking," said Mary's mother smiling.

"I do not have a chance to say anything about your cooking, I'm too busy eating it," said Mary's father. "She is the best cook in the world you know," he told them.

"Of course I'm not," replied Mary's mother.

"Well you taught me all I know about cooking," said Mary.

After they had eaten breakfast Mary and her daughter Elizabeth washed the dishes, whilst William Jr took Pip outside and Mary's parents searched in the sideboard for some old photographs.

A short time later Mary's twin sister Beth arrived with her two daughters and as soon as she saw Mary she just screamed with delight.

"Oh, Mary, come and sit down. We have got so much to talk about," said Beth, beaming with happiness.

Later that day they all sat in the garden drinking tea and talking about old times and it brought back so many happy memories for Mary.

Mary and William stayed in Newcastle for the next two weeks, but then the day arrived when it was time to leave to travel back to Yorkshire.

"I do not want to go home, I want to stay here with Grandma and Grandpa," said Elizabeth.

"You have to come home with us," said Mary.

"Why? You said yourself Grandma could do with some help around the house now that she has got arthritis," said Elizabeth.

"We have only just got enough money to get home. If we leave you here we will not be able to afford to get you back," said Mary.

"I don't mind. I want to stay here and then I'll have time to show Grandma and Grandpa how good I am at oil painting," said Elizabeth.

Mary looked at William not knowing what to do.

"It is not up to me," William told her.

"Oh let her stay; then we can get to know each other better," said Mary's mother.

"But it is not fair on your brother, William. You know he will not be able to stay here as well because the Lockwoods need him to help on their farm," Mary told Elizabeth.

"Oh I don't mind. Let Elizabeth stay here, I will get some peace then," said William Jr smiling.

"Oh thank you very much," said Elizabeth sarcastically.

"Well at least William did not argue about it, not like Beth's two daughters; they are always arguing," said Mary's mother.

"Please can I stay?" begged Elizabeth.

"Only if your grandparents are in agreement," her father told her.

"Of course you can stay with us," said Mary's mother.

"That's settled then," said Mary's father.

"Oh thank you, I promise I'll be really good," Elizabeth told her parents.

"We had better get going now," said William.

They all said their goodbyes, then Mary, William and William Jr went on their long journey back to Yorkshire.

"I'm so pleased you let me stay here with you. Is there anything you would like me to help you with?" Elizabeth asked her grandmother.

"Yes, actually there is. I was just about to bake some bread. Would you like to help me make it?" she asked.

"Oh, yes please," replied Elizabeth.

Elizabeth spent the morning helping her grandmother in the kitchen and she even helped to make a lovely vegetable stew for dinner.

"Ummm, this stew is delicious, good cooks must run in the family," said Elizabeth's grandfather.

"Wait until you taste the steamed jam pudding we have made," Elizabeth told him.

"I had better save some room for that then," said her grandfather smiling.

"He likes his food, dear, as you can tell," said her grandmother.

Elizabeth just laughed and continued to eat up her dinner.

As the next few weeks passed Elizabeth had settled in with her grandparents extremely well and, although she missed her parents and brother very much, she still had no intention of returning to Yorkshire, not that she could even if she wanted to.

"I'm going to do some painting today. Is that alright by you?" Elizabeth asked her grandmother.

"Of course, dear, you go ahead," she told her.

Elizabeth walked outside and decided to paint a picture of the flowers that were in the garden. She knew how much her grandmother loved the flowers, so she wanted to paint the picture for her as a gift. As Elizabeth started to mix the colours together she noticed a young girl standing by the gate watching her.

"Hello," said Elizabeth.

But the girl did not answer her; she just ran away. Then a short time later the young girl appeared at the gate again.

"Hello, my name is Elizabeth. What is your name?" she asked.

But the girl still did not answer so Elizabeth walked towards her, but the girl ran away again. So Elizabeth went indoors to see her grandmother to find out who the girl was.

"All I know about her is that her parents are extremely strict and they will not allow her to associate with any other children," her grandmother told her.

"Why ever not?" asked Elizabeth.

"I heard she was bullied by some children once so her father stopped her from having friends altogether," replied her grandmother.

"That's a bit unfair, isn't it?" said Elizabeth.

"Well her father makes the rules so it is not for us to interfere," said her grandmother.

Elizabeth then went back outside to do some more painting, but she did not see the young girl again that day. However, a few days later the girl stood by the gate again, but this time Elizabeth did not say anything to her as she did not want to frighten her away again. Elizabeth just continued with her painting and made out she had not seen the girl. After some time had passed Elizabeth stood back slightly to admire her painting, even though it was not quite finished.

"You are very clever. Aren't you?" said the girl.

"Thank you," replied Elizabeth.

"My name is Emily. I'm not really supposed to be talking to you," she told Elizabeth.

"Well I won't tell if you won't," said Elizabeth with a smile. "Would you like to come in the garden and watch me paint?" she asked Emily.

"No I had better not because if my father catches me he will be really angry," replied Emily.

"Why?" asked Elizabeth.

"He just will. That's all," said Emily rather abruptly. "Anyway I had better be going now," she said.

"Maybe I will see you again tomorrow," said Elizabeth.

"Yes, I would like that," replied Emily, as she quickly hurried away.

Elizabeth could not understand why Emily's father was being so strict. *Yes she was bullied but not all children are nasty and cruel*, she thought.

The next day Elizabeth took her painting outside again but she did not see Emily. *Maybe Emily's father saw us talking together yesterday and now she is being made to stay indoors*, thought Elizabeth.

Later that afternoon whilst Elizabeth and her grandmother were having a cup of tea there was a loud knock at the door. Elizabeth went all hot and started to panic, as she thought it was probably Emily's father come to tell her to stay away from his daughter. But it was not Emily's father, it was Emily.

"Quick, you have to come with me; it's my ma she is having the bairn," shouted Emily.

"Where is your father?" asked Elizabeth's grandmother.

"He is at work. Please come quick, she is in a lot of pain," cried Emily.

Elizabeth and her grandmother quickly followed Emily back to her house and they could hear Emily's mother screaming before they even entered the house.

"Get some fresh linen for me and I'll check on your mother," Elizabeth's grandmother told Emily.

She then walked into the bedroom to see how far in labour Emily's mother was.

"My goodness, you have not got much further to go. I can see the head already," said Elizabeth's grandmother.

"Please just help me get it out," cried Emily's mother.

"Come on, let's have some big pushes from you and it will soon be all over," Elizabeth's grandmother told her.

"I can't I'm too tired," said Emily's mother.

"Nonsense, you can do it, now push," said Elizabeth's grandmother.

"Aaaaaaaaah," she screamed as she pushed as hard as she could.

"Come on, just a little bit more," said Elizabeth's grandmother.

Emily's mother pushed again and at last the baby was born.

"You have another daughter," Elizabeth's grandmother told her.

"Oh thank you," said Emily's mother as she wept tears of joy.

"I'll just clean the bairn up and then you can hold her," said Elizabeth's grandmother.

Elizabeth and Emily heard the baby cry so they rushed into the bedroom.

"Oh look, I've never seen anything so tiny," said Elizabeth.

"It's a girl," said Emily's mother.

Elizabeth's grandmother cleaned the baby then wrapped her in a blanket and gave her to Emily's mother to hold.

"What are you going to call her?" asked Elizabeth.

"We decided if it was a girl we would call her Eve, that way both of our daughters' names begin with the letter E," replied Emily's mother.

"Can I hold her, Mother?" asked Emily.

"Of course, but mind her head as you hold her," she told Emily.

They all stood admiring baby Eve for a while, then Emily's father returned home.

"Father, it's Mother, she has had the bairn," shouted Emily.

Emily's father rushed upstairs and into the bedroom and he looked shocked as he saw his newborn daughter.

"This kind lady helped me give birth, I don't know what I would have done without her," Emily's mother told him.

Emily's father looked at Elizabeth's grandmother and smiled at her.

"Thank you," he said.

"You are very welcome," she told him. "We had better be going now, Elizabeth, as mother and bairn need their rest," said Elizabeth's grandmother.

"Congratulations on the bairn," said Elizabeth as she left the bedroom.

As they both walked back home all Elizabeth could talk about was the baby and how tiny she was.

"If you had come into the room a minute earlier you would have seen her be born," said her grandmother.

"I always seem to get there too late," said Elizabeth.

"Why do you say that?" asked her grandmother.

"Well even when I was a lot younger my friend Ernest had a foal born whom he named Admiral and although I saw it when it had just been born, I didn't actually see the birth," replied Elizabeth.

"Oh I'm sure one day you will eventually see the real thing," her grandmother told her.

The next day to Elizabeth's surprise Emily knocked at the door.

"My parents sent me here to say thank you again for helping my mother and my father has now allowed me to spend time around here with you," she told Elizabeth.

"Oh that's good," said Elizabeth's grandmother.

"It has taken my father a long time to trust anyone since I was bullied," said Emily.

"Why anyone would want to bully you I'll never know, you are a lovely girl and yet some people can be so cruel," said Elizabeth's grandmother.

Emily had long blonde hair but she was not the prettiest of girls, rather a plain Jane type and this was why she used to be bullied by other children; and yet she had a nice side to her that others did not always get the chance to see.

"Come inside, Emily don't stand there on the doorstep," Elizabeth's grandmother told her.

. "My grandma and I have just made some biscuits. Would you like to try one?" asked Elizabeth.

"Only if that is alright," replied Emily.

"Of course it is, help yourself," said Elizabeth's grandmother.

Emily took one of the biscuits then sat down on a chair. She was even polite enough to hold her hand open to catch any crumbs that almost fell on to the floor.

"How are your mother and bairn?" asked Elizabeth's grandmother.

"They are both very well, thank you," replied Emily.

"Maybe in a few days I will be able to visit her as I would love to see Eve again," said Elizabeth.

"Yes maybe, but I will have to ask my mother first to see if that is alright by her," said Emily.

"Yes, of course," said Elizabeth.

The two girls sat talking for a while then they went outside so Elizabeth could finish her oil painting.

"Why do you live with your grandparents? Are your parents dead?" asked Emily.

"No, of course not, my parents live in Yorkshire but when we came here for a holiday I decided I wanted to stay on here for a while," replied Elizabeth.

"You are so lucky, my parents would have never allowed me to do something like that," Emily told her.

"Yes, I suppose I am, I have really lovely parents," said Elizabeth.

As the girls spoke and laughed together Elizabeth's grandmother watched from the window; she was really pleased that Elizabeth had found a friend of her own age and she was also happy that Emily's parents trusted Elizabeth enough to let Emily come round and make a friend at last.

Over the next few months Elizabeth and Emily became very close friends and they saw each other every day. Elizabeth's grandmother taught them both how to sew and Elizabeth started to teach Emily how to read and write as she was not very good. They even both helped Emily's mother with chores as it was not easy for her having a young baby to look after.

One day when Emily arrived to see Elizabeth, Elizabeth got very excited.

"Look, I have almost finished this portrait of my grandparents, but don't tell them as it is a surprise," said Elizabeth.

"But surely they must know, because I thought you had to sit when you have a portrait painted," said Emily.

"No, because I have used some of these old photographs to get a good likeness of them both and some of it just comes from memory," said Elizabeth.

"That is really good. You are so talented, not like me, I cannot do anything," said Emily.

"How can you say that? Of course you are talented. Over the last few months you have learnt to read and write, my grandmother has taught you how to sew and you have even learnt how to cook and you could not do any of those things when I first met you," Elizabeth told her.

"Yes, but those are everyday things that I should have been able to do anyway. I haven't got any other talents like you have. I have not even got the looks that you have got," said Emily.

"But you have, you just lack confidence," Elizabeth told her.

"Take my word for it, Elizabeth, I'm a nobody," she said.

Elizabeth did not know what to say to her friend, but it was obvious that since Emily had been bullied years before it had made her very bad impact on how she saw herself. She did not have any friends apart from Elizabeth and she was feeling very low about her appearance, which made her lack confidence and start to feel that she had nothing good going for her. Then one day Elizabeth had an idea that might help Emily gain confidence in herself. She asked her how she felt about going to find employment together; that way Emily would not only be doing something to occupy herself, but she would also be associating with other people which might get her confidence back. But when she put it to Emily she started to get rather suspicious.

"Why on earth do you want to go and find employment?" she asked.

"Well I cannot live off of my grandparents forever and the extra money would come in very useful," replied Elizabeth.

"But why do you want me to come with you?" asked Emily.

"I just thought it would be good for us to both get employment together, otherwise we will not see each other as often as we do now," replied Elizabeth, thinking rather quickly.

"Oh, I don't know," said Emily.

"Come on, it will be good for us and I'm sure your parents could do with some extra money coming in each week," Elizabeth told her.

"Oh alright," said Emily, rather reluctantly.

"Good, we'll start looking tomorrow. Shall we?" said Elizabeth.

Emily just looked at Elizabeth and curled her lip up in disapproval. But the following day they went together to look for employment. The first place they went to was a bakery shop which had an advertisement in the window looking for staff, but they were only looking for one person to employ and as Elizabeth and Emily wanted to work together they decided not to bother. The next place they went to was a large house where they were looking for cleaners, but Emily was not keen on doing cleaning for a living, so Elizabeth also refused to go there.

"Well I don't know where else we can go because we do not have any experience to do anything else," said Elizabeth.

"Maybe we should just forget about working then," said Emily.

"Don't be silly, we have to find work eventually, so now is as good time as any," Elizabeth told her.

Elizabeth's grandfather overheard the two girls talking so he told them about a place that was looking for staff.

"Flagerty's are looking for seamstresses if you are interested," he told the girls.

"Where is that?" asked Elizabeth.

46

"It is in that huge factory down by the mill," replied her grandfather.

"Well it is worth a try. What do you think?" she asked Emily.

"I suppose that is better than cleaning and we already know how to sew, so yes, let's go down there and see what they say," said Emily.

The next morning both girls took a walk down to Flagerty's factory and were lucky enough to both get employment as there were two vacancies left.

"You can both start first thing in the morning and do not be late otherwise you will have some of your pay deducted," said Mr Flagerty.

"Thank you, sir," said Elizabeth as she left the building.

"That Mr Flagerty is a miserable old so 'n' so, isn't he?" said Emily.

"Well at least he gave us a job, which was kind of him," replied Elizabeth.

"Why are you always so nice about everything and everyone?" Emily asked her.

"Well it was kind of him to give us both work," said Elizabeth.

"You are too nice for your own good. Take it from me, people can be pretty nasty when they want to be. Do not trust anyone," Emily told her.

Elizabeth just raised her eyebrows at Emily and continued to walk back to her grandparents' house.

"Well how did it go at Flagerty's?" asked Elizabeth's grandfather.

"We start first thing tomorrow morning," replied Elizabeth.

"Good, just make sure you mind your manners because Mr Flagerty is not a man to be crossed," said her grandfather.

"I will, Grandpa, you have no worries there," replied Elizabeth.

The next day Elizabeth and Emily arrived for work bright and early and were introduced to the rest of the staff that worked at Flagerty's. Then they were shown what they had to do. Elizabeth and Emily were kept busy for the rest of the day and they were not allowed to even speak whilst they worked, apart from if they had a problem with what they were doing. As the bell rang at the end of the day Elizabeth was quite exhausted and was glad to be going home. But as the next few weeks passed Elizabeth did not feel so tired, as she had started to get used to her work and it just became routine to her.

FOUR YEARS LATER

One day as the girls were walking to work Emily started to point at a young man working at the mill nearby.

"Look at him, he is gorgeous," said Emily.

"Emily, it is rude to point," Elizabeth told her.

"Come on, let's go and say hello to him," said Emily.

"We have got to go to work. Or have you forgotten?" said Elizabeth.

"Oh we have got loads of time yet, come on," Emily told her.

The two girls then walked towards the mill and Emily started to whistle at the young man; he looked up and Emily started to giggle, so the young man smiled at them.

"Good morning, I have not seen you around here before," said Emily.

"No, you wouldn't have, I have not long moved to this area, I'm staying with my aunt," said the man.

"I'm Emily by the way and this is my friend Elizabeth. We are just on our way to work at Flagerty's," she told him.

"Yes and if we do not hurry up we are going to be late," said Elizabeth.

"My name is Freddie. I think your friend wants to go to work," he told Emily.

"Oh come on then, Elizabeth," said Emily. "Maybe we will see you again," she told Freddie.

"Yes, maybe you will," he said as he smiled.

"Oh my goodness, Elizabeth, I think he likes me," said Emily all excitedly.

"He does not even know you," Elizabeth told her.

"Oh stop being such an old misery guts, of course he likes me," said Emily.

Elizabeth just looked at Emily and shook her head slightly, as if to say you are raving mad. As the girls sat working that day all Emily kept doing was sitting grinning at Elizabeth and Elizabeth knew why she was grinning, because she knew Emily was still thinking about Freddie.

"Aaaaaaaaah," shouted Emily all of a sudden.

Everyone in the factory looked around to where Emily was sitting and noticed blood pouring from her finger.

"Quick, someone help me, the needle has gone through my finger!" she screamed.

Elizabeth rushed towards Emily but her finger was not as bad as it looked, although it was still very painful.

"If you were concentrating more on what you were doing, instead of thinking about Freddie, this would never have happened," said Elizabeth.

"Maybe it is a good thing that it happened, because Freddie might kiss it better now," said Emily.

"You are impossible," said Elizabeth as she bandaged Emily's finger. "Now get on with your work," she told her.

Every day after that whilst Elizabeth and Emily were walking to work, Emily would always go and have a quick chat with Freddie and poor Elizabeth had no choice but to go along with her.

By now Elizabeth had worked at Flagerty's for quite a number of years and whilst working she had managed to put some of the money that she had earned aside. She did not know what she was going to do with the money, but she knew it would come in handy for a rainy day.

But one day unexpectedly Elizabeth received a letter from her parents asking her to return home and she was told to use the money that she had saved for her fare. Elizabeth was devastated at the thought that she had to return to Yorkshire, as she had made a new life for herself in Newcastle. But her grandparents did explain to her that she knew her stay in Newcastle would not be permanent and that she had to return home as her parents missed her deeply.

"Yes, I understand that and I also miss them, but I do not want to leave you both and I will never find a friend like Emily again," explained Elizabeth.

"My dear, I know how you feel, but it is time for you to see your parents, after all they have missed quite a number of years of watching you grow up," said her grandmother.

"It does not look like I have got a lot of choice then. Does it?" said Elizabeth abruptly.

"It is for the best, you know it is," said her grandfather.

When Elizabeth spoke with Emily and told her the news that she had to return to Yorkshire Emily was just as devastated.

"But you are my only real friend," said Emily.

"That's nonsense, you have made lots of friends since working at Flagerty's," said Elizabeth.

"Yes, but not a true friend like you," she told Elizabeth.

"Well what about Freddie? He is your friend," said Elizabeth.

"But I never hardly see him, well only for a quick chat before I go into work and anyway you know as well as I do that he is too old for me," said Emily.

"I am really sorry, Emily, but I do not have any choice. I have to do what my parents ask and anyway we can still keep in touch," said Elizabeth.

"But it won't be the same. Will it?" said Emily.

"I know," replied Elizabeth.

A few days later Elizabeth gave her notice in at Flagerty's but had to work there for the rest of the week. She also arranged for Emily to spend an evening with her before she left and invited her for dinner.

"Oh, Elizabeth, you have only got two days left here," said Emily.

"Yes, I know, so stop reminding me," Elizabeth told her.

"Elizabeth, be a good girl and take your grandfather a nice cup of tea," said her grandmother.

"Where is he, Grandma?" asked Elizabeth.

"He is lying down upstairs as he felt a bit poorly earlier," replied her grandmother.

Elizabeth took the tea upstairs to her grandfather whilst Emily and Elizabeth's grandmother sat talking downstairs.

"Don't look so down, dear, you will see Elizabeth again one day," said Elizabeth's grandmother.

"I doubt that very much as neither of us have much money, so we are never going to be able to afford to travel to see one another," said Emily.

"Oh I'm sure you will," said Elizabeth's grandmother with a friendly smile.

"Grandma, it's Grandpa, he's not moving," shouted Elizabeth.

Elizabeth's grandmother rushed upstairs as fast as she could and, lying dead on the bed, was Elizabeth's grandfather, he had died from a stroke earlier that evening.

"It is no use trying to wake him, he has gone," cried Elizabeth's grandmother.

"But he can't have gone. I was only talking to him a few hours ago," shouted Elizabeth. "Wake up, Grandpa," she told him.

"It's too late, Elizabeth, he is not going to wake up," said Emily.

Elizabeth's parents were notified as soon as possible and Elizabeth used the money that she had saved to pay for her parents' travel expenses, so that they could return to Newcastle for the funeral. When they arrived they could hardly believe how much Elizabeth had changed; she had gone from a young girl into a beautiful young lady.

"My goodness, Elizabeth, just look at you," said her father.

Elizabeth hugged her parents and she wept as she spoke about how she had found her grandfather lying lifeless on the bed.

"That must have been awful for you," her mother told her.

"Where is young William?" asked Elizabeth's grandmother.

"He decided to stay in Yorkshire as there is quite a lot of work to do on the Lockwoods' farm. We did not think it was fair for all of us to up and leave when there was so much to do," said William.

"I was really looking forward to seeing him again," said Elizabeth's grandmother.

"Yes, so was I," said Elizabeth.

"Well you will see him soon enough, Elizabeth, when you travel back with us," her father told her.

"But I can't go back with you now, otherwise grandma will be left on her own," said Elizabeth.

"We'll talk about this after the funeral," her mother told her.

Elizabeth stayed silent not knowing what was to happen now, but she was hoping that her parents would change their minds and let her stay on in Newcastle.

After the funeral Elizabeth's parents made the arrangements to take them all back to Yorkshire, but Elizabeth begged them to let her stay with her grandmother so eventually they agreed.

CHAPTER FOUR

Once Elizabeth's parents had returned to Yorkshire, Elizabeth started to get quite down in the dumps, not just because they had left but because the house seemed rather empty now that her grandfather was no longer there. But a few weeks later things did start to get better for Elizabeth; she managed to get her job back at Flagerty's which took her mind off losing her grandfather and she still had Emily for companionship. But it was Elizabeth's grandmother who was now feeling the pressure. She would sit at home on her own whilst Elizabeth was at work and felt very alone most of the time. She could not even do a lot around the house anymore to keep herself occupied, as the arthritis that she had was now in her hands. Beth her other daughter still used to visit her every day, but she did not realise how down and lonely her mother was really feeling.

"Hello, Grandma, I'm home," said Elizabeth as she got in from work.

"Hello, dear. Did you have a good day?" asked her grandmother.

"Yes, I did as it happens. Jessica at work has invited a few of us for tea tonight as it is her birthday, so please do not do me anything to eat," replied Elizabeth.

"Well at least you are getting out a bit more," said her grandmother.

"I had better go and get washed and changed otherwise I'll be late," said Elizabeth.

Elizabeth's grandmother was pleased for her granddaughter that she was making new friends, but she felt sad because she was not seeing as much of Elizabeth as she would have liked, especially now that her husband was no longer with her, and she did not have much to do to pass the time. But she would also smile to herself when she thought of Elizabeth, as she was no longer the little girl that she had first met. She was growing up fast into an attractive young lady.

"How do I look, Grandma?" asked Elizabeth, as she twirled around in her frock.

"You look lovely, dear," her grandmother told her. "But haven't I seen that dress somewhere before?" she asked.

"Yes, it used to belong to Aunt Beth. She was having a clear out and she asked me if I would like it," replied Elizabeth.

"I knew I recognised it. I made that dress for Beth when she was about your age," said her grandmother.

"It still looks like new, doesn't it?" asked Elizabeth.

"Yes, it does. You look lovely," her grandmother told her.

"I had better get going now, as I have got to knock for Emily," said Elizabeth.

"Oh Emily is going as well, is she?" asked her grandmother.

"Yes, she is," replied Elizabeth.

"That's nice, I'm really pleased she is making more friends now," said her grandmother.

"I'll see you later then. I won't be too late," said Elizabeth.

When Elizabeth and Emily arrived at Jessica's house they were both surprised when Freddie answered the door.

"Hello, Freddie, I didn't know you would be here this evening," said Emily.

"Well, I live here so of course I'd be here," Freddie told her.

"You mean you live here at Jessica's house?" asked Emily.

"Yes, her mother is my aunt," replied Freddie.

"Maybe Jessica can put a good word in for you to Freddie," whispered Elizabeth to Emily.

"Yes, maybe she can," said Emily with a huge grin upon her face.

"Hello, come and sit down," said Jessica when she saw her friends. "My mother is just finishing the sandwiches," she told them.

"You did not tell me you had such good-looking friends, Jessica," said a young man.

"Take no notice, you two. This is my brother Charlie, he's a bit of a charmer. Well, he likes to think he is, anyway," said Jessica.

"Sisters, they like to embarrass you but I'll get her back," said Charlie.

"I do not embarrass you, you do quite a good job of that by yourself," said Jessica.

They all started to laugh, then Jessica's mother walked into the room carrying a tray of sandwiches.

"Hello, girls, I'm glad you could make it. Help yourself to some food and I'll get you all something to drink," said Jessica's mother.

"It doesn't look like Nelly is coming, she always lets me down," said Jessica.

"Is Nelly the girl with the turned-up nose?" asked Charlie.

"Yes. You had a crush on her remember?" said Jessica.

"Will you stop making me look bad, your friends will get the wrong impression of me," said Charlie.

"Yes, Jessica, stop making your brother look like a right Charlie," laughed Freddie.

"Don't you start as well, us men are supposed to stick together," laughed Charlie.

"See what I have to put up with? Not only a mad brother but a mad cousin as well," said Jessica smiling.

They all sat laughing and after they had eaten Jessica's father started to sing and they all joined along with him, apart from Elizabeth, who felt slightly embarrassed to sing with them.

"Are you alright, Elizabeth? Only you seem rather quiet," said Freddie.

"Yes, I'm fine, thank you, it's just that I do not normally sing very much," she told him.

"Would you like to sit in the garden for a while?" asked Freddie.

"Yes, alright, I'd like that," replied Elizabeth.

As they both went outside, Freddie put his arm around Elizabeth.

"What are you doing?" she asked.

"I'm sorry, I thought that you would not mind if I put my arm around you," said Freddie.

"Well, I do mind, and so will Emily if she finds out what you just did," said Elizabeth.

"What has Emily got to do with it?" asked Freddie.

"You must realise that she really likes you," Elizabeth told him.

"Does she? But it isn't Emily that I am interested in, it's you," said Freddie.

"What are you two doing? Sneaking off like that?" asked Charlie, as he caught them both in the garden.

"Nothing at all, I just wanted some air, that's all," replied Elizabeth.

"Don't look so worried, I was only teasing you," said Charlie.

Elizabeth started to feel quite uncomfortable, not only because Charlie had seen her with Freddie, but she was also worried how Emily would react if she found out that Freddie was not interested in her. After all Emily had liked Freddie for a very long time and Elizabeth did not want to jeopardise their friendship for anyone, especially a young man.

"I think I had better be going home now," said Elizabeth.

"I'll walk you home. If that is alright by you?" said Charlie.

"Yes, alright," replied Elizabeth.

She then looked over at Freddie and he did not look very happy because she had accepted to walk with Charlie and yet she had turned down his advances towards her.

"Wait there, I'll just get my coat," said Charlie.

Whilst Elizabeth stood in the garden Freddie walked towards her.

"Please think about what I said to you. I really like you," he told her.

"But I have already told you that Emily likes you so go inside and speak with her," said Elizabeth.

"No, because it is not her I want to be with, it is you," said Freddie. "Just think about it that is all I am asking," said Freddie.

Just as he said that Charlie came out from the house.

"I had better go and say goodbye to everyone and thank your mother for having me," said Elizabeth.

Whilst Elizabeth was inside saying goodbye to everyone Charlie and Freddie stood outside together.

"Let me walk Elizabeth home, Charlie, I really like her," said Freddie.

"No chance. I like her as well and, besides, she has already said I can walk her home," Charlie told him.

"You are not interested in Elizabeth. You only want to walk her home because I asked you if I could," said Freddie raising his voice.

"Calm down, you know that isn't true," Charlie told him.

"If you like Elizabeth that much, then why were you with that girl Katie last week?" asked Freddie.

"I had not met Elizabeth then. Had I?" said Charlie.

"Well I doubt if Elizabeth will be interested in someone like you anyway," said Freddie.

"What is that supposed to mean?" asked Charlie.

"Just take a look in the mirror and work it out for yourself," shouted Freddie.

With that Charlie just exploded in anger and hit Freddie in his mouth, so Freddie hit him back and a big fight erupted.

"What are you doing?" shouted Elizabeth. "Stop it!" she told them.

After a few minutes the two young men got up off of the ground and Elizabeth just stared at them both in disgust.

"Why are you two fighting? You should not be hitting one another, especially as you are related to each other," Elizabeth told them.

"We were fighting over you, Elizabeth," said Freddie.

"You are worth fighting for," Charlie told her.

"Well you had both just better forget about me, because I do not want to be associated with anyone that has to use violence to get his own way," shouted Elizabeth.

Elizabeth walked away feeling quite angry and yet quite sad that this had happened because of her.

Later that night, Emily came to see Elizabeth as she had heard what had happened between the two young men.

"I just wanted to make sure you were alright," said Emily.

"Yes, I am fine, thank you. I am so sorry, Emily, I did not do anything to encourage Freddie. I would never do anything to hurt you and I even told him how much you like him," said Elizabeth.

"Don't worry, Elizabeth, it was not your fault. I should have known Freddie would not be interested in me, anyway," said Emily.

"Oh please don't think that," said Elizabeth, as she hugged Emily. "What did Jessica's parents say when they found out what happened?"

"They were absolutely furious with them and Jessica's father has told them both that they have got to apologise to you," said Emily.

"This is awful and on Jessica's birthday as well," said Elizabeth.

"Yes I know, but at least I know exactly how Freddie feels about me now," said Emily.

"I think you had a lucky escape, Emily, after all, who wants someone that has to use violence to get what they want," said Elizabeth.

"Yes, I think you are right," Emily told her.

As they sat talking together there was another knock at the door; it was Freddie and Charlie to see Elizabeth.

"Yes," said Elizabeth rather abruptly.

"I am so sorry, Elizabeth I did not mean for any of this to happen," said Charlie.

"I'm also very sorry and I do not blame you if you never speak to me again," said Freddie.

"I do not want to fall out with either of you, but I hope you both realise that we can never be more than just friends," Elizabeth told them.

"I understand," said Charlie.

"Good. I accept your apologies but I must ask you both to leave now," said Elizabeth and she shut the door.

As time passed, Elizabeth did see both men again but she only spoke to them in passing; she never became really good friends with either of them and in time Emily eventually got over her feelings for Freddie.

"Hurry up, Emily, Elizabeth is waiting for you to go to work," Emily's mother told her.

"I'm ready now," Emily replied.

As the two girls walked to work they suddenly heard the sound of people shouting and jeering, so they both walked towards where the noise was coming from and it was then that they saw a crowd of people throwing things at a man whom had been put in stocks.

"Why are those people throwing things at that man?" asked Elizabeth.

"He must have done something wrong and this is his punishment," replied Emily.

"I heard he is being punished for non-payment of fines," said a lady standing nearby.

"But this is so cruel. Surely he does not deserve this," said Elizabeth.

"Of course he does," replied the lady.

"Well, I think it is disgusting to treat anyone in this way and, I think anyone who can stand here and watch such a terrible thing, should also be punished," said Elizabeth as she walked away.

Emily quickly pushed through the crowd to catch up with her friend.

"Elizabeth, wait!" she called.

"How can all those people just stand there and watch such a thing?" asked Elizabeth.

"They are probably used to it, it happens every now and again," Emily told her.

"Well, I think it is quite sickening," said Elizabeth.

"Come on, we had better be getting to work," said Emily.

"I feel quite ill now," said Elizabeth.

"Why don't you go home. I'll make some excuse to Mr Flagerty why you could not make it into work today," said Emily.

"No, I'll be alright and besides I cannot afford to lose a day's pay," Elizabeth told her.

Whilst Elizabeth was at work all she could think about was the man in the stocks and she was glad when she finally heard the bell ring for the end of the day. When she arrived home she sat down in a chair and spoke with her grandmother about the terrible thing she had witnessed and, her grandmother told her that she had felt the same way, the first time she saw such an awful thing.

"Is this what the world is really like? Are people really this cruel?" asked Elizabeth.

"Only some people are cruel, dear, that is just the way things are," replied her grandmother.

"I have not been able to take my mind off of that poor man all day," said Elizabeth.

"Well, I have something to tell you that will probably take your mind off him, but it is not going to make you very happy, I'm afraid," her grandmother told her.

"What could be as terrible as what I witnessed today?" asked Elizabeth.

"I really don't know how to say this without upsetting you," said her grandmother.

"What has happened? Is it mother Or father?" asked Elizabeth.

"No it is nothing like that," her grandmother told her.

"Then what is it? What is wrong?" asked Elizabeth.

"I have decided to give up my house and move in with your Aunt Beth," replied her grandmother.

"But why?" asked Elizabeth.

"It is my arthritis, it has got so bad lately I cannot get about very well and I cannot do things around the place like I used to do," she told Elizabeth.

"But you never mentioned to me that it was this bad," said Elizabeth.

"I did not want to worry you," said her grandmother.

"What will happen to me, though?" asked Elizabeth.

"You will have to return to Yorkshire, I'm afraid," she told her.

"But I do not have any friends there, everyone I know are here," cried Elizabeth.

"But your family are there," her grandmother told her.

"But you are my family," said Elizabeth.

"I am only your grandmother, it is not the same thing as having your parents with you," said her grandmother.

"What if I give up work so that I can help out more, then I won't have to leave," said Elizabeth.

"Then we would not be able to afford anything and where would that leave us?" asked her grandmother.

"Well, can't Aunt Beth spend more time here? And I will do everything else when I get home from work," pleaded Elizabeth.

"Your Aunt Beth does enough around here as it is. I cannot expect her to do anymore as she has a home of her own to run," replied her grandmother.

"But I do not want to leave you," cried Elizabeth.

"But you knew that your stay here was only supposed to be on a temporary basis. You have been here a lot longer than anticipated," she told Elizabeth.

"Don't you want me here then?" asked Elizabeth.

"Of course I do. I want that more than anything else, but the time has come for certain changes," replied her grandmother. "Look, I did not want to show you this, but I think you should see it," said her grandmother.

She then pulled up her sleeve and showed Elizabeth a burn on her arm. Elizabeth's grandmother had spilt boiling water over her arm whilst trying to make a pot of tea.

"Oh my goodness," said Elizabeth, looking shocked.

"That's not all, take a look at my leg. This bruise was caused by me falling over," she told Elizabeth.

"I did not realise," said Elizabeth.

"My legs keep giving up on me and I cannot hold things very well. Now, do you understand why I have had to make this decision?" she asked.

"Yes I do, but it does not change the fact that I do not want to leave you," replied Elizabeth.

"I know, dear, but it is for the best and your parents need you, they have not seen you for ages and as for your brother, William, well he will not even recognise you anymore," her grandmother told her.

"When are you thinking of going to Aunt Beth's to live?" asked Elizabeth.

"In about a week. That way it will give you time to work out your week's notice at Flagerty's," replied her grandmother.

"Yes, alright," replied Elizabeth.

Elizabeth went to bed later that evening feeling extremely sad, but she knew deep down, that her grandmother had to be looked after properly and even though Elizabeth was hurting inside she tried to make the best of her last week in Newcastle. One of the hardest things she had to do was tell Emily and when she told her the news the following morning Emily hugged her and wept like a child.

"What am I going to do without you?" asked Emily.

"You will be fine and anyway you have got plenty of friends at Flagerty's now," said Elizabeth.

"But I won't have my best friend, will I?" said Emily.

"Oh don't say that, Emily, it is hard enough for me to leave as it is," Elizabeth told her. "Anyway, I will get another job and I will save up the money to come and visit you, you will not get rid of me that easily."

"Oh, Elizabeth, I am going to miss you so much," said Emily.

"I know and I will miss you too, but I have to go as I do not have any choice," said Elizabeth.

"Yes, I know," said Emily.

Elizabeth went into work that day and gave a week's notice of leave and, although Mr Flagerty could be a funny old so 'n' so, he was really sad to hear that Elizabeth was leaving as she was one of his best workers.

The rest of the week seemed to go so quickly for Elizabeth and before she knew it the day had arrived for her to leave Newcastle. As the carriage waited outside for her Elizabeth said her goodbyes to Emily and her grandmother.

"You will keep in touch, won't you?" asked Emily.

"Of course I will," Elizabeth told her.

"I have a little something for you, Elizabeth. It isn't much, but you should be able to afford to buy yourself some more oil paints and when you do your next painting you can think of me," said her grandmother, as she gave her some money.

"I cannot take this, you might need it," said Elizabeth.

"Nonsense, you take it dear, I want you to have it," her grandmother told her.

"Thank you," said Elizabeth.

Elizabeth climbed into the carriage with tears streaming down her face and she waved to Emily and her grandmother as the carriage pulled away.

Elizabeth sobbed and sobbed for most of the journey home, but once she was at her parents' house she went inside, washed her face, changed her clothes and then made her way to the Lockwoods house to see her family.

CHAPTER FIVE

As Elizabeth walked through the Lockwoods' garden towards their house, a gentleman smiled at her, so trying to be polite Elizabeth smiled back at him, even though she did not know him. She then made her way into the house to find her mother and when her mother saw her she just screamed with delight.

"Oh, Elizabeth, it is so good to have you back, you do not know how much I have missed you," said her mother.

"It feels quite strange being back here after all these years," said Elizabeth.

"Yes, I suppose it does, but you will soon get used to it. Now sit down and I'll make you a cup of tea," said her mother.

"How is everyone?" asked Elizabeth.

"Everyone is just fine and they are looking forward to seeing you, especially your brother as he has not seen you since you first went away," replied her mother.

"I'm a bit nervous to see him because I might not even know him anymore," said Elizabeth.

"Well, I'm not going to say he has not changed, because he has, but he is still the same William inside," her mother told her.

"Where are father and William now?" asked Elizabeth.

"They are working near the stables; they are making a barn for some chickens that are soon to arrive," replied her mother.

"When I have drunk my tea I'll go and see them," she told her mother.

"Would you like me to make you something to eat first? You must be hungry after that long journey," asked her mother.

"No, thank you, I have already eaten. Grandma gave me some food to take on my journey," replied Elizabeth.

"After you have spoken to your father and William, perhaps you could go and see Mr and Mrs Lockwood. I know they are dying to see you," said her mother.

"Yes, of course I will," replied Elizabeth.

Once Elizabeth had drunk her tea, she made her way towards the stables, but it brought back terrible memories for her from when her brother John died in the stable fire. She looked across at the stable and saw her father working nearby, so she walked towards him. Elizabeth then crept up behind him and put her hands over his eyes to surprise him.

"I know those soft hands, they belong to my little girl," he said.

"Father," said Elizabeth, all embarrassed.

Her father turned around picked Elizabeth up and swung her around like a rag doll.

"Father, put me down!" she screamed.

William saw his father with Elizabeth, but he was not sure if it was really her as she had changed so much since he had last seen her.

"William, come over here and give your little sister a hug," his father told him.

"My little sister, I don't think you can say that anymore. Just look at you all grown up," said William beaming with happiness.

"Hello, William. How are you?" asked Elizabeth.

"I'm fine. Oh my goodness, I can't get over how good you look," said William.

"Well, look at you, you are taller than father now, but not quite as handsome," she joked.

"Still the same old Elizabeth, always teasing me," laughed William. "Come here," he told her as he hugged her.

Elizabeth stood talking with her father and brother for quite a while, then she noticed the gentleman that had smiled at her earlier.

"Who is that young man over there?" she asked.

"Why, don't you recognise him? That is Ernest Lockwood. Surely you remember him, Elizabeth?" said her father.

"Is it really? My goodness he is quite a handsome young man, isn't he?" she told them.

"I'll call him over, shall I? Then you can speak with him," said her father.

"No, don't you dare! replied Elizabeth.

"Oh, you are not shy are you, Elizabeth?" said her brother teasingly.

"No, of course I'm not," she replied with a smile.

William and his father both looked at each other and grinned.

"She is shy," they both said together.

"Will you two stop it, you are embarrassing me," Elizabeth told them.

"We had better get back to work now and finish off that barn," William told his father.

"Yes we had. We will see you a bit later, Elizabeth," said her father. "It is good to have you back," he whispered in her ear.

Elizabeth just smiled then she took a walk around the garden recognising things she had not seen for many years. Then she suddenly remembered someone she had not seen for years, and she got very excited. Elizabeth started to run as fast as she could back towards the stables and as she entered them standing inside was Ernest Lockwood's horse Admiral. Elizabeth recognised him straight away.

"Hello, boy, I bet you do not remember me anymore? But I remember you and you are still as gorgeous as when I last saw you," she said.

Elizabeth stood stroking Admiral but she suddenly jumped as she saw Ernest Lockwood walk into the stable.

"Hello, Ernest," she said.

Ernest looked at her but could not remember who she was.

"Do I know you?" he asked politely.

"Yes you do. I'm Elizabeth Oakendale," she replied.

"Elizabeth Oakendale. Not tiny Elizabeth that used to stand and watch me ride Admiral years ago?" he asked.

"Yes, that's me," she giggled.

"Oh my goodness me, Just look at you, you are beautiful," he told her.

"Thank you," said Elizabeth, blushing with embarrassment.

"I wondered who you were when I first saw you and now that you are in here with Admiral, I should have known. You never forgot him then?" asked Ernest.

"How could I? He is gorgeous," said Elizabeth.

"Have you seen my parents yet? Or don't they know you are here?" he asked.

"No, I haven't seen them yet, I was just having a look around first, getting to know the place again," replied Elizabeth.

"Well, if you want to come and see them, I'll walk with you," Ernest told her.

"Yes, alright," she said.

Elizabeth felt quite nervous walking beside Ernest because she felt like she did not know him anymore and what made it even worse was that she thought how very handsome he was. But he chatted away to her as if he had always known her and, to him, it was as though she had never been away.

As they walked together Ernest picked a rose from the garden and gave it to Elizabeth.

"A beautiful flower for a beautiful lady," he told her as he gave it to her.

"Thank you," said Elizabeth smiling.

Once they were inside the house Ernest took Elizabeth into the drawing room; he then asked his parents to join him and when they entered the room and saw Elizabeth standing there they were absolutely thrilled to bits.

"You remember Elizabeth, don't you, Mother?" he asked.

"Of course I do. You are even prettier now than I remember," said Mrs Lockwood.

"How are you, Elizabeth?" asked Mr Lockwood.

"I am very well, thank you," she replied.

"My goodness, it has been quite a few years since we last saw you. I remember you as this little girl running around and falling asleep in stables," laughed Mrs Lockwood.

"Oh yes, so I did," smiled Elizabeth.

"What about your oil painting? Do you still do that?" asked Mr Lockwood.

"Yes I do, and I am getting a lot more experienced now that I'm older," replied Elizabeth.

"Oh I am pleased. I remember when you first started painting, I think you had more on your clothes than on the painting itself," laughed Mr Lockwood.

"Yes, I know, stop reminding me," said Elizabeth with a giggle.

"Would you like a drink? Maybe a sherry or something else?" asked Mrs Lockwood.

"I'll have a cup of tea please, I'm not old enough to drink just yet," replied Elizabeth.

"Well, you look old enough to me. You are a proper young lady now," said Mrs Lockwood.

"Mother, stop embarrassing Elizabeth," Ernest told her.

"I'm so sorry, I just got a bit carried away with all the excitement of seeing you again," Mrs Lockwood told her.

"That's alright, you do not have to apologise to me. It must be quite strange for you seeing me all grown up, because it is quite strange for me as well, seeing my brother looking so different, then seeing Ernest all grown up and looking so handsome," said Elizabeth.

"Yes, well Ernest gets his looks from me," said Mr Lockwood smiling.

"I do not look anything like you. I'm much better looking," laughed Ernest.

"You men are unbelievable, you are so big-headed," said Mrs Lockwood.

"Oh, but you love us really," Mr Lockwood told her.

"Yes, and all the women love me," said Ernest jokingly.

"See what I have to put up with, Elizabeth? Two grown men who have never really grown up at all," said Mrs Lockwood.

They all started to laugh and Elizabeth started to feel a bit more at ease whilst in Ernest's company, but that was probably because Mr and Mrs Lockwood had broken the ice for her slightly.

"So what do you intend to do work-wise now that you are back?" asked Mrs Lockwood.

"I have not had chance to think about that yet, but I would not mind going back to being a seamstress, because that was what I was doing before I left Newcastle," replied Elizabeth.

"Well, there is always work here for you if you need a job. Just come and see me if you decide not to be a seamstress anymore," Mrs Lockwood told her.

"Thank you, I'll keep that in mind if I do not find any work else where," said Elizabeth.

"Good, I will be only to pleased to help you," said Mrs Lockwood.

After Elizabeth had spoken with the Lockwoods she made her way back home so that she could unpack her belongings and then she cooked dinner for her family, because she thought it would be nice for her mother to have a break when she returned home.

"Something smells good," said Elizabeth's father as he entered the house.

"I have made a vegetable stew for dinner. Grandma taught me how to make it," said Elizabeth.

"Well, it smells delicious," her father told her.

"Ah but does it taste as good as it smells?" asked her brother William.

"Well you won't know that until you try it. Will you?" replied Elizabeth jokingly.

That evening all the family sat talking about everything that had happened over the years and Elizabeth's parents told her how pleased they were to have her back living with them once more.

Elizabeth spent the next few days looking for employment, but she was unsuccessful in finding work as a seamstress.

"Why don't you take up Mrs Lockwood's offer of employment? After all we could do with another cleaner around the place," said her mother.

"A cleaner?" said Elizabeth.

"Yes. What is wrong with that?" asked her mother.

"I do not really want to be a cleaner," replied Elizabeth.

"There is nothing wrong with cleaning, after all, your mother has done it for most of her life," her father told her.

"No offence, Mother, but cleaning is not something I want to do for the rest of my life," said Elizabeth.

"It does not look like you have much choice. There is a perfectly good job going at the Lockwoods', so go and speak to Mrs Lockwood about it before someone else gets it," her father told her.

"Do I have to do it?" asked Elizabeth.

"Yes, you do. All us Oakendales work and you are no exception," said her father.

Elizabeth reluctantly went to see Mrs Lockwood later that day and she was given a job as a cleaner and asked to start straight away, but she hated it.

When Elizabeth had her afternoon off from work she would sometimes watch Ernest riding his horse Admiral, or she would sit in the grounds of the Lockwoods' home and continue with her oil paintings.

"Your work is very good," said Ernest one day as he stood admiring her painting.

"Thank you," she replied blushing slightly.

Elizabeth had started to get quite a crush on Ernest, but she knew deep down he would never be interested in her, not just because she was still quite young, but because she thought he would never want to walk out with a cleaner on his arm.

Ernest Lockwood was studying to be a lawyer and spent a lot of time away from home, but when he did return back to his family Elizabeth would get very excited and her heart would miss a beat.

"Elizabeth, your father has been asked to go into town for Mr Lockwood. Why don't you go with him and buy yourself a new evening dress as we have been invited to the butler's ball next weekend," said her mother.

"But I do not know what type of dress to buy," said Elizabeth.

"Something elegant, but if you are not sure the assistant will help you decide," her mother told her.

Elizabeth climbed on to the back of the cart and went with her father to town and whilst he was shopping for groceries for the Lockwoods, Elizabeth searched for a dress. There were plenty of nice dresses to choose from but most of them were out of Elizabeth's price range, so Elizabeth had to choose one that was a little less glamorous.

On the evening of the butler's ball the Oakendales smartened themselves up so that they looked presentable and were taken by carriage to the butler's ball. When they arrived Elizabeth was extremely impressed by all the handsome-looking guests that were there and she thought how beautiful the ladies looked in their ball gowns. The ladies' gowns were not quite as extravagant-looking as what the upper-class well-to-do people wore, but to Elizabeth they all looked stunning. Elizabeth watched as the ladies and gentlemen danced the night away; she had never seen anything so grand before. As she sat watching quite a few young gentlemen approached her and asked her to dance, but Elizabeth politely declined their offer, not because she was being rude but because she did not know how to dance. One gentleman introduced himself to her and asked if he could sit beside her; Elizabeth agreed and they sat talking for quite sometime. But as the ball came to a close the gentleman asked if he could possibly see Elizabeth again, but she refused as all she could think about was Ernest Lockwood as he was the one man she had feelings for.

A few weeks later Elizabeth was asked to take tea into the drawing room for the Lockwoods and they asked her to bring an extra cup with her as Ernest had brought along his lady friend for the afternoon. Elizabeth felt quite sick when she heard that Ernest was seeing another lady, but there was nothing that she could do. Elizabeth took the tray of tea to the drawing room, but as she left she saw Ernest walking along the hallway with his lady friend.

"Good afternoon, Elizabeth," said Ernest.

"Good afternoon," she replied.

She then looked at Ernest's lady friend and she could see why he liked her; she was very beautiful with long flowing blonde hair and very smart in her appearance. Elizabeth walked away to continue with the rest of her chores, but she could not stop thinking about Ernest and how she wished it was her sitting by his side drinking tea.

At the end of the day Elizabeth waited outside for her mother as they always walked home together. Whilst waiting Elizabeth noticed Ernest walking with his lady friend through the garden and she felt very envious. As they got a bit closer to Elizabeth the lady called to her.

"Elizabeth, isn't it?" she asked.

"Yes, that's right," she replied.

"Well, Elizabeth, don't you realise it is rude to stare?" said the lady.

"I am extremely sorry, I did not mean to stare. I was just admiring how pretty you look," replied Elizabeth.

"Pretty," said the lady sarcastically. "You do not know what the word pretty means, just look at the state of you," she told Elizabeth.

She then linked her arm in Ernest's arm and walked away. Elizabeth was quite upset by how the lady had spoken to her and she was even more upset that Ernest just stood there and let her speak to her in that way.

"Are you alright, dear?" asked her mother as she came out from the house.

"Yes, I am fine," replied Elizabeth.

But she was not fine at all, she was very upset and she could not believe how someone like Ernest could like someone as rude as the lady he was with.

The next day Ernest apologised to Elizabeth for his friend's behaviour and he told her no matter what anyone says to her, he thought she was very pretty. This made Elizabeth's day and she kept smiling to herself every time she thought about what he had said to her.

A few days had passed and whilst Elizabeth was scrubbing the doorstep she heard a carriage pull up outside; when she looked she saw Ernest's lady friend being helped out from the carriage. Elizabeth looked straight down as she did not want to be accused of staring again, but she could hear the lady walking towards her. As the lady got almost to the door she picked up a handful of dirt and threw it over the doorstep.

"Oh dear, it looks like you will have to clean it again now," said the lady, as she smirked.

Elizabeth could feel herself boiling with anger inside, but she knew she dare not say anything through fear of losing her job. The lady just walked away laughing, so Elizabeth cleaned the mess up without saying a word.

The next day was Elizabeth's afternoon off from work, so she decided to go up by the little stream and do some painting as it was very quiet and peaceful up there. As she stood painting the ducks and swans she heard a horse galloping towards her and when she looked to see who it was, she saw Ernest's lady friend riding the horse. As soon as the lady saw Elizabeth she pulled up on the horse and dismounted and walked towards where

71

Elizabeth was painting. Elizabeth tried to just ignore the lady and continued to do her painting.

"What is this rubbish?" asked the lady as she looked down at the painting.

Elizabeth did not answer her; she just continued with what she was doing.

"I asked you a question, girl," said the lady.

She then started hitting Elizabeth with her riding crop, but as she did this Elizabeth fell and knocked her painting to the ground. This made the horse frightened and he started to bolt upright and, as the lady tried to get at of the way of the horse, she stepped back and slipped straight into the little stream.

"Look what you have done, just look at the state of me!" shouted the lady. "Well don't just stand there, help me out of here," she told Elizabeth.

Elizabeth just looked at the lady and started to laugh.

"Sorry I cannot help you, it is my afternoon off," she told the lady.

Elizabeth then picked up her painting and walked away leaving the lady struggling to get out from the little stream.

"You just wait, I'll get you for this!" shouted the lady.

Elizabeth did not say anything she just carried on walking. But the next day she was dreading going into work in case the lady had made a complaint against her. But as the day went by everything seemed to be fine, the Lockwoods were speaking perfectly normal to her and Ernest seemed to be his usual happy self, so obviously the lady had not said anything about the incident.

As Elizabeth was cleaning a rug outside with a carpet beater she heard someone call to her; when she looked she saw Ernest's lady friend standing inside the house.

"I am very sorry for the way that I have treated you, perhaps we can call it a truce," she told Elizabeth.

"Yes, of course. I never had anything against you in the first place," said Elizabeth.

"I know I was rather horrible to you, but perhaps I can make it up to you in some way," said the lady.

"No, it is alright, I would rather just forget about it," Elizabeth told her.

"Well, perhaps I can help you out in some way," said the lady.

"How do you mean?" asked Elizabeth.

"Well what types of things do you like doing?" asked the lady.

"Well apart from painting I do like reading, but that's about it I'm afraid," said Elizabeth.

"Perhaps I can lend you some books to read from the library. I'm sure Mr and Mrs Lockwood would not mind," said the lady.

Elizabeth thought for a few seconds and then refused the lady's offer to borrow the books; she still was not sure whether or not to trust her, and she did not want to be accused of stealing them.

"Alright forget about the books, but at least have a cup of tea with me, after all, I would like to make amends for the way I treated you," she told Elizabeth.

"Yes, alright I would like that," said Elizabeth.

"You go and make the tea then and I will meet you in the drawing room," said the lady.

Elizabeth felt quite relieved that she was now on good terms with the lady, so she made a pot of tea and took it into the drawing room.

"Come in," the lady told Elizabeth as she stood holding the tray.

Elizabeth walked into the drawing room and as she put the tea tray on the table, a gentleman came in after her; he then closed the door and locked it.

"Do not look so worried, Elizabeth, this is my brother, he won't hurt you," said the lady.

"No, of course, I won't hurt you, I rather like young girls," said the gentleman.

"Yes, especially slave girls, isn't that right?" the lady asked her brother.

"What do you mean by that?" asked Elizabeth.

"Oh come on now, you know exactly what I mean, after all, you are a slave girl yourself," replied the lady.

"No, I'm not, I just clean that's all," said Elizabeth.

73

"Ah, but are you clean or, are you a dirty girl?" asked the lady's brother.

"I think I had better go now, so please unlock the door," said Elizabeth.

"But you have not had your tea yet," said the lady.

"That's alright, your brother can have it," Elizabeth told her.

"But I do not want it, I have not had chance to work up a thirst yet," said the gentleman.

By now, Elizabeth knew that she had been tricked by the lady; she did not want to call a truce at all, all she wanted was to get back at Elizabeth for not helping her out of the little stream.

"If you do not unlock the door I shall scream," said Elizabeth.

"And who will hear you? Mr and Mrs Lockwood are out and Ernest is out riding on his horse," said the lady.

"My mother will hear me," replied Elizabeth.

"Your mother is working down in the kitchen; she cannot hear anything from there," said the lady.

The lady's brother walked towards Elizabeth and started to stroke her hair. He then moved his hand down her face and put his hand over her mouth so that she could not make a noise.

"Quick, lay her on the floor," shouted the lady.

Elizabeth tried to struggle free; she grabbed at the gentleman's hand but he was to strong. He pulled Elizabeth down on the floor and the lady grabbed her arms above her head. Elizabeth then tried kicking the man so he sat on her legs so she could not move.

"Quick, put something in her mouth," said the lady.

The man pulled out a handkerchief and stuffed it in Elizabeth's mouth so that he silenced her; he then started to unbutton her dress and, whilst he was doing this, he just grinned at her. Elizabeth was absolutely petrified but she could not do anything to free herself. The man then started to kiss Elizabeth's neck and he slowly made his way down towards her breast, but suddenly a voice called out the name Rosemary. It was Ernest looking for his lady friend. The man quickly jumped off Elizabeth, and Rosemary let go of her arms, Elizabeth then did her buttons up and the man unlocked the door.

"If you breathe a word of this to anyone I will kill you," Rosemary told her.

Elizabeth did not say a word she just ran towards the door, opened it and ran out of the room. She then saw Ernest, but ran straight past him.

"Elizabeth!" called Ernest as he could see something was wrong.

But Elizabeth did not answer him she just kept running, she then ran out of the house and all the way home. Ernest continued to walk towards the drawing room where Elizabeth had just came out from and when he got there he asked Rosemary and her brother what was wrong with Elizabeth.

"The stupid girl spilled tea all over my clothes so I told her off," replied Rosemary.

"Well, it was probably just an accident," Ernest told her.

"Why are you taking her side?" asked Rosemary.

"I'm not. I just know Elizabeth would never have done it on purpose," said Ernest.

"Just look at my clothes, they are ruined; the stupid girl should be more careful," said Rosemary.

Rosemary had tipped the tea over herself just to make it look good in front of Ernest and her brother backed up her story.

"I think you had better go home and change your clothes," Ernest told her.

"I'll come with you," said her brother.

By now, Elizabeth was at home and still shaking from her ordeal, but she knew she could not tell anyone what had happened because she thought everyone would probably believe Rosemary against her. Elizabeth sat down and began to sob as she knew there was nothing that she could do and, even if she did tell someone, she knew that Rosemary had already warned her that she would kill her.

When Elizabeth's parents arrived home they instantly knew there was something wrong with Elizabeth, but she made an excuse that she was feeling unwell. For the next few days Elizabeth stayed in her room; she did not even go to work at the Lockwoods. Then one day, there was a knock at the door and when Elizabeth looked out from the window she saw Ernest standing there. Elizabeth came downstairs and opened the door to him to see what he wanted.

"Hello, Elizabeth. I came here today to see if you are alright. I was told by Rosemary that you spilled tea over her and that she told you off, and I have noticed that you have not been into work since," said Ernest.

"No, I have been feeling a bit under the weather, but it had nothing to do with Rosemary telling me off," said Elizabeth.

"Oh, that is good to hear. I thought she had frightened you away," said Ernest.

"No, of course not," replied Elizabeth.

"Well, just to let you know, Rosemary will not be around for a while as she has gone away for a month or so, so get better soon and I will see you when you come back to work," said Ernest.

"Thank you, I will probably be back tomorrow," Elizabeth told him.

"I'll see you there," said Ernest.

Elizabeth could not believe how deceitful Rosemary was, and to blame her for spilling tea down her knowing what she and her brother had done was just unbelievable. Elizabeth felt sick but she was also relieved that Rosemary would not be around for a while, which would make life a lot easier for her.

CHAPTER SIX

Elizabeth had been back at work for quite sometime now, and she had not seen or heard from Rosemary since that awful incident she had been put through. Elizabeth felt much better in herself, although she still had not forgotten what Rosemary and her brother had done to her. She knew that Rosemary was back from her travels as she had heard the Lockwoods talking, but now that Ernest was away studying, it meant that Rosemary would not be around so often, which pleased Elizabeth.

One day whilst Elizabeth was oil painting in the garden a gentleman approached her.

"That is really good," he told her as he admired her work.

"Thank you," she replied.

"Have you done many paintings before?" he asked.

"Yes, I have done quite a few," replied Elizabeth.

"Would it be possible for you to bring some here to show me? Only I work in London and I know quite a lot of art collectors that might be interested in your work," he told her.

"Yes, I can bring some here tomorrow to show you. If tomorrow is alright by you?" asked Elizabeth.

"Yes, tomorrow will be fine. I'm Edward Thomas by the way. I am a friend of Mr Lockwood. I will be here for a few more days," he told Elizabeth.

"I am Elizabeth Oakendale. It is very nice to meet you, Mr Thomas," she said.

"It is very nice to meet you too, Elizabeth. I will see you tomorrow then," said Edward.

Later that evening, Elizabeth looked through her paintings and picked out a few of her best ones and took them to work with her the next day to show Mr Thomas.

When she arrived at work she saw Mr Thomas standing talking with Ernest so she walked towards him.

"Hello, Elizabeth," said Ernest.

"Hello, I did not realise you were back home," she told him.

"Yes, I travelled back a few days ago with Edward, he has been giving me some advice about becoming a lawyer," said Ernest.

"Oh I see," said Elizabeth feeling rather disappointed in case Rosemary came back on the scene.

"Yes, we lawyers have got to stick together and, from what I have seen, Ernest is doing remarkably well," said Mr Thomas.

"I have brought in a few paintings for you to look at, Mr Thomas," said Elizabeth.

"Oh yes, of course, let me take a look," he told her.

Mr Thomas was very impressed by what he had seen and so was Ernest as he also stood admiring Elizabeth's work, especially one painting that she had done as it was of Ernest's horse, Admiral.

"Would you be interested in selling this painting to me?" asked Ernest.

"No. Sorry, what I meant to say was, you can have it as a gift, I could not possibly take money from you for it," said Elizabeth.

"That's nonsense, you have got a beautiful painting here and I would like to buy it from you," said Ernest. "I want you to take this," he told her as he gave her a pouch of money.

"Thank you," said Elizabeth.

"No, thank you, this painting is just magnificent," he told her.

"These paintings are really very good. Would you mind if I took some of them back to London with me? I am sure many of my friends will be very interested to see them," said Mr Thomas.

"No, I do not mind at all," replied Elizabeth.

"I will bring them back to you in about three weeks," said Mr Thomas.

"Yes, alright," she replied.

Elizabeth walked away feeling pleased with herself as someone had taken an interest in her work and this made her feel really special. But then she thought of Rosemary coming back around and this started to worry her.

"Mother," she called as she entered the Lockwoods' house.

"Yes, dear," replied her mother.

"Look what Ernest has given me; he gave me all this money for one of my paintings," she said excitedly.

"My goodness, you are lucky," her mother told her.

"Here, Mother you take it," said Elizabeth.

"I cannot take that from you, you earned that money by all the hard work you put in painting that picture," said her mother.

"I don't care, I want you to have it," Elizabeth told her.

"Well, only if you are really sure; that money would come in handy, though," said her mother.

"Of course I'm sure, now take it," said Elizabeth.

"Thank you. I am so proud of you, you are a good girl," her mother told her.

A short time later Elizabeth took a tray of tea up to the Lockwoods and when she entered the room, she saw everyone admiring her work.

"These paintings are really quite breathtaking, Elizabeth," said Mr Lockwood.

"Thank you, sir," she replied.

"Would it be possible for you to do a painting of Mrs Lockwood and me at all?" he asked.

"Yes, of course, I would love to do one of you both," replied Elizabeth.

"I will pay you well, of course," said Mr Lockwood.

"Oh no, sir, I could not possibly take payment from you," said Elizabeth.

"My dear girl, if you are going to spend hours, days or even weeks, painting our portrait, I do not expect you to do it for free," he told Elizabeth.

"Alright, but I'll only charge a small fee," said Elizabeth.

"You will do no such thing! I will pay you a good price and that's that," said Mr Lockwood.

"Alright, when would you like to sit for me?" asked Elizabeth.

"How about tomorrow evening?" said Mr Lockwood.

"Yes, tomorrow evening it is then," she replied.

Elizabeth left the room feeling very happy indeed. Not only had she sold a painting that day and been booked to paint for the Lockwoods, but she also thought that she might even get more offers of work once Mr Thomas had shown her paintings around London.

Elizabeth spent the next few weeks working all hours; she not only had done her cleaning job at the Lockwoods, she also spent most of her evenings painting for them. But once she had finished the portrait, the Lockwood's were so pleased with it, it made Elizabeth feel that all the hard work she had put in was worthwhile.

As the days passed, Elizabeth had forgotten all about Edward Thomas, until one day he arrived at the Lockwoods and asked to speak with her.

"Hello, Elizabeth, I have some very good news for you," he told her. "I have spoken to a number of people in London and shown them your paintings and they are very keen to meet you," said Edward.

"Oh, that is good news," replied Elizabeth.

"Yes, it is, but you will have to travel to London to meet with them," Edward told her.

"Oh, I do not think I can do that, because I have commitments here," said Elizabeth.

"Oh, I'm sure I can have a word with Mr Lockwood, to give you some time off work, after all, this is a good opportunity for you to show off more of your paintings," said Edward.

"But I do not think my father would approve of me going. And where would I stay?" asked Elizabeth.

"Why you could stay with me; I have a very large house and I can show you around London," replied Edward.

"I will have to speak with my father first," said Elizabeth.

"It would be a good opportunity for you, Elizabeth, one that you should not miss out on," he told her.

"Yes, I know. I will speak with my father and get back to you," said Elizabeth.

"I will be here for a few days and then I will have to travel back to London as I also have work commitments," he told her with a smile.

"That soon?" asked Elizabeth.

"Yes, I'm afraid so. So you had better see your father as soon as you can, as you have not got much time to decide," Edward told her.

"Yes, alright, I shall go and speak with him now," said Elizabeth.

"You do realise that you will be away for a few months though, don't you?" said Mr Thomas.

"Yes, alright," replied Elizabeth.

Elizabeth was so excited about the thought of travelling to London she almost jumped on her father when she saw him working on the farm.

"Slow down, Elizabeth, I cannot understand a word you are saying, because you are talking so fast," said her father.

"Mr Thomas has arrived back from London. You remember him, the man who took some of my paintings to show to people?" said Elizabeth.

"Oh yes, I remember," said her father.

"Well, these people that he knows, want to meet with me, but I will have to travel back to London with Mr Thomas if I am interested," said Elizabeth.

"Travel to London with a complete stranger, I do not think so," said her father.

"But Mr Thomas told me it would be a good opportunity for me to show off more of my work," said Elizabeth.

"And where would you stay whilst you are in London?" asked her father.

"Mr Thomas said I can stay at his house with him," replied Elizabeth.

"So you think it is a good idea to travel to London with a man you hardly know, and to stay alone in his house with him?" asked her father.

"But he might have a wife living with him," replied Elizabeth.

"I have met Mr Thomas on the odd occasion and, I know for a fact, he is not married," her father told her.

"But he seems like a proper gentleman. I think he generally wants to help me," said Elizabeth.

"Or help himself to something," said her father.

"How can you say such a thing, you hardly know him," said Elizabeth.

"My words exactly, you hardly know him either," replied her father.

"Please, I am begging you let me go!" cried Elizabeth.

Elizabeth's father could see how much she really wanted to go to London, so he told her he would speak with Mr Thomas first before he made his final decision.

"Thank you," she said.

Later that day, Elizabeth's father did speak with Mr Thomas, but he was still not convinced that it was a good idea for his daughter to go to London with someone she hardly knew.

"But, Father, you have to let me go," said Elizabeth.

"I do not have to do any such thing," he told her.

"But surely you must know how much I want this and, I thought you, of all people, would understand how that feels," said Elizabeth.

"What do you mean by that?" asked her father.

"Well you wanted Mother all those years ago and you know how you felt when your father refused to let you see her. But that did not stop you. Did it?" asked Elizabeth.

"She has a point, dear," said Elizabeth's mother.

"Yes, and I have made my point quite clear. I do not know if I can trust a man alone with my daughter," said Elizabeth's father.

"Well, if you have any doubts, why don't you go and speak with Mr Lockwood, after all, he has been friends with Mr Thomas for many years and I am sure he will tell you if he is trustworthy or not," said Elizabeth's mother.

"Yes, I suppose I could do that," said her father.

Elizabeth's father did speak with Mr Lockwood and he could understand how William felt, but he had known Mr Thomas for a very long time and he had the highest respect for him.

"I can assure you that Mr Thomas has no interest in your daughter that way; all he is trying to do is help Elizabeth make use of the talent that she has," said Mr Lockwood.

Elizabeth's father knew that Mr Lockwood would never say anything that he did not mean, so this made his mind up for him.

As Elizabeth waited patiently outside, whilst her father spoke with Mr Lockwood, she prayed hard that her father would let her go to London.

"Elizabeth, I have made my decision and I have decided to let you go to London with Mr Thomas, but if anything happens to you, I will hold Mr Thomas entirely responsible," he told her.

"Oh thank you, Father," said Elizabeth.

Elizabeth was thrilled to bits that her father had decided to let her go to London; she also knew that by going she would not have to face Ernest's lady friend Rosemary for a while either. But she was sad that she would not see as much of Ernest as she would have liked, as she still had strong feelings for him.

"You had better start packing your belongings then, as Mr Thomas will be leaving in a day or so," her father told her.

"Oh thank you, Father, you have made me the happiest girl alive," said Elizabeth.

"Yes, well I hope I do not live to regret it," said her father.

"You won't, I promise," said Elizabeth.

The next few days could not go quick enough for Elizabeth and, on the evening before she was due to leave, she was so excited that she could hardly sleep.

"Come and eat your breakfast, Elizabeth," her mother told her.

"I'm so excited I cannot eat anything," said Elizabeth.

"But you have a long journey ahead of you so you have to eat something," said her mother.

"I really can't eat anything, but I will have a cup of tea," Elizabeth told her.

After sometime had passed there was a knock at the door.

"That must be Mr Thomas," shouted Elizabeth excitedly.

"Have you got everything that you need?" asked her mother.

"Yes, I think so," she replied.

Elizabeth opened the door and there stood Mr Thomas with a huge smile upon his face.

"Are you ready?" he asked.

"Yes, I am," replied Elizabeth.

Elizabeth hugged her mother and brother William, whilst her father put her belongings on to the carriage outside.

"Mother, please do not cry. I will only be away for a month or so," said Elizabeth.

"I know, dear. But that does not mean I am not going to miss you," she told her.

Elizabeth then walked towards her father and as he hugged her he whispered into her ear.

"Don't forget I love you," he told her.

"Don't worry, I won't," said Elizabeth.

Elizabeth climbed into the carriage and waved to her family as the carriage slowly moved away. Even Pip their pet dog started to bark as if he were trying to say goodbye.

"We have to stop off at the Lockwoods' first as they want to see you before you leave," said Mr Thomas.

"Yes, alright," replied Elizabeth.

When they arrived at the Lockwoods' house Mr and Mrs Lockwood were waiting outside for them; even Ernest was there as well.

"Hello, Elizabeth, we will not keep you too long. We just wanted to wish you well on your journey," said Mrs Lockwood.

"Thank you," said Elizabeth.

"Make the most of your time in London, Elizabeth. I am sure once everyone sees your paintings they will love them," said Mr Lockwood.

"Here you are, Elizabeth, I have a little something for you," said Ernest, as he gave her a rose.

"I remember when I first came back here and you gave me a rose then," said Elizabeth smiling.

"Oh you remembered then?" asked Ernest.

"Yes I did," she replied.

"Well, I have given you this one so that you do not forget me," he told her.

"How could I ever forget you," she giggled.

Ernest leaned towards Elizabeth and gave her a kiss on her cheek. She then suddenly had a thought come to her.

He does like me after all, she thought.

Elizabeth waved to Ernest and his parents and she wiped the tears that flowed down her face. She then looked down at the rose that Ernest had given to her and she smiled to herself as she pictured him in her mind.

"Are you alright, Elizabeth?" asked Mr Thomas.

"Yes, I'm fine, thank you. It's just the thought of leaving everyone that has upset me, that's all," she replied.

"Don't worry, you are going to have a wonderful time," Mr Thomas told her.

Edward Thomas was in his mid-thirties; he was thin, smart-looking and still very attractive for his age. He had never been married but he kept himself busy with his work as a lawyer. He did not go out very often as most of his spare time was used up studying law, but he did on the odd occasion invite close friends around for dinner.

"How long have you lived in London?" asked Elizabeth.

"All of my life. My father was a lawyer there and his father before him, so really I had no choice but to follow them," replied Mr Thomas.

"How do you know Mr Lockwood then? Because he lives in Yorkshire," asked Elizabeth.

"He was a close friend of my father's for many years and that is how we met. But we had not seen each other for quite some time, well not until recently when I started giving Ernest some advice about law," replied Mr Thomas.

"You must be very clever to be a lawyer," said Elizabeth.

"I had good teachers," he told her with a smile.

After travelling for quite some time Mr Thomas stopped the carriage so that the horses could have a drink and so he and Elizabeth could both stretch their legs for a while.

"Oh that's better, I was starting to get cramp, just then," said Mr Thomas.

Elizabeth started to giggle.

"What is so funny?" he asked.

"You are, the way you are hobbling about," laughed Elizabeth.

"Yes, well I am not as young as I used to be," said Mr Thomas.

"You are not that old," Elizabeth told him.

"Well, I feel old when I am around young people like you and one day you will know exactly what I mean," said Mr Thomas.

"Oh no I won't, because I am never going to get old," said Elizabeth.

Mr Thomas just smiled to himself and shook his head slightly, as if to say you will one day.

A few hours later they stopped at an inn that was nearby so that they could get something to eat and some rest for the night.

As they entered the inn Mr Thomas asked for his horses to be taken to the stables for the night and then he asked for two rooms, for Elizabeth and himself.

"Would you like an evening meal?" asked the innkeeper.

"Oh yes please, I'm starving," replied Elizabeth.

Mr Thomas started to laugh at Elizabeth; it was just the way she answered the innkeeper that made him laugh, but Elizabeth could not understand what was so funny.

"I'll show you to your rooms, said the innkeeper.

"When you have freshened yourself up, Elizabeth, I will meet you downstairs and we shall have something to eat," said Mr Thomas.

"Yes, alright," she replied.

As Elizabeth entered the room she thought how dark and dingy it was and how very cold. But as she was only there for one night she tried to make the best of it.

After having a wash Elizabeth met Mr Thomas downstairs and they both had a meal.

"At least the food tastes good," said Mr Thomas.

"Haven't you been here before?" asked Elizabeth.

"No and from what I have seen of my room, I shall not be coming here again," he replied.

Elizabeth did not comment as she did not think it was her rightful place, but she could see Mr Thomas' point as she also thought that her room was awful.

Later that night, Elizabeth lay in bed but she could not sleep very well through all the noise outside. She could hear the sound of horses running by and drunken men shouting in the street and a short time later the wind started howling and it rained quite heavily on the window.

As she lay in bed Elizabeth started to think of Ernest Lockwood and she remembered the rose that he had given to her. She then climbed out of bed and picked up the rose and smelt it. Elizabeth then climbed back into bed and after a while she finally fell asleep still holding the rose in her hand.

The next morning Elizabeth and Mr Thomas were up bright and early to continue on their journey to London. When they arrived in London, Elizabeth was shocked and gasped at how big everything was.

"My goodness look at the size of those buildings," she told Mr Thomas.

Mr Thomas who had lived in London all of his life did not take any notice of the things around him; he was too busy looking at the expressions on Elizabeth's face as she took everything in about this great city.

"It's like being in another world," she told Mr Thomas.

He just smiled at Elizabeth and watched the excitement on her face.

Elizabeth looked at all the smartly-dressed people walking around and she thought how elegant the ladies looked in their expensive clothes.

"Those people must be very wealthy to be able to wear clothes like that," said Elizabeth.

"Yes they probably are," replied Mr Thomas.

Mr Thomas pointed to some buildings that he could see in the distance and he explained to Elizabeth what they were used for, but it was all too much for her to take in all at once and her eyes just seemed to be everywhere.

"I could never have imagined a place like this. I've never seen anything quite like this before in my life," said Elizabeth.

"London is a very big city and there is a lot more to see than just this," said Mr Thomas.

"Well I think it's wonderful," said Elizabeth smiling.

A short time later they arrived at Mr Thomas' house; it was a huge detached place with plenty of ground around it.

"Is this really where you live?" asked Elizabeth.

"Yes, it is," he replied.

"You mean you live in this great big house all by yourself?" said Elizabeth.

"Yes," replied Mr Thomas.

"Oh it's beautiful and just look at the garden, it is so pretty," said Elizabeth.

"I'll just take the horses to the stable and then I'll show you around," said Mr Thomas.

Elizabeth climbed out from the carriage and wandered around whilst Mr Thomas saw to the horses. As she looked around she could not believe that for the next few months she would be staying in a place that looked so grand, and even though she had seen a big house like the Lockwoods had, that was nothing compared to this one.

"Are you ready to go inside?" asked Mr Thomas as he walked along the gravelled pathway.

"Oh yes, I can hardly wait," replied Elizabeth excitedly.

As they entered the house Elizabeth gasped as she saw the huge staircase, and the hallway was just magnificent with beautiful crystal chandeliers along the walls and going up the staircase.

"I'll take you to your room first, then you can unpack your belongings and freshen up," said Mr Thomas.

Elizabeth followed Mr Thomas upstairs and once she reached the top all she could see were lots of closed doors.

"You can have this room, Elizabeth," said Mr Thomas.

The bedroom that Elizabeth was given was the best guestroom in the house; it had a four-poster bed inside and beautiful oak furniture.

"You mean this will be my room whilst I am here?" asked Elizabeth looking shocked.

"Yes. Do you like it?" asked Mr Thomas.

"Like it, I absolutely love it. It is beautiful," replied Elizabeth.

"I'll leave you to it then. I'll see you downstairs in a little while," Mr Thomas told her.

Elizabeth was absolutely thrilled with the room that she had been given and as she looked around she now understood why Mr Thomas was so disappointed with the room he had been given at the inn. After all if this was the kind of place he was used to living in, then obviously he would have been disappointed going from this to a dark, cold and dingy room.

A short time later Elizabeth came downstairs, but there were so many different rooms that she did not know where to go, so she called to Mr Thomas.

"Come this way," Mr Thomas told her.

"I can see I am going to get lost in this place, it is so big," said Elizabeth.

"You will soon get used to it," he told her.

"Would you like me to get you anything, sir?" asked Elizabeth.

"No, of course not, you are here as my guest," replied Mr Thomas.

"Oh I really don't mind, sir," she said.

"Elizabeth, I do not expect you to wait upon me and I do not expect you to call me sir either," he told her.

"Yes, alright, Mr Thomas," she said.

"Please call me Edward," he told her. "Now would you like something to drink?" he asked.

"Could I have a drink of milk please?" asked Elizabeth.

Edward went to the kitchen and made himself a pot of tea and gave Elizabeth some milk to drink and a short time later he made Elizabeth and himself something to eat.

"Don't you have any staff working here for you?" asked Elizabeth.

"Yes I do. But I gave them time off whilst I was away. All my staff will be back working in the morning but they do not live in; they start at six and leave here at six in the evening," replied Edward.

"I did not think that you cleaned a big house like this by yourself," laughed Elizabeth.

"I do like to be organised but when it comes to cleaning I'd rather leave that to someone that knows what they are doing," smiled Edward.

"It is a really beautiful house that you have here," said Elizabeth.

"Thank you," said Edward.

Elizabeth and Edward sat talking until quite late, but as Elizabeth started to fall asleep Edward asked her to go to bed.

The following morning Elizabeth woke to the smell of breakfast being cooked. She got dressed and washed then made her way downstairs.

When Elizabeth finally found where the breakfast room was she saw Edward already up and sitting at the table.

"Good morning, Elizabeth, come and sit down," Edward told her.

Elizabeth felt quite awkward and embarrassed as she was being waited upon. She had never been treated in this way before. It was usually her waiting on other people.

"Relax, Elizabeth, and stop fidgeting," Edward told her.

Elizabeth started to giggle as she knew Edward was right; she was fidgeting and she did not feel very relaxed at all being waited upon.

"Help yourself to food and if there is anything else that you would like you only have to ask," said Edward.

Elizabeth started to get slightly nervous as one of the maids poured her a cup of tea.

"Are you alright?" asked Edward.

"Yes, I am fine, thank you. Well actually no, I am not fine. I feel a bit awkward having all these people waiting upon me," she replied.

Elizabeth, my staff are here to help you, they will not bite," said Edward.

"Yes, I know. It just feels strange me sitting here whilst they do all the work," said Elizabeth.

"It is their job, that is what I pay them for, so please just relax and get used to it," Edward told her.

Whilst Elizabeth ate her breakfast Edward sat reading the newspaper; he then folded it up and looked across the table at Elizabeth.

"How would you like me to show you around London today?" he asked.

"Oh, yes please, I would love that. But haven't you got to go to work?" she asked.

"I am my own boss, Elizabeth, so I can go into work when I please. Besides I have not got to see any clients until tomorrow," replied Edward.

"It must be really nice being your own boss," said Elizabeth.

"Yes, I suppose it is. I do have five people working for me and a secretary, so if I am not around they will make my appointments for me," said Edward.

After breakfast Edward took Elizabeth around London. He showed her many of the sights there and they ate out for lunch.

"Have a look at the menu, Elizabeth, and when you have decided what you would like to eat I shall order it for you," said Edward.

"Oh I don't know what to have, everything is so expensive," said Elizabeth.

"Forget about the cost, it is not important; just choose what ever you want," Edward told her.

"What are you going to have?" asked Elizabeth.

"I am going to have jam and scones with a pot of tea," replied Edward.

"Well I'll have the same as you then," she said.

"After we have eaten lunch I want to take you to a few shops," said Edward.

"Alright," replied Elizabeth.

"I think you will like the shops I want to show you," said Edward.

"Why? Do they sell oil paintings?" she asked.

"No, they don't," replied Edward.

"Then what type of things do they sell?" asked Elizabeth.

"You will have to wait and see," replied Edward with a cheeky grin upon his face.

"Oh, Edward, just tell me," laughed Elizabeth.

"You will see all in good time," he told her.

A short time later Edward took Elizabeth to a ladies' dress shop.

"Why on earth would you want to bring me here? They only sell ladies' clothes," said Elizabeth.

"Yes, I know. I thought that you could do with some new clothes," said Edward.

"But I cannot afford anything that they sell in here. Just look at the quality of these clothes, they must cost a fortune," said Elizabeth.

"It is a good job that I shall be paying for them. Isn't it?" said Edward.

"I cannot let you do that, Edward, besides the clothes I have are not worn out yet," she told him.

"Elizabeth, I do not want to sound rude when I tell you this, so please do not take offence by what I am about to say," said Edward.

"What? What is it?" asked Elizabeth.

"Tomorrow evening I am taking you to meet some friends of mine, one of whom is a bank manager. Now when you meet these types of people you have to look the part, which is why I need to buy you some new clothes. You could not possibly wear the clothes that you have already, otherwise you will be looked down upon," said Edward.

Elizabeth looked down at her dress and she could understand what Edward was saying to her.

"If you want people to be interested in your work, Elizabeth, especially high-class people, then you have to dress to their level," he told her.

"Yes, alright," said Elizabeth looking quite disappointed with herself.

"Cheer up, this is going to be fun, I promise," said Edward.

Elizabeth smiled at Edward; he then gave her his arm to hold and he led her into the dress shop.

As Elizabeth looked around the shop she was spoilt for choice, as all the clothes were really smart and elegant looking.

"Have you seen anything that you like?" asked Edward.

"Yes, everything," laughed Elizabeth.

"Would you like some help?" asked the shop assistant.

"Yes, I think that is a good idea. My friend here cannot decide what she wants, so perhaps you can help her choose what will suit her best," said Edward.

"Come with me, I am sure we have something that will look lovely on you," the assistant told Elizabeth.

Elizabeth tried on dozens of different outfits and also shoes and hats and eventually with the help from the assistant she chose the clothes that suited her best.

"I cannot believe you have spent all that money on me," she told Edward as she left the shop with him.

"It was money well spent. But there is one thing that you have to do for me now," said Edward.

"Yes, what is it?" asked Elizabeth.

"When we get back home you have to show me what you look like in all your new clothes," he told her.

"Of course I will. I cannot wait to show you," said Elizabeth excitedly.

"Best we go home now then," said Edward smiling.

"Thank you for everything that you have done for me, Edward, and I do not just mean the clothes you have bought for me. I mean thank you for bringing me here to London and giving me a chance to show off my work as well," said Elizabeth.

"You are more than welcome," said Edward.

When they arrived home Elizabeth ran upstairs to her room and put on one of her new dresses to show Edward and when she came back downstairs Edward was shocked when he saw her.

"My goodness, Elizabeth, you look so grown up. You have also changed your hair," said Edward.

"Yes, I know. I thought I would look more sophisticated with my hair pinned up," she told him.

"You look lovely, Elizabeth," said Edward.

CHAPTER SEVEN

It was the evening that Elizabeth was meeting some of Edwards's friends and she was extremely nervous. As she got ready upstairs she kept checking herself in the mirror just to make sure that her hair was in place as she wanted to make a good impression.

"Are you ready, Elizabeth? As we have to leave in a few minutes," called Edward.

"Yes, I'm just coming," she replied.

Edward waited downstairs and when he saw Elizabeth he smiled at her as she looked beautiful.

"I have got butterflies in my stomach because I am so nervous," said Elizabeth.

"Stop worrying, you will be fine," Edward told her.

"But what if your friends do not like me?" said Elizabeth.

"Of course they will. Just be polite, speak clearly, but most of all be confident," he told her.

Elizabeth took some of her paintings to show Edward's friends and they were more than interested in her work.

"Your work is extraordinary, Miss Oakendale," said one gentleman as he looked at her paintings.

"Thank you," replied Elizabeth politely.

That evening Elizabeth got quite a few offers from clients wanting portraits painted and she was thrilled at how pleased they were with her work.

"I do not know why I was so worried earlier tonight. Your friends were really nice to me," said Elizabeth as she travelled home with Edward.

"See I told you that you had nothing to worry about and you have been offered plenty of work for the next few weeks," said Edward.

"Yes, I know and it is all thanks to you," said Elizabeth.

"No it isn't, because you are the one that did all the hard work with your paintings," he told her.

"Yes, I know. But if it were not for you I would not have been given this chance to do more paintings and to earn money from them," said Elizabeth.

"Well, you might even get some more clients tomorrow, as I have invited some people around for dinner," said Edward.

"My goodness you are trying to keep me busy. Aren't you?" said Elizabeth.

"A little bit of help goes along way," replied Edward.

The next evening Elizabeth met some more of Edward's friends, but this time is was not just gentlemen that she spoke with; there were quite a few ladies as well.

"Have you always been interested in oil painting?" asked one of the ladies.

"Yes, ever since I was quite young," replied Elizabeth.

"You have a very special talent," said another lady.

"Thank you," replied Elizabeth.

"So how do you and Edward know each other?" asked one gentleman.

"Oh, Elizabeth is a friend of someone that I know in Yorkshire; that is how we got introduced to one another," said Edward quickly interrupting.

"Oh I see," said the gentleman.

"How long will you be staying in London?" asked one lady.

"Only for a few months," replied Elizabeth.

"Is that all?" asked the lady.

"Yes, because I have work commitments back in Yorkshire," replied Elizabeth.

"Oh I see, you have a lot more paintings to do for other clients do you?" asked the lady.

"Oh no, I have to go back because of my cleaning job," replied Elizabeth.

Edward put his hand up to his face as he knew Elizabeth had made a big mistake by telling his friends that.

"You are a cleaner?" asked the lady looking horrified.

"Yes, I am. But my first love is obviously oil painting," replied Elizabeth.

"Oh Edward, how could you possibly let us eat at the same table as a cleaner?" asked the lady.

"I am sorry you feel that way, but Elizabeth is my friend and she will be treated with respect," said Edward.

"I thought I was your friend, but you obviously prefer to put a cleaner first," shouted the lady.

The lady then got up out of her chair and asked to be excused.

"Oh come on, Maud, don't be like that. Miss Oakendale has most obviously got a talent that neither you nor I have," said her husband.

"But she is a cleaner, she should be in the servants quarters," replied the lady.

"Please apologise to Elizabeth, I will not have you speak about her in that way," said Edward.

"I shall not," said the lady.

"Then please leave my house as you are no longer welcome here," Edward told her.

"Oh really," said the lady as she walked out in a huff.

"I am so sorry, Edward, I really do not know what has got into Maud," the lady's husband told him.

"Pure snobbery I guess," replied Edward.

"We had better be going as well," said another of Edward's guests. "But that is not because we have anything against Miss Oakendale. We will definitely be in touch to have some paintings done," he told Edward and Elizabeth.

"Thank you," said Edward.

"We shall see ourselves out," said the gentleman.

Elizabeth was mortified by the way she had been spoken too. She just looked at Edward and burst into tears.

"It is alright, Elizabeth, you have done nothing wrong," Edward told her.

"But I have ruined everything," said Elizabeth.

"No, you haven't. You still have people interested in having paintings done for them. It was just one person that spoilt this evening and that was Maud Wood," said Edward.

"But if only I had not opened my big mouth and told them I was a cleaner none of this would have happened," cried Elizabeth.

"You do not have to be ashamed of what you do; besides cleaners work extremely hard and I bet you have worked harder in your short life than Maud has in the whole of her life," said Edward.

"You are really angry with her, aren't you?" asked Elizabeth.

"Yes I am. What right has she got to judge anyone? After all we are all born the same and we go out the same way, with nothing," said Edward.

"Thank you for standing by me this evening, Edward, I felt really humiliated, but when you told Maud what you thought of her I felt like laughing out loud," said Elizabeth.

"It served her right, the batty old woman," said Edward.

Elizabeth started to laugh at Edward and watching her made him laugh.

"Let's just forget about her, Elizabeth. People like her are not even worth bothering with," Edward told her.

"Well at least we had the last laugh on her," said Elizabeth smiling.

"That's the spirit. Don't let her get to you, after all she is just one small-minded person, but I bet there are a lot more people out there that are interested in your work, regardless of who you are or what you do," said Edward.

"Yes, I think you are probably right. I'm certainly not going to lose my confidence just because of her. I have come all this way to make something of myself and I am not going to give up now," said Elizabeth.

"Good for you. That is exactly what I needed to hear," said Edward.

As the next few weeks passed word got around about Elizabeth's oil paintings and she was starting to get inundated with work.

"Edward, I think I am going to have to cancel some of my work, as I have got too much to do and only a short time to do it in," said Elizabeth.

"Why? You could make a fortune from your oil paintings," Edward told her.

"Yes I know. But I will be going back to Yorkshire soon and I just won't have the time to finish them all," said Elizabeth.

97

"But you could if you stayed on in London more permanently," said Edward.

"Oh, I do not think my father would allow me to do that," said Elizabeth.

"Why? Once he knows how well you are doing I am sure he will understand," said Edward.

"Do you really think so?" asked Elizabeth.

"Well I cannot see why not and it is not as if you have anything to go back to Yorkshire for apart from your family," Edward told her.

"I suppose I could write to him to see what he says," said Elizabeth.

"Yes, I think you should. This is a great opportunity for you to better yourself and I am sure your father will be in agreement," said Edward.

Elizabeth did write to her father and explain her situation and, just as Edward had told her, her father decided it was in her best interest if she stayed on in London to further her career.

Elizabeth was thrilled at the news as she really enjoyed her work and she also loved being in London as well and to be earning a great deal of money for doing something that she enjoyed was a bonus.

Elizabeth spent the next few months working all hours just to complete her paintings and she did not see Edward very much as he also had his own work to be getting on with. But when they did eventually see each other Edward always made time to sit and speak with Elizabeth and to find out how her work was going.

"There is a letter here for you, Elizabeth, it came earlier today," said Edward one evening.

Elizabeth opened the letter and sat down and read it out loud to Edward; it was from her parents wishing her a happy birthday.

"You did not tell me you had a birthday coming up," said Edward.

"To be honest, Edward, with all this work that I have had, I totally forgot myself," she told him.

"Well we will have to do something about that," said Edward.

"What do you mean?" asked Elizabeth.

"You are working far too hard so on your birthday I do not want you to make any appointments for that day, as I am going to take you out for the day," he told her.

"Where are we going?" asked Elizabeth.

"I am hardly going to tell you that. Am I? It is your birthday so I will surprise you," said Edward.

On Elizabeth's birthday Edward helped her into a carriage and off they went for their special day out.

"Please tell me where you are taking me, Edward," said Elizabeth.

"Be patient, all will be revealed very soon," he told her.

As the carriage stopped for them both to get out Elizabeth looked around and she gasped as she saw this huge building in front of her.

"I have never seen anything so beautiful," she told Edward.

Edward had taken Elizabeth to visit Crystal Palace. It was a large building that stood in Hyde Park and it was made entirely of glass and cast iron to house the Great Exhibition. There were over 14,000 exhibits including the first gas cooker, a stuffed elephant, a 24-ton lump of coal, a railway engine and the Koh-i-noor Diamond from India, to name but a few.

They both spent the whole day looking around the Great Exhibition and Elizabeth could not believe half the things she saw there.

"Oh, Edward, this has just been the best birthday ever," said Elizabeth.

"I am so pleased that you have enjoyed today," Edward told her.

"Oh I have," she said with a smile.

Later that evening whilst Elizabeth lay in bed thinking about the day that she had had, she could not help but think how generous Edward had been to her. Then she started to wonder why Edward had never been married, as he was such a kind and loving person and still extremely attractive. Elizabeth never asked Edward this question through fear that he might think she was prying and she did not want to lose the friendship that she had with him, as they had formed an extremely close bond between them over the months.

As Elizabeth was earning quite a lot of money she could now afford to buy the expensive clothes she had only ever dreamed of. She had also almost forgotten what it was like to be poor, but she had never forgotten her family and she always made sure they were well provided for and she often sent money to them to help them out financially.

One morning as Elizabeth was just about to leave the house Edward called to her.

"Elizabeth, I shall be working from home today as I think I have a touch of flu coming on," he told her.

When Elizabeth saw Edward he looked quite poorly.

"Would you like me to stay home with you?" she asked.

"No, of course not, you go ahead and do what you have to do, I will be fine," replied Edward.

"But I really don't mind. I would prefer to stay home just to make sure you are alright," said Elizabeth.

"I will be fine, Elizabeth, trust me," he told her.

Elizabeth left the house to go to see her client but she could not stop thinking about Edward for most of the day, so as soon as she got the chance to come home that is exactly what she did.

"Hello, Elizabeth, you are home early this evening," said Edward.

"Yes, I know, I was worried about you," said Elizabeth.

"Oh I am fine. In fact I feel a lot better now. I do not think I have flu after all, maybe it is just a cold," said Edward.

"But you looked terrible this morning, that was why I was so worried and you seemed very wheezy," Elizabeth told him.

"Yes, I know. But I do sometimes suffer with asthma," said Edward. "Anyway how was your day?" he asked.

"It went very well, thank you, Edward. I have been asked to paint a picture of an elderly lady's pet dog, I just hope it sits still long enough for me to paint it," she laughed.

Elizabeth sat speaking with Edward for quite some time and he told her about a dog he once had when he was a child, so she spoke of her family's pet dog Pip.

Edward then started to tell Elizabeth some of the silly things he used to get up to when he was quite young, like when he put eggs into his cousin's shoes and how his cousin repaid him by putting worms inside of his bed. Elizabeth sat giggling as

Edward told her the stories. She also told him about some of the things she had done as a young child, like when she used to watch Joseph and Ernest Lockwood riding their horses and how she had always dreamed of one day having a horse of her very own. As they both sat talking they did not realise the time; it was almost 1 o'clock in the morning and they could not believe they had both been talking for so long.

"I think I had better get some sleep now as I have an early start in the morning," said Elizabeth.

"Thank you for tonight, Elizabeth, I really enjoyed our little chat. It brought back lots of happy memories for me as my cousin and I were quite close once," said Edward.

"Yes, I know what you mean," said Elizabeth as she started to think about Ernest Lockwood.

"I am sorry I kept you up so late though. I did not realise the time," said Edward.

"That's alright, I enjoyed myself," she told him.

As Elizabeth lay in bed she started to think about Ernest again; she wondered what he was doing and if he was still courting that awful lady Rosemary. She also smiled to herself as she thought of Ernest's horse Admiral and remembered the day that he was born. As the thought of Ernest went through her mind Elizabeth finally fell asleep, but when she awoke the next morning she did not feel at all like getting up as she was still very tired.

"Good morning, Edward, I hope you feel a lot better today," said Elizabeth.

"Yes I do, thank you very much," he told her. "And how do you feel this morning?" he asked.

"Very tired," replied Elizabeth.

"Well, that will teach you for keeping me up half the night," laughed Edward.

"Yes, I think I had better have an earlier night tonight," said Elizabeth as she started to yawn.

As Elizabeth walked to her client's house she started to feel a bit more awake; it was quite warm outside and Elizabeth looked up at a tree as she heard birds singing loudly. Elizabeth did not mind walking to work when the weather was mild, but she dreaded the winter returning.

As she walked through the cobbled streets she noticed a hat in a shop window and she thought how pretty it was. But she was suddenly distracted by a noise coming from down the street, so she went to see what was happening. It was then she saw a boy being held quite roughly by people who were pushing and shoving him. Apparently the boy had been caught pickpocketing from people as they walked past him. Elizabeth did not stand with everyone else as they watched; she walked away as she was quite appalled at the way he was being treated. Elizabeth knew that the boy had done wrong taking from other people, but she could not help but feel sorry for him and she wondered how desperate he must have been to do such a thing.

When Elizabeth returned home that evening she spoke to Edward about the boy and what he had done and she told him that she thought people were cruel to mistreat him in such a way. Elizabeth was shocked when Edward told her about some of the punishments that used to go on in prior years, like when men were tied to the back of carts and dragged up the streets and whipped at the same time for stealing. He also told her how people were also hanged for their crimes and how up to two thousand people would stand and watch.

"Hanging still goes on even now," he told her.

"Oh that's terrible," said Elizabeth.

"Do you know in the 1820's some people were put in a cage and hung up from the front of buildings?" he told her.

"Oh, Edward, that is so cruel," said Elizabeth.

"Yes, I suppose it is. But if people do these crimes then they have to expect to be punished for them," said Edward.

"Yes I agree, but I still think some of these punishments are a bit harsh," said Elizabeth.

That night Elizabeth could hardly sleep through thinking about all the different punishments that went on in Britain and because she had a late night the night before made it even worse. The next morning Elizabeth felt exhausted and she decided not to go into work, as she was just too tired.

"It is not like you to take time off from work," said Edward.

"I have not had much sleep for two nights now. If I go to work I will only make a mistake and I cannot afford to do that because it could mess the whole picture up," said Elizabeth.

"Well, why don't you get some sleep now and later this afternoon I will come back early and we'll go on a picnic," said Edward.

"Yes, alright, that sounds nice, as long as I get some sleep now though," she told him.

"You go ahead then and I will see you later this afternoon," said Edward.

Elizabeth went straight back to bed whilst Edward went to work and when she woke up about five hours later she felt much better.

Later that afternoon Elizabeth and Edward went on their picnic and they took a basket of food with them, which Elizabeth had asked the cook to prepare earlier that day. They both travelled to the countryside and Elizabeth thought the view was breathtaking.

"It is lovely here. Isn't it?" she told Edward.

"Yes it is. I used to come here quite a lot when I was a child," said Edward.

As Elizabeth stood on top of a very steep hill she could see for miles. The grass was full of daisies and it was so quiet and peaceful, a lot different to the noise that they were used to in the busy city.

After they had eaten Elizabeth and Edward went for a long stroll and whilst they were walking they saw some squirrels and rabbits.

"I think I need to sit down for a while," said Edward, as his back started to ache.

"Oh come on, Edward, we haven't even walked very far yet," said Elizabeth.

"Well it is far enough for me. I am not as young as you are," he told her.

"Oh, any excuse for a sit down," laughed Elizabeth.

"Well that is rather laughable seeing as you have been in bed asleep for a good part of the day," said Edward.

"Oh, alright, you win, let's sit down then," said Elizabeth with a smile.

"I knew I would get my own way in the end," laughed Edward.

"Oh, that's it. You can get up now and start walking again," said Elizabeth jokingly.

"I'm sorry, I'm sorry, I did not mean it," laughed Edward.

"It is a good job I am a forgiving person, or else I might have made you walk home," said Elizabeth.

As they watched the sun go down Edward decided that it was time they were heading back home, so he packed up the picnic basket and put it inside of the carriage. Whilst travelling home Elizabeth started to get quite tired and even though she fought to keep her eyes open, she could not quite manage it and by the time they got home she was sound asleep. Once they were home Edward carried Elizabeth from the carriage to inside the house and as he sat her gently in a chair she woke up.

"Oh, Edward, how rude of me, I am so sorry for falling asleep," said Elizabeth.

"Don't be silly, you have nothing to apologise for," Edward told her.

"But you had the decency to take me out for the afternoon, so the least I could do was stay awake," said Elizabeth.

"It does not matter, so stop worrying," said Edward.

"I still feel rather tired. Would you mind if I retired to my room?" asked Elizabeth.

"No of course not, you go ahead," replied Edward.

"I will see you in the morning and thank you for a lovely day," said Elizabeth.

"You are very welcome. Good night, Elizabeth," said Edward.

The next morning Elizabeth woke up feeling so much better for having a good night's sleep; she ran downstairs all bubbly and lively and met Edward in the breakfast room.

"Good morning, Edward," she said.

But Edward just looked at her seriously.

"Are you alright, Edward?" she asked.

"Elizabeth, sit down please as I have something to tell you," said Edward.

"What is it?" asked Elizabeth as she sat down opposite him.

"I am afraid it is not good news. I have received a letter from your father this morning and there is no easy way for me to tell you this," said Edward.

"Oh, please do not tell me he wants me to go back to Yorkshire," said Elizabeth.

"It is about your grandmother. She has passed away. I am so sorry, Elizabeth," Edward told her.

"No, she can't have!" cried Elizabeth.

"I am afraid it is true. I am so sorry," said Edward.

Elizabeth ran out of the room in tears; she ran upstairs and into her bedroom and closed the door. Elizabeth threw herself on to her bed and wept and wept. She could not believe the news that her grandmother had gone and the more she thought about it the more hysterical she became.

Edward left Elizabeth to be alone but he could hear her crying from downstairs and he became extremely worried about her. After an hour or so had passed, Edward decided to go upstairs to see if Elizabeth was alright. He knocked at the door and Elizabeth opened it; as she looked up at Edward her eyes were very swollen through crying so much and tears were still flowing down her face.

"Oh come here," said Edward as he put his arms around her.

"I cannot believe it. I cannot believe that I am never going to see her again," said Elizabeth.

"I know," said Edward, trying his hardest to comfort her. "Why don't you come downstairs and have a strong cup of tea?"

"Yes, alright," said Elizabeth with her voice trembling.

Edward held on to Elizabeth and helped her downstairs. He then asked for some tea to be brought into the drawing room for them both.

"Elizabeth, your father has requested that you attend the funeral next week," said Edward.

"Yes, of course," replied Elizabeth.

"I will escort you to Newcastle if that is alright by you," he told her.

"Yes, of course. I do not think I could cope with travelling alone," said Elizabeth.

Edward made all the arrangements to take time off from his work and he also cancelled all of Elizabeth's appointments with her clients for the time being.

When they both arrived in Newcastle Elizabeth's parents and brother William were already there and although they were all pleased to see each other, they all would have preferred to have met up again on a happier day.

At the funeral Elizabeth met up with her friend Emily again. They had both grown up a lot since they last saw each other and Emily could not believe how smart and elegant Elizabeth looked in her expensive clothes.

"I am so pleased that everything is going so well for you in London," said Emily.

"You will have to come and visit me when you get some free time," Elizabeth told her.

"I would love to come to London to see you, but on what I earn I do not think I could ever afford to leave Newcastle," said Emily.

"Don't worry about the cost of the fare. If you want to come to London just let me know and I will arrange everything," said Elizabeth.

When Elizabeth and Edward travelled back to London Elizabeth could not stop thinking about her grandmother and she hardly said two words to Edward all the way home.

When they arrived at the house Edward helped Elizabeth out of the carriage and he asked Elizabeth if she needed anything.

"No, thank you," she replied. "I think I shall have a lie down for a while," she told him.

As the next few days passed, Edward started to get rather concerned about Elizabeth, because she hardly ever came out from her room and she had not touched any food for days. Edward knew how close Elizabeth had been to her grandmother and how deeply her death had affected her, but he did not know what to do to ease the pain that she was going through. Then one day Edward had an idea. He knocked on Elizabeth's bedroom door and told her he had a surprise for her.

"What is it?" she asked.

"Come with me and I'll show you," said Edward.

Elizabeth followed Edward downstairs, then he told her to close her eyes. He then led her outside into the garden.

"You can open your eyes now," he told her.

Elizabeth opened her eyes and standing in front of her was a black horse; it looked rather like Ernest Lockwood's horse, Admiral.

"He is all yours," said Edward.

Elizabeth gasped and then turned and threw her arms around Edward.

"Oh thank you, he is beautiful," said Elizabeth.

"It is my pleasure," said Edward. "Now all you have to do is learn to ride him," he told her.

"I have never ridden on a horse before," said Elizabeth.

"Well, let me help you upon him and I shall teach you," said Edward.

Elizabeth spent the whole day learning how to ride, but by the evening she felt very stiff and ached all over.

"What are you going to call him?" asked Edward.

Elizabeth thought for a few seconds until at last she had thought of a name.

"I think I shall call him Midnight," she told him.

"That is a fine name," said Edward.

Over the next few weeks Elizabeth had learnt to ride very well and every evening when she arrived home from work she would go straight out to see Midnight and take him for his daily run around. Edward would often watch Elizabeth riding from his window and he would smile to himself as he could see the joy on Elizabeth's face and he was thrilled that he had made her dream come true by giving her a horse of her very own.

CHAPTER EIGHT

One evening after Elizabeth had been out riding on her horse she came home to find a letter on the table. After she had opened the letter she turned to Edward and told him that she had been invited to attend the wedding of her brother William to Alice Clifford. The wedding was taking place in a few weeks' time. Elizabeth was thrilled at the news but also surprised, as she could hardly believe that her brother was actually going to be married.

"I had better go shopping soon as I will need something new to wear," she told Edward.

Elizabeth arrived in Yorkshire a few days before the wedding and she was really pleased to see her family again and at least this time it was for a happy occasion.

Elizabeth was introduced to her brother William's intended and they both hit it off straight away.

Alice Clifford was a very petite lady with fair hair and extremely quiet spoken and Elizabeth took an instant liking to her.

As Elizabeth witnessed the wedding between her brother William and Alice, it brought tears to her eyes and it also made her think of Ernest Lockwood. Even though Elizabeth had not seen Ernest for a very long time, she still often thought about him and her feelings for him had never changed.

After the wedding and the celebration that followed Elizabeth travelled back to London and she could not wait to tell Edward all about Alice and how beautiful she had looked in her dress.

"I am so pleased that the wedding went well," said Edward. "I also have some good news to tell you."

"What is it?" asked Elizabeth.

"I have also had an invite to a wedding. I have been invited to attend the wedding of Ernest Lockwood and Rosemary Thornton," said Edward.

Elizabeth just stood there and froze. She had suddenly heard the words which she had dreaded hearing and what made it worse was the thought of Ernest marrying someone as horrible as Rosemary Thornton.

"Well aren't you pleased?" asked Edward.

"Oh, yes, of course I am. It was just a bit of a shock that's all," replied Elizabeth.

"It takes place in six weeks," said Edward.

"That is good news," replied Elizabeth, feeling rather sickened by the announcement.

"Oh yes before I forget, I have invited a few friends around for dinner this evening," said Edward.

After hearing the news that Ernest was going to be married, Elizabeth certainly did not feel in the mood to socialise with people that evening, but she knew she had to do it for Edward's sake.

As Elizabeth sat at the table with Edward's friends she was extremely quiet and hardly touched her food, but because everyone was talking and laughing they hardly noticed Elizabeth's strange behaviour, although Edward had.

"Are you alright, Elizabeth? Only you seem like you are somewhere else," said Edward.

"No, I do not feel well, I have the most terrible headache. Could I possibly be excused?" she asked.

"Yes, of course. You should have said something earlier," said Edward.

Elizabeth left the table and went up to her room; she sat down on her bed and just could not stop thinking about Ernest. Knowing that he was to be married had come as a complete shock to her and she was broken-hearted as she had really loved him for a very long time.

How could Ernest even think of marrying someone as awful as Rosemary, she thought. *If only he knew what she was really like.*

Later that night Edward knocked at the door but Elizabeth was fast asleep so he did not bother to wake her. The next morning Elizabeth came downstairs and sat with Edward at the breakfast table but she did not eat very much; the thought of Ernest getting married still sickened her inside and because of this she had lost her appetite.

"Are you alright, Elizabeth? Only you did not eat very much last night and you have hardly touched your breakfast this morning," said Edward.

"I still have a slight headache as I did not sleep very well last night," replied Elizabeth.

"Well, when I came up to see you last night you were sound asleep," Edward told her.

"I did sleep a bit but I was also quite restless," said Elizabeth.

"There is nothing worrying you is there?" asked Edward.

"No, of course not," replied Elizabeth.

Elizabeth could hardly tell Edward how she felt about Ernest as she felt embarrassed and she knew that Ernest was going to be married whether she liked it or not and there was nothing that she could do; she had to just get on with her life and accept it.

As the day got nearer to Ernest's wedding Elizabeth tried hard not to think about it and she kept herself busy by working very long hours doing her paintings.

"Elizabeth, I do not feel to well today. I think I must have a cold coming and I also have a chill," said Edward.

"But you cannot get ill now, after all you have got to attend Ernest Lockwood's wedding in a few days," said Elizabeth.

"The way I feel now I do not know if I want to travel all that way to Yorkshire," said Edward.

"But they will be expecting you there," said Elizabeth.

"I know. I suppose I cannot really let them down. Can I?" asked Edward.

"Well if you are not feeling up to travelling then maybe you should stay here. I am sure Ernest will understand," said Elizabeth.

"Do you really think so?" asked Edward.

"Of course he will," said Elizabeth.

The real reason Elizabeth was trying to convince Edward not to go to the wedding was because she did not want to be on her own; it was bad enough Ernest was getting married, but to be alone as well would give her more time to think about it which she did not want.

"I shall see how I feel in a day or so, but if I still feel ill then I shall stay here," said Edward.

Over the next couple of days Edward did not get any better; he was full of cold and had now caught a cough as well, so he decided not to attend Ernest's wedding after all.

Once the wedding day arrived Elizabeth was feeling very low, but she now knew the man she loved had committed himself to another and she realised that she could no longer live in the past; she had to accept the situation and move on with her life.

Quite a few months had passed since Ernest's wedding and Elizabeth did not think about him as much as she used to do.

As the dark nights drew in and the weather started to get colder Elizabeth woke one morning and to her surprise there was a deep layer of snow outside. She ran downstairs to tell Edward but he had already left for work a bit earlier because of the weather conditions. Elizabeth put on her winter coat, but it was looking a bit shoddy, so she decided it was time to treat herself to a new one. Once she had purchased her new coat she decided to wear it straight away, but as she admired herself as she walked past a shop window Elizabeth slipped on some ice and fell to the ground outside a jewellery shop. Suddenly a gentleman came running out from the jewellers and helped her up.

"Are you alright?" he asked.

"Yes I think so but my arm hurts," she told him.

"Would you like to come inside the shop for a moment?" asked the gentleman.

"No, thank you, I'll be fine," replied Elizabeth.

But just as Elizabeth was about to walk away she slipped again and almost fell over for a second time.

"I think you had better come inside and sit down for a while," said the gentleman.

He then held Elizabeth's arm and helped her into the shop.

"Let me take a look at your arm," said the gentleman.

Elizabeth pulled back her sleeve and let the gentleman check her arm for any broken bones.

"Well, it is not broken, but it is badly bruised," he told her.

The gentleman then made Elizabeth a cup of tea and he told her she should not have come out in such bad weather. As Elizabeth sat drinking her tea she noticed a pocket watch inside a glass cabinet.

"Could I possibly have a closer look at that watch?" asked Elizabeth as she pointed to it.

"Yes, of course," he replied.

Elizabeth had a good look at the watch and decided to purchase it as a special gift for Edward. Edward had done so much for Elizabeth over the last few years and bought her so many nice gifts that she felt it was her turn to treat him to something nice for a change.

"Is this for someone special?" asked the gentleman.

"Yes it is. It is for a very special friend," replied Elizabeth.

"I hope he likes it," said the gentleman.

"Oh I am sure he will," said Elizabeth. "I ought to be going now, but thank you very much for helping me when I fell," she said.

"Alright but be careful not to fall again," he told her.

"Don't worry, I won't," said Elizabeth.

The gentleman helped Elizabeth to her feet and then opened the door for her.

"I am Albert Turner by the way; it was very nice to meet you," he told her.

"I'm Elizabeth Oakendale. Thank you for all your help," she said as she left the shop.

When Elizabeth arrived home Edward was sitting in front of the fire trying to keep warm.

"Hello, Elizabeth, come and sit here you must be freezing," said Edward.

"No, I am fine, honest," said Elizabeth.

"How can you say that? It is freezing outside, now come and get warm," said Edward as he took hold of her arm.

"Ouch!" said Elizabeth.

"What? I did not do anything," said Edward.

"It wasn't your fault, Edward. I fell over on some ice whilst I was out and I hurt my arm, but luckily a kind gentleman from Turner's the jewellers helped me up," she told him.

"Oh, that was very thoughtful of him," said Edward.

"Yes, it was. His name is Albert Turner and he was very kind to me. He even let me sit down inside his shop and he made me a cup of tea," said Elizabeth.

"He sounds like a very nice gentleman. I'll have to call into see him when I am passing that way to thank him," said Edward.

"Oh, I almost forgot. I bought you something whilst I was in the jewelers," said Elizabeth as she gave the watch to Edward.

"You should not be buying me gifts, Elizabeth, you should be spending your money on yourself," said Edward.

"It was the least I could do after everything that you have done for me," Elizabeth told him.

"Oh, Elizabeth, it is absolutely beautiful, thank you very much," said Edward.

"You are very welcome," said Elizabeth.

"I will treasure this forever," Edward told her.

Over the next few days the weather got much worse and the snow was still falling heavily. Elizabeth and Edward stayed at home because of the weather conditions, as it was quite dangerous for anyone to walk out in.

"I think I'll go and check on Midnight, just to make sure he is alright," said Elizabeth.

"Just be careful. Won't you?" said Edward.

"I will," she replied.

After a while Elizabeth came back into the house and she stood in front of Edward with a huge grin upon her face. Edward held down the newspaper that he was reading and just stared at her.

"What is so funny?" he asked.

"Nothing," replied Elizabeth still smiling.

"Then why are you smiling?" he asked.

Elizabeth walked towards Edward and stood beside him, she then put a handful of snow down the back of his neck.

"Why you…" said Edward as he jumped out from his chair.

Elizabeth quickly ran out of the house with Edward chasing after her. She then picked up another handful of snow and threw it at Edward, so he did the same and they both ended up having a huge snowball fight. Elizabeth ran around giggling as Edward chased her, but he eventually caught her and he picked her up and threw her down in a huge pile of snow.

"Oh, Edward, I am soaking wet," she laughed.

"That will teach you for putting snow down my shirt," he told her.

Eventually they both got very cold so they went back inside the house to change their clothes and get warm. Edward made them both a warm drink and they both sat in front of the fire.

"Do you know, Elizabeth, you definitely bring out the worst in me," said Edward. "If people that I know could see me playing out in the snow they would have thought I was mad," he told her.

"Well it does not hurt to have a bit of fun sometimes. Does it?" said Elizabeth.

"No I suppose not," said Edward smiling.

As the night went by Elizabeth developed a chill and by the morning she was full of cold.

"Good morning, Edward," she said with her nose rather blocked.

"Good morning, Miss Red Nose," said Edward.

"Oh stop teasing me, Edward, I feel awful," said Elizabeth.

"Well, I do not think you should be going out at all today especially in your condition and besides the weather is extremely bad outside as it has snowed all night," said Edward.

"No, I won't. I think I'll just sit by the fire and keep warm," said Elizabeth.

Edward left the house to go to work, but it was not long before he returned home again.

"The weather is absolutely terrible out there. I cannot get through the snow to get to work," he told Elizabeth.

Edward stayed at home for the rest of the day and continued with his paperwork from home. Elizabeth sat by the fire for most of the day reading some books that Edward had lent her and by the evening it had stopped snowing but there was still a deep layer of snow outside.

"How are you feeling now?" asked Edward.

"A lot better thank you. My chill has now gone, but I still have a blocked nose," she told him.

"Just make sure you keep warm," said Edward.

"Yes, I will," said Elizabeth.

The snow seemed to last for ages but after a few days Elizabeth and Edward returned back to work. It was still very slippery outside so Elizabeth left the house a bit earlier, as she was afraid that if she rushed to get to her client's house she might slip over again.

Elizabeth was making quite a name for herself in London as a professional artist and she was never short of clients.

Just before she left for work Edward called to her as he had something to tell her.

"Elizabeth, before you go, I just wanted to mention that I have had an invite to the Mayor's annual ball which is being held in three weeks' time. The invitation is for me and a guest. So I was wondering if you would like to come with me as my guest?" asked Edward.

"Thank you, Edward, but I do not think I can make it," said Elizabeth.

"Why ever not?" he asked.

"I just do not think it is my kind of thing," replied Elizabeth.

"Of course it is, you will love it," said Edward.

"No, I won't," said Elizabeth.

"Why? What is the problem?" asked Edward.

"I just do not want to go," Elizabeth told him.

"There has to be a reason. So come on, Elizabeth, tell me the truth. Why don't you want to go?" asked Edward.

"If I tell you, you will laugh," said Elizabeth.

"Of course I won't," said Edward.

"Well, if you must know it is because I do not know how to dance," said Elizabeth.

"Is that all?" laughed Edward.

"See I told you that you would laugh." said Elizabeth.

"I am not laughing at you, Elizabeth. I am laughing because it is such a silly thing to be worrying about," said Edward.

"Yes, well I think it is rather embarrassing. I remember once when I went to a butler's ball, I had to sit down all night and just watch everyone else dancing," said Elizabeth.

"I think this ball will be a lot grander than a butler's ball," said Edward.

"Yes, exactly. That is why I would rather not go," said Elizabeth.

"What if I teach you how to dance? Then will you come with me?" asked Edward.

"Would you really do that for me?" asked Elizabeth.

"Yes, of course I will, but only if you promise that you will attend the ball with me," said Edward.

"Alright, I promise," said Elizabeth.

"Good, I will start teaching you as from tonight," Edward told her.

Later that evening after they had finished their dinner Edward got up from his chair and took hold of Elizabeth's hands.

"What are you doing?" asked Elizabeth.

"I am going to teach you how to dance," he told her.

"What now?" she asked.

"Yes, there is no time like the present," said Edward.

He then showed Elizabeth a few dance steps, but as she tried to copy him she kept standing on Edward's feet. So Edward showed her again and again, but still Elizabeth could not do it.

"It is no good, Edward, I am useless. I am never going to be able to learn to dance," she told him.

"Yes, you will. It just takes practice," Edward told her.

Edward held on to Elizabeth as she tried to pull away, but he was not going to let her go anywhere; he was there to teach her how to dance and she had no choice in the matter. He then told her to count her steps as she moved, but Elizabeth was still clumsy and almost fell over as she tripped on to his feet.

"I am so sorry, Edward, I just cannot do it," said Elizabeth.

"Yes, you can, you are not going to give up so easily," he told her.

Edward made Elizabeth dance with him for quite a few hours and every evening after that he made her practise again and again, until eventually she finally got it right.

On the evening of the Mayor's ball, Elizabeth returned home quite late and as she entered the house Edward called to her.

"You had better hurry up and get ready for the Mayor's ball, Elizabeth, we have to leave within the hour," he told her.

Elizabeth suddenly realised that because of her busy work schedule she had forgotten to buy a new ball gown.

"Oh, Edward, I will not be able to come with you, I have been so busy that I have forgotten to buy a gown for the ball tonight," she told him.

"Oh, Elizabeth, you have worked so hard learning how to dance," he told her.

"Yes, I know. I am really sorry," said Elizabeth.

"Never mind, you had better go and get changed out of your work clothes anyway," he told her.

Elizabeth felt terrible because she had let Edward down and especially as he had spent so much time teaching her how to dance. Elizabeth went up to her room and as she opened the door to her surprise there was a beautiful golden ball gown laid out across her bed. There was also a message beside the gown which read, 'With regards from your friend, Edward'. Elizabeth put the gown on and pinned her hair up and then walked downstairs. Edward was standing at the bottom of the staircase and he just smiled up at her.

"You look stunning," he told her.

"Oh, Edward, it is beautiful, thank you so much," said Elizabeth.

"Wait a minute, there is something missing," said Edward.

Elizabeth looked down at her gown but she could not understand what Edward meant. Edward then held out a box and inside was a beautiful gold necklace.

"Is this for me?" she asked.

"It most certainly is. Now let me put it on for you," said Edward.

"You should not be buying me all these things, Edward," Elizabeth told him.

"Now you look perfect," said Edward.

He then stepped back and had a good look at Elizabeth, but then he started to frown.

"What is wrong?" she asked.

"There is still something missing," said Edward.

"What else could possibly be missing?" asked Elizabeth looking rather puzzled.

"Come with me," said Edward, as he led her into the drawing room.

As Edward opened the door Elizabeth was stunned to see Albert Turner the man from the jewellers standing in the room.

"Hello, Mr Turner. What are you doing here?" she asked.

"I think I had better explain," said Edward. "I have asked Mr Turner to escort you to the ball this evening. I think you would look better with someone your own age," he told her.

"But I want to go to the ball with you," said Elizabeth.

"I am afraid it is not really my cup of tea, Elizabeth, but rather than let you down, I thought that it would be nice if Mr Turner went with you," said Edward.

"Are you really sure you do not want to go?" asked Elizabeth.

"I am positive. Now you both go and enjoy yourselves," Edward told them.

Mr Turner gave Elizabeth his arm and he led her out of the house to a waiting carriage outside. When they arrived at the Mayor's ball Elizabeth became quite nervous and as she entered the hall she gasped as she could not believe how big it was. A waiter came towards Elizabeth and Mr Turner and offered them both a drink from his tray; they then went to find a seat to sit down on.

Elizabeth was amazed by how beautiful the ladies looked and the whole place was so completely different from the butler's ball she had once attended.

Elizabeth did not dance straight away; she sat and watched everyone else for a while first. Mr Turner did not mind, he was just pleased to be sitting with the prettiest lady at the ball and he could not take his eyes off of her.

When Elizabeth saw the food that was laid out she thought that it was out of this world. There was salmon, lobster and caviar to name but a few and Elizabeth had never tasted anything like it before in her life.

After some time had passed, Elizabeth eventually plucked up enough courage to have her first dance and she danced extremely well and all the gentlemen at the ball could not help but glance over at her as she looked absolutely stunning. Mr Turner felt rather proud as he knew that Elizabeth was definitely the most radiant lady at the ball and he could see the envy on the other gentlemen's faces. As they both danced together Elizabeth was approached by other gentlemen trying to get her to dance with them, but Elizabeth politely refused as she did not want to hurt Mr Turner's feelings. But Mr Turner was not prepared to let anyone take Elizabeth from him either and he told quite a number of gentlemen that Elizabeth was with him and that he was not prepared to share her with anyone. Elizabeth danced the night away with Mr Turner and, for the first time in her life, she felt really special and she felt as though the night belonged to her.

As the ball came to a close Mr Turner escorted Elizabeth back home and as he walked her to the door he asked if he could possibly see her again. Elizabeth politely accepted his offer. They arranged to meet the following evening and Mr Turner told Elizabeth he would call at the house to see her about seven.

"Thank you for a lovely evening, Mr Turner," said Elizabeth.

"No, thank you," he told her. "I had a lovely time, but please call me Albert."

Elizabeth said goodbye to Albert and then went inside the house where she saw Edward sitting in a chair waiting for her.

"Oh, Edward, I had such a wonderful time this evening. I did not think I could ever be this happy," she told him.

"I am really pleased for you, Elizabeth. And what was Mr Turner like?" he asked.

"Oh, Albert was the perfect gentleman and I am going to see him again tomorrow evening," said Elizabeth.

"Good, I am really pleased everything went so well for you," said Edward.

"Oh it did, it was just wonderful!" said Elizabeth.

"Did you dance at all this evening?" asked Edward.

"Yes, I danced almost all night and I never made any mistakes," laughed Elizabeth.

"See, I told you that you could do it," said Edward with a smile.

"Oh, thank you, Edward, for making this night possible. If it had not been for all your help, I would have probably not have even gone to the ball tonight," said Elizabeth.

"It is my pleasure just to see you happy, Elizabeth," he told her.

"I had better go and take my gown off as I do not want to ruin it, but thank you again, Edward, and I shall see you in the morning," said Elizabeth.

"Good night," said Edward.

Elizabeth could hardly sleep that night as she kept thinking about how wonderful the Mayor's ball had been and she could not wait to see Albert again. As she woke the next morning she sat in front of the mirror brushing her hair and she felt so happy to be alive.

"I am really pleased that you and Mr Turner got along so well last night. It is about time you started associating with people more your own age," said Edward.

"Why do you always say things like that? Just because you are older than me does not mean I do not like your company. You are my closest friend, Edward, and I would not change that for anything," she told him.

"But you still need to have people your own age around you, instead of sitting here with an old fool like me," said Edward.

"You are not an old fool. I love being with you," said Elizabeth.

Later that evening Albert arrived to see Elizabeth and she got all excited.

"Would you like to stay for dinner, Mr Turner, as Elizabeth and I have not eaten yet?" asked Edward.

"No, thank you, I would prefer to take Elizabeth out to dinner," replied Albert.

"Just as you wish," said Edward.

Elizabeth spent the whole evening out with Albert and over the next few months there was not a day that went past where they did not see each other.

Albert Turner's father owned the jewellers' shop which Albert worked in and he was about to open another one in Paris.

"Does that mean that you will be moving away to Paris?" asked Elizabeth.

"No, not at all, I will still be managing the jewellers here in London, whilst my father works over in Paris," said Albert. "Would you like to meet my parents before my father goes away?" he asked.

"Yes, I would love to meet them," replied Elizabeth.

"I will speak with them later tonight and maybe we can arrange for you to come to dinner," said Albert.

"Yes, I would like that very much," Elizabeth told him.

Albert Turner was not a very tall man; he was about five foot eight in height and he had dark brown hair and a thin moustache. He was very smart in appearance, but he was also very outspoken.

When the day arrived for Elizabeth to meet his parents she was extremely nervous.

"What if they do not like me?" said Elizabeth.

"Of course they will, they will love you," Albert told her.

As Elizabeth entered their house Albert took her coat and hat from her and led her into the room where his parents were.

"Hello, my dear. Please sit down," said Albert's mother.

"Would you like some tea? Or would you prefer something a bit stronger?" asked Albert's father.

"Tea will be fine, thank you, if it's no trouble," replied Elizabeth.

"It is no trouble at all. We don't bite, you know," Albert's mother told her.

Elizabeth looked up and smiled at them both. She then started to tell them all about the work that she did and even offered to one day show them some of the paintings that she had done.

"I would be very interested in seeing them," said Albert's father. "But you will have to bring them around here quite soon, as I am off to Paris in a week or so," he told her.

"Oh yes, Albert mentioned that you were opening another shop in Paris. You must be rather excited," said Elizabeth.

"Yes, I am rather looking forward to it, although I am rather worried about leaving my wife for to long, as she has breathing problems and has been quite poorly lately," said Mr Turner.

"Oh, I am really sorry to hear that," said Elizabeth.

"It is nothing, my dear. Mr Turner fusses too much over me," said Mrs Turner.

"Dinner is ready. Shall we go through?" asked Albert.

Albert took Elizabeth's arm and as they walked into the next room together he whispered in her ear.

"I think they like you," he told her.

"I really hope so," said Elizabeth with a smile.

As the evening went on Elizabeth became more relaxed and ended up having a really enjoyable evening. Elizabeth had made a very good impression on Albert's parents and they were only too pleased to invite her back again when she had some free time.

As Christmas was only a few weeks' away Edward asked Elizabeth what plans she had for over the festive season, as he did not know whether she was going to visit her parents in Yorkshire, being that she had not seen them for quite some time. Elizabeth decided that she wanted to stay in London for Christmas as she did not want to leave Edward on his own and she also wanted to spend some time over Christmas with Albert as well.

Edward had started to notice a difference in Elizabeth as she was now a lot more grown up in her ways and a lot more independent. He could also tell that Elizabeth and Albert were becoming a lot closer over time and he knew that at some stage she could quite easily leave.

On Christmas Eve Elizabeth invited Albert around for the evening, but he refused as he wanted to spend the evening with his mother as his father was still away in Paris.

"You do not have to stay at home with me, Elizabeth. If you want to go to Albert's house, I really don't mind," said Edward.

"No, I am not going to leave you on your own on Christmas Eve," said Elizabeth. "Anyway, I think Albert will be popping in just for a few minutes to wish me a Merry Christmas a bit later."

Elizabeth sat drinking sherry with Edward whilst he drank some brandy and they tucked into some mince pies that the cook had made for them earlier that day.

"It is a shame that Albert's father has not come home from Paris for Christmas, isn't it?" said Edward.

"Yes it is. Why don't we invite Albert and Mrs Turner for Christmas dinner tomorrow?" suggested Elizabeth.

"Yes, what a nice idea," said Edward.

When Albert arrived to wish Elizabeth a Merry Christmas, she asked him if he and his mother would like to come Christmas for dinner, but he refused.

"Why won't you come? I think it is a lovely idea," said Elizabeth.

"I suppose it was Edward's idea, wasn't it?" asked Albert.

"No, actually it was me that suggested it," replied Elizabeth. "Why on earth would you think it was Edward's idea?" she asked.

"I just thought that perhaps he was trying to keep you all to himself over Christmas, because it is quite obvious why you are spending Christmas here instead of with me," said Albert.

"Edward is not trying to do anything of the sort. In fact he even told me to spend Christmas with you and your mother, but it was my choice not to leave Edward on his own," Elizabeth told him.

"You will not leave Edward on his own, but you can leave me," said Albert.

"But you have your mother with you, Edward has nobody," said Elizabeth.

"Yes, he does, he has the woman that is supposed to be with me," said Albert raising his voice.

"Oh, Albert, you are just being petty now. You know Edward and I are just good friends," said Elizabeth.

"I'm so sorry, what am I thinking?" said Albert.

"So will you come to Christmas dinner tomorrow? Seeing that it was my idea and not Edward's," asked Elizabeth.

"Yes, alright. I will see you then," he told her.

Elizabeth spent the rest of the evening helping Edward decorate their Christmas tree and it looked beautiful once it was finished and it stood over six feet tall.

"Here you are, Elizabeth, put these presents under the tree," said Edward.

"Oh, I just love Christmas, don't you?" she asked.

"Yes, I do," replied Edward.

The next morning Elizabeth was up bright and early, but she did not touch the presents under the tree as she wanted to wait until Albert had arrived.

"Merry Christmas, Elizabeth," said Edward as he kissed her on her cheek.

"Merry Christmas to you," said Elizabeth.

"What time are Albert and his mother arriving?" asked Edward.

"I think they will be here around midday," replied Elizabeth.

"I think I'll just go and see if cook is alright with everything, after all she has a lot to do today," said Edward.

"Oh, I'm sure cook has got everything under control," said Elizabeth.

"Well, I think I'll just go and check anyway," said Edward smiling.

"Oh I know what you are up to, you are going to ask her for a slice of turkey, aren't you?" asked Elizabeth.

"Now would I do something like that?" said Edward.

"Yes, you would, you know you would," laughed Elizabeth. "I can't say I blame you, it smells delicious. I think I'll come with you," she said smiling.

Later that morning Albert Turner arrived with his mother and they all sat down with a drink before having Christmas dinner.

"That's a large sherry, are you trying to get me drunk?" Mrs Turner asked Edward.

"No, of course not," replied Edward smiling.

"Well, you know what they say, Mother, a large sherry makes you merry," said Albert.

"Oh it looks like dinner is being served, so let's go through," said Edward.

"I have been looking forward to this all morning," said Elizabeth.

They all sat down for their dinner and after they had eaten they could hardly move.

"Let's go and look at the presents now," said Elizabeth.

They all went into the other room and Elizabeth gave Albert and Edward their presents from her. She had bought Albert a new wallet and Edward some new cufflinks.

"Thank you, Elizabeth, these are just what I needed," said Edward.

"Yes, thank you, Elizabeth," said Albert.

Albert was quite disappointed with the present that Elizabeth had given him; he seemed to think that he should have had the cufflinks instead of Edward, as he thought they were a more expensive gift.

"Here is your present from me," said Edward to Elizabeth.

"No, wait a minute. I want you to have mine first," said Albert.

Edward did not say a word although he was thinking how rude Albert was for interrupting him like that. Elizabeth did not seem to notice; she was to busy trying to find out what Albert had bought her.

"Oh Albert, these are lovely," said Elizabeth as she held up a pair of earrings.

"Now you can have my present, Elizabeth," said Edward.

Elizabeth was very excited and when she saw what Edward had bought her, she just beamed and gasped at the same time.

"Oh Edward, this must have cost you a fortune. It is really beautiful and it is something that I have always wanted," said Elizabeth, as she admired a gold charm bracelet which was full of all different charms.

"Oh that is lovely, isn't it dear?" said Mrs Turner.

Albert looked furious. He did not like the thought of Edward giving Elizabeth something better than he had given her and he looked across the room at Edward and gave him the most terrible, filthiest look ever. What made things even worse was that Elizabeth just could not stop looking or even talking about the charm bracelet. Edward was aware of the look that Albert had given him, but he did not say anything as he did not want to spoil everyone's day; he just carried on as if nothing had happened.

"Let's all have a drink, shall we?" asked Elizabeth.

"I'll just have a small sherry this time, thank you," said Mrs Turner.

"Yes, we wouldn't want you getting drunk and falling over, otherwise we might have to sue Edward," said Albert. "I can just imagine that in the newspapers, a lawyer being sued," he said rather sarcastically.

Edward still did not comment but he knew that Albert was deliberately trying to provoke him, however, Elizabeth was still oblivious to the situation.

"Let's have a toast," said Elizabeth as she held up her glass. "A Merry Christmas to all," she said.

"Yes, a Merry Christmas to all and a kiss for my beautiful Elizabeth," said Albert, as he kissed her on her cheek.

But as Albert kissed Elizabeth he looked at Edward with a sarcastic grin upon his face, but Edward just drank his drink and tried to ignore him.

"Would you like a cigar, Albert?" asked Edward.

"No, thank you, I do not touch them, it is a filthy habit," replied Albert.

"Yes you do, you used to smoke them all the time," said Mrs Turner.

"Yes, exactly, Mother. I used to smoke them but not anymore," he told her rather rudely.

"Edward does not smoke them either, he only saves them for his special guests," said Elizabeth.

"I must be your special guest then, am I Edward?" asked Albert.

"Of course you are," replied Elizabeth.

"It is very noble of you to say so, my dear," said Albert, as he put his arm around Elizabeth's waist.

Edward was starting to get rather agitated with Albert; he could see right through him and his sarcastic remarks, but he did not retaliate as he knew this was what Albert wanted him to do.

Edward was quite relieved as the evening came to an end; he had had just about all he could take from Albert for one day.

"Maybe tomorrow you will come to us for dinner?" Albert told Elizabeth.

"Yes, I would like that," she replied.

"What about Edward? I am sure he would like to join us as well," said Mrs Turner.

"Oh, I am sure Edward has other plans, Mother. I am sure he doesn't want to sit there and watch Elizabeth and I all night," said Albert.

"But I will be there if he needs someone to talk to," said Mrs Turner.

"Well your age group have a lot more in common with each other, don't they?" said Albert.

"I'll just get your coats," said Edward.

Edward, by this time, felt like he was about to breath fire all over Albert. He then gave them both their coats and saw them to the door.

"Would you help my mother into the carriage? Whilst I say goodbye to Elizabeth," asked Albert.

Edward held Mrs Turner's arm and led her to the carriage and once she was inside he waited for Albert. As Albert came towards him Edward grabbed hold of his arm, but he made sure Elizabeth could not see from where she was standing.

"I do not know what you think you are playing at, but whatever it is, it is not very amusing," said Edward.

"Oh come on, Edward, I am not playing at anything. You are the one who tried to win Elizabeth over by buying her a expensive charm bracelet. But let's face it, Edward, she would never be interested in you. You are an old man trying to buy a lady's affection," said Albert.

"That is utter nonsense and you know it. I would never do anything like that to Elizabeth," said Edward.

"Let's face it, you will never get the chance to do anything with Elizabeth, old man. She is mine, just remember that," Albert told him.

Edward let go of Albert's arm and he climbed into the carriage, Edward just stood and stared at him as the carriage pulled away.

"Don't just stand there, Edward, it is freezing out here," shouted Elizabeth.

"I am just coming," he told her.

"It went rather well today, didn't it?" asked Elizabeth.

"Yes, it did," replied Edward.

127

"You are going to come to Albert's parents' house tomorrow, aren't you?" she asked.

"I don't know, Elizabeth, I think I might just stay home," he told her.

"Why?" asked Elizabeth.

"I am just not one of those people who enjoys going to other peoples houses, that's all," replied Edward.

"Well, if you change your mind, just let me know," Elizabeth told him.

"Yes, alright," said Edward.

Edward tried to put on a brave face for Elizabeth's sake, but deep inside he was not only angry he was also very hurt by what Albert had said to him. All Edward had ever tried to do was be a friend to Elizabeth and yet he was being accused of trying to buy her love and Edward felt ashamed that someone could think of him in that way.

CHAPTER NINE

Over the next six months or so Elizabeth had started to get even closer to Albert and although Edward disapproved there was nothing he could do about it. Albert was still very jealous of Edward's close relationship with Elizabeth and whenever he saw Edward he let him know it, but he put it in such a way so as not to let Elizabeth find out how he felt. Edward on the other hand wanted Elizabeth to find out just what kind of person she was getting herself involved with, but he could not tell her himself in case she did not believe him and the last thing Edward wanted was for Elizabeth to turn against him.

"Elizabeth, I have something to tell you," said Albert one day.

"What is it?" she asked.

"It is my mother. Her health has deteriorated," said Albert.

"Oh, Albert, I am so sorry to hear that," said Elizabeth.

"I think my father has decided to sell his shop in Paris as he wants to be closer to my mother. It is such a shame as that shop is doing extraordinary well over there," said Albert.

"Why can't your father employ someone else to run it for him?" asked Elizabeth.

"I do not think my father will trust anyone else to do it, as he lost a lot of money once through trusting other people with his businesses," replied Albert.

"Oh, that is a shame," said Elizabeth.

Later that evening Elizabeth told Edward the terrible news about Mrs Turner's health and about having to sell the jewellery shop in Paris.

"Oh that is a shame. I am really very fond of Mrs Turner," said Edward.

"Yes it is awful, isn't it?" said Elizabeth. "And to think Mr Turner has worked so hard as well building up his business in Paris and now he has to sell it all."

Edward suddenly had an idea but he was not sure how Elizabeth would react when he told her.

"If Mr Turner needs to be closer to his wife, he could always take over the shop he already has in London and let Albert manage the other shop in Paris," said Edward.

"But I would hardly ever see him if he does that," said Elizabeth.

"Of course you would. Paris is not that far away and Mr Turner seems to do alright travelling back and forth," said Edward.

"Oh, I don't know," said Elizabeth.

"I think it is a very good idea and, that way Mr Turner will not lose one of his businesses," said Edward.

"Well, yes, when you put it like that, I suppose that is the best solution for everyone," said Elizabeth.

"Then why don't you put the idea to Albert. He can only say no if he does not like the idea," said Edward.

Edward had suddenly realised that this was his only way of separating them both. He knew Albert was a bad sort and certainly not good enough for Elizabeth, but he could not tell her that. He was just praying that his plan would work and that Albert would take the manager's job in Paris.

The next day Elizabeth put the idea to Albert but he looked quite shocked at her suggestion.

"Are you trying to get rid of me?" he asked.

"No, of course not. I was just thinking of a way to save your father's business, that's all," replied Elizabeth.

"But we would not see each other very often," said Albert.

"I know that. But we could still keep in touch, after all your father manages to do it," said Elizabeth.

"Well, I suppose I could have a word with my father. He will probably think it is a good idea. Anything to get me out of the way," said Albert smiling.

"Don't be so ridiculous. If he likes the idea that's probably because he wants to save his business," said Elizabeth.

"Yes I know, I am only joking," said Albert.

"Well, Edward thought it was a good idea, so I expect your father will as well," said Elizabeth.

"You have spoken to Edward about this?" asked Albert.

"Well yes. In fact it was his idea," replied Elizabeth.

"You mean it was his idea for me to go to Paris?" asked Albert.

"Yes," replied Elizabeth.

I bet it was, thought Albert.

Albert was absolutely furious with Edward. He knew why Edward wanted him out of the way. Well at least he thought he did. He thought Edward wanted Elizabeth all to himself, but Edward only wanted Albert out of the country because he knew he was bad for Elizabeth.

I'll show him, thought Albert.

Later that evening, Albert paid Edward a little visit.

"Good evening, Albert. I did not realise you were coming here this evening," said Elizabeth.

"I would like to speak with you and Edward," said Albert.

"Come through, Edward is in here," said Elizabeth.

Albert followed Elizabeth into the room and when Edward saw Albert he immediately stood up.

"Albert would like to speak with us both," said Elizabeth.

"Go ahead," Edward told him.

"I have spoken with my father about going to Paris to manage the shop there and he thinks it is a wonderful idea," said Albert.

"That is good news," said Edward.

"Yes, I thought you might say that. But my only concern is that I will not see as much of Elizabeth as I would like," said Albert.

"But we will still see each other, just not as often," said Elizabeth.

"That is not good enough," said Albert. "So the reason I am here is to ask you something, Elizabeth," he said.

"What is it?" asked Elizabeth.

"How would you feel about coming to Paris with me?" he asked.

"Oh, Albert, I could not possibly go to Paris. I have my work commitments here," she told him.

"Yes, but just think how well you are doing in London. You could start all over again in Paris. The people there would love your work," said Albert.

"It is very tempting, I suppose," said Elizabeth.

"Well, I do not think it is a very good idea," said Edward.

"Why? After all there is nothing to keep Elizabeth here. Is there Edward?" asked Albert with a sudden change in his tone of voice.

"Elizabeth has made many friends here, she might not make friends easily over in Paris," said Edward.

"She has made new clients here or the odd acquaintance, they are not real friends," said Albert.

"I still do not think it is a good idea for Elizabeth to leave here. And besides where would she live? After all she most certainly could not live with you," said Edward.

"Edward does have a point," said Elizabeth.

"Well, once we are out there we could get married straight away, then there will be nothing stopping us living together," said Albert.

"Over my dead body!" Edward told him.

"I am sure Elizabeth can think for herself, she is an adult after all," said Albert. "Just think, Elizabeth, all those romantic evenings in Paris and it will be just you and me there to enjoy it," said Albert.

"Oh it sounds lovely," said Elizabeth.

"I think you are rushing into things rather too quickly, Elizabeth, you should take time to really think about what you are doing," said Edward.

"Time is not on our side, Edward. If Elizabeth wants to come with me she will have to give me an answer straight away, as I shall be leaving for Paris within the next day or so," said Albert.

"You cannot expect Elizabeth to give you an answer straight away, after all this could affect her whole life," said Edward.

"Yes it could. Just think about it, Elizabeth, your whole life with me. That is what you want, isn't it?" asked Albert.

"Well, I suppose so," she replied.

"See Elizabeth did not say yes to you; that's because she is not sure it is what she wants," said Edward.

"You do love me don't you?" asked Albert.

"Yes, of course I do," replied Elizabeth.

"Well, if you really love me, then you would say yes," Albert told her.

Elizabeth looked over towards Edward and he just stared at her. He was praying that she would not say yes to Albert.

"Well, Elizabeth, what is it to be?" asked Albert.

"Yes, alright, I will come with you to Paris," she replied.

As Albert lifted Elizabeth off the floor and swung her around, Edward slumped himself down in his chair in despair. He knew by now that Elizabeth was about to make the biggest mistake of her life and there was nothing that he could do about it.

"Would you get my coat for me, Elizabeth?" said Albert.

Whilst Elizabeth was out of the room Albert walked towards Edward and smirked at him.

"Looks like the best man won," he told Edward.

"You might have won this time, but I can assure you that in time Elizabeth will see right through you for what you really are," said Edward.

"Yes, of course she will. She will see that I am the better man and you are nothing but a sad, lonely old man," said Albert.

When Albert left Edward sat down with Elizabeth and tried his hardest to change her mind about going to Paris with him, but she had all these romantic thoughts in her head about how Paris would be and there was nothing Edward could do or say that would change things.

Albert made all the arrangements for them both to travel to Paris and he did this as quickly as possible before Elizabeth had a chance to change her mind. Elizabeth packed her belongings and was so excited about going to Paris, but it made Edward feel like he hardly existed.

"Hurry up, Elizabeth, the carriage is here to take us to the port," said Albert, as they were about to leave.

"I am just waiting for Edward," said Elizabeth.

"Why? He is not coming with us, is he?" asked Albert.

"Yes, he is coming to see us off," replied Elizabeth.

"Then tell him to hurry up or else we will be late," said Albert, rather abruptly.

When they arrived at the Port, Elizabeth and Albert both collected their belongings together, then Elizabeth walked towards Edward to say her goodbyes to him.

"Come on, Elizabeth, we have not got time for all this," said Albert, as he grabbed her arm.

Edward was just about to give Elizabeth a kiss on her cheek, but before he had the chance Albert had pulled her away from him.

"Goodbye, Edward," shouted Elizabeth, as Albert led her away.

Edward was extremely upset by the way Albert was acting towards him; all he wanted to do was say goodbye to Elizabeth, but Albert had not even given him the chance to do so.

As they both climbed the steps to the huge cruise liner Elizabeth pushed passed some of the passengers, as she wanted to get to the front so that she could wave to Edward.

"Where is Edward? I cannot see him," said Elizabeth.

"Oh, just forget about him, you are with me now," Albert told her.

"Yes, I know that. But I still want to wave goodbye to Edward, as this might be the last time I see him," said Elizabeth.

"Edward, Edward, Edward. That is all I ever hear," said Albert.

"That's not true. All I want is to say goodbye to him," said Elizabeth.

"Goodbye and good riddance if you ask me," said Albert.

"How can you say that? Edward has been really good to me these past few years. At least let me have this one opportunity to say goodbye to him," said Elizabeth.

Elizabeth turned away from Albert and looked through the crowd of people that were standing waving goodbye to their loved ones.

"I can see him. There he is!" said Elizabeth as she pointed to him.

Elizabeth started to wave like mad at him but Edward could not see her. She then saw Edward wiping his eyes with a handkerchief.

"Oh poor Edward, look he is crying," said Elizabeth.

"He is not crying. He is probably just wiping his eyes because of the wind blowing," said Albert.

"No, look, he is crying, I can see him," said Elizabeth.

"Well, he cannot see you, so come on, let's go inside," said Albert.

"No, I want to stay here and wave to Edward," Elizabeth told him.

"If Edward means so much to you, why don't you just stay here with him," said Albert angrily.

"Yes, maybe I should!" said Elizabeth.

"I am so sorry, Elizabeth, I did not mean that," said Albert.

"Then why did you say it?" she asked.

"It's just that you keep going on and on about Edward and it is starting to annoy me," replied Albert.

"You are not jealous of him are you?" asked Elizabeth.

"Don't be so ridiculous. Me jealous of him, I do not think so," he replied.

"It seems to me that you are," Elizabeth told him.

"Just shut up about him. Now get your belongings and come downstairs," said Albert looking extremely angry.

"How dare you speak to me like that. I am not going anywhere with you," said Elizabeth, as she pushed past him.

"Where do you think you are going?" asked Albert.

"I am going home where I belong," she replied.

"What, back to Edward? But you do not belong to him, you belong to me," shouted Albert, as he grabbed hold of her arm.

"Let go of me, you are hurting me!" said Elizabeth.

"No, I won't. You are not going anywhere with him, you are staying right here with me," shouted Albert.

"Let go!" shouted Elizabeth.

Albert held on to Elizabeth's arm as tightly as he could and he pulled her towards him, so Elizabeth suddenly slapped him across his face, but this made Albert even more angry. He then punched Elizabeth in her face and made her fall to the ground. Within seconds a gentleman came running towards Albert and grabbed his arms behind his back and another gentleman who was standing nearby helped Elizabeth to her feet.

"Are you alright, my dear?" asked the gentleman.

135

"No, I have to get off, please help me to the stairs," said Elizabeth.

The gentleman took Elizabeth's arm and walked with her; he then helped her down the steps and she pushed past everyone so that she could find Edward. Elizabeth looked everywhere but Edward was nowhere to be seen. She then started to panic and got very upset and people around her just stared at her as the tears flowed down her face.

Where are you, Edward? she thought.

Elizabeth then came to a tea room, but as she was about to enter it she noticed her reflection in the window. Her face was very swollen where Albert had hit her, and her dress was torn where she had struggled to free herself from Albert.

Oh look at the state of me, she thought.

But just as she started to walk away she heard a voice call to her. It was Edward who had come out from the tea room. Elizabeth turned around and when she saw Edward she just threw her arms around him and sobbed bitterly in his arms.

"Elizabeth. What on earth has happened to you?" asked Edward.

"It was Albert, he did this to me," cried Elizabeth.

"Where is he now?" asked Edward.

"I don't know. I think he has been arrested," replied Elizabeth.

"Well, if I get my hands on him, I'll..." Edward paused before he said something he might regret.

"All I wanted to do was wave goodbye to you and Albert suddenly went berserk," said Elizabeth.

"Let's go inside the tea room, I think you need to sit down," said Edward.

Edward took Elizabeth's hand and helped her into the tea room and everyone in there started to stare at her.

"Sit down, Elizabeth, before you fall down," Edward told her.

"How could he do this to me? Look at my face!" cried Elizabeth.

"I think Albert is extremely jealous of my relationship with you, although I have never given him cause to be," said Edward.

"What makes you think that?" asked Elizabeth.

136

"He was angry with me at Christmas because I bought you a charm bracelet. He also told me I was trying to buy your affection and he said that he was a better man than me and that I was a sad, lonely old man," said Edward.

"But why would he say such awful things to you?" asked Elizabeth.

"He thought that I wanted you for myself, which is why he asked you to go to Paris with him. It was his only way of getting you away from me," said Edward.

"Why didn't you tell me all of this before? I never realised he despised you so much," said Elizabeth.

"If I had told you all the horrible things that Albert had said to me you probably would have never believed me," said Edward.

"But I trust your honesty, you know I do," said Elizabeth.

"But I was afraid to say anything in case I turned you against me," said Edward.

"That would never have happened. You mean the world to me. You know that," said Elizabeth.

"I just could not take that risk. The thought of you going to Paris with that vile man almost tore me apart, but it was better that you went with him, than losing your friendship altogether," Edward told her.

"I am so sorry, Edward. This is all my fault," said Elizabeth.

"Of course it isn't your fault. He had you fooled all along," Edward told her.

"How could I have been so blind? And for him to say such terrible things about you is unforgivable," said Elizabeth.

"Never mind about me, what he has done to you is unforgivable," said Edward.

Elizabeth put her hand up to her face and touched where Albert had hit her.

"I'll go and get a wet towel to put on your face; it will bring the swelling down," said Edward.

Elizabeth sat drinking her tea whilst Edward asked for a towel. Her body was still trembling through shock. A minute or so later Edward walked back to the table where Elizabeth was sitting and he gently held the wet towel on her face. Elizabeth just stared at Edward but some how something changed inside of her. She suddenly saw Edward in a different light. Here was a gentleman who was kind, gentle and considerate and who would do anything for Elizabeth. He had given her hope for the future, a new way of life, but most of all he had given her trust, love and understanding. The man of her dreams was sitting right in front of her and it had taken her all these years to realise that.

"Your face is very swollen," said Edward.

"So are your eyes," said Elizabeth.

"Oh yes, the wind blew some dust into them earlier," said Edward.

But Elizabeth knew that Edward was trying to put on a brave face. She knew deep down he had been crying, but she did not say that to him as she wanted to spare him any embarrassment.

"Let's go home, shall we?" said Edward.

"Yes," replied Elizabeth.

When Elizabeth and Edward returned home the police were outside the house; they wanted her to give them a statement about why Albert had assaulted her.

"I do not want to say anything, I would rather just forget about him," said Elizabeth.

"But, Elizabeth, this man attacked you; surely you are not going to let him get away with that?" said Edward.

"I do not wish to press charges against Mr Turner," she told the police.

"But, Elizabeth, please!" said Edward.

"Just take me inside," she told Edward.

Edward did what Elizabeth asked and the police went away. But Edward still thought that Elizabeth was making a big mistake.

Later that evening there was a knock at the door; it was Albert's father, Mr Turner. He had come to apologise for his son's behaviour.

"The police were here earlier, but I told them that I did not want to press charges against Albert," said Elizabeth.

"Yes, I know. But the police are still going to prosecute him for breech of the peace," said Mr Turner.

"Oh, I see," said Elizabeth.

"It is alright. I know you were not to blame. My son has a terrible temper and he deserves all he gets," said Mr Turner.

Mr Turner did not stay very long at Edward's house; he was afraid that his wife might find out what Albert had done. He had kept it from her as she was very poorly and he did not want to worry her.

When Mr Turner had left, Elizabeth burst into tears. She told Edward that she did not think that she could ever trust another man.

"There are only two gentlemen in my life that have never hurt me; one is you and the other is my father," said Elizabeth.

"Why do you say that? Have you been hurt before?" asked Edward.

Elizabeth then poured her heart out to Edward about Rosemary Thornton's brother whom had once tried to rape her, but only to be stopped due to Ernest Lockwood turning up unexpectedly.

Edward was lost for words; he could not believe Elizabeth had been so badly treated like that and he vowed never to visit Ernest again all the while he was married to Rosemary.

Edward felt very sad for Elizabeth. He never realised how troubled her life had been before she moved to London, but he also felt honoured that she had trusted him enough to confide in him about Rosemary's brother, as she had kept that secret to herself for many years.

Elizabeth sobbed bitterly as she told Edward about the terrible things that Rosemary had done to her and how frightened she had been when her brother assaulted her. Edward put his arms around her to comfort her, but she just sobbed and sobbed.

"Oh, Elizabeth, I am so sorry to hear such awful things, but I feel I am to blame as well," he told her.

"What do you mean? You are not to blame for any of this," said Elizabeth.

"I played a big part in getting Albert around here. If I had not asked him to escort you to the Mayor's ball, you would not be sitting here now with a swollen face," said Edward.

"Edward, you are the kindest, most generous person I have ever known and I certainly do not blame you for anything. You only did what you thought was right, so please do not blame yourself," Elizabeth told him.

Edward looked at Elizabeth and wiped the tears from her face; he had never seen her look so unhappy and he did not know what to do to ease her pain. Edward had grown very fond of Elizabeth and just the thought of anyone hurting her made his blood boil.

Elizabeth stayed home for the next few days as she did not want anyone to see her with a swollen face, but once she started back at work on her paintings she tried to put Albert out of her mind and get on with her life.

CHAPTER TEN

After a few months had passed Elizabeth received a letter from her brother William, telling her the good news that his wife Alice had given birth to a little boy whom they had named Benjamin. As Elizabeth read the letter a huge smile came upon her face.

"Is it good news?" asked Edward.

"Yes it is. I cannot believe it!" screamed Elizabeth.

"What is it?" asked Edward.

"My brother has written to inform me that his wife Alice has not long given birth to their son. I cannot believe I am actually an aunt," said Elizabeth excitedly.

"Oh that is good news. Why don't you take some time off work and visit them? After all, you have not seen your family in quite a while," said Edward.

"Yes, I think I might just do that. But I think I will leave it for a week or so; that way it will give William and Alice a bit of time to get used to the idea of being parents," said Elizabeth.

Edward smiled to himself as he could see that Elizabeth was genuinely excited about becoming an aunt and he was pleased that she had received some good news at last, after all the terrible things she had been through over the past few months.

A few weeks later Elizabeth travelled to Yorkshire to see her family again and when she arrived her brother and his wife were already at her parent's house waiting for her.

"Where is he then? Where is my new nephew?" asked Elizabeth.

"He is asleep over there," replied William as he pointed to a cradle.

Elizabeth walked towards him and when she saw him she could hardly believe how tiny he was.

"Oh he is just so beautiful," said Elizabeth, smiling from ear to ear.

"Isn't it about time you were married, Elizabeth? Then you could have a child of your own," said William.

"Oh no, I am much too busy for that," replied Elizabeth.

"Well, isn't there anyone special in your life?" asked William.

"No, well not yet, anyway," she replied.

"Will you stop asking Elizabeth personal questions, you are embarrassing her," Alice told him.

"Elizabeth does not mind, do you?" asked William.

"Well yes, actually I do," she replied jokingly.

"Who would like some tea?" asked Elizabeth's mother.

"Umm, yes please," replied William.

"Sit down, Mother, I'll make it," said Elizabeth.

"Have you planned anything for tomorrow, Elizabeth?" asked Alice.

"No not really. Why?" asked Elizabeth.

"I was wondering if you would like to come shopping with me?" asked Alice.

"I would love to," Elizabeth told her.

The next day Elizabeth and Alice spent the whole day looking around the town and Elizabeth spent a lot of money buying lots of things for her new nephew Benjamin. The two ladies got along really well with each other; it was as if they had known each other all their lives.

Before Elizabeth returned to London she travelled to Newcastle as she wanted to pay her friend Emily a visit and when Emily saw who it was knocking at her door she just screamed with excitement.

"What are you doing here?" she asked.

"I have been to Yorkshire to visit my family as my brother and his wife have not long had a little boy. Before I return to London I thought it would be nice to see you again," replied Elizabeth.

"Come in, come in," said Emily. "Look who is here!" Emily told her mother.

Emily's mother walked into the room and just looked at Elizabeth.

"It's Elizabeth. Don't you recognise her?" asked Emily.

"Oh yes, so it is. I am awfully sorry, Elizabeth, you look so different and so grown up" said Emily's mother.

"How are you all?" asked Elizabeth.

"We are all fine, thank you," replied Emily's mother.

"Come and sit down, Elizabeth, and tell me all your news," said Emily.

Elizabeth sat talking with Emily for hours and she trusted her enough to tell her all about Albert and the awful way he had treated her.

"That's terrible," said Emily. "What did Edward say?" she asked.

"He was furious and he wanted me to have him prosecuted, but I refused as all I wanted was to just forget about him," replied Elizabeth.

"How is Edward anyway?" asked Emily.

"He is fine," replied Elizabeth.

"When I met him at your grandmother's funeral he seemed really nice," said Emily.

"Yes he is, he is the perfect gentleman," Elizabeth told her.

"Elizabeth is there something that you are not telling me?" asked Emily with a smile.

"What do you mean?" asked Elizabeth.

"Oh you know. I can see that look in your eye. You have fallen in love with him, haven't you?" she asked.

"Don't be so ridiculous" replied Elizabeth.

"I think you are telling fibs. So what if you have, he is a good-looking gentleman and you said yourself how kind and generous he is," said Emily.

"Edward is just a friend that's all. But yes, I do have feelings for him, but not in the way that you think," said Elizabeth.

"I don't believe you," said Emily.

"Trust me, there is nothing going on between Edward and I," Elizabeth told her.

"I bet given half the chance Edward would not say no," laughed Emily.

"How can you say such a thing? Edward would never do any such thing," said Elizabeth.

"All men would if they were given half the chance," said Emily.

"Not Edward," said Elizabeth.

"I'm not so sure. I saw the way he looked at you at your grandmother's graveside. He had love in his eyes for you," said Emily.

"Now you are just being silly," Elizabeth told her.

"I am telling you the truth. I cross my heart and hope to die," said Emily.

"Do you really think so?" asked Elizabeth.

"I am telling you so. He loves you and even though you will not admit it, I can tell you feel the same way about him," said Emily.

Elizabeth did not admit to anything, she just raised her eyebrows at Emily and gave her a cheeky grin.

"So when are you going to come and stay with me in London?" asked Elizabeth.

"Oh I don't know. I don't really have the money anyway," replied Emily.

"Forget about the money that is the least of your worries. Just hurry up and visit me," Elizabeth told her.

"I'll try," said Emily smiling.

"You had better," said Elizabeth jokingly.

Elizabeth stayed at Emily's for a few days and whilst she was in Newcastle she also visited her Aunt Beth and her cousins.

When she returned to London Elizabeth crept into the house to surprise Edward.

"Oh, Elizabeth, it is so good to see you. You were away so long, I did not think that you were ever coming back," said Edward.

"I'm sorry, I should have let you know when I was coming back, but I did not know myself. Whilst I was away I decided to go to Newcastle as well to see my friend Emily," said Elizabeth.

"As long as you enjoyed yourself, that's all that matters," Edward told her.

"Yes I did. It was so good to see my family again and little Benjamin is absolutely gorgeous," said Elizabeth. "And how have you been, Edward?" she asked.

"I have been working hard as usual, but I still missed you very much. It has been extremely quiet here without you," said Edward.

"I have missed you too," said Elizabeth.

Elizabeth went back to work on her paintings the following day and she worked until late in the evenings. She was trying to catch up with her paintings as she had been away for quite a number of weeks and had many more clients to see.

"Elizabeth, you look exhausted," said Edward, one evening.

"I am. But I have so much to do," she told him.

"You need to rest more, it is not good for you to work all these hours," said Edward.

"Yes I know, but I have to," said Elizabeth.

"Well, you can come home a bit earlier tomorrow as I have two tickets for the opera and I would like to take you to it," said Edward.

"Really?" asked Elizabeth.

"Yes. Would you like to come with me?" he asked.

"Yes, I would love to. I have never been to the opera before," said Elizabeth smiling.

"We will have to leave about seven," said Edward.

"I'll be here," she told him excitedly.

On the evening of the opera Elizabeth got herself all dressed up and she was very excited about going to the opera, as she had not had a night out in quite a while due to her work commitments. As she walked downstairs Elizabeth looked at Edward and she thought how smart and dashing he looked in his suit.

"Well just look at you, you look beautiful," Edward told her.

"Thank you. You look quite dashing yourself," she said with a smile.

Elizabeth did not really know what to expect that evening as she had never been to an opera before, but she thoroughly enjoyed herself. As she sat watching she could sense Edward was looking at her, but she did not let him know that she knew. Edward was watching the expressions on Elizabeth's face and he smiled to himself as he could see that she was enjoying every minute of it.

As the curtain closed for the end of the show Elizabeth and Edward made their way towards the exit, but as they walked downstairs Elizabeth tripped on her dress, so Edward quickly grabbed her arm to save her from falling.

"Oh, thank you, Edward, if you hadn't of grabbed hold of my arm I might have fallen all the way down these stairs," said Elizabeth.

"Good evening, Edward," said a voice.

Edward looked around and saw an old client of his whom he had represented in court just a few weeks ago.

"Good evening," said Edward to the man.

"Jolly good show, wasn't it?" said the man.

"Yes, it was very good," replied Edward.

Edward noticed that the man was very unsteady on his feet as he had been drinking and he also noticed that he kept staring at Elizabeth.

"Well aren't you going to introduce me to this beautiful young lady?" asked the man as he looked at Elizabeth.

"This is Elizabeth Oakendale, she is a very dear friend of mine," replied Edward.

"She is a friend? Oh that's what they all say," said the man. "But don't worry, your secret is safe with me," he told Edward as he tapped his nose.

"No she really is a friend," said Edward looking rather embarrassed.

"Yes, yes, of course she is," said the man jokingly. "They say the young ones are the best. Is that true?" he asked Edward.

"Excuse me, I have to go," said Edward looking quite angry.

"Oh I see, you cannot wait to get her home and who can blame you. If I were with a lovely lady like her I would want to get her home as well," said the man.

"Oh, be quiet, you do not know anything," said Edward raising his voice.

"I know one thing, you are on a good thing with her, you lucky devil," said the man.

Elizabeth felt extremely embarrassed by what the man was implying and she could see that Edward was beginning to get very annoyed and agitated by what the man was saying.

"Come on, Edward, let's go," she told him.

"Enjoy the rest of your evening, won't you?" said the man as he laughed out loud.

Edward did not answer the man he just took Elizabeth's arm and led her away. Elizabeth could tell that Edward was boiling with anger just by the look on his face and he did not say one word to her all the way home. She knew it was not through anything she had done; it was because of the foolish man's rudeness towards them both that had annoyed him.

When they arrived back home Edward poured himself a brandy and drank it down all in one mouthful; he then poured himself another one and did exactly the same thing.

"Steady on, Edward, you'll get drunk," Elizabeth told him.

"I'm sorry, but I needed that after the night I have had," said Edward.

"Well, I enjoyed myself very much," said Elizabeth.

"Yes so did I, until I set eyes on that rude little man," said Edward, as he poured himself yet another drink.

"Can I try some?" asked Elizabeth.

"Yes, you are welcome to try it, but I do not think you will like it," Edward told her.

He then poured Elizabeth a brandy and she downed it in one mouthful just like Edward had done.

"Ahhhhhhhh!" she said as she shuddered.

Edward just stood there and laughed.

"I did warn you," he told her.

"At least you are laughing now," said Elizabeth smiling. "You looked so angry when we left the theatre tonight."

"Yes, I was very angry with that stupid-minded little man," said Edward.

"You should not let people get to you like that and anyway he was probably only jealous," said Elizabeth.

"Yes, most probably, but there is still no excuse for rudeness," said Edward.

"Well, it does not bother me what people think. In fact, I felt very proud being with you tonight," said Elizabeth.

"But people like him can cause a lot of trouble with their silly rumours," said Edward.

"Then they obviously have such boring lives if they have to make up such stories like that," said Elizabeth.

"Yes that is so true," said Edward.

"You have been a really good friend to me, Edward, and if people cannot accept that, then they are just foolish," she told him. "At least you treat me with respect, which is more than I can say about Albert or even people like that man tonight," said Elizabeth.

"You are so sweet, Elizabeth, and I know what you are saying, but when people start spreading rumours like that it is very hard for others to believe the real truth and it would be awful if people started pointing their finger at you and started talking about you just because of a malicious rumour, wouldn't it?" said Edward.

"I do not care what people say. I'll just tell them to mind their own business," said Elizabeth.

"But I care, Elizabeth, and I would not want anyone talking about you in that way," he told her.

"I think I'll go to bed now, but thank you for a lovely evening," said Elizabeth.

"You are very welcome, goodnight," said Edward.

Later that night Elizabeth was woken by the sound of thunder which she hated and, as the thunder got louder, she hid her head underneath the blankets that were on her bed. But after a while the rain started to get heavier and the thunder started to get worse and because Elizabeth was so petrified of thunder she decided to go downstairs and sit with Edward, as she felt safer being with him. Elizabeth looked in most of the rooms downstairs but she could not find Edward, so she thought he must have retired to bed. Then she thought that he might be in his study doing some paperwork, so she had a look in there but he was not in there either. As she was about to leave the study she noticed a book lying open on his desk, so she had a look at it not realising that it was Edward's diary.

I took Elizabeth to the opera tonight and what an enjoyable evening we had. As I sat next to her I watched as her beautiful eyes sparkled like diamonds and those funny little expressions she pulled made me laugh. Elizabeth is the most important thing in my life and yet people with their illicit thoughts try to spoil that. I would never knowingly do anything to hurt her and if only I were twenty years younger I could tell her how I felt about her, but I know I must not say anything as I might lose her altogether and if I lose her friendship I might as well lose my life it said.

Elizabeth could not believe what she was reading; she never realised that Edward felt that way about her, but she was pleased because she also had feelings for him. Then she remembered what her friend Emily had told her; she said that Edward loved Elizabeth as she could see it in his eyes and just by the way he looked at her.

Suddenly there was another loud clap of thunder so Elizabeth ran out from the study, ran upstairs and woke Edward with her screams.

"Are you alright, Elizabeth?" asked Edward as he came out of his bedroom.

"No, I cannot sleep because of the thunder," she told him.

"Yes, it is keeping me awake as well," said Edward.

"Shall I make us some tea?" asked Elizabeth.

"That would be lovely," replied Edward.

After Elizabeth had made some tea she sat down in front of the fire and could not help but look at Edward. She kept thinking about what he had written in his diary about her and yet she still found it hard to believe that he did actually love her.

"You are rather quiet, Elizabeth. Is there anything wrong?" asked Edward.

"I just do not like thunder that's all," she replied.

"Don't worry, it will soon pass," Edward told her.

But it did not pass for quite some time. The thunder seemed to get louder and louder as it came overhead and Elizabeth sat shaking with fear.

Edward took out the tea tray from the room and when he came back he brought a blanket with him for Elizabeth to keep her warm. By then Elizabeth was sitting on the floor in front of the fire, so Edward put the blanket around her and sat on the floor next to her.

"That's better. I feel a bit warmer now," said Elizabeth.

"Just keep that blanket around you and you'll be fine," he told her.

Elizabeth was still very quiet as she did not know what to say to Edward; all she kept thinking about was the diary.

After some time had passed the thunder had gone and Edward was just about to say to Elizabeth about retiring to bed when he suddenly realised she had fallen asleep on the floor. Edward tried to carefully move her without waking her, but she started to wake so he let go of her. Elizabeth then got comfortable again, but as she laid back down she laid across Edward and he could not move. Edward looked down at Elizabeth and just kept thinking how beautiful she was, but he certainly did not have the courage to tell her how he felt, as he knew deep down he did not stand a chance with her.

A while later Edward had to move as he had cramp in his leg where Elizabeth had been lying on him, but as he moved she woke up.

"I am so sorry, I did not mean to wake you," he told her as he rubbed his leg.

"It is alright," said Elizabeth.

Elizabeth had started to get cold again and Edward had noticed her shivering, so he wrapped the blanket around her shoulders, but as he did this Elizabeth looked at him and put her hands up to his face and tried to kiss him. Edward quickly pushed her hands away and stood up.

"What are you doing, Elizabeth? This is wrong," he told her.

"I'm sorry, but I thought it was what you wanted," she said.

"What made you think that?" he asked.

"It does not matter," replied Elizabeth.

She then ran out of the room feeling extremely embarrassed and Edward just stood there not knowing what to do next. He could not understand why Elizabeth had tried to kiss him, after all he had never given her reason to do that. Edward had always kept his feelings to himself, but he now knew Elizabeth had feelings too, and he did not know how to deal with it. Edward knew that he had to put a stop to it but he did not want to hurt her. Even though Edward did love her he knew they could not possibly be together because too many people would start to gossip and although that did not bother him as such, he still had to protect Elizabeth from such scandal.

The next day Edward went out early in the morning as he did not want Elizabeth to feel anymore embarrassed than she already did. But when Elizabeth got up and realised that Edward was not there, she blamed herself for frightening him away.

What did I do so wrong? she thought. "I thought he loved me, in fact I know he loves me. So what is so wrong with us kissing?" she said to herself.

After breakfast, Elizabeth decided to go riding on Midnight as she needed to get out to clear her head, but it was hard for her to think about anything else apart from Edward and by now she was so confused over it all she did not know what to think.

Elizabeth spent most of the day out on her own either riding Midnight or just sitting down thinking about what happened between her and Edward the night before.

"I just don't know what to think anymore," she told herself.

As she sat down by a tree she could see someone walking towards her, but because the sun was in her eyes she could not see who it was.

"Elizabeth," said a voice.

Elizabeth stood up and when she saw who it was she was rather shocked. It was Albert Turner, the man who had hit her a few months before.

"Stay away from me!" Elizabeth told him.

"I am not going to hurt you," said Albert.

"What do you want then?" she asked.

"I just saw you there and I wanted to apologise for what I did to you. It was unforgivable," said Albert.

"Yes it was," said Elizabeth. "It was also unforgivable about the way you treated Edward. He is my friend and you had no right to accuse him of anything," she told him.

"I'm sorry, but I was jealous. All you seemed to do was talk about him and it made me angry," said Albert.

"It does not matter anymore. You have said your apologies, so please leave me alone," said Elizabeth.

"Don't worry, I will not be around here for much longer anyway. I have since moved to Paris and I am only back for my mother's funeral" said Albert.

"You mean your mother has passed away?" asked Elizabeth.

"Yes, last week," replied Albert as he started to weep.

"Oh, Albert, I am so sorry to hear that, your mother was such a lovely lady," said Elizabeth.

Albert just stood weeping even more, so Elizabeth walked towards him and put her arms around him to comfort him.

"Come on, Albert, stop crying, everything will be alright," said Elizabeth.

"Nothing is ever going to be alright. First I lost you, now my mother. It just gets worse and worse," said Albert.

"It just takes time to get over it that's all," said Elizabeth.

"But I will never get over losing you," said Albert.

Elizabeth just stared at him then Albert pulled her closer to him and kissed her.

"Stop it. What do you think you are doing?" shouted Elizabeth.

"Oh come on, Elizabeth, you know you still love me and I love you," said Albert.

"No, you are wrong, I do not love you anymore," said Elizabeth.

"But you were going to marry me once and spend your life with me in Paris. So how can you say you do not love me?" asked Albert.

"That was a long time ago. Things have changed since and I have changed," said Elizabeth.

"What things have changed?" asked Albert.

"Just things," replied Elizabeth.

"I bet this has something to do with Edward, doesn't it?" asked Albert.

"I don't know what you are talking about," Elizabeth told him.

"Yes, you do. You are in love with him and I bet this was going on when we were together, wasn't it?" said Albert.

"No, it was not. But yes, I am in love with Edward now," replied Elizabeth.

"I knew it, you little slut! You let him near you, but you would never let me!" said Albert.

"Nothing like that has happened," said Elizabeth.

"So you are telling me you are still pure," said Albert.

"Yes, I am. Not that it is any of your business," shouted Elizabeth.

"I do not believe you. You are just like all the others, a cheap slut!" shouted Albert.

"You had better shut your mouth before I shut it for you," said a voice.

Elizabeth looked around and there stood Edward; he had heard everything.

"Oh look, it is lover boy come to Elizabeth's rescue, or should I say dirty old man who takes advantage of young girls," said Albert.

Edward was fuming by Albert's remarks. He suddenly flew at Albert and punched him right in his face. Albert fell to the floor so Edward grabbed him by his collar and hit him again and again.

"Edward, that's enough, you'll kill him!" shouted Elizabeth.

Edward suddenly came to his senses and stopped hitting Albert. He then walked over to Elizabeth to see that she was alright.

"I shall be seeing you in court for this," shouted Albert.

"Feel free to do so. I have many friends that are lawyers and judges so you will not stand a chance and, do not forget, you still have a criminal record from when you hit Elizabeth that day," said Edward.

"I was not taken to court by Elizabeth," said Albert.

"But you were still prosecuted for breech of the peace and that has not been forgotten," said Edward.

"Just go home, Albert, you are not wanted around here anymore," said Elizabeth.

"Looks like the best man won after all," said Edward.

"You do not love her. You are just a filthy man getting what he can," said Albert.

"That is where you are wrong. I do love Elizabeth yes, but I have never ever laid a finger on her," said Edward.

"Come on, Edward, we do not have to explain ourselves to him," said Elizabeth.

"No, we do not," said Edward as he looked at her and smiled.

Edward then grabbed hold of Midnight's reins and he took hold of Elizabeth's arm with his other hand and they walked back home together. Albert walked away with not only a hurt face; his feelings were hurt as well and it was his own fault for being such a selfish fool.

As Elizabeth walked with Edward she kept looking at him and smiling.

"What, what is so amusing?" asked Edward.

"Is it true what you said to Albert about being in love with me?" asked Elizabeth.

"Oh!" replied Edward looking rather embarrassed.

"Well, is it?" asked Elizabeth.

"Yes it is. I do not know how it happened, it just did, but not to worry. I will not embarrass you by telling anyone else," smiled Edward.

"I would not be embarrassed. I would be very flattered if you told everyone," said Elizabeth.

"Would you?" asked Edward.

"Yes, I would. I love you, Edward, and I do not care who knows it," said Elizabeth.

"But I am so much older than you. It would cause a lot of gossip," said Edward.

"People are not going to gossip. They know we already live in the same house together and they do not think anything of it," said Elizabeth.

"Yes, but that is different. If people find out our feelings have changed towards each other they will not like us living in the same house, as we will be accused of all sorts," said Edward.

"So what?" said Elizabeth.

"Elizabeth, it does not matter how we feel we cannot be together," said Edward.

"Why not?" asked Elizabeth.

"You know why. I am old and you are young," he told her.

"You might be older than me but you are certainly not old. Anyway, what does it matter as long as it is what we want," said Elizabeth.

"It is not a good idea, Elizabeth. We should just forget about it," said Edward.

Elizabeth walked home with Edward and he took Midnight to the stable. When he came inside the house Elizabeth cleaned up his hand as it was cut and swollen through hitting Albert.

"It looks rather sore," said Elizabeth as she looked at his hand.

"I don't know what came over me. I have never hit anyone like that before," said Edward.

"It serves him right, he deserved that for hitting me before," said Elizabeth.

"Violence does not solve anything," said Edward.

"Well, with some people like Albert, violence is all they know," said Elizabeth.

Elizabeth cleaned Edward's hand and then lifted his hand up so that she could kiss it.

"Elizabeth, no!" said Edward as he pulled his hand away.

Elizabeth went quite red. She then walked out of the room with the bowl of water she had just used to clean Edward's hand.

What is wrong with me? Why have I let this happen? said Edward to himself.

Elizabeth could not understand what she was doing wrong either. One minute she hears Edward saying he loves her and the next he says it is wrong for them to be together.

I know he loves me. So why won't he let his feelings out? she thought.

I cannot let this happen. Elizabeth has to find someone her own age. I love her so much but I cannot let her waste her youth on me, thought Edward. *And what would people say? They would accuse me of taking advantage of her*, he thought.

Elizabeth did not mention anything else to Edward that day as she felt that he was throwing her feelings right back at her and she felt quite humiliated by it all.

"Edward, there is a letter here for you," said Elizabeth a few days later.

Elizabeth sat down and started to eat her breakfast when suddenly she saw Edward's face change.

"What is wrong?" she asked.

"I've had bad news about my cousin. He has passed away," replied Edward.

"Oh, Edward I am so sorry," said Elizabeth.

"Yes, so am I," he told her.

"Is that the cousin that you told me about? The one that you were really close to at one time?" asked Elizabeth.

"Yes, it is," replied Edward. "I think I'll go for a walk for a while as I need some fresh air," he told her..

"Would you like me to come with you?" she asked.

"No, I'll be fine on my own," replied Edward, as he left the house.

Edward had been out for most of the day and Elizabeth had started to get quite worried about him.

Where can he be at this time? she thought.

Another two hours had passed and Edward was still not home and, by now, Elizabeth was pacing up and down the room. Then suddenly she heard the door slam shut, so she quickly ran out into the hallway and lying on the floor was a drunken Edward.

"Oh, Edward, look at the state of you!" said Elizabeth.

"I'm sorry," he said.

Elizabeth helped Edward upstairs and laid him down on his bed and he fell asleep. She then sat beside him just to make sure he was not sick, as she thought he might choke. When Edward woke the next morning he had rather a bad headache. He sat up and when he saw Elizabeth asleep in his room he was not sure what to think.

"Elizabeth, wake up," he told her.

"Good morning, Edward. How are you feeling?" asked Elizabeth.

"Never mind about me, what were doing sleeping in my room?" he asked.

"You were drunk so I slept in the chair, I wanted to keep an eye on you in case you were sick," replied Elizabeth.

"Oh, I see," said Edward.

"Oh Edward, you did not think I took advantage of you when you were drunk. Did you?" laughed Elizabeth.

"Don't be silly," he told her. "I was more worried in case I had done something wrong to you," he told her.

"But it would not be wrong, would it?" asked Elizabeth.

"Elizabeth, I think you ought to go downstairs now," Edward told her.

Elizabeth took one big breath and sighed as she was not getting anywhere with Edward; she then walked towards the door. As Elizabeth opened the door she saw the maid outside, so she quickly closed it so that the maid did not see her in Edward's bedroom.

"What is it?" asked Edward as he looked at Elizabeth.

"The maid is outside the door," she whispered.

"Oh my goodness! This is all we need," whispered Edward as he started to panic.

Elizabeth put her hand over her mouth as she started to giggle; she thought it was hilarious and it made things even worse when the maid knocked at the door.

"Sir, I have come to clean your room," said the maid.

"Leave it today please as I am still in bed. I feel a bit under the weather," Edward told her.

Elizabeth looked at Edward with a huge smirk upon her face, but Edward shook his head as if to say it's not funny.

"Now what are we going to do? You cannot stay in here all day," said Edward.

"Why ever not?" asked Elizabeth cheekily.

"Will you behave, I have to get you out of here," said Edward.

"I am only teasing you," said Elizabeth.

Elizabeth opened the door again and the maid had gone, so Elizabeth quickly ran out of Edward's room before being seen by anyone.

A few minutes later Edward came downstairs and when he walked into the breakfast room Elizabeth had a huge grin upon her face.

"Will you stop it, it is not funny," said Edward.

"We did not do anything wrong. So why are you worrying so much?" she asked.

"I just do not like people gossiping that's all," Edward told her.

"Where did you go yesterday? I was really worried about you," said Elizabeth.

"I went to see a friend of mine who knew my cousin years ago. We had a few drinks and I came home," replied Edward.

"A few too many drinks more like," said Elizabeth with a smile.

"Yes, I did have a bit too much, didn't I? And I am paying for it now," said Edward.

"Well, it is not often that you drink like that. In fact, I do not remember ever seeing you drunk before," said Elizabeth.

"It is not that often that I get such terrible news either," Edward told her.

"When is the funeral?" asked Elizabeth.

"In a few days time," replied Edward.

"Would you like me to come along with you?" asked Elizabeth.

"No thank you. I do not like ladies seeing me cry," smiled Edward.

"So what if you do cry, that does not matter. You were there for me when my grandmother passed away and I would like to be there for you," said Elizabeth.

"I do not mean to sound ungrateful, but I would prefer to go on my own," said Edward.

"You are not ashamed of me are you?" asked Elizabeth.

"No, definitely not. Why would you think such a thing?" asked Edward.

"It's just that ever since you told Albert you loved me and I told you I felt the same, you have been very distant towards me," said Elizabeth.

"I do not mean to be distant from you. I am just frightened of being close to you," said Edward.

"You are really strange," said Elizabeth.

"No, I am just being sensible," Edward told her.

On the day of the funeral Elizabeth watched as Edward left the house; he looked so sad as if he had the whole world upon his shoulders. Elizabeth was there for him when he returned, but Edward was not in the mood for company; he just went to his study and closed the door.

Later that evening, Elizabeth knocked at the door but Edward told her he wanted to be alone for a while. Elizabeth did not want to push Edward into talking if he did not want to, so she just left him alone and went up to bed. A few hours later Elizabeth was woken by a loud bang, so she got up and knocked on Edward's bedroom door, but there was no answer so she went downstairs. Elizabeth found Edward sitting downstairs on his own.

"What are you doing down here?" he asked.

"I was woken by a loud bang," replied Elizabeth.

"Oh, that must have been when I dropped the shovel on the hearth. I was putting some coal on the fire and they just slipped out of my hand," said Edward.

"Look, you have got coal everywhere," said Elizabeth. "I'll clear it up for you," she told him, as she bent down and picked up the shovel.

"You will do no such thing," said Edward as he took the shovel from her hand.

As Edward took the shovel he looked at Elizabeth and without even thinking he leaned towards her and kissed her.

"I'm so sorry," said Edward after they stopped kissing.

"I'm not," said Elizabeth as she cupped his face in her hands and kissed him again.

"I do not think we should be doing this," said Edward.

Elizabeth put her finger over Edward's mouth to silence him. She then held both his hands and they sat down in front of the fire together. Edward cuddled Elizabeth and she felt so safe just lying in his arms and a short time later she fell asleep. Edward could not take his eyes off of her and he stroked her face as she slept.

"You are so beautiful," said Edward.

But as he said that Elizabeth woke up.

"Am I dreaming? Or am I really lying here with your arms around me?" asked Elizabeth.

Edward smiled and then kissed Elizabeth once more, but this time more passionately. He then laid her down on the floor and kissed her again whilst Elizabeth unbuttoned her dress.

"Elizabeth, I am not sure about this," said Edward, looking worried.

"Why? You know it is what we both want," she told him.

"Are you sure it is really what you want?" asked Edward.

"I have never been so sure about anything before," replied Elizabeth.

"But I promised your father I would not do this," said Edward.

"Yes, I know. But I was rather young then. I am a grown woman now and my father cannot tell me what to do anymore," said Elizabeth.

Elizabeth then pulled Edward closer to her and as hard as he had tried Edward could not help but give in to his feelings for her.

Edward kissed Elizabeth on her lips and slowly moved down to her neck; he then undressed her and he gently made love to her. After that they fell asleep in front of the fire together.

When Edward awoke the next morning he looked at Elizabeth and kissed her cheek, he then covered her naked body with a blanket. A few minutes later Elizabeth woke up and she looked at Edward and gave him a beautiful smile.

"Are you alright?" he asked.

"I have never felt better," she replied.

Edward kissed Elizabeth again and he started caressing her naked body once more and they made love for a second time.

"What on earth do you see in an old man like me?" asked Edward.

"You are everything to me and more," she told him.

"You are so beautiful, Elizabeth, and I love you more than anything," he told her.

"I had better go and get dressed before the staff arrive and catch us together," said Elizabeth.

She then wrapped the blanket around her and went up to her bedroom to put some clean clothes on. Elizabeth was so happy she could hardly believe this was happening to her. She had now found the man of her dreams who also loved her just as much, and she felt on top of the world.

CHAPTER ELEVEN

As the next few weeks passed, Elizabeth and Edward became more devoted to one another than ever before. There was not a single thing they would not do for each other, and they both felt as if they were sixteen again.

"Elizabeth, there is something I would like to ask you," said Edward one day. "I was wondering how you would feel about sharing my room with me, but only if that is alright with you," he said.

"I would love to," she replied.

"It's just that we cannot keep sleeping on the floor in front of the fire, because we might oversleep one day and get caught out by one of the staff," said Edward.

"Yes I know, and that would be so embarrassing," said Elizabeth.

"Yes, it would. So you are in agreement then?" he asked.

"Yes, of course I am," replied Elizabeth.

She then leaned over Edward's shoulders from behind him, wrapped her arms around him and kissed him.

"I do not think I have ever been this happy, Elizabeth," said Edward.

"I know how you feel because I feel exactly the same. It is a really good feeling, isn't it?" she said.

"It is the best feeling in the world," replied Edward.

"I should be home early today because I only have one client to see and I should have his painting finished within a few hours," said Elizabeth.

"Well, I will not be here as I am in court today representing someone. I will probably be home late this afternoon," said Edward.

"Oh that is alright. I think I shall write a letter to my friend Emily whilst I have time. I want to know when she is coming to London to see me," said Elizabeth.

"Yes, it would be nice for her to have a change of scenery and it will do you good to take some time off work and spend some time with Emily whilst she is here," said Edward.

"Yes, I know, I have already thought of that," said Elizabeth.

Elizabeth sent Emily a letter asking her to come to London and she also enclosed the cost of the fare as well.

Emily replied to the letter within a few weeks. But she told Elizabeth she was still not sure whether she could get time off from her seamstress job. Elizabeth was quite disappointed as she was really looking forward to seeing Emily again and she also wanted to show her the sights of London.

"I am sure Emily will come here when she can, so do not look so downhearted," said Edward.

"I hope so, because I really want to see her again. But I would prefer it if she came here rather than I go to Newcastle, because it will give her a nice break," said Elizabeth.

"Just be patient, I am sure things will all work out good in the end," said Edward.

A month or so later Emily arrived unexpectedly as she wanted to surprise Elizabeth.

"Elizabeth is out working at the moment I'm afraid, but she should not be too late home," said Edward.

"Actually I was hoping Elizabeth was not here because it will be a nice surprise for her when she returns home," said Emily.

"It certainly will. Elizabeth will be absolutely thrilled to see you," said Edward.

"This is a beautiful house you have here," said Emily.

"Thank you, I rather like it too," smiled Edward.

One of the maids brought Emily something to eat and drink; she then sat talking with Edward until Elizabeth finally arrived home.

"That sounds like Elizabeth now. She always manages to slam the door," laughed Edward.

Emily did not say anything she just smiled back at Edward.

As Elizabeth walked through the door Emily was hiding behind it so that Elizabeth did not see her straight away.

"Please close the door, Elizabeth, it is rather drafty in here," said Edward.

When Elizabeth saw Emily standing behind the door she just screamed; she then threw her arms around her friend and hugged her.

"Oh my goodness, I cannot believe you are really here!" said Elizabeth excitedly. "What time did you arrive?" she asked.

"Earlier this afternoon," replied Emily.

"Oh we have got so much to talk about, sit down and tell me everything that has been happening in Newcastle," said Elizabeth.

"I think I'll leave you ladies to it, you have obviously got a lot to discuss," said Edward.

Edward went to his study and whilst in there he could hear Elizabeth and Emily talking and giggling like a couple of children. Edward smiled to himself; he was just glad Elizabeth was happy.

"So what has been happening here in London?" asked Emily.

"Oh not a lot really, I have just been busy working," replied Elizabeth.

"Haven't you met anyone yet?" asked Emily.

"No," said Elizabeth, trying hard to hold back her smile.

"You have, haven't you?" laughed Emily.

"Yes, actually I have," replied Elizabeth.

"Tell me more," giggled Emily.

"Well he is very rich and handsome," said Elizabeth.

"Oh you get all the luck," Emily told her.

"He is also kind, generous and the perfect gentleman and he adores me," said Elizabeth.

"My goodness he sounds a bit like Edward. So what is his name?" asked Emily.

"Actually his name is Edward," replied Elizabeth.

"What a coincidence," laughed Emily.

Elizabeth just looked at Emily and gave her a cheeky grin.

"Oh my goodness, it is Edward we are talking about, isn't it?" said Emily.

"Yes," replied Elizabeth.

"I knew it. I told you he was in love with you, but you did not believe me," said Emily. "So tell me all the details. Have you, you know?" she asked.

"Emily, you cannot ask me something like that and expect me to answer you," said Elizabeth.

"I take it that's a yes then," laughed Emily.

Elizabeth started to laugh and that made Emily laugh even more.

"Well, what was it like?" asked Emily.

"I'm not going to tell you that, you will have to wait until you try it yourself," replied Elizabeth with a smile.

"I doubt if that will ever happen. I have never had anyone even slightly interested in me before," said Emily.

"Of course you will, eventually," Elizabeth told her.

"So where do you sleep then?" asked Emily.

"In Edward's room with him, but we have to keep it quiet so that the staff do not find out, otherwise they will start to gossip," said Elizabeth.

"If I had someone like Edward making love to me I certainly would not be able to keep quiet. I would be screaming the house down," laughed Emily.

"Will you stop it," said Elizabeth smiling.

"I am so pleased for you, Elizabeth, Edward is really nice," said Emily.

"Yes he is, and I am absolutely mad about him," said Elizabeth.

Edward joined Elizabeth and Emily later in the evening and he laughed as they spoke of the things they had done together when they were younger.

"I think I shall have to go to bed in a minute, I can hardly keep my eyes open," said Emily.

"Yes, I am quite tired as well," said Elizabeth.

"Elizabeth, could I have a private word with you please?" asked Edward.

Elizabeth followed Edward into the hallway and stood in front of him.

"I do not think it is a very good idea for us to share the same bedroom whilst Emily is staying here with us," said Edward.

"Why? I have already told Emily all about us," said Elizabeth.

"What!" said Edward looking rather shocked.

"It is alright, Emily will not say anything. In fact, she is really pleased for us," said Elizabeth.

Emily came out of the room as she really wanted to go to bed and Edward suddenly went quite red.

"You have not got a problem with Edward and I sleeping in the same room whilst you are here. Have you?" asked Elizabeth.

"Not at all, you go and enjoy yourselves," laughed Emily.

Edward just wanted to curl up and die with embarrassment and he was getting redder by the second.

"Oh look, Elizabeth, you have embarrassed the poor man now," said Emily.

"Don't you mean you did?" said Elizabeth. "Come on, I'll show you to your room," she told Emily.

As the two ladies went upstairs they started laughing even more. Edward just walked back into the room; he felt very uncomfortable about the whole situation and extremely humiliated. He sat down in a chair and waited for Elizabeth to come back down, but when she did finally walk into the room Edward just looked at her rather crossly. Elizabeth knew why Edward was cross but she did not feel like she had done anything wrong.

"I'm sorry, Edward, I did not mean to embarrass you," said Elizabeth.

"Why on earth did you tell Emily about us? What we do should be kept private," said Edward.

"Oh, Edward, I could not help myself. I am so in love with you and I was just bursting to tell someone," replied Elizabeth.

"But you did not have to tell her everything," said Edward.

"I didn't, she guessed," said Elizabeth.

"What am I going to do with you?" said Edward as he hugged her.

"Take me to bed and I'll tell you," said Elizabeth smiling.

"You are impossible. Do you know that?" smiled Edward.

"Come on, let's go to bed," said Elizabeth, as she giggled.

Over the next few days Elizabeth showed Emily around London. Emily absolutely loved the city and she told Elizabeth how much she envied her.

"I wish my life had been a lot different. I am dreading going back to Newcastle and back to that awful job that I hate," said Emily.

"It is not that bad," Elizabeth told her.

"Yes it is. You are so lucky, Elizabeth, you have everything," said Emily.

"Well I hope you are not going back before my birthday, it is only in two days time," said Elizabeth.

"Of course I'll be here for that. That is if Edward does not mind about me staying here," said Emily.

"Of course Edward does not mind. He is the most easy-going person I know," said Elizabeth.

As Elizabeth and Emily walked through the streets of London it started to rain, so they headed for the nearest tea room and stayed there until the rain eased up a bit.

"We had better be making a move home in a minute, before the rain comes down again," said Elizabeth.

As the ladies walked down the street it suddenly started to get quite overcast and within a few minutes the rain came down again. Elizabeth and Emily started to run as they wanted to get home quicker before they both got soaked, but Elizabeth slipped and fell straight into a huge puddle. Emily stood there and just burst into fits of laughter and even though Elizabeth was filthy and wet, she could not help but laugh with her friend as well.

When they did finally arrive home Edward was already there waiting for them and when he saw the state of the ladies, especially Elizabeth, he also burst into laughter. Their hair and clothes were just dripping from the rain and Elizabeth had splashes of mud all up her dress.

"You had both better go and get dried and changed," said Edward smiling.

"Stop laughing, Edward, I am freezing," said Elizabeth.

"I am so sorry, I do not mean to laugh but you do look funny," said Edward.

"Come on, Emily, let's get out of these wet clothes," said Elizabeth.

They both went upstairs together and went to their own rooms to get changed, but it took Elizabeth longer to get cleaned up, because she had splashes of mud up her legs. When she came downstairs Emily was already down there talking to Edward, but as soon as Elizabeth walked into the room Edward and Emily both suddenly went quiet.

"What are you two whispering about?" asked Elizabeth.

"Nothing," replied Edward.

"I was just telling Edward what a lovely time I have had since I have been here," said Emily.

But just by looking at Edward, Elizabeth could sense that something was not right, but she did not know why they were both acting so secretively. Later that evening, Elizabeth left the room for a few minutes and when she returned the same thing happened again; Edward and Emily both went quiet as soon as she walked into the room. Elizabeth did not say anything but she was starting to feel rather agitated by their behaviour. When Elizabeth went to bed that night she asked Edward again what Emily and he had been whispering about, but Edward told her that she was imagining things. Elizabeth lay in bed with all different thoughts going through her head. She thought that perhaps Edward was more interested in her friend Emily than her. Then she looked at Edward whilst he was sleeping and she knew it could not possibly be that, as Edward had never given her reason to doubt him and she knew he loved her dearly. Then she thought perhaps Emily had made some sort of pass at Edward, after all, she already knew that Emily was envious of her and Emily had already told her that she had never met anyone special of the opposite sex before. Elizabeth also knew that Emily was dreading returning to Newcastle and to her job as a seamstress, so by trying to come on to Edward, maybe she saw a way of being able to stay on in London. Elizabeth had all these thoughts going through her head and there was obviously something strange going on, but they would not tell Elizabeth what it was.

The next morning, Elizabeth tried to act as normal as possible, even though she still had a feeling that something was not right. But she could not say anything as she had no proof.

Once Edward went off to work Emily asked Elizabeth if she would like to go out for the day, but Elizabeth declined her offer as she was just not in the mood.

"Are you alright? Only you seem awfully quiet," asked Emily.

"Yes, I am fine," replied Elizabeth rather abruptly.

Emily just looked at her friend as she was rather shocked that she had spoken to her so rudely.

"I am going to go out for a walk. You do not want to come then?" asked Emily.

"I already said no, didn't I?" replied Elizabeth.

"Alright, there is no reason to speak to me like that," Emily told her.

"I'm sorry, I am a bit tired and I have a headache," said Elizabeth.

"I will see you when I get back then," said Emily.

"Yes, alright," replied Elizabeth.

Once Emily had left the house Elizabeth burst out crying; she felt quite bad about the way she had spoken to Emily and yet she still felt as though she had a reason to be angry with her.

As the day went on Elizabeth tried to pull herself together. She did not want Edward and Emily to find out that she was suspecting them of anything, just in case she was wrong. After all she had known them both a very long time and she did not want to lose either of them, especially over something that might not be true anyway.

Edward was the first to arrive home and when Elizabeth saw him she threw her arms around him and hugged him as tightly as she could.

"What is all this for?" asked Edward.

"I just wanted to show you how much I love you," replied Elizabeth.

"I think I already knew that anyway," smiled Edward.

"But perhaps I have not shown you enough recently, especially as I have been spending a lot of time with Emily. I just did not want you to think I was neglecting you," said Elizabeth.

"I never thought any such thing," said Edward, as he kissed her on her cheek.

That evening they all sat and had dinner together and things seemed to go really well. Edward and Emily behaved quite normally without whispering at all and Elizabeth seemed more relaxed as she thought that perhaps she had just been imagining things.

"How do you feel Elizabeth? Is your headache gone now?" asked Emily.

"Yes, I feel fine, thank you," replied Elizabeth.

"You did not tell me you had a headache earlier," said Edward.

"I did not want to worry you," said Elizabeth.

"Perhaps you need to go to bed a bit earlier tonight," said Emily.

"No, I am fine now," Elizabeth told her.

Edward and Emily smiled at each other and this time Elizabeth knew she was not imagining things.

"Why are you two smiling at each other?" asked Elizabeth.

"We're not," replied Emily.

"Yes you were, I saw you both," said Elizabeth.

"Oh, Elizabeth, now you are just being silly," said Emily.

"If you want me out of the way you only have to say," said Elizabeth. "After all, you have already said that I should go to bed a bit earlier," she told Emily.

"Oh, come on, Elizabeth, you are getting all worked up over nothing," said Emily.

"Am I really? Well, perhaps I should just go to bed then," said Elizabeth.

She then walked out of the room and pulled the door so that it was still slightly ajar. Elizabeth then stood behind the door so that she could listen to them talking, as she wanted to hear in case either of them said anything that was inappropriate.

"I think Elizabeth is getting a little bit suspicious. She has already asked me what we were whispering about yesterday," said Edward.

"What did you tell her?" asked Emily.

"I told her that she was imagining things, but Elizabeth is no fool you know," said Edward.

"That is true, there is definitely no fooling her," said Emily.

"I do not think she knows what we are up to though," said Edward.

Elizabeth could not believe what she was hearing; she never thought Edward would treat her this way. She felt totally betrayed but not only by Edward the man she loved, but also by Emily, the person that she trusted and whom had been one of her closest friends for many years.

Elizabeth ran upstairs to her bedroom and wept, but when Edward came up to bed she pretended to be asleep as she did not want him anywhere near her.

The next morning, Elizabeth got up extra early as she could not sleep and she went out before Edward and Emily were up.

"Where is Elizabeth?" asked Edward as he walked downstairs.

"I thought that she was still in asleep. I was just about to bring her up her breakfast in bed," said Emily as she held a tray full of food.

"She must have gone out early today. I did not even get the chance to wish her many happy returns," said Edward.

"You will just have to wait until tonight," said Emily.

"Oh well. I had better have my breakfast and then get off to work, but I shall be home a bit earlier tonight," said Edward.

Elizabeth felt extremely upset. She was now certain that Edward and Emily were having an affair and it broke her heart even to think about it. She walked the streets for hours then eventually she sat in a tea room when it finally opened. After an hour or so Elizabeth had an idea; she thought that if she bought an expensive dress and made herself look beautiful Edward would still find her attractive and would not look twice at Emily, so that is what she did. She spent the whole day going from shop to shop, until eventually she found the dress she liked.

When she arrived home Edward and Emily were extremely worried about her.

"Where have you been all day? I have been sitting here worried out of my mind," said Emily.

"Yes, so have I. I did not even get the chance to see you this morning and I really wanted to wish you many happy returns," said Edward looking worried.

"Look what I have bought you," said Emily as she gave Elizabeth a pair of gloves.

"Thank you," said Elizabeth as she kissed her friend.

Elizabeth had forgotten all about her birthday with everything else that had been going on in her life.

"Many happy returns, Elizabeth," said Edward, as he gave her a box.

Elizabeth opened the box and inside was a pretty diamond broach.

"Oh, Edward, it is beautiful!" Elizabeth told him.

"Go and get changed and put the broach on and I will see you in the dining room," said Edward.

Elizabeth was thrilled with her presents but she still felt upset at the thought that Edward and Emily were having an affair. She then washed and put on her new dress and left her hair down so she looked extremely feminine. She also knew that Edward loved her hair down, so she did this for him as she just wanted him to like her again. She then pinned the broach that Edward had bought her onto her dress and made her way downstairs and into the dining room.

"Oh, Elizabeth, you look beautiful. In fact, you look so stunning I am lost for words," said Edward.

"Do I really?" she asked.

"Yes you do," he told her.

"Where is Emily?" asked Elizabeth.

"She will be here soon so sit down," Edward told her.

Elizabeth sat down at the table and Edward sat opposite her. She then realised that the table was only laid out for two people.

"Isn't Emily eating with us tonight?" asked Elizabeth.

"No she is not," replied Edward.

"Why?" asked Elizabeth looking worried.

Emily suddenly walked into the dining room dressed as a maid.

"Good evening," she said.

"What are you doing?" asked Elizabeth.

"You and Edward have been so kind to me since I have been here, so it is my turn to do something for you. As it is your birthday I am going to be waiting on you tonight, so just relax and enjoy yourselves," said Emily.

Emily then walked out of the dining room and Elizabeth turned towards Edward with a puzzled look upon her face. Within a few minutes Emily came back with a bowl of soup for them both; she left it on the table and then left the room again. After Elizabeth and Edward had eaten their soup Emily brought them in their second course, which was lobster and side salad.

"Ummm, this tastes delicious," said Elizabeth.

"I only get the best for you," said Edward. "Would you like some champagne?" he asked.

"Oooooo, yes please," replied Elizabeth.

Edward poured out two glasses of champagne for them both and gave one glass to Elizabeth; he then held up his glass and made a toast.

"Many happy returns, Elizabeth, and thank you for just being you," said Edward.

Elizabeth smiled and then took a sip of her drink, but as she drank her drink she noticed something in the bottom of the glass.

"Edward, there is something floating in my drink," she told him.

"Is there?" he asked.

"Yes, look. It looks like a ring," said Elizabeth.

Edward took the glass from Elizabeth and poured her champagne into a bucket, he then picked up the ring that was in her glass.

"See, I told you that there was a ring in my glass," said Elizabeth.

Edward dried the ring on a napkin and then walked towards Elizabeth. He then bent down on one knee and just smiled at her.

"What are you doing?" she asked.

"Would you do the honour of becoming my wife?" asked Edward.

"You mean you want to marry me?" asked Elizabeth.

"Yes, I do. So will you marry me?" he asked again.

"Yes, yes, I would love to marry you!" she screamed.

Edward then stood up and placed the ring on Elizabeth's finger and he kissed her on her lips.

"You have made me the happiest man in the world," said Edward.

"I cannot believe this. I thought one of the maids had accidentally lost their ring in my glass, but you had planned this all along, hadn't you?" asked Elizabeth.

"Yes, I did. I wanted your birthday to be a birthday to remember," said Edward smiling.

"Does Emily know about this?" asked Elizabeth.

"Of course she does. That is why you saw us whispering, because I was telling her what I was planning to do tonight," explained Edward.

"Now I know why it is just you and me here for dinner," said Elizabeth.

"Well, I wanted it to be romantic, but I did not want to leave Emily out, so she suggested that she wait on us both," said Edward.

"Oh, Edward, this is just the best birthday I have ever had and just look at this ring. It is beautiful!" said Elizabeth.

"It is ruby and diamonds," said Edward.

"It is out of this world," smiled Elizabeth.

Emily suddenly came back into the room to take out their plates so that she could then bring in their dessert, and as she walked towards the table Elizabeth smiled at her and held up her hand so that Emily could see her ring.

"Oh you said yes then," smiled Emily excitedly.

"Of course I did. You did not think that I would have turned Edward down, did you?" asked Elizabeth.

"No, of course not. You would have been a fool if you had," said Emily. "Congratulations to you both," she told them.

"Thank you," said Elizabeth as she kissed her friend.

"Join us for a glass of champagne, Emily," said Edward.

"Oooooo lovely, I won't say no to that," giggled Emily.

Elizabeth just sat admiring her ring. She felt so happy and yet guilty at the same time. She felt guilty for even thinking that Edward and Emily were having an affair and all they were secretly doing was planning a surprise engagement for her.

"I am so happy and I just want to say thank you to my two best friends in the whole world, Edward and Emily," said Elizabeth.

"I am happy for you as well. Well in fact I am not only happy. I am also jealous as well because you have all the luck," smiled Emily.

"Just tell me this is not a dream. It is really happening, isn't it?" asked Elizabeth.

"Of course it is. So when is the big day?" asked Emily.

"We have not had chance to decide yet," replied Edward.

"I would like a summer wedding. What about you Edward?" asked Elizabeth.

"I really do not mind. I will let you decide what you want," Edward told her.

"I think you are dreaming, Elizabeth, and I am in your dream as well, because I have never met any man quite like Edward in real life before. He is kind, generous, good-looking, rich and he will do anything for you. I just want to kick you because I did not find him first," laughed Emily.

"It is me who is the lucky one finding the lady of my dreams. I still cannot believe anyone as beautiful as you could be in love with me," Edward told Elizabeth.

"Oh stop it you two, I am going to start crying in a minute," said Emily.

"I shall have to write to my family and tell them our good news," said Elizabeth.

"I would prefer it if you did not do that. I think we should go to Yorkshire so that I can ask your father for your hand in person," said Edward.

"Yes, alright let's do that then," said Elizabeth.

The next day Emily had to return home to Newcastle much to her disappointment, but she promised to keep in touch.

"Let me know when the wedding is," said Emily.

"Of course we will. We cannot have our wedding without you there," smiled Elizabeth.

"I should hope not," said Emily jokingly.

"I will write to you soon with all the details," Elizabeth told her.

"Take care of yourself, Edward, and look after Elizabeth for me," said Emily.

"Oh yes, I intend to," smiled Edward.

A few weeks later Elizabeth and Edward travelled to Yorkshire so that Elizabeth could see her family again. Once they arrived they all sat talking for a while and a short time later Edward and Elizabeth's father went for a stroll together.

"You have done wonders for Elizabeth. I do not think I can remember when I have ever seen her so happy," said Elizabeth's father.

"She is a beautiful young lady," said Edward.

"Do I detect that you would like to ask me something?" asked Elizabeth's father.

"Ur no, well nothing that cannot wait until later," replied Edward nervously.

"You want to marry my daughter, don't you?" asked Elizabeth's father.

"Yes, I do, very much. But how did you know that?" asked Edward.

"It was not hard to see that you are both in love. I could just tell by the way you both looked at each other and the ring on Elizabeth's finger also gave me a clue," said Elizabeth's father smiling.

"Oh, the ring, I forgot about that," said Edward.

"Edward you do not need my permission to marry Elizabeth; she is old enough to make her own decisions," said her father.

"Yes I know that, but it would be nice if I could have your approval," said Edward.

"Edward, when you first suggested taking Elizabeth to London I was against the idea because I was afraid for her being alone in a house with a single gentleman. But I have since respected you for the way you have treated her and I know everything that she has done is all thanks to you," said her father.

"Well, that is not entirely true, as Elizabeth has worked extremely hard to get where she is today. I just gave her a little help along the way," said Edward.

"You did not just give her a little help, you gave her a new way of life and no one can thank you more than I. That is why I just want to say I would be very happy for you to take my daughter's hand in marriage. I do not think she could have picked a nicer person than you. Elizabeth is a very sensible young lady and she has chosen her future husband well," said Elizabeth's father.

"Thank you, thank you very much," said Edward.

"You could have just asked me you know, instead of telling me it can wait until later," laughed Elizabeth's father.

"I was a bit nervous about how you would react, especially because of the age difference," said Edward.

"Who am I to judge anyone? I chose the woman who I wanted to spend the rest of my life with regardless of what my own father thought and we are still as much in love today as we were when we first met. So take it from me, if you are happy then do not let anyone stand in your way," said Elizabeth's father.

"We had better go and tell the others the news," said Edward.

Elizabeth's father patted Edward on his back and they both walked back to the house together.

Elizabeth's mother and brother were thrilled to hear the news and they shook Edward's hand and congratulated them both.

"We are hoping to get married sometime in the summer," said Elizabeth.

"Will you be getting married in London?" asked her mother.

"No, Edward thought it would be nice if we married in my home town," replied Elizabeth.

"Elizabeth only wants a small wedding, but I do not mind either way," said Edward.

"Elizabeth got you under her thumb already has she, Edward?" joked Elizabeth's brother, William.

"No, not at all. I just want Elizabeth to be happy and I shall make her very happy," said Edward.

"I hope you are going to invite the Lockwoods to the wedding," said Elizabeth's mother.

"No!" shouted Elizabeth.

Edward looked at Elizabeth and understood why she had said 'no' so abruptly. He knew that if the Lockwoods were invited, then Ernest and his dreadful wife Rosemary might come too.

"Why ever not?" asked Elizabeth's mother.

"I have not seen them for years and I hardly know them anymore," said Elizabeth.

"But they would love to see you get married. They have known you since you were born," said Elizabeth's mother.

"Yes and you are also good friends with the Lockwoods. Aren't you, Edward?" said Elizabeth's father.

"Yes I am, but it is Elizabeth's decision," replied Edward.

"Please think about it, dear. The Lockwoods would love to see you again, especially on your wedding day, and it's not as if you have got to invite Joseph and Ernest Lockwood because they are working away," said Elizabeth's mother.

"Alright, but only Mr and Mrs Lockwood because I do not want lots of people that I do not know," said Elizabeth.

"Oh, this is so exciting, my own daughter getting married," smiled Elizabeth's mother.

They all started to laugh and then Elizabeth's father poured them all a drink and he made a toast to congratulate his daughter and Edward on their engagement.

"If there is anything that I can do to help please let me know," said Alice.

"Well, yes, there is one thing you can do. I was wondering if you would be my matron of honour," said Elizabeth.

"Yes, I would love to," said Alice.

"I am also going to ask my friend Emily to be a bridesmaid," said Elizabeth.

"Well, that does not leave a lot for me to do. I shall just have to eat all the food instead," said Elizabeth's brother, William.

"How would you like to be my best man?" asked Edward.

"Really, I would be honoured," replied William. "Oh, yes, then when I do my speech I shall be able to tell everyone just what Elizabeth was like as a child and the awful things she used to get up to," said William laughing.

"Take no notice of him, Edward, he is just teasing me," said Elizabeth.

"Oh no I am not. You were a right little bully when we were younger," laughed William.

"No I was not," laughed Elizabeth.

"Will it be alright if I prepare the food and make the wedding cake?" asked Elizabeth's mother.

"Yes, of course," replied Elizabeth. "My mother makes the best cakes ever," she told Edward.

"Perhaps whilst we are here we could go and see the vicar and book up the church," said Edward.

"Yes, what a good idea," said Elizabeth.

The next day Elizabeth and Edward went to the church and they booked their wedding for the 23rd July.

The next few months could not go quick enough for Elizabeth. She was so excited but had so much to organise. She had dresses and suits to buy, flowers to order and not forgetting invitations to send to everyone.

On the eve of their wedding, Edward slept at Elizabeth's brother's house and Elizabeth stayed with her parents. Alice did Elizabeth's hair in ringlets which she kept in overnight and both Alice and Emily had their hair pinned up the same. When Elizabeth was ready Alice and Emily came downstairs in their lemon bridesmaid dresses and they all waited for Elizabeth to come down last. As Elizabeth made her way downstairs her mother wept when she saw how beautiful her daughter looked and her father just stood there with a lump in his throat.

"You look absolutely beautiful. If I were not your father I would marry you myself," said Elizabeth's father.

Elizabeth just smiled and then Emily gave her a bouquet of flowers to hold.

"Good luck," said Emily beaming from ear to ear.

As everyone left to make their way to the church Elizabeth stood alone with her father.

"I must be the proudest father in the world," said her father. "I hope you are going to be really happy. In fact I know you will be, just like your mother and I," he told her.

"Thank you. Now stop getting all sentimental or you will have me in tears and I will look awful before I even arrive at the church," said Elizabeth with a smile.

"Well, this is it. We had better not keep Edward waiting any longer," said her father.

When Elizabeth arrived at the church she started to get very nervous and her father sensed that, so he squeezed her hand just to let her know he was there for her. Elizabeth looked at him and gave him a slight smile and he winked back at her. He then walked her through the church doors and up the aisle and everyone turned around to watch as she made her way towards Edward. Edward was stunned as he watched his bride-to-be walking towards him. He even had to wipe the tears from his eyes as his emotions got the better of him.

After they were married everyone went back to Elizabeth's parent's house where they held the reception and as William read his speech Elizabeth and Edward could not take their eyes off each other.

"Where are you going for your honeymoon?" asked Emily.

"I did ask Elizabeth if she wanted to travel abroad to Switzerland but she preferred to stay in England. She decided that she wanted to spend sometime at the seaside, so we both agreed to go to Ramsgate and Margate for a few weeks," said Edward.

"I would like to make a toast to the happy couple," said Elizabeth's brother. "May my sister and her new husband be really happy and healthy in their new lives together. To Elizabeth and Edward," said William as he held up his glass.

Elizabeth and Edward cut their cake and then thanked everyone for making their day special.

"Congratulations to you both. I am so pleased for you," said Mrs Lockwood.

"Yes, so am I. You make a lovely couple," said Mr Lockwood.

"It does not seem that long ago that you were a little girl running around the farm," said Mrs Lockwood smiling.

"Yes, running around and getting all muddy in the pigpen, as I remember," laughed Mr Lockwood.

"Oh don't remind me, that was awful!" laughed Elizabeth.

"Well, Mrs Thomas, I think we should get going soon as we have a long journey ahead of us," said Edward.

"Oh that sounds funny, you calling me Mrs Thomas," laughed Elizabeth.

"You'll soon get used to it," Edward told her.

Everyone watched as Elizabeth and Edward climbed into the carriage and they wished them luck for their honeymoon.

Elizabeth and Edward waved goodbye to their family and friends as the carriage pulled away and then Elizabeth snuggled up to Edward as they travelled the long distance to Kent.

When they arrived in Margate they stayed in a guest house not far from the seaside. They were both shown to their room where they had a wash and changed for dinner; then after they went for a walk along the seafront.

"It is quite quiet here, isn't it?" said Elizabeth as she stood watching the sea.

"Yes it is. It is quite different to the noise we are used to in London," replied Edward.

"I could just stand here forever," said Elizabeth as she cuddled up to Edward.

Edward put his coat around Elizabeth's shoulders as it started to get a bit chilly; then a short time later they made their way back to the guest house.

The following day they both walked to Margate town and they could not believe how small it was compared to London. The next day they went to Ramsgate which was about five miles away from Margate. They had a look around the town and then they made their way to the harbour to look at the boats. They stayed in Ramsgate for about six hours then made their way back to Margate. As they travelled back they passed St Lawrence church and saw a couple coming out of the church that had just got married.

"I hope they will be as happy as we are," said Edward.

"I do not think anyone could be as happy as us," smiled Elizabeth.

Elizabeth and Edward stayed in Kent for the next month then they travelled back to London. When they arrived home there were quite a number of letters for them both from family and friends wishing them both well for the future.

Edward carried Elizabeth over the threshold and took her upstairs. He then gently laid her on the bed.

"Welcome home, Mrs Thomas," he said.

Edward leaned forward and kissed Elizabeth; she then threw her arms around him and kissed him back.

CHAPTER TWELVE

Elizabeth and Edward went back to work a few days after returning to London, but Elizabeth found it quite strange when her clients called her Mrs Thomas and it took her a while to get used to it.

Edward came home from his first day at work with a present from his colleagues; they had all put a collection together and had bought Elizabeth and Edward a crystal vase.

"It's beautiful, isn't it?" said Elizabeth.

"Yes, it is, but it looks rather empty," said Edward as he pulled out some flowers from behind his back.

Elizabeth smiled as she took the flowers from Edward. She then arranged the flowers in the vase and put them on to the table; but as she turned, Elizabeth suddenly felt quite dizzy. She held on to the table for support and just stood still for a few minutes.

"Are you alright?" asked Edward.

"Yes I think so. I just felt a bit dizzy, that's all," replied Elizabeth.

"Come and sit down," said Edward.

Edward helped Elizabeth to a chair and got her some water to drink and she soon felt much better.

After they had eaten their dinner they both took a slow walk up to the stables as Elizabeth wanted to see her horse, Midnight.

"I can still remember when you first gave me Midnight. I could not believe how lucky I was and now look at me. I must be the luckiest lady in the world," said Elizabeth.

"I am the lucky one," said Edward.

He then took Elizabeth's hand and kissed it and they slowly made their way back to the house. As they almost reached the door Elizabeth felt dizzy again and was very unsteady on her feet.

"I am going to get a doctor out to have a look at you, because there is obviously something not right," said Edward.

"No, don't do that. I will be fine," said Elizabeth.

But as Elizabeth walked into the house she suddenly fainted and Edward only just managed to catch her before she hit the floor. He carried Elizabeth upstairs and put her into bed and then he got a doctor to come and see her. When the doctor arrived he went upstairs to examine Elizabeth but Edward stayed downstairs. Edward was extremely worried about Elizabeth as he did not have a clue what was wrong with her. The doctor was with Elizabeth for about ten minutes and then he walked downstairs to speak to Edward.

"What is wrong with my wife?" asked Edward.

"She just needs plenty of rest. I think she has been over-doing things recently," replied the doctor.

Edward saw the doctor out and then went upstairs to see Elizabeth.

"How are you feeling now?" he asked.

"I am fine, so stop looking so worried," Elizabeth told him.

"But what did the doctor say was wrong with you? All he told me was that you needed plenty of rest," said Edward.

"Come and sit down," said Elizabeth.

Edward sat on the edge of the bed and looked at Elizabeth.

"Well what did he say?" asked Edward again.

Elizabeth took Edward's hands and kissed them she then looked up at Edward and smiled.

"There is a little baby Thomas on the way," she told him.

"You mean I am going to be a father?" he asked.

"Yes that is exactly what I mean," replied Elizabeth, with a huge smile upon her face.

"Oh, that is wonderful news. You will have to take things easy now. Is there anything I can get you?" asked Edward excitedly.

"Just calm down a bit, I am not ill, you know," said Elizabeth.

"I am sorry, I just got a bit carried away, but I am still very concerned about you," Edward told her.

"Yes, I know. But I am going to be fine and I do not want you worrying," said Elizabeth.

Within the next month Elizabeth started to get morning sickness, but she still continued with her paintings, as she was not going to let anything interfere with her work. A few months later she started to put on quite a lot of weight and her mood changed for the worst, but Edward took everything in his stride and never once argued back with her.

"Elizabeth, what are you going to do about your work once the baby is born?" asked Edward one day.

"I had not really thought about that," she replied.

"Well, if you do decide that you would still like to continue with your paintings, we will have to seriously think about getting a live-in nanny," said Edward.

"Well, I would like to continue with my work, but I do not really like the idea of a stranger looking after our baby," said Elizabeth.

"But if you continue painting you cannot take a baby with you," Edward told her.

"I know," said Elizabeth looking rather disappointed.

"Just think about it and we can decide what to do later," said Edward.

A few days later Elizabeth came up with an idea that would solve her problem about going back to work, so she told Edward about it.

"Why don't we employ Emily as a nanny, that way I can still go back to work and I know our baby will be left with someone that we can trust," said Elizabeth.

"Well, yes, I suppose that is a good idea. But would Emily want to move to London?" asked Edward.

"Of course she will. She loved it when she was here before and I think she would be only too pleased to give her job up at Flagerty's. He is a right miserable old so 'n' so," replied Elizabeth.

"Well, it is fine by me, so go ahead and ask her," said Edward.

"I'll write a letter to her tonight," said Elizabeth excitedly.

Emily was thrilled when she heard the news that Elizabeth was expecting her first child and she was only too pleased to accept the offer of employment as a nanny for their baby. She arrived in London a month before Elizabeth was due to give birth and by that time Elizabeth had already given up work for a few weeks, as she got very tired quickly and her legs had got quite swollen through her pregnancy.

"What are you hoping for, a boy or girl?" asked Emily.

"We do not really mind as long as the baby is healthy," replied Elizabeth.

"Have you decided on any names yet?" asked Emily.

"Well, we have both come to an agreement that if it is a girl I shall name her and if it is a boy then Edward shall choose his name," replied Elizabeth.

"But we have not chosen any names as yet" said Edward.

"Just remember, Elizabeth, Emily is a nice name," said Emily with a smile.

"I knew you would say something like that," laughed Elizabeth.

"Why don't you go and lie down for a while, Elizabeth, you look worn out," said Edward.

"I'm alright, honest," Elizabeth told him.

Emily helped out as much as she could and Elizabeth was pleased to have her friend around, especially whilst Edward was at work, because it was company for her. Before Emily had arrived in London Elizabeth had got quite bored sitting around the house all day, as she was used to being independent.

In the last two weeks of her pregnancy Elizabeth started to feel very uncomfortable, as the baby was quite low down by this time and she knew she did not have much longer to wait before giving birth. Elizabeth often spoke to Edward about her fear of giving birth, but even though Edward was also worried for her, he tried to reassure her that everything would be alright.

"But what if there are any complications?" asked Elizabeth.

"Just try not to worry, I am sure everything will be fine," Edward told her.

"You get off to work, Edward, I am here for Elizabeth if anything happens," said Emily.

"Just make sure Elizabeth gets plenty of rest," said Edward.

"Of course I will. I will not let her out of my sight and I will make her sit in that chair all day if I have to," laughed Emily.

Edward kissed Elizabeth goodbye and went off to work as usual.

"Is there anything I can do for you?" asked Emily.

"Yes, actually there is. You can swap places with me if you want," laughed Elizabeth.

"I do not mind helping around the home but I cannot perform miracles," said Emily.

They both began to laugh but suddenly Elizabeth had a sharp pain. She then gasped and looked at Emily.

"Are you alright?" asked Emily.

"I don't know. I had a pain but it has gone now, so maybe it was nothing more than wind," said Elizabeth.

But a few minutes later Elizabeth had another pain and more followed, each one getting stronger by the minute.

"It is definitely not wind. I think the baby is coming. Let's get you upstairs," said Emily.

Elizabeth managed to get upstairs and Emily made her as comfortable as possible. She then got a midwife to come out in case something went wrong.

By this time the contractions were extremely strong and Elizabeth started to get quite distressed, but Emily stayed by her side and wiped the sweat from her forehead.

"How much longer is it going to be?" asked Elizabeth.

"Unfortunately you have got quite a way to go yet," replied the midwife.

Elizabeth began to cry as the pain became unbearable; she then started to scream as the contractions gripped her stomach.

A few hours later Edward walked into the house returning home from work and he knew straight away what was happening to Elizabeth because he could hear her screams from outside. He ran upstairs and saw Emily carrying some fresh linen in the hallway.

"Is Elizabeth alright?" he asked.

"She is having the bairn. Quick go in and sit with her," said Emily.

Edward walked into the bedroom and Elizabeth was so relieved when she saw him.

"Thank goodness you are here," said Elizabeth.

Edward held her hand and sat down beside her. Elizabeth started to squeeze Edward's hand really tightly as she got another contraction and this time she started to push.

"Aaaaaaah!" she screamed. "Edward I'm scared."

"You are going to be fine, you are doing really well," Edward told her.

"You won't leave me, will you?" she asked.

"I am not going anywhere," said Edward.

Elizabeth began to push again and again and the more she pushed the more she screamed. Edward tried to be as helpful as possible. He rubbed Elizabeth's back for her and encouraged her to push when the midwife asked her to.

"How much longer will this take?" asked Edward.

"Your wife is almost there. I can see the head now, just a few more pushes should do it," said the midwife.

"Come on, Elizabeth, the baby is almost here," said Edward.

Elizabeth gave a few more pushes and at last the baby was born.

"You have a son!" said the midwife.

The midwife wrapped the baby up and gave him to Elizabeth to hold and she wept as she looked at her newborn son.

"He has got your eyes," said Edward smiling.

"He is perfect, isn't he?" said Elizabeth.

"Yes, he is. Thank you," said Edward as he kissed her.

Emily saw the midwife out and left Elizabeth and Edward to be alone for a while. She even shed a few tears herself. She could not believe Elizabeth was now a mother as it had not seemed that long ago that they were just children themselves.

"How do you feel now?" asked Edward.

"Tired, but relieved that it is over," replied Elizabeth.

"I am so proud of you," said Edward.

About an hour later Emily knocked at the door holding a tray of tea and biscuits.

"Can I come in?" she asked.

"Of course you can. Come and look at him, he is beautiful," said Elizabeth.

"He is like you, Edward, but I can see that he has Elizabeth's eyes," said Emily. "So what are you going to call him?" she asked.

"That is up to Edward. So have you chosen a name yet?" asked Elizabeth.

"Yes I have. What do you think about the name Adam?" he asked.

"Adam Thomas, yes I like that. But how do you feel about having William as his middle name? That way he will also have my father's name," said Elizabeth.

"Adam William, yes that is a strong name for a strong little boy," said Edward.

Edward sat beside Elizabeth until she finally fell asleep; then he crept out of the room trying hard not to wake her or baby Adam.

"I can hardly believe I am actually a father!" Edward told Emily.

"You should be very proud, he is beautiful," said Emily.

"Yes, I am, I am extremely proud," said Edward.

As soon as Elizabeth was feeling well enough she contacted her parents to let them know that they had a second grandson and they were delighted with the news and Elizabeth's father was also very proud to hear that William was the baby's second name.

A few months later Elizabeth invited her family to witness the christening of her and Edward's son and that was the first time they all saw baby Adam. After the christening Elizabeth's parents presented their grandson with a holy Bible and Elizabeth's father wrote a small message inside of it, which made Elizabeth very emotional.

As the next few months past Adam got his first tooth and by six months old he could sit up unsupported; he was also walking on his own by the time he was just eleven months old.

Adam was the image of his father Edward, but like his mother he loved horses and he got quite excited whenever Elizabeth took him up to the stables to see Midnight. Elizabeth would hold him in her arms and Adam would stroke him and giggle when the horse licked him.

One hot summer's day when Adam was about sixteen months old, Elizabeth took him into the garden to let him have a run about. Emily was out shopping that day and Edward was in his study busy with his paperwork, so Elizabeth spent some time with her son alone. Whilst Elizabeth was in the garden, she noticed a bird's nest in a tree and the nest had baby birds inside it, so she pointed to it to show Adam. After a few minutes had passed, Elizabeth ran into the house to tell Edward to come and have a look but Edward did not hear her calling, so Elizabeth picked Adam up and went to his study to get him. When Elizabeth entered the study she could hear Edward coughing, so she walked towards him and she saw that he looked quite poorly.

"You look terrible," said Elizabeth.

Edward was coughing quite badly and he was sweating with a fever, so Elizabeth rubbed his back for him.

"Is it your asthma?" she asked.

"No, I think it is more serious than that," replied Edward.

Elizabeth did not hesitate, she immediately got a doctor out to see Edward and when he arrived she waited outside the bedroom whilst he examined him. After about twenty minutes of waiting the doctor finally came out of the room and he had quite a serious look upon his face.

"What is it? What is wrong with Edward?" she asked.

"I am afraid it is not good news. Edward has got tuberculosis and I do not expect him to last more than two weeks," said the doctor.

Elizabeth could not believe what she was hearing. She just froze on the spot and went completely white.

"Are you going to be alright?" asked the doctor.

"I don't know," cried Elizabeth.

"You can go in and see your husband, but please put a handkerchief over your mouth," he told her.

Just as the doctor had said that, Emily walked into the house. Emily walked in smiling away to herself until she saw the look on Elizabeth's face and then it dawned on her that something was wrong.

"What has happened?" asked Emily as she ran upstairs.

Elizabeth did not answer her; she just burst into tears and hugged her friend.

"What is it? What is wrong?" Emily asked the doctor.

"Edward has tuberculosis and I am afraid there is nothing that I can do for him," replied the doctor.

"Oh my god. No!" said Emily.

"I have to go now, so please look after your friend," said the doctor.

"Yes, of course I will," said Emily.

"What am I going to do without him?" cried Elizabeth.

"Elizabeth, listen to me. Edward needs you more now than ever, so go in the bedroom and sit with him," Emily told her.

"But I do not want him to die," sobbed Elizabeth.

"I know, but you have to be strong for him as well," said Emily, as the tears flowed down her face.

"Yes, I do," said Elizabeth as she stood up straight and wiped her face.

"Go on, go in there, he needs you," said Emily.

Elizabeth looked at Emily and she tried hard to hold back her tears. She then opened the bedroom door and just stared at Edward as he lie helpless in bed. She sat down beside Edward and held his hand as he slept and it was then that she could no longer hold back her tears. Elizabeth cried and cried and it was not long before Edward opened his eyes and saw her. Edward could not bear to see Elizabeth so upset, so he squeezed her hand as if to say don't worry.

"I know I am dying, Elizabeth, but I need you to be strong for Adam's sake. It is not going to be easy for either of you, I know that, but Adam is still young and he is going to depend on you to be there for him," said Edward.

Elizabeth did not say anything; she just looked at Edward and wiped the tears from her face.

"Elizabeth, I would like you to remember two things. The first is, please remember how much I love you. I have always loved you more than anything else in the world. The second thing I would like you to remember is, be happy in your life, just as I have been in mine," he told her.

"But how can I be happy without you!" said Elizabeth.

"You will find a way and, whatever happens, I will always be there with you," said Edward.

Elizabeth started to weep again as she could not bear the thought of losing Edward. She then leaned across him and hugged him, whilst Edward closed his eyes and fell asleep once more.

Over the next few days Elizabeth did not leave Edward's side. She hardly ate and she did not even spend any time with her son, Adam. She felt that her priority was to be with Edward and she tried to make his last few days as special as possible.

By now Elizabeth was exhausted herself as she had hardly slept for days and as she was so tired her eyes just gave up and she was forced to go to sleep. But as she slept beside Edward she was soon woken by the sound of him coughing, so she sat up and grabbed a handkerchief for him as he had began to cough up blood. Elizabeth wiped Edward's mouth and gently eased his head back on to the pillow. She then held his hand and laid down beside him. Edward squeezed her hand and Elizabeth gently squeezed his hand back and then Edward gave her a huge smile. But suddenly his hand went limp, so Elizabeth sat up and when she looked at Edward she knew he had gone.

"No, no, you can't leave me! I need you!" she screamed.

But it was too late, Edward was gone and there was nothing that Elizabeth could do to change that. Elizabeth started to sob uncontrollably and Emily heard her crying from downstairs, so she ran upstairs and into the bedroom as she had guessed that Edward had gone.

"Come on, Elizabeth, come downstairs," said Emily.

"No, I don't want to leave him!" cried Elizabeth.

"Elizabeth, listen to me. Edward would not want you to be like this," said Emily.

"I can't help it. I love him," said Elizabeth.

"Just come downstairs with me," said Emily.

"Alright, but let me cover Edward with the blanket because he looks cold," said Elizabeth.

Elizabeth stood up and tucked one of his arms inside the blanket; she then walked around to the other side of the bed and as she lifted his other arm to tuck it inside, she heard something fall onto the floor. Elizabeth looked down to see what had fallen on to the floor and it was then she noticed it was the pocket watch she had bought him years before. Elizabeth realised that

Edward died holding the pocket watch. She then remembered what Edward had once told her when she first gave him the watch. Edward had said that he would treasure it forever and that is exactly what he had done. Elizabeth suddenly fell to her knees beside the bed and cried hysterically, so Emily walked over to her and helped her to her feet. She then put her arm around Elizabeth and led her downstairs.

"Why did this have to happen?" asked Elizabeth.

"I don't know. But at least Edward is not suffering any more," said Emily.

"He should not have suffered in the first place, after all he was a good man and he never did anything wrong in his life ever!" shouted Elizabeth.

"I know, that is why you have got to remember the good things that Edward has done," said Emily.

"But I do not want just memories. I want Edward here with me now. What am I going to do without him, Emily?" cried Elizabeth.

"You are going to wipe your face and go and see Adam because he needs you right now," said Emily.

"Where is Adam?" asked Elizabeth.

"He is playing in the garden" replied Emily.

Elizabeth walked over to the window where she could see Adam playing. Adam looked up at her and smiled; he did not have a care in the world and he was too young to know what was going on.

"Look at him, he is so innocent. I do not know what I am going to tell him when he asks where his father has gone," said Elizabeth.

"You will just have to explain as best as you can that his father has gone away for a while, then when he is old enough to understand you can tell him the truth," said Emily.

Elizabeth contacted her family to tell them the sad news about Edward and Emily helped Elizabeth with the funeral arrangements.

On the day of Edward's funeral, hundreds of people gathered the streets to pay their respects to him, as Edward was very highly thought of in the community. Edward was taken through the streets of London by a horse-drawn carriage and one of the horses that led the carriage was Elizabeth's horse, Midnight, the horse that Edward had given her years before. Midnight looked proud as he walked along with a plume attached to him.

After the funeral everyone went back to Elizabeth's house for the wake, but although Elizabeth was not in the mood to socialise she put on a brave face and did Edward proud. After everyone had left the house Elizabeth went up to her room and sobbed and she did not come out until the next morning. Elizabeth's parents stayed in London for the next two weeks, as they did not want to leave their daughter in the state that she was in. Elizabeth's father also went with his daughter to the reading of Edward's will and as Elizabeth was Edward's next-of-kin he left her everything, from the house the contents and also a large sum of money. Edward also left his son Adam £500.00 to be given to him when he marries, or when he reaches the age of twenty-five. He also left his son the pocket watch that Elizabeth had bought him, but it was only to be given to him when he was old enough to appreciate it. Elizabeth was also handed a letter written to her by Edward only a few days before he died. Elizabeth held on to the letter but did not open it until she got home. Elizabeth took the letter upstairs so that she could read it aloud; she sat on her bed and opened it and the letter read:

To my dearest Elizabeth,

In the beginning you were like the daughter I never had, but I was so proud when you eventually accepted my proposal of marriage and I could finally call you my wife. You brought so much happiness into my life and I thank you for that.

Elizabeth, please do not cry over me as you have your whole life ahead of you. You are very gifted and have so many special qualities about you. I love you so much, my darling, and it is so hard for me to know I have to leave you soon, but I have left part of me with you and that is in our son, Adam. Please take good care of him and let him know how much he meant to me. You both are the most precious things I ever had.

Please be wise and careful, Elizabeth, but most of all, enjoy your life just as I have mine with you.
Goodbye, my darling.

I love you always
Edward.

Elizabeth cried bitterly after reading the letter and she stayed in her room for quite some time after.

A while later she went downstairs to speak with her parents whom were very concerned for their daughter.

"Could I possibly come back to Yorkshire with you for a while? I just need to get away from London and this house," said Elizabeth.

"Of course you can. You can stay with us as long as you like," replied her mother.

"What about Adam? Will you be bringing him with you?" asked her father.

"Yes, of course," replied Elizabeth.

"I think it will be a good idea if Emily also comes with you, that way she can help you with Adam," said her mother.

"Yes, whatever you think is best," replied Elizabeth.

Whilst Elizabeth was in Yorkshire she never left the house. Her parents tried their hardest to get her to go out, even if it was just for a short walk, but Elizabeth was not having any of it.

"I am really worried about Elizabeth. She just sits in the chair all day and hardly says a word," said her mother.

"I have tried talking to her but she seems to just want to be left alone," said Emily.

"She needs time to get over Edward; we just have to be patient with her," said Elizabeth's father.

When Elizabeth did finally return to London she decided to give up her painting job, as her heart was just not in it anymore.

A few months later Elizabeth had come to a decision about what she wanted to do with the rest of her life. She sat Emily down as she wanted to tell her about the changes that she had decided to make.

"I have decided to sell the house and move back to Yorkshire to be closer to my family," said Elizabeth.

"Why? Everything that you had with Edward is here," said Emily.

"Yes, I know. But Edward is not here anymore and I cannot bear to be in this house without him," said Elizabeth.

"Why don't you just buy another house, that way you could still stay in London," said Emily.

"Because I came here to London with Edward and now that he has gone it seems pointless me staying here. Besides now that Edward has gone, it has made me realise just how short life is and I might not have my own parents here much longer. So I want to be able to spend as much time with them as I can, as I have missed out so much of my life with them already," said Elizabeth.

"I suppose that means you will not need me here any longer," said Emily.

"Of course I need you with me. I am not going anywhere without you," said Elizabeth.

"You really mean that?" asked Emily.

"Of course I do. You are my best friend and you have always been there for me, so stop worrying because you are definitely coming to Yorkshire with Adam and me," said Elizabeth.

"But what if your parents do not want me living at their house?" said Emily.

"They will not mind, you know they think the world of you and, besides I will not be living with my parents forever, it will only be until I have sorted everything out and then I shall buy my own house again," said Elizabeth.

"As long as you are certain this is what you want, because once you have sold this house there is no going back," Emily told her.

"I know that, and I am not saying that I do not love this house because I do, but it is not the same anymore without Edward. It just feels too empty," said Elizabeth.

"Yes, I know what you mean," said Emily.

CHAPTER THIRTEEN

Once Elizabeth was back in Yorkshire with her family, she started to feel a whole lot better in herself and within a few weeks she started to look at different properties to purchase. Elizabeth eventually found a nice five-bedroomed Tudor cottage, which was only about ten minutes' walking distance from her parent's house.

"Oh, Elizabeth, this house is absolutely beautiful and just look at the garden. It is perfect for Adam to play in," said her mother.

"I'll have the smallest bedroom as I do not have much to put in it," said Emily.

Although by this time, Elizabeth was extremely wealthy she decided not to employ any staff, as she wanted to do everything herself and she was certainly not afraid of hard work.

One evening whilst Adam was fast asleep in bed Elizabeth told Emily that she wanted to have a change of career.

"What are you thinking of doing?" asked Emily.

"I have decided to design my own clothes and I was wondering if you would like to help me. I will draw the designs of the clothes and we could make them together as we are both experienced seamstresses," said Elizabeth.

"It sounds like a good idea," said Emily.

"I thought that we could make clothes that are similar to what they sell in London shops, but we could sell them at a more reasonable price," said Elizabeth.

"But who would look after Adam whilst we are doing this?" asked Emily.

"I am sure my mother or even Alice would help out and, when Adam is old enough, he will go to boarding school as I want him to have the best education," replied Elizabeth.

"It looks as though you have thought everything through properly," said Emily.

Over the next few weeks Elizabeth drew lots of different designs and when she had done what she thought was enough to get her started, she then bought the material and sewing machines and then Emily and she got to work on their new venture.

Elizabeth and Emily worked extremely hard, sometimes until the early hours of the morning just to get the outfits completed. Even Elizabeth's mother was keen to see their finished work.

"Is there anything that you like?" Elizabeth asked her mother.

"They are all nice," she told her daughter.

Elizabeth and Emily started to get plenty of orders from the local people; they thought that the clothes were extremely good value for the price that was charged. For the next few months the orders came pouring in and Elizabeth and Emily found it hard to cope with the demand, so Elizabeth decided to expand the business. She purchased a small factory and with the help from Emily they ran the business between them and they employed about twenty staff to help them.

One day, whilst Elizabeth was at work, she heard a rumour that one of her staff called Joan Manning had been stealing material to sell for her own benefit.

"I think you should get the police involved and have her arrested," said Emily.

"No, I do not want to involve the police and besides I have no proof that she has stolen anything. It might just be a rumour," said Elizabeth.

"But what if it is true? Are you going to just stand there and let her get away with it?" asked Emily.

"No, of course not, but I need to have proof before I can approach her," said Elizabeth.

"I will have a quiet word with the other ladies and if they see anything suspicious I will get them to inform me," said Emily.

A few days later one of the ladies told Emily that she had seen Joan Manning rolling up some material and putting it up her dress, so Emily went straight to Elizabeth to explain the situation.

"Alright, I will deal with her myself," said Elizabeth.

Elizabeth walked from her office into the factory and asked Joan Manning if she could speak with her. Joan Manning went very red as she had guessed that she had been caught out.

"Close the door please," said Elizabeth.

Joan Manning did what she was asked and then she turned to face an angry-looking Elizabeth.

"Would you mind showing me what you have tucked up inside your dress?" said Elizabeth.

Joan took the material from inside her dress and held it in her hand. She then looked down at the floor in disgust.

"Why are you stealing from me? Don't I pay you enough wages?" asked Elizabeth.

"I am so sorry but I was desperate. My husband is ill you see. He has got miner's lung and he has not got much longer to live. Since he has been out of work, I have struggled to keep a roof over my head and I also have four children to feed. I did not mean to steal from you, but I just saw a way to make an extra bit of money for my family," said Joan.

"Why didn't you just come to me if you were having difficulties?" asked Elizabeth.

"Because I am not a charity case and I do not want your pity," replied Joan.

"I could dismiss you on the spot you know and then where would you be?" asked Elizabeth.

"Oh please, I am begging you do not sack me," said Joan.

"Give me one good reason why I should keep you on here? Because I doubt if I will ever be able to trust you again," said Elizabeth.

"Please keep me on here, if not for me do it for my children," begged Joan.

Elizabeth then thought about her own son, Adam, and what would have happened if she had still been poor when Edward had died and then she thought about what the police would do to Joan if she contacted them. She could still remember how badly people were treated when they were caught stealing and Elizabeth did not want that on her conscience.

"I have decided to give you another chance but on the understanding that as soon as you have sorted your finances out you will pay me back every bit of money that you owe me," said Elizabeth.

"Yes of course," said Joan.

"But if this happens again I will have no choice but to involve the police and you will definitely be dismissed from your position," said Elizabeth.

"What am I going to tell the other ladies? They know that I stole from you and they might start being nasty to me," said Joan.

"I will speak to them, just leave it with me," said Elizabeth.

"Thank you," said Joan as she left the office.

A few minutes later Emily came back into the office and Elizabeth told her that she was not going to take the matter any further.

"Are you mad? That woman stole from you, you cannot let her get away with that!" said Emily.

"She had her reasons so I am willing to give her another chance," said Elizabeth.

"Well I suppose you are the boss," said Emily. "Oh, there is a gentleman waiting to make an order for a dress for his mother," she told Elizabeth.

"Could you send him in please," she asked Emily.

The gentleman came into Elizabeth's office and she showed him some of her designs.

"What type of dress are you looking for?" asked Elizabeth.

"Something for my mother to wear out for the evening, only it is her birthday soon and I promised to treat her to a dress and to a night out," said the gentleman.

"What about something like this?" asked Elizabeth as she pointed to an evening gown.

"Oh yes, I think she would really like that," replied the gentleman.

"You will have to bring your mother in to see me so that I can take her measurements and once you have decided on a colour, I can get started on the dress," said Elizabeth.

"Thank you, I will try and bring my mother here tomorrow," said the gentleman.

"I look forward to it," said Elizabeth as she shook his hand.

"Would you mind if I asked you something?" asked the gentleman.

"That depends on what you are going to ask me," replied Elizabeth.

"Would you care to walk out with me one evening?" he asked.

"I am sorry, but no thank you," said Elizabeth politely.

"Oh I do beg your pardon, I did not realise that you were already married," said the gentleman as he looked at Elizabeth's wedding ring.

"I am a widow, but I am not interested in anyone else just yet," Elizabeth told him.

"What about the lady outside with the blonde hair? Is she single?" he asked.

"My goodness, you certainly do not waste any time. Do you?" said Elizabeth.

"I just have a good eye for a pretty lady, although the lady outside is nowhere near as pretty as you," said the gentleman.

"Do not let Emily hear you saying that, she will be mortified," said Elizabeth.

"Oh, her name is Emily, is it?" asked the gentleman.

"Yes it is, and no she is not courting at the moment," replied Elizabeth.

"Thank goodness for that. I had better go and use my charm on her then, but I still much prefer you," he told Elizabeth with a smile.

Elizabeth just shook her head as if to say, 'Who on earth do you think you are?' The gentleman then approached Emily and they stood talking for a while, then he left the building and Emily rushed into Elizabeth's office all excitedly.

"Oh my goodness, Elizabeth, that gentleman that was just here, has only gone and asked me to walk out with him tomorrow night," said Emily.

"Well, did you say yes?" asked Elizabeth.

"Of course I did. After all it is not often I get asked out by a gentleman," she said smiling.

"He seemed really nice," said Elizabeth.

"Yes, he did, didn't he?" said Emily.

The next day the gentleman came to the factory with his mother and whilst his mother was being measured for her dress, the gentleman stood talking to Emily.

"My name is Howard Madison," he told her.

"Yes, I know, I saw your name on the order book," said Emily.

"Oh, checking up on me, were you?" he laughed.

"Obviously, I have to know whom I am walking out with," said Emily giggling.

"I will pick you up about seven. Is that alright?" he asked.

"Yes, that is fine," replied Emily.

That evening Emily rushed home from work and Elizabeth could hardly keep up with her.

"Slow down, will you," Elizabeth told her.

"I have to get home quick because I have not got much time before Howard gets here," said Emily.

Elizabeth smiled to herself because she could see how excited Emily was at the thought of walking out with someone at long last.

Howard knocked at the door at exactly seven o'clock and Emily rushed to the door to meet him.

"Hello," she said when she saw him.

"Have a nice time," shouted Elizabeth.

"So where are you taking me?" asked Emily.

"I thought we could have a walk in the park seeing as it is such a lovely evening," replied Howard.

"Yes, alright," said Emily.

Emily put her arm in Howard's and they took a slow walk through the park, but Emily's feet started to hurt so they found a bench to sit on.

As they sat talking Howard put his arm around Emily and she could not believe her luck.

"What type of work do you do?" asked Emily.

"I am a teacher but I am hoping to one day be a headmaster," replied Howard.

"Is it very hard keeping all the children under control?" asked Emily.

"Not at all. We are rather strict but that is the only way to get respect and although the children probably resent discipline, in the end they will realise it is for their own good," replied Howard.

"I do not think I could cope with working with lots of children; one or two, yes, but not lots of them. It is bad enough trying to keep lots of ladies in line where I work, let alone children," laughed Emily.

"I can assure you it is not that bad and the children do have fun as well," said Howard.

"I still would not want to do that, you must be awfully brave," said Emily.

"And you are awfully beautiful," said Howard as he held Emily's head and kissed her.

Emily felt on top of the world. She could not believe that someone was actually interested in her.

"Shall we go somewhere a little more private?" asked Howard.

"Where do you suggest we go?" asked Emily.

"Come with me and I'll show you," he told her.

Howard took Emily's hand and led her to an empty house at the bottom of the park.

"Are you sure we are allowed in here?" asked Emily.

"Of course we are. Nobody lives here anymore; it has been empty for ages," replied Howard.

Howard put his hand through a broken piece of glass in the door so that he could open it and they both went inside.

"What are we supposed to do now?" asked Emily.

Howard then pulled Emily closer to him and kissed her again. He then put his hand up to her face and stroked it gently, but he slowly moved his hand down to touch her breast.

"What are you doing?" asked Emily.

"I thought it was what you wanted, but if you do not like me, then I shall leave," said Howard.

"Of course I like you and I certainly do not want you to leave," said Emily.

"Well, if you really like me then, let me touch you," said Howard.

He then started to kiss Emily again and he slowly put his hand inside her dress so that he could feel her breasts. Emily was quite nervous but she did not try to stop him; she was afraid he might walk away from her and as Emily had never walked out with anyone before, she thought that it was the right thing to do.

"Oh Emily, you are so beautiful," said Howard as he started to kiss her neck.

"Do you really think so?" she asked.

"I never say anything that I do not mean," he told her.

Suddenly Howard put his hand on Emily's bottom and he pulled her closer to him; he then slowly lifted up her dress and put his hand inside her undergarments. Emily was still feeling very nervous but her nerves stopped as she started to enjoy herself.

"Lay down on the floor," he told her.

Emily being the naive lady that she was did exactly what Howard told her. He then started to pull down her undergarments and no sooner had he taken them off he was making love to her.

"Oh, Emily, I think I am in love with you," said Howard as he got what he wanted.

Emily laid on the floor and let Howard do whatever he wanted to her. She was just thrilled that someone had taken an interest in her.

"I had better be taking you home now," said Howard as he tucked his shirt in.

"What already? But we have not been out for very long," said Emily.

"Oh, didn't I tell you that I have a lot of books to mark tonight?" asked Howard.

"No, you never," replied Emily.

"Oh, I am so sorry," said Howard.

"That's alright, as long as you promise to see me again tomorrow," said Emily.

"You can count on it," said Howard.

Howard then walked Emily home and he kissed her goodnight before leaving.

"Thank you for a lovely evening," said Emily.

"I will see you tomorrow about the same time," he told her.

Emily walked into the house all excitedly and she threw her arms around Elizabeth as she sat reading in a chair.

"I take it you had a nice evening then?" asked Elizabeth.

"Yes, it was the best ever!" replied Emily.

"So what does he do for a living?" asked Elizabeth.

"He is a teacher but he wants to be a headmaster one day," replied Emily.

"Oh, so you might one day be married to a headmaster," said Elizabeth smiling.

"We have not talked about marriage yet, silly," laughed Emily.

"I should hope not, you hardly know him," smiled Elizabeth.

As Elizabeth said that, Emily started to think. But then she remembered that Howard had told her he loved her, so she did not care what she had done earlier as she felt very happy.

The next day Emily got up feeling extremely bubbly; she was in such a good mood that nothing was going to be able to upset her that day.

Whilst Emily was at work the next day all she could think about was Howard, but she kept making mistakes with some of the orders.

"Emily, will you concentrate on what you are supposed to be doing, only you have mixed up three orders already," said Elizabeth.

"Oh, I am so sorry. It's just that I keep thinking about Howard," Emily told her.

"Well, try not to think about him because we cannot afford to make mistakes," said Elizabeth.

Later that evening, Emily got all dressed up and waited for Howard to call at seven o'clock. She waited and waited for him, but he did not arrive.

"Where is he?" asked Emily.

"Perhaps something has happened at home and he has been delayed," replied Elizabeth.

"But if something has happened surely he could let me know," said Emily.

"Perhaps he cannot get here. I am sure he will have a reasonable explanation," said Elizabeth.

"Or perhaps he just does not want to see me again," said Emily.

"Oh, I am sure he does. Why wouldn't he want to see you again?" asked Elizabeth.

Emily just looked at Elizabeth and burst into tears, but Elizabeth could not understand why.

"What is it? Why are you getting so upset?" asked Elizabeth.

"I think Howard hates me," cried Emily.

"Of course he does not hate you. Why are you thinking that?" asked Elizabeth.

"Because I let him have his way with me the other night," replied Emily.

"You did what?" asked Elizabeth looking shocked.

"I thought he liked me and he even told me he loved me," cried Emily.

"You silly little fool. Why did you let him do that? He has ruined you now and you hardly even know him," shouted Elizabeth.

"I did it because I thought he would like me more and it's not as if I have had many other offers. Is it?" said Emily.

"Oh, Emily, I cannot believe you have been so stupid. No man is worth losing your virginity to, especially on the first night," said Elizabeth.

"How can you stand there and say that to me? Knowing that you gave yourself to Edward before you were married," said Emily.

"But that was different, we were in love and we had known each other for years," replied Elizabeth.

"But I thought that Howard loved me, that is why I did it," said Emily.

"How could you possibly think that Howard loved you when he hardly knew you?" asked Elizabeth.

"Alright, so I made a mistake. But you do not have to keep shouting at me because of it," said Emily.

"I'm sorry. It is as much Howard's fault as it is yours. You both should have known better," said Elizabeth.

"Do you think that is why he has not come here tonight?" asked Emily.

"Yes, probably. After all he has got what he wanted. Hasn't he?" said Elizabeth.

"Why doesn't anything good ever happen to me? Why couldn't Howard have loved me?" asked Emily.

"It just wasn't meant to be. Later you will meet someone that will really love you and then you will wonder what you ever saw in Howard," said Elizabeth.

"But when is it going to happen for me, Elizabeth? No one is ever interested in me!" said Emily.

"It will happen one day and when it does you will be the happiest person in the world," said Elizabeth.

Emily sat down in a chair and cried her eyes out and although Elizabeth was quite disgusted with her for what she had done, she still tried to comfort her and make her feel better.

A week or so later had past and Emily had still not heard from Howard, so she now knew by now that he had just used her for sex.

As Elizabeth sat looking through her order book she soon realized that Howard and his mother were due in that day, as his mother had to try on her dress to see if it fitted properly. Elizabeth also knew that if Emily saw him she might cause a scene in the factory, so she had to think of something quick to get Emily out of the way.

"Emily, you look quite tired today. Why don't you take the rest of the afternoon off. I can finish off here by myself," said Elizabeth.

"No, I feel fine," said Emily.

"But you do not look fine, you look extremely tired and I would prefer it if you went home," Elizabeth told her.

"Alright, but there is nothing wrong with me," argued Emily.

A short time after Emily had left the factory Howard arrived with his mother and, although Elizabeth wanted to tell Howard just what she thought of him, she kept her thoughts to herself as she did not want to embarrass his mother.

"Come this way as your dress is ready for you to try on," said Elizabeth.

Howard's mother went into one of the changing rooms to try on her dress and she was thrilled with the finished product. Elizabeth then folded up the dress for her and placed it into a box.

"I'll just get your bill for you," said Elizabeth.

"You wait outside, Mother, I'll be out in a few minutes," Howard told her.

Howard then followed Elizabeth to her office and closed the door.

"I am pleased I have managed to get you on your own, as I would like to have a quiet word with you," said Elizabeth.

"If it is about Emily then I do not want to talk about her," said Howard.

"How could you treat her like that? She was innocent until you took that away from her," said Elizabeth.

"I did not force myself upon her, she was quite willing to lay with me," said Howard.

"Only because you told her that you loved her!" shouted Elizabeth.

Howard suddenly started to laugh, but Elizabeth started to get even more angry.

"What is so amusing?" she asked.

"You are. I rather like a lady who is a bit feisty, like you," replied Howard. "I always did prefer you to Emily anyway. After all, Emily is not exactly the best-looking girl in the world, is she?" he told Elizabeth.

"Then why didn't you tell Emily that? Instead of making her do something you knew she would regret," asked Elizabeth.

"I do not remember her having any regrets, in fact, from what I can remember, she loved every minute of it," said Howard.

"Oh, you disgust me!" said Elizabeth.

"Now don't be like that, I really do like you and I would like to get to know you better, if you allowed me to," said Howard.

"No, thank you, I'm really not that desperate," said Elizabeth.

"You are not turning me down are you? I am really not as bad as you think," said Howard.

"Why should I believe anything that you say? After all, you have already humiliated my friend," said Elizabeth.

"But it is not her I want, it is you," said Howard as he walked towards Elizabeth.

Elizabeth was not as naive as Emily. She knew that Howard was just another man out for what he could get and she had met his type before. But Elizabeth decided to play along with him, as she wanted to get him back for the way he had treated her friend.

"Is that true that you want me and not Emily?" asked Elizabeth.

"Yes, it is. You are much more prettier than she is and I like the way you speak your mind," replied Howard.

"Then what are we going to do about it?" asked Elizabeth.

"What about if I meet you tonight?" asked Howard.

"Oh no. I am busy this evening." replied Elizabeth. "But I am not busy now," she told him.

Howard gave Elizabeth a slight grin and then walked even closer to her; he then put his arms around her and tried to kiss her, but before he could do that Elizabeth brought up her knee and hurt Howard in his private parts.

"Don't ever play games with me again, I am not stupid enough to fall for the rubbish that flows out of your mouth and, don't even think about trying to get your way with me. I would rather die than have your body anywhere near me!" shouted Elizabeth.

"You will regret that," said Howard, as he bent over holding himself.

"I do not regret anything. Now get out of my factory and take your custom elsewhere," said Elizabeth.

"Do not think you have got away with this because you have not!" said Howard.

Suddenly the office door opened and in walked Howard's mother.

"Hurry up, dear, I am cold waiting for you outside and do not forget your wife will be home soon," his mother told him.

"Oh, I did not realise you had a wife," said Elizabeth sarcastically.

"Oh yes, but he has only been married for a few months," said Howard's mother.

Howard did not know what to say but his face said it all. He was frightened in case Elizabeth said anything out of turn to his mother, so he quickly rushed her out of the factory and Elizabeth never heard from him again. But a few weeks later Elizabeth caught Emily crying, but when Elizabeth asked her what was wrong Emily could not get her words out properly as she was sobbing.

"Come and sit down and tell me what it is that is bothering you," said Elizabeth.

Emily just looked at Elizabeth and started to sob even more.

"Emily, what is it?" asked Elizabeth.

"I am with child," replied Emily.

"Oh no, please tell me this is not true," said Elizabeth.

"I can't because it is true," said Emily.

"Does anyone else know?" asked Elizabeth.

"No, no one," she replied.

"I think you need to see a doctor; he might be able to take the baby away from you," said Elizabeth.

"How?" asked Emily.

"I do not know exactly. But whilst I was living in London I once heard these two ladies talking. One of them must have been with child, because I heard the other lady telling her that she knew someone that could remove it for her if she did not want to keep it," explained Elizabeth.

"Will it hurt?" asked Emily.

"I do not know. We will just have to ask the doctor and see what he has to say," said Elizabeth.

"Please do not tell anyone about this, Elizabeth, I could not bear the thought of everyone talking about me as if I were some kind of loose woman," said Emily.

"Don't worry, your secret is safe with me. But you do need to see a doctor as soon as possible," Elizabeth told her.

Later that evening, Elizabeth got a doctor to come out and examine Emily and he confirmed that she was definitely with child.

"My friend does not want the baby, so would it be possible for you to take it away from her?" asked Elizabeth.

"What kind of doctor do you think I am?" he shouted.

"I am sorry, I do not understand. What have I said that is so wrong?" asked Elizabeth.

"Do you realise what you are asking me to do is illegal?" asked the doctor.

"No, I did not realise that," replied Elizabeth.

"Well, what am I going to do now?" asked Emily.

"I am afraid that you have got yourself in a mess and there is nothing that I can do," replied the doctor.

"But I cannot have this bairn. What will people say?" cried Emily.

"Then you should have said 'no'," the doctor told her angrily.

After the doctor left, Emily burst into tears, so Elizabeth sat with her to try and comfort her.

"I honestly thought that the doctor could help you. I never realised that it was illegal to take a baby out of someone," said Elizabeth.

"What am I going to do? Everyone will look down at me," said Emily.

"It does not matter what people think. You still have a home here with me and I shall look after you," Elizabeth told her.

"I do not deserve your kindness, I deserve to be punished," said Emily.

"Now you just listen to me and stop this silly talk. You were innocent in all of this and did not know any better, but Howard did know better and he is as much to blame, if not more so," said Elizabeth.

Emily continued to work with Elizabeth at the factory, but over the next few months as Emily started to put on weight the ladies in the factory started whispering about her. Emily could sense that she was being talked about and Elizabeth had also started to notice the change in the atmosphere at work.

"Could all you ladies stop working for a moment as I would like to say a few words," said Elizabeth one day.

"I have noticed a lot of you whispering and sniggering behind Emily's back and we all know why you are doing this without me even mentioning it. But I would just like to say that I want it to stop because Emily is a very dear friend of mine and I am not going to tolerate her being humiliated in my own premises. If any of you continue to whisper and I find out, I will have you dismissed without a second warning. Is that understood?" asked Elizabeth.

"Yes, miss," replied the ladies.

Elizabeth then walked back into her office with Emily following behind her.

"You did not have to do that for me. It is my own fault why they are talking about me," said Emily.

"They are here to work, not to discuss other peoples private business and I will not tolerate them talking about you in that way," said Elizabeth.

"But it is still my own fault and I expected it," said Emily.

"You made one mistake, that is all and, yes, you are paying for it, unlike Howard who was just as much to blame, but he just walks away," said Elizabeth.

"You are such a good friend to me, Elizabeth. I do not deserve your kindness," said Emily.

"I have never forgotten all the things you have done for me in the past. Like when I gave birth to Adam you helped me through it and you were there for me when Edward died and now it is my turn to be there for you when you need a friend," said Elizabeth.

"Thank you," said Emily as she hugged Elizabeth.

The gossip soon stopped at the factory and things gradually got back to normal. Emily continued to work until she was about seven months pregnant and she would have continued to have worked longer, but Elizabeth advised her against it. Elizabeth's sister in-law, Alice, was also expecting her second child, so she often kept Emily company, although her baby was not due for another six months yet.

"Aren't you getting ready to come to church with me?" asked Elizabeth, one Sunday.

"No, I feel too tired to go out," replied Emily.

"Would you like me to stay home with you?" asked Elizabeth.

"No, you go and join your family at church, I will be fine," replied Emily.

"But I do not like leaving you on your own," Elizabeth told her.

"Just go, I will be fine, honest," said Emily.

Elizabeth left the house and met up with her family at the church, whilst Emily sat at home with her feet up and had a sleep. About half an hour later Emily was woken by severe pains in her stomach and the pains got stronger by the minute. Emily started to panic as she knew that the baby was coming, but she was frightened because she was on her own. After a few minutes had passed, Emily decided to walk to the church so that she could get help from Elizabeth, but she had only walked a short distance when she suddenly collapsed in agony. Emily started to shout and scream but there was no one around to hear her; but a short time later a man came along riding a horse. The gentleman saw Emily lying on the ground so he pulled up and dismounted.

"Are you alright?" he asked.

"No, I am having my bairn," replied Emily.

The man picked Emily up from the ground and sat her on his horse.

"Where do you live?" he asked.

210

"In that cottage just across the field," replied Emily.

The man took Emily home and helped her inside the house, but as the pains got worse she began to scream really loudly.

"Is there anyone home?" asked the gentleman.

"No, everyone has gone to church," replied Emily.

The man then carried Emily upstairs and made her as comfortable as he could.

"I had better go and find someone that can help you," he told Emily.

"No, you cannot leave me!" she shouted.

"Alright, calm down, everything is going to be fine," he told her.

"I think the bairn will be here soon," said Emily.

"Oh my goodness, I have never done anything like this before," said the gentleman.

"Just be here for me, that is all I ask," said Emily.

Emily took off some of her clothes and started to push, but the man just stood there not knowing what to do.

"I think the head is coming out," said Emily as she pushed again.

"What already?" he asked.

"Quick help me!" Emily told him.

The man looked down and saw the baby's head coming out, so he told Emily to push again as he eased the baby out.

"It's a girl," he told her.

"Oh thank you," cried Emily.

"You are welcome. She is beautiful," said the gentleman.

When Elizabeth arrived home she called to Emily as she could not find her downstairs, so Emily shouted back to her and told her that she was upstairs in her room. Elizabeth came upstairs and when she walked into Emily's bedroom she had the shock of her life, as she saw her friend sitting in bed holding her baby.

"Oh my goodness, you have had the baby already," she said.

"Yes, and this kind gentleman helped me," replied Emily.

"I had better be going now, anyway," said the gentleman.

"Thank you for being there for my friend, I'll see you out," said Elizabeth.

Elizabeth walked back downstairs with the gentleman and saw him to the door.

"I have just got to get my horse; he is tied up on the fence around the side of the house," said the gentleman.

Elizabeth walked round with the gentleman and watched as he untied his horse, but Elizabeth had to look twice when she saw the horse as she thought she recognised it.

"Excuse me. Is that horse called Admiral?" she asked.

"Yes he is. How do you know that?" asked the gentleman.

"Ernest, is that you?" asked Elizabeth.

"Yes. Do I know you?" he asked.

"It's me, Elizabeth Oakendale. Well, actually, I'm Elizabeth Thomas now as I was married," replied Elizabeth.

"Well I never. You look extremely well, I must say," said Ernest.

"So do you," Elizabeth told him.

"I had better be going now as everyone will be wondering where I am," said Ernest.

"Thank you again for all your help," said Elizabeth.

"It was nothing, I do that kind of thing everyday," he laughed.

Elizabeth watched as Ernest rode away on his horse and it brought back lots of memories to her from when she was a child, when she used to often watch Ernest riding his horse. Elizabeth then rushed back inside the house and ran upstairs to see Emily.

"I am so sorry I was not here for you," said Elizabeth.

"Never mind, she is here now and we are both alright," smiled Emily.

"I take it she is a girl then?" said Elizabeth.

"Yes, isn't she just adorable?" said Emily.

"Yes she is, she is beautiful," replied Elizabeth.

"I cannot believe that I even thought about getting rid of her before," said Emily.

"I am so pleased you are thinking that way, because I was not sure how you were going to react to her once she was born," said Elizabeth.

"I absolutely love her and I do not care anymore what anyone has to say about me, just as long as they do not say anything nasty about her," said Emily.

"So what are you going to call her?" asked Elizabeth.

"I have decided to name her after you, but I am going to shorten her name to Lizzie so we do not get confused," smiled Emily.

"Can I hold her?" asked Elizabeth.

"Yes, of course," replied Emily, as she gave her daughter to Elizabeth.

"Doesn't it make you feel proud when you hold your own baby for the very first time?" said Elizabeth.

"Yes it does. I know I made a mistake, Elizabeth, but I would not part with her for the world," said Emily.

A short time later Elizabeth went downstairs so that Emily could get some rest, but she kept checking on Emily every hour or so, just to make sure that she was alright. The next day Elizabeth's sister in-law came around to see if Emily was alright as Elizabeth had to go to work and she was rather surprised to hear that Emily had already given birth to a daughter.

"Oh, she is lovely. I hope when I have my baby that I have a daughter this time," said Alice.

When Elizabeth returned home from work she cooked Emily a dinner and took it up to her room for her.

"How are you feeling?" asked Elizabeth.

"I am still a bit tired but Lizzie has been awfully good. She has hardly cried at all today," replied Emily.

"Well eat your dinner before it gets cold as you need to keep your strength up. I will come up and see you again later," said Elizabeth.

CHAPTER FOURTEEN

A few days later, whilst Elizabeth was sitting downstairs reading one evening, there was a knock at the door; when Elizabeth answered it she saw Ernest standing outside.

"Good evening. I have just called around to see how the lady with the baby is doing," said Ernest.

"Oh, you mean Emily," said Elizabeth. "You had better come in," she told him.

Ernest walked into the house and just stood in the middle of the room.

"You can sit down, you know," smiled Elizabeth.

"So how is Emily?" asked Ernest.

"She is fine and the baby is also doing well," replied Elizabeth.

"I am really pleased to hear that. She looked so frightened when I found her yesterday. I do not know what would have happened to her if I had not come along," said Ernest.

"Thank you again for all your help," said Elizabeth.

"How are you, Elizabeth?" asked Ernest.

"I am very well, thank you," she replied.

"I was really sorry to hear about Edward's death, it came as quite a shock," said Ernest.

"Yes, it was awful when he passed away. I found it very difficult being on my own. That is one reason why I moved back here," said Elizabeth.

"I was very surprised when I heard that you and Edward were getting married, and I was even more shocked when I was not even invited to your wedding," said Ernest.

"Oh, I am sorry about that, but we decided to have just a small wedding with as less people as possible," said Elizabeth.

"Have you any children?" asked Ernest.

"Yes, Edward and I have a son called Adam. He is like his father in many ways," replied Elizabeth. "What about you? Do you have any children?" asked Elizabeth.

"No, I have never been married," replied Ernest.

"But I thought you were married to Rosemary Thornton; only you did send Edward an invite to your wedding," said Elizabeth.

"Yes, we were due to get married but I had a lucky escape," said Ernest.

"Why, what happened? Oh, excuse me for being so rude, you do not have to tell me if it is too personal," said Elizabeth.

"No, it is alright if you know. Everyone else around here knows what happened anyway. Rosemary made a complete fool out of me. She had an affair with my parents' gardener. I caught her romping with him in the stables one day and apparently it had been going on for months," said Ernest.

"I am really sorry, Ernest, I did not realise," said Elizabeth.

"No, don't be, I'm not. I am just relieved I found out when I did, because I now know what a nasty person she really is," said Ernest.

"Do you ever see her anymore?" asked Elizabeth.

"No, I have not seen her recently, but I do occasionally see her parents," replied Ernest.

"What did your parents think when they found out what she had been up to with their gardener?" asked Elizabeth.

"They were absolutely disgusted with her and they told her so. They also sacked their gardener as well," replied Ernest.

"I often wondered what you ever saw in her; you were much too nice for her," said Elizabeth.

"What makes you think that?" asked Ernest.

"Oh, it does not matter now," replied Elizabeth.

"No, come on. You obviously dislike Rosemary, so please tell me why?" asked Ernest.

"When I worked for your parents many years ago, Rosemary used to bully me quite often and, one day she asked me to bring her tea into the drawing room, which I did. But when I got there Rosemary was there with her brother and they locked me inside the room. They then held me so that I could not move and Rosemary's brother tried to force himself upon me, but they only released me when they heard you call Rosemary's name. If you had not come along when you did, I think he would have raped me," said Elizabeth.

"My God, Elizabeth. Why on earth didn't you report them to my parents?" asked Ernest.

"Because I did not think that anyone would believe me. After, all I was just a maid then and Rosemary was a well-to-do lady," replied Elizabeth.

"What an evil woman she is," said Ernest.

"I have never told anyone about what Rosemary and her brother did to me, apart from Edward. Now you know the real reason why we did not invite you to our wedding, because we thought that you had married Rosemary and we did not want her there that day," said Elizabeth.

"Well, that is understandable to say the least," said Ernest.

"I have never hated anyone in my life, Ernest, but I hated her and I still do," said Elizabeth.

"I do not blame you at all. But God works in mysterious ways, because she is certainly paying for her sins now," said Ernest.

"What do you mean by that?" asked Elizabeth.

"She is now married to a man called George Todd. He drinks quite a lot and I have heard that he often beats her in drunken rages, so I think God must be punishing her for the cruel things that she has done in the past. Her brother was also killed in a riding accident a few years ago, so he has also paid for his crime," said Ernest.

"It serves them both right," said Elizabeth.

"Yes, my words exactly," said Ernest.

"I would prefer it if you did not mention what I have told you to anyone else, as I have kept this secret to myself for all these years, well apart from when I confided in Edward of course," said Elizabeth.

"Do not worry, I will not say a word to anyone, my lips are sealed," Ernest told her.

"Thank you," said Elizabeth.

"You have really changed since I last saw you, for the better of course. I have also heard that you are doing really well for yourself," said Ernest.

"Yes, I made a living from selling my paintings whilst I was in London and now I have my own dressmaking business," said Elizabeth.

"I am really pleased for you," said Ernest.

"So, what have you been doing these past years?" asked Elizabeth.

"I have been really busy studying law and now I am a qualified lawyer. Edward gave me some good advice in the past; I wish he was here now so that I could thank him," said Ernest.

"What about your brother Joseph, is he married yet?" asked Elizabeth.

"Yes, he is married with two children and he now lives in London. He works in a bank and hopes to one day be a bank manager," replied Ernest.

"So quite a lot has changed since I last saw you?" said Elizabeth.

"Yes, I suppose it has. Mind you, I was surprised that you still recognised my horse, Admiral, after all this time," smiled Ernest.

"How could I ever forget him? I can still remember the day he was born and I can remember standing there watching you riding him. I was so envious of you because I always wanted a horse of my own, but my wish did come true because Edward kindly bought me my own horse whom I named Midnight," smiled Elizabeth.

"Perhaps we could go riding together one day when you are not too busy," said Ernest.

"Yes, I would really like that," said Elizabeth.

"How about this Saturday?" asked Ernest.

"Yes alright," she replied.

"Good, I'll call here about eleven o'clock in the morning. I'll also bring a picnic and we can make a day of it," said Ernest.

"That's if it does not rain," smiled Elizabeth.

"Do you know I have been sitting here for a few hours and you have not even offered me a drink," said Ernest jokingly.

"I see that you are still as cheeky as ever," laughed Elizabeth.

"I'm not cheeky, just thirsty," he laughed.

"Alright, I will make you a cup of tea," said Elizabeth jokingly.

Elizabeth and Ernest sat talking for hours and it was only when the clock chimed twice that they realised that it was two o'clock in the morning.

"My goodness, I did not realise it was this late!" said Ernest.

"Neither did I. I have got to be up for work in a few hours as well," said Elizabeth.

"Oh, I am alright because I have got court tomorrow and I have not got to be there until about eleven," smiled Ernest.

"Lucky you," said Elizabeth sarcastically, but with a smile.

"Now don't be like that. You are the one that kept me here half the night," laughed Ernest.

"And you are the one that I am going to kick out right now," laughed Elizabeth.

"Alright, alright, I'm going. I know when I'm not wanted," said Ernest jokingly.

When Ernest left Elizabeth kept smiling to herself as he had made her laugh and she felt a lot better in herself for being able to have confided in him about everything that had happened with Rosemary years before.

Elizabeth went upstairs to bed but it seemed that no sooner had she been asleep when it was suddenly time to get up again. When she arrived at work Elizabeth had a lot of orders to sort out and she was really missing Emily's help. When she arrived home that evening Emily was sitting downstairs nursing her baby.

"Hello, you must be feeling a lot better now, seeing as you are up," said Elizabeth.

"Yes, I am. I could not stay in bed a minute longer," smiled Emily. "I have also cooked us both a dinner so sit down," Emily told her.

"You should not be doing things like that, you have to rest, after all, it has only been a few days since you gave birth," said Elizabeth.

"I had to do something or I would have gone mad. Mind you, I did get a bit of help from Alice," laughed Emily.

"Oh yes, before I forget, Ernest came around here last night to see how you and Lizzie were, but as you were asleep I did not want to disturb you," said Elizabeth.

"That was nice of him. I don't know what I would have done if he had not found me the other day. He was so nice to me and, although I was frightened, he made me feel quite at ease," said Emily.

"And how is my favourite girl today?" asked Elizabeth.

"She has been really good, I have hardly known that she was here," replied Emily.

"Well, make the most of it because it will not last, as you know from when Adam was a baby. Once he was walking he was into everything," smiled Elizabeth.

"Yes, I can remember. He was rather mischievous. Wasn't he?" said Emily.

"Mischievous is not the word I would use. More like a little monster," laughed Elizabeth.

"He does look like Edward though. Don't you think?" asked Emily.

"Yes, he gets more like him every day. I just wish Edward was here to see him growing up," replied Elizabeth.

"You still miss him don't you?" asked Emily.

"Only every minute of the day," smiled Elizabeth.

Just after Elizabeth and Emily had eaten their dinner there was a knock at the door; it was Ernest.

"Hello, come in," said Elizabeth.

Ernest walked into the room and saw Emily holding her baby.

"Hello, you look well. How is the baby?" he asked.

"Lizzie is fine, thank you," replied Emily.

"She looks very contented," said Ernest.

"Would you like to hold her?" asked Emily.

"Yes, I would love to," he replied.

As Ernest took Lizzie in his arms he looked down at her and smiled.

"It was quite an emotional experience for me to actually witness her birth; it is something that I shall never forget," said Ernest.

"Whilst you are here, Ernest, I would like to ask you and Elizabeth something. I was wondering how you would feel about being Lizzie's godparents when I have her christened?" she asked.

"I would be deeply honoured to be her godparent; thank you for asking me," replied Ernest.

"What about you, Elizabeth?" asked Emily.

"You just try and stop me," said Elizabeth as she gave Emily a hug.

"Did Elizabeth tell you I called around last night to see how you were?" asked Ernest.

"Yes, she did. I am sorry I missed you but I was rather tired," said Emily.

"I expect Elizabeth is tired as well today. Did she also tell you she kept me up half the night talking?" laughed Ernest.

"No, she did not," replied Emily.

"It was Ernest that actually kept me up half the night and I had to be at work early today," she laughed. "It was quite hard at work today as well as I have had so many orders this week. I am certainly finding it difficult without you there to help me, Emily," said Elizabeth.

"Oh yes, before I forget, Alice has offered to look after Lizzie for me if I decide to go back to work and I do want to go back because I need the money," said Emily.

"You do not need to come back straight away though, only when you feel strong enough," said Elizabeth.

"I had better be going now. I only called around here because I was passing and I expect you two ladies could do with an early night anyway," said Ernest.

"Well I could," laughed Elizabeth.

"Thank you for coming to see us," said Emily.

"I am busy for the rest of the week so I doubt if I will get time to come around again, so I will see you on Saturday at eleven," said Ernest.

"Yes, alright, I shall see you then," said Elizabeth, as she saw Ernest out.

"What is all this then? You keeping secrets from me are you?" asked Emily.

"What are you talking about?" asked Elizabeth.

"You did not mention to me that you had planned to see Ernest on Saturday," laughed Emily.

"Oh, is that all? We are only going horse riding together," said Elizabeth.

"Well there is nothing wrong with that, he seems really nice," said Emily.

"Before you start getting ridiculous ideas into your head Ernest and I are just friends; we have known each other since we were children," said Elizabeth.

"He is rather handsome though, even you have to admit that," said Emily.

"I never said he was not handsome," replied Elizabeth.

"Is he married?" asked Emily.

"No," said Elizabeth sarcastically.

"So, he is a handsome bachelor, ummmm," said Emily smiling.

"Will you stop it? I am not interested in Ernest in that way, we are just friends," said Elizabeth.

"Of course you are," laughed Emily.

"I am not even going to speak to you whilst you are behaving like this," said Elizabeth.

"I am only teasing you. Do you think he will kiss you on Saturday?" laughed Emily.

"Oh you!" said Elizabeth, as she chased Emily with a fork.

Even though Elizabeth used to have strong feelings for Ernest, a lot had changed since then; she was still not over Edward's death and was certainly not looking for another partner.

Ernest arrived for Elizabeth just before eleven o'clock on the Saturday morning and they both rode off on their horses together.

"Your horse is almost as handsome as mine, but not quite," laughed Ernest.

"You think you are so funny, don't you?" said Elizabeth.

"I don't think it, I know it," joked Ernest.

"I'll race you to that big oak tree," said Elizabeth as she rode off before him.

"You cheated," shouted Ernest as he tried to catch up with her.

Elizabeth kept looking around as she rode her horse, just to see where Ernest was. But it was not long before he rode straight past her and laughed as he went by.

"Hurry up!" shouted Ernest as he rode past.

Elizabeth was not as experienced at riding as Ernest was and although she tried she just could not keep up with him.

"See I knew I would beat you in the end and I did not cheat," shouted Ernest as he pulled his horse up by the big oak tree.

Elizabeth just rode towards him smiling to herself; then as Ernest stood laughing at Elizabeth a bird that was in the tree messed right upon his head.

"Oh no!" shouted Ernest.

Elizabeth pulled up her horse and when she saw Ernest's head covered in bird muck she laughed so much she almost fell on to the floor.

"I do not know why you are laughing, it is not even funny," smiled Ernest.

"It might not be funny to you but it is to me," laughed Elizabeth.

Ernest then chased Elizabeth around the tree; she then ran away from him towards some nearby grass, but he soon caught up with her and started tickling her.

"Stop it, Ernest, I cannot breathe," laughed Elizabeth.

She then sat down on the grass and Ernest sat down beside her.

"Oh this is so nice," said Ernest as he laid in the sun.

Elizabeth picked a glade of grass and tickled Ernest's face with it and then she poked it up his nose. Ernest sat up quickly as he rubbed his nose, whilst Elizabeth sat laughing at him.

"Now who thinks they're funny?" said Ernest smiling.

Elizabeth did not say anything. She just sat next to Ernest giggling.

"Look there is a squirrel up in that tree over there," pointed Ernest.

"Oh yes, I can see it," said Elizabeth.

"Oh look, there is also a mouse," said Ernest.

"Where?" asked Elizabeth.

"Right next to your hand," replied Ernest.

Elizabeth quickly jumped up and screamed, whilst Ernest sat on the ground and fell about laughing.

"I am only joking with you, there is not a mouse really," he told her as he laughed.

"Oh you!" shouted Elizabeth as she smiled.

Ernest then stood up and untied a bag from his horse. He then brought the bag over to Elizabeth and took out some sandwiches for them to eat.

"Ummm, these are nice," said Elizabeth.

"I made them myself," said Ernest.

"Did you really?" she asked.

"No, I am just kidding with you, the cook made them for us," laughed Ernest.

"Can't you ever be serious?" asked Elizabeth with a smile.

"Alright, I will," said Ernest as he made a serious face.

"You are mad," laughed Elizabeth.

After they had eaten Elizabeth laid down with the sun burning on to her face, whilst Ernest sat picking daisies.

"Here you are, I have made you a daisy chain," said Ernest.

"I think I am a bit old to wear a daisy chain," said Elizabeth.

"Alright, I'll just have to wear it myself," he told her with a smile.

"Shall we go for a walk?" asked Elizabeth.

"No, let's just sit here and relax," replied Ernest.

"Stop being so lazy, now get up," said Elizabeth, as she pulled his arms.

"You are quite bossy, aren't you?" said Ernest.

"Of course, that is just how a lady should be," she told him jokingly.

Ernest then grabbed hold of Elizabeth and lifted her up into the air and started to swing her around.

"Stop it, just put me down, I am going dizzy," screamed Elizabeth.

Ernest gently stood Elizabeth on to her feet again and then took her hand as they went for a walk together.

"You do not have to hold my hand you know, I am not a little girl about to wander off somewhere," said Elizabeth.

"I just thought that you might like holding my hand," smiled Ernest.

"I don't think so," said Elizabeth jokingly.

Elizabeth collected cones as she walked as she wanted to put them into a basket for decoration, whilst Ernest stood throwing a stick up into a tree trying to knock down conkers. A while later they walked back to where their horses were tied up.

"So where are you living now?" asked Elizabeth.

"I still live with my parents. I did purchase a house a few years ago but I got lonely living on my own, so now I just rent it out," replied Ernest.

"It must be awfully lonely living on your own. I know when Edward died my house seemed really empty, but at least I had Emily living with me, which was a great comfort," said Elizabeth.

"But you are happy now. Aren't you? After all, you do have your family around you now," said Ernest.

"Yes, I suppose I am, but I still miss Edward very much," replied Elizabeth.

"What about your son? Does he ask about Edward?" asked Ernest.

"Yes, he does sometimes. I try and talk about Edward as often as I can when Adam is around, but now that he is at boarding school I do not see him very much," replied Elizabeth.

"I will have to come and meet young Adam the next time he comes home. If that is alright by you?" asked Ernest.

"Yes, of course it is. Actually Adam is due home next weekend for a while, so you can meet him then," said Elizabeth.

"I will not be able to make it on Sunday as it is my parents' anniversary and they are having a garden party with some of their friends. Well actually, why don't you and Adam come along as well," said Ernest.

"Oh no, not if it is your parents' anniversary, they will not want me there," said Elizabeth.

"Of course they will. They will be thrilled to see you and to meet Adam," said Ernest.

"I don't know, but I will think about it," said Elizabeth.

"Well, if you do decide to come it starts about one in the afternoon," said Ernest.

"Yes, alright," replied Elizabeth.

"Come on, let's get the horses and I'll race you home," said Ernest.

"You only said that because you know you are going to beat me," said Elizabeth.

"Not necessarily. I might just let you win," he laughed.

As they pulled up to the house Elizabeth dismounted and walked Midnight to the stable; Ernest just stood waiting for her to come back.

"Would you like to come inside and have a cup of tea?" asked Elizabeth.

"Yes, if it is no trouble," replied Ernest.

"The only thing that is trouble around here is you," laughed Elizabeth.

"How can you say such a thing and after I made you all those sandwiches as well?" laughed Ernest.

"You really are quite mad, aren't you?" said Elizabeth.

"Hello. How was your day?" asked Emily.

"Very nice, thank you," replied Elizabeth.

"Yes, it was very nice, Emily, apart from when Elizabeth decided to put a blade of grass up my nose and then insulted me by telling me that I am mad," laughed Ernest.

"Oh and I laughed because a bird left its droppings on Ernest's head," said Elizabeth, as she burst out laughing again.

"Well it sounds to me like you had a good time, but it does not sound very romantic," said Emily.

"It was not meant to be romantic, Emily. We just went out for the day, that's all," said Elizabeth rather abruptly.

Ernest looked at Emily and raised his eyebrows as if to say I think you said the wrong thing, but Emily just smiled back at him as she thought it was funny.

"So what else did you do whilst you were out?" asked Emily.

"I raced Elizabeth to the big oak tree, but I won of course, even though Elizabeth tried to cheat," said Ernest.

"And Ernest made me a daisy chain, but I would not wear it," smiled Elizabeth.

"I don't think I would have either," said Emily looking at Ernest rather weirdly.

"There is nothing wrong with wearing a daisy chain," said Ernest, as he showed his off to Emily.

"Now you know why I think he is mad," laughed Elizabeth.

After Ernest had gone home Emily put Lizzie upstairs and then sat with Elizabeth for a while.

"You and Ernest seem to be getting along very well," said Emily.

"Yes, we are, as friends," she told Emily.

"Yes, alright I think you have made yourself quite clear that there is no romance," said Emily.

"Then stop making little remarks about us, especially in front of Ernest because it is very embarrassing," said Elizabeth.

"I do not think Ernest was embarrassed because I saw him smiling to himself," said Emily.

"I mean it, Emily, it is not funny. All I want is a friend, that's all," said Elizabeth.

"I am only teasing you. Where is your sense of fun?" said Emily.

"I had fun today, if you must know," said Elizabeth.

"Did Ernest try and kiss you?" asked Emily.

"Emily, will you stop it!" Elizabeth told her.

"I am only asking," said Emily.

"Well if you must know, no he did not," said Elizabeth.

"Oh how boring is that," said Emily.

"Ernest was not boring at all. In fact, I had a really lovely day and he made me laugh a lot," smiled Elizabeth.

"Good, I am really pleased for you. It is about time you enjoyed yourself," said Emily. "Ernest seems like a really nice gentleman," she told Elizabeth.

"Yes, he is," said Elizabeth.

"Your mother came around earlier with Alice; she thought that Lizzie was gorgeous," said Emily.

"She is not wrong, Lizzie is gorgeous," said Elizabeth.

"Oh, by the way, I made some soup earlier and there is still some in the pot if you would like it," said Emily.

"I might have it a bit later as I am not that hungry at the moment. I think I'll go and get washed and changed and then sit in the garden for a while," said Elizabeth.

"I think I might join you," said Emily.

A short time later Elizabeth and Emily sat in the garden together drinking wine.

"Don't you just love these nice warm evenings?" said Elizabeth.

"Yes, it is nice to just sit here and relax," replied Emily.

"Adam is back from boarding school this weekend. I cannot wait to see him," said Elizabeth.

"He is certainly a lovely boy and I have noticed that he is getting more like Edward every time I see him," said Emily.

"Yes, I know. Ernest has asked if he can meet him. He has invited us to his parents' house on Sunday, as they are having a garden party to celebrate their anniversary," said Elizabeth.

"Oh, that will be nice for you both," said Emily.

"I am not sure whether I am going to go yet," said Elizabeth.

"Why? It will do you good to go and it is not as if you do not know Ernest's parents," said Emily.

"I know. But I might feel out of place," said Elizabeth.

"Oh, just go and enjoy yourself. I am sure Ernest's parents will be only too pleased to see you again," said Emily.

"That is what Ernest said, but I told him I would think about it," said Elizabeth.

"I think Ernest is a really nice gentleman and I would like to think that you two might get together one day," said Emily.

"That is not going to happen. But that does not mean that I do not like him because I do. I did have feelings for him once, but I have grown up a lot since I last saw him," said Elizabeth.

"You never told me that you once had feelings for Ernest," said Emily.

"I never told anyone because they probably would have laughed at me; after all, he was from a high-class family and I was just a maid then," said Elizabeth. "I can still remember when Edward got an invite to his wedding. I was absolutely devastated," said Elizabeth.

"Oh I did not realise that Ernest was once married," said Emily.

"He did not get married in the end, but I have only just recently found that out. I am pleased that he never married

227

Rosemary she was the nastiest person that I ever met and she always looked down upon me," said Elizabeth.

"But Ernest treats you as an equal. He does not look down upon you," said Emily.

"I know he doesn't, he has always treated me with respect," said Elizabeth.

"Well, I think if you do get a chance to be with him you should take it, after all you both seem to get along really well together," said Emily.

"We are just friends, Emily. The feelings I had for Ernest are in the past now. I still love Edward and nothing will ever change that," said Elizabeth.

"I know how much you and Edward loved each other because I saw it with my own eyes, so I understand what you are saying," said Emily.

"Then stop going on about Ernest, because it is never going to happen," Elizabeth told her.

THE FOLLOWING SUNDAY

"Are you going to see Ernest today at his parents' house?" asked Emily.

"No, I do not think I shall bother going because I want to spend some time with Adam," replied Elizabeth.

"But Ernest has invited Adam to go along as well, so stop making excuses not to go," said Emily.

"I am going around to Uncle William's house later as I want to see Benjamin," said Adam.

"But I thought that we could spend some time together here," Elizabeth told him.

"But I have already told Benjamin that I will see him later today and I cannot let him down," said Adam.

"Well, if Adam is going to see his cousin, then there is no reason why you cannot attend the garden party," said Emily.

"Oh alright I shall go, but only for a little while," said Elizabeth rather reluctantly.

When Elizabeth arrived at the Lockwoods house there were a lot of people gathered around in the garden, but Elizabeth felt slightly awkward as she did not know anyone. But as she walked around Ernest noticed her so he walked towards her.

"Hello, Elizabeth. I am really pleased you made it here," said Ernest. Where is Adam?" he asked.

"He decided to go and visit his cousin Benjamin, that is why I have come here on my own," replied Elizabeth.

"Come with me and I will get you something to drink," said Ernest.

Elizabeth stood next to Ernest drinking her drink, when suddenly she heard a voice call out her name. When she looked around she saw Mr Lockwood walking towards her.

"Hello, sir, it is lovely to see you again," said Elizabeth.

"It is lovely to see you, but you do not have to call me sir," smiled Mr Lockwood.

"It seems quite funny being back in your garden after all these years," said Elizabeth.

"Yes, I can still remember when you were a child and you would sit out here for hours busy doing your paintings," said Mr Lockwood.

"It seems like a lifetime ago," said Elizabeth.

"Yes, a lot has definitely happened since then. I was sorry to hear the sad news about Edward. How are you coping without him?" asked Mr Lockwood.

"A lot better than I was in the beginning. But I still shed the odd tear or two when I am on my own sometimes," said Elizabeth.

"Edward was a good man and a very dear friend of mine and I still cannot believe he has gone," said Mr Lockwood.

"Yes, I know. I sometimes wake up in the morning and hope it was all just a bad dream, but then it suddenly hits me that it really has happened," said Elizabeth.

"Anyway, on a brighter note, how is that young son of yours?" asked Mr Lockwood.

"He is very well, thank you. He is actually at my brother's house as we speak. He has got some time away from boarding school," replied Elizabeth.

"Well, you tell young Adam when you see him later that he is welcome at my house whenever he wants to come here, as my wife and I would be delighted to meet him," said Mr Lockwood.

"Thank you," said Elizabeth.

"Talking of mother, where is she?" asked Ernest.

"Oh, she is around here somewhere. You know your mother; she is probably talking to someone because that is what she does best," laughed Mr Lockwood.

"I shall tell her you said that when I find her," said Ernest.

"I had better go and find somewhere to hide then," laughed Mr Lockwood. "You two go and enjoy yourselves," he told them both.

"Let's have a look around to see if I can find my mother. I know she is just dying to see you again," said Ernest.

A few minutes later Ernest saw his mother standing talking to a couple of ladies whom she had known for years.

"Sorry to have to interrupt you, Mother, but look who is here," said Ernest, as he stood with Elizabeth.

"Well I never. How are you?" asked Mrs Lockwood.

"Very well, thank you. How about you?" asked Elizabeth.

"I am all the better for seeing you here today. I am so glad you came," said Mrs Lockwood.

"Thank you," said Elizabeth.

"Come and sit down with me as I want to know everything you have been doing these past few years," said Mrs Lockwood.

"I'll come back in about six hours then, shall I?" laughed Ernest.

"Don't be so cheeky," smiled Mrs Lockwood. "You can go and get Elizabeth something to eat whilst we two sit and chat," she told Ernest.

"My father was right, she never stops talking," laughed Ernest.

"Oh, just leave us be," said Mrs Lockwood jokingly.

Elizabeth and Mrs Lockwood sat talking for quite some time and they both laughed as they spoke about when Elizabeth was a child.

"You are certainly a beautiful young lady, Elizabeth, mind you, even as a child you were always pretty," said Mrs Lockwood.

"It is lovely to see you all and to see Ernest again after all this time," said Elizabeth.

"Ernest is very fond of you, you know, he is always talking about you," said Mrs Lockwood.

"I am also very fond of him; he is a good friend," said Elizabeth.

"Between you and me, I think Ernest would like to be more than just friends with you, but he keeps his feelings very close to his chest because of the way he was treated in the past," said Mrs Lockwood.

"I know Ernest was hurt badly by Rosemary in the past because he told me, but I do not think that Ernest sees me as more than just a friend," said Elizabeth.

"I know my son, Elizabeth, and I know he has only just got acquainted with you again recently, but I can tell you now he is falling in love with you, and who can blame him, you are beautiful," said Mrs Lockwood.

"But I am not looking for someone to fall in love with at the moment; I am still in love with Edward," said Elizabeth.

"I know you are, dear. But you have to remember that Edward is gone and you still have a life to live and Ernest is a good man and I know he would look after you," said Mrs Lockwood.

"I understand what you are saying, but I am not ready to let go of the past just yet," said Elizabeth.

"But you have to let go sometime, dear. Just don't leave it too late," said Mrs Lockwood, as she squeezed Elizabeth's hand. "You are a lovely girl and you deserve some happiness in your life after what you have been through, so just think about what I have told you."

"Come on, Elizabeth. You are not still talking to my mother are you? She is a bad influence you know," laughed Ernest.

"Where is Elizabeth's food? I asked you to get her some," said Mrs Lockwood.

"I have left it on a table over there. I knew if I brought it over here I would never get Elizabeth away from you," said Ernest jokingly.

"See what I have to put up with, Elizabeth? He needs a woman to put him in his place," said Mrs Lockwood with a smile.

"Will you stop trying to get me married off with everyone you speak to?" said Ernest.

"Well I do not want you living with me for the rest of your life," laughed Mrs Lockwood.

"Come on, Elizabeth, let's go over there and eat our food, I think my mother has said quite enough for one day," smiled Ernest.

"Goodbye, Mrs Lockwood," said Elizabeth.

"Enjoy yourself, dear," Mrs Lockwood told her.

"What exactly has my mother been saying to you?" asked Ernest.

"Oh nothing much," replied Elizabeth.

"I can just imagine," said Ernest. "I know my mother," he told her with a smile.

Elizabeth sat down with Ernest and had something to eat and then he took Elizabeth to meet some of his parents' guests.

"This is my Aunt Ellen, she is my mother's sister," said Ernest.

"It is very nice to meet you. I am Elizabeth," she told her.

"Are you Ernest's new lady friend?" asked Aunt Ellen.

"We are old friends," replied Elizabeth.

"Yes, we have known each other since we were children," said Ernest.

"Has Ernest told you that I am having a dinner party in a few weeks?" asked Aunt Ellen.

"No, he has not mentioned it," replied Elizabeth.

"You men are so useless when it comes to ladies. Why haven't you invited Elizabeth to my dinner party?" asked Aunt Ellen.

"I forgot about it," replied Ernest.

"Forgot my foot, you probably just got cold feet," Aunt Ellen told him. Well, Elizabeth, I am inviting you to my dinner party. It is two weeks on Saturday. Ernest will bring you along so do not worry about coming to my house alone," she told Elizabeth.

"Can you see the similarities between my aunt and my mother? They are both very pushy aren't they?" asked Ernest.

Elizabeth did not comment she just smiled politely, although she was getting rather embarrassed by everyone trying to pair her up with Ernest and, although Elizabeth was very fond of him, she was just not ready to get involved with anyone quite so soon.

After a few hours had passed Ernest walked Elizabeth home and it was then that he finally met Adam, Elizabeth's son.

"My goodness he is just like Edward, but he has got your eyes," said Ernest.

"Yes, I know. Everyone says that," said Elizabeth.

"Did you have a nice time with Benjamin today?" asked Elizabeth.

"Yes, it was alright," replied Adam.

"I think Adam and Benjamin had a bit of a disagreement," said Emily.

"Oh I see. I wondered why Adam was so quiet," smiled Elizabeth.

"Never mind, Adam, you will soon be friends again. When I was your age I was always having arguments with my brother Joseph, but we soon made friends again, but only because I used to be scared of him," laughed Ernest.

"Stop telling fibs. You and Joseph always got on well together," said Elizabeth.

"Yes, I know. I was just trying to make Adam feel better, but now you have gone and spoilt everything," laughed Ernest.

"That will teach you for telling lies," said Adam.

"Oh, I can see you are your mother's son; cheeky just like her," said Ernest.

Everyone started to laugh. Even Adam cheered up and laughed with Ernest.

"I had better be going now but I will call around sometime next week. Thank you for coming to my parents' house today, Elizabeth, I think it made their day to see you," said Ernest.

"I am glad I went; I really enjoyed myself," said Elizabeth.

"Well, do not forget that you have been invited to my aunt's dinner party; she will never forgive me if I do not bring you along," said Ernest.

"Don't worry, I will not forget," said Elizabeth with a smile.

After Ernest had left Elizabeth made some tea and then sat down with Emily.

"How did it go at Ernest's parents' house today?" asked Emily.

"Yes, it went really well apart from when Mrs Lockwood started saying that Ernest and I should be more than just friends," said Elizabeth.

"Why did she say that?" asked Emily.

"I don't know. She just started saying that Ernest never stops talking about me and she seems to think that he would like to be more than just friends with me," replied Elizabeth.

"What did you say?" asked Emily.

"I told her I was not ready to get involved with anyone as I still love Edward, but I do not think she was really listening to me, because all she kept saying was how well Ernest would treat me if we were together," said Elizabeth.

"Well, at least you know that she approves of you," said Emily.

"All I want is to be friends with Ernest. Why can't everyone understand that?" asked Elizabeth.

"Maybe they cannot understand you," said Emily.

"What do you mean?" asked Elizabeth.

"Well just take a look at Ernest. He is single, handsome, hard working, and he obviously thinks a lot of you otherwise he would not be bothering to come around here and yet you do not seem to care about how he feels; just how you feel about Edward," said Emily.

"That is not fair, Emily, of course I care how Ernest feels. It's just that I do not feel the same way anymore. Anyway Ernest has not even said he has feelings for me; it is everyone else, including you, that are saying all these things," said Elizabeth.

"Well, if I am saying it and Mrs Lockwood is saying it, we cannot both be wrong," said Emily.

"Perhaps I should just make things easier for everyone and not see Ernest anymore and then perhaps all this nonsense will stop," said Elizabeth.

"Oh stop being so pig-headed. So what if Ernest likes you. It is not a crime, is it? You should be flattered, not sitting there moaning about him," said Emily.

"I am not moaning about Ernest, I really like him. I am moaning about everyone assuming that there is more to our friendship than there really is," said Elizabeth.

"Well, I think you like Ernest more than you are letting on, but the only reason you will not admit it is because you think you are betraying Edward; but Edward is not here anymore and if he were he would want you to be happy," said Emily.

Elizabeth did not say anything she just walked outside into the garden and slammed the door behind her. Emily knew then that what she had just said to Elizabeth had obviously hit a nerve. She then thought it was true Elizabeth does still have feelings for Ernest, but she is not letting anyone know as she felt as though she was betraying Edward.

Emily decided not to mention too much about Ernest to Elizabeth, as she realised the more she mentioned things, the more Elizabeth was backing away.

Ernest came around a few times the following week, but he did not stop very long as he had been extremely busy at work and was very tired. Elizabeth had also been very busy as she did not have Emily at work to help her. Emily had already spoken to Elizabeth about returning to work, but Elizabeth told her to wait a few more weeks.

"Are you still going to that dinner party at Ernest's aunt's house next weekend?" asked Emily.

"Yes, I am. Not that I really want to go. It's just that I do not want to disappoint Aunt Ellen," said Elizabeth.

"No, you cannot do that," said Emily as she secretly smiled to herself.

Elizabeth put on a long red dress and pinned up her hair as she got ready to go to the dinner party with Ernest.

"How do I look?" she asked Emily once she was ready.

"You look lovely. Is that a new dress?" she asked Elizabeth.

"Yes, it is. I wanted to make a good impression on Aunt Ellen," said Elizabeth.

"Are you sure you are not trying to impress anyone else?" asked Emily smiling at her.

"No, of course not. Why would I?" asked Elizabeth.

"Oh, no reason," replied Emily sarcastically.

Ernest called to pick up Elizabeth about seven thirty that evening and when he saw Elizabeth he almost fell over his lip as his mouth opened so wide. He thought she looked absolutely stunning as he had never seen her properly dressed up before.

As they arrived at Aunt Ellen's, Ernest's face suddenly changed when he saw someone that he knew.

"Is there anything wrong?" asked Elizabeth.

"No, everything is perfectly fine," replied Ernest.

But Elizabeth could sense that something was not quite right.

"Good evening, Elizabeth. I am so glad you could come here tonight," said Aunt Ellen as she greeted them at the door.

Ernest gave Elizabeth a drink as she stood talking to Aunt Ellen, whilst he went and spoke to a couple of gentlemen whom were standing nearby. As Elizabeth stood talking she noticed three gentlemen standing together who kept staring at her, but she tried not to take any notice. A few minutes later one of the gentlemen approached Elizabeth and offered her a drink but she politely refused as she already had one in her hand.

"Oh, go on, have another one," the gentleman told her.

But Elizabeth still refused. By this time Ernest had noticed that Elizabeth seemed a bit uncomfortable so he walked over to her, took her by her hand and led her away to the other side of the room.

"Are you alright?" he asked.

"I am now, thank you," she replied.

"Sorry I left you on your own, but I thought you would like to get to know my Aunt Ellen better," said Ernest.

"You have nothing to apologise for, it was not your fault that gentleman would not take no for an answer," said Elizabeth.

"I will make sure I do not let you out of my sight again this evening," said Ernest smiling.

"You do not have to do that, I do not expect you to have your evening spoilt by having to watch me all night," said Elizabeth.

"Watching you all night would definitely not spoil my evening," laughed Ernest.

Elizabeth looked at Ernest and started to laugh as well.

"You look even prettier when you laugh, but you do not laugh enough," Ernest told her.

Elizabeth did not say anything; she just gave Ernest a slight grin.

"Oh, Elizabeth, there you are. Come over here and meet some of my friends," said Aunt Ellen.

"I'll come with you," said Ernest.

"This is ladies' talk. You can go and get Elizabeth another drink," said Aunt Ellen.

Ernest just stood still not knowing what to do, after all he had promised not to let Elizabeth out of his sight.

"It is alright, I will be fine," whispered Elizabeth.

Ernest smiled back at her and then went to get another drink, whilst Elizabeth met some of Aunt Ellen's friends.

"This is Elizabeth, she is Ernest's new lady friend," said Aunt Ellen.

"Hello, Elizabeth, it is very nice to meet you. I just hope you treat Ernest better than my daughter did," said the lady.

"I am sorry but I think you have got the wrong idea about Ernest and I. We are just old friends that's all," said Elizabeth.

"Oh, I did not mean to offend you, dear. It's just that when Ellen said you were Ernest's new lady friend I thought you were courting. I was just trying to explain that Ernest was treated badly in the past by my daughter, Rosemary," said the lady.

When the lady said that Elizabeth knew straight away who she was talking about. She was talking about her daughter Rosemary Thornton. Elizabeth suddenly got quite scared at the thought of being associated with anyone that was related to Rosemary, but she could not be rude so she had to just stand there and make polite conversation.

"What type of employment do you do, Elizabeth?" asked Mrs Thornton.

"I have my own dressmaking business. I design them and make them in my factory," replied Elizabeth.

"Oh, you have your own factory, do you? Where about is that then?" asked Mrs Thornton.

"It is along Nash Lane, the blue factory at the end," replied Elizabeth.

"Oh yes, I have heard of it. Many of my friends have purchased clothes from you. I shall have to pay you a visit sometime," said Mrs Thornton.

Ernest walked towards Elizabeth carrying their drinks and he almost fell on to the floor when he saw who Elizabeth was talking to.

"Excuse me, I have got you a drink here, Elizabeth," said Ernest.

"Oh, thank you," said Elizabeth.

Elizabeth gave Ernest a funny look as if to say get me away from her, but she did it discreetly so that Mrs Thornton was not aware of it.

"Excuse me whilst I take Elizabeth away from you, only I need to have a quiet word with her," said Ernest.

"That is quite alright, Ernest. I know you do not want to stand talking to us old ladies, but at least be honest about it," said Mrs Thornton jokingly.

Ernest just smiled at her and then pulled Elizabeth to one side to speak with her.

"Did you know that Rosemary's mother was invited here tonight?" asked Elizabeth.

"No, I did not. But I did notice her as we arrived," said Ernest.

"Why didn't you tell me?" asked Elizabeth.

"I did not think it would matter. Mrs Thornton is nothing like Rosemary, so you have nothing to worry about," said Ernest.

"You still should have warned me. Do you realise how nervous I felt once I knew who she was?" said Elizabeth.

"I am sorry. I just thought it was best not to mention it to you," said Ernest looking quite worried.

"Oh, it is not your fault, you have not done anything wrong. It's just that every time I think about Rosemary I remember all those terrible things that she did to me. It is still so clear in my mind even though it was all those years ago," said Elizabeth.

"She really has affected you badly, hasn't she?" asked Ernest.

"Well, she did used to beat me and her brother did try to rape me," said Elizabeth.

"I am so sorry, Elizabeth. I wish I had not brought you here now. Would you like me to take you home?" asked Ernest.

"No, I cannot let your Aunt Ellen down," replied Elizabeth.

"Are you sure?" asked Ernest.

"Yes. Just keep her away from me, that is all I ask," said Elizabeth.

"Of course," said Ernest.

As they all entered the dining room Ernest managed to seat Elizabeth as far away from Mrs Thornton as possible and he sat opposite Elizabeth so that he could keep an eye upon her.

"Are you alright?" whispered Ernest as they ate they dinner.

"Yes, I am fine, thank you," replied Elizabeth softly.

After dinner everyone made their way into another room and they listened to a gentleman playing the piano, but all Elizabeth could think about was Rosemary's mother; she was not enjoying herself at all.

"Would you like to go for a walk outside?" asked Ernest.

"Yes, I would, but I do not want to offend your aunt," replied Elizabeth.

"My aunt is over there singing. I do not think she will notice if we disappear for a while," said Ernest.

"Alright, let's go outside then," said Elizabeth.

Ernest put his coat around Elizabeth's shoulders to keep her warm; he then led her outside into the garden.

"I am really sorry about this evening, Elizabeth, you know I would never upset you intentionally," he told her.

"I know," said Elizabeth. "Stop worrying, it is not your fault," she told him.

"I am glad that I have got you on your own because there is something that I would like to say to you," said Ernest.

"What is it?" asked Elizabeth.

"Well, we have been friends for many years now, and I know we have only been in contact with each other for just a short time, but I would just like to say that I am mad about you, Elizabeth. In fact, I think I am in love with you," said Ernest.

"Oh, Ernest, I wish you had not said that," said Elizabeth.

"Why? I am just telling you how I feel," said Ernest.

"It is too soon for me, I am not ready for all of this," replied Elizabeth.

"Is it because of Edward?" asked Ernest.

"Yes it is. I still love him and I always will," replied Elizabeth.

"But you have to move on with your life at some stage and I am sure Edward would understand that," said Ernest.

"I am not sure if I want to move on," said Elizabeth.

"But you cannot go on with the rest of your life living on just memories; but if that is what you want to do, then I suppose I cannot change that," said Ernest.

"It is not that I do not like you, Ernest, because I do. I just need more time," Elizabeth told him.

"I understand," said Ernest.

"Would you mind if I went home now? Only I do not particularly want to go back inside because of Mrs Thornton being in there," said Elizabeth.

"Of course not. Come on, I'll walk you home," said Ernest.

CHAPTER FIFTEEN

Over the next few months Ernest did not come around so often; he only visited Elizabeth about once a week.

Although Ernest's feelings had not changed towards Elizabeth, he felt that he should give her some time on her own and he never spoke about how he felt to her again; but he had not given up hope.

"Where is Alice, she should have been here by now? I am going to be late for work," said Emily.

"I hope nothing has happened to her," said Elizabeth.

"Shall I go and see her to make sure everything is alright?" asked Emily.

"No, you take the keys and open up the factory, whilst I take Lizzie to my mother's and then I shall go and see if Alice is alright," said Elizabeth.

"Alright," replied Emily.

After Elizabeth had taken Lizzie to her mother's house, she arrived at her brother's house shortly after. Elizabeth knocked at the door but there was no answer, so she went around the back of the house and opened the door.

"Alice, are you here?" called Elizabeth.

But there was still no answer, so Elizabeth walked from the kitchen into the hallway and lying unconscious in the hallway was Alice.

Elizabeth did not try and move Alice in case she had a broken back, but she did get a doctor to her instead.

"Quick, it is my sister-in-law I think she must have fallen down the stairs," said Elizabeth. "She is also expecting a baby in a few weeks," she told the doctor.

The doctor examined Alice but she was not badly hurt; she did have a broken leg though and a concussion.

"Alice, can you hear me?" asked the doctor.

Alice started to come round but she just mumbled to the doctor.

"Let me get her upstairs," said the doctor as he carried her.

"Is she going to be alright?" asked Elizabeth.

"Yes, I think so, but I need to check on the baby," he replied.

"I need to contact my brother as he is Alice's husband. Can you stay with Alice until I get back?" asked Elizabeth.

"Yes, of course. But please be as quick as you can," replied the doctor.

Elizabeth ran as fast as she could to the Lockwoods' house and when she got there the first person she saw was Ernest.

"Is everything alright, Elizabeth?" he asked.

"No, I need to find my brother because Alice has fallen downstairs and she is due to give birth in just a few weeks," replied Elizabeth.

"You go back to Alice whilst I find William for you," Ernest told her.

"Oh, thank you," said Elizabeth as she ran off again.

When Elizabeth returned to the house she could hear Alice screaming, so she ran upstairs to see what was happening.

"Alice has gone into labour, I'm afraid," said the midwife.

"The baby will be alright though, won't it?" asked Elizabeth.

"I really cannot say at this precise moment. All I know is that it is not good to give birth prematurely," she told Elizabeth.

"But the baby will only be a few weeks early, surely it will survive," said Elizabeth.

"I will do everything I possibly can," said the midwife.

A few minutes later William arrived with Ernest; they had ridden together on Ernest's horse, Admiral.

"How is Alice?" asked William looking extremely worried.

"She has broken her leg but she is alright. The main concern is the baby because Alice has gone into labour," replied Elizabeth.

William sat beside Alice and stroked her hair, whilst Alice held on to his hand.

"Everything is going to be alright," said William.

"Is there anything that I can do?" asked Ernest.

"Yes, actually there is. Could you go to the factory and explain to Emily what has happened and tell her that I will not be able to get to work today as I have to be here for Alice. Also can you remind her that Lizzie is at my mother's, so she will have to collect her from there when she finishes work," said Elizabeth.

"Yes, of course, I'll do it straight away," said Ernest.

"Help me William," screamed Alice as the contractions got worse.

William felt terrible as there was nothing that he could do to ease Alice's pain; all he could do was just sit and watch.

As the hours passed, Alice started to scream more and more, but Elizabeth was there to try and comfort her.

"Come on, Alice, push a bit harder," Elizabeth told her.

"I cannot do it anymore, I am too tired," said Alice.

"Yes you can, now push!" Elizabeth told her.

The midwife examined Alice once more to see how far the baby's head was, but she suddenly had a worried look upon her face which Elizabeth noticed.

"What is wrong?" whispered Elizabeth.

The midwife then left the room so Elizabeth quickly followed her.

"What is it? What is wrong?" asked Elizabeth again.

"I am afraid Alice is not dilated enough to give birth, but the baby is coming rather quickly," replied the midwife.

"So what does that mean?" asked Elizabeth.

"I might have to force her pelvic bones apart, but if I do this Alice is going to be in a lot of discomfort," replied the midwife.

"Oh my God, it is going to be extremely painful for her, isn't it?" asked Elizabeth.

"Yes I am afraid so," replied the midwife. "But if I do not do it we could lose both mother and child," she told her.

"You will just have to do what you have to do. As long as they are both safe, that is all that matters," said Elizabeth.

"I do not think it is a good idea to tell your brother just yet, as it will only worry him," said the midwife.

"But he is in the room with her, so he will know what you are doing," said Elizabeth.

"I think it is for the best that you get him downstairs," said the midwife.

By now Ernest had returned so Elizabeth explained to him what was happening, she then asked Ernest to try and keep William downstairs whilst the midwife tried to do everything she could to save Alice and the baby.

"Alice, I am going to have to help the baby out as you are not dilating enough, but you might experience some discomfort whilst I am doing this," said the midwife.

Alice looked petrified when the midwife explained to her what she had to do, but Elizabeth tried to comfort her as best as possible.

"I am just going to put this piece of wood inside your mouth; if you need to bite just do it as hard as you like," said the midwife.

Elizabeth wiped the sweat from Alice's head and then held both of her hands. The midwife then started to pull Alice's bones apart and Alice bit down on the piece of wood as hard as she could, whilst going bright red in the face through the pain. This took the midwife quite a few minutes to do and Alice was in so much pain that the sweat was just dripping off her by now.

"I am so sorry, Alice, for having to put you through this, but it is the only way to save you and your baby," said the midwife.

Alice suddenly spat the piece of wood out of her mouth and screamed, but by this time her heart was beginning to fade.

"You have to hurry as Alice does not look very good," said Elizabeth.

The midwife looked up and could see that Alice was struggling with the pain, so she just pushed her bones as hard as she could and pulled the baby out.

"It is alright, Alice, it is all over now," said Elizabeth.

But Alice had experienced so much pain she had almost lost consciousness.

"You have a little girl, Alice," said the midwife.

Alice gave a slight smile but she was so weak she could hardly do anything.

"Take the baby downstairs to show her father, whilst I clean Alice up and examine her," said the midwife.

A few minutes later Elizabeth came back upstairs to ask the midwife if it was alright for William to see his wife now.

"Alice is extremely weak as she has had a terrible shock to her body. She may get a fever within a matter of hours, so she will need someone with her at all times to bath her. She will also need as much rest as she can get, so if possible perhaps someone can look after her baby for her," said the midwife.

"Yes, of course. I will stay here to help with the baby," said Elizabeth. "Alice is going to be alright though, isn't she?" she asked.

"She is very weak, Elizabeth," replied the midwife.

"That is not what I asked. Is she going to be alright?" asked Elizabeth.

"I am so sorry, her heart is too weak; she will probably not last the night," said the midwife.

"Oh my God, no!" cried Elizabeth.

"Just make her as comfortable as possible; that is all you can do," said the midwife.

The midwife then left the house leaving Elizabeth standing upstairs on the landing. Elizabeth tried to compose herself before entering the bedroom; she then sat beside Alice and stroked her hair. After a few minutes Alice opened her eyes and looked at Elizabeth.

"Where is William and where is my baby?" she asked.

"I shall go and get them for you," Elizabeth told her.

Elizabeth went downstairs and spoke with her brother and Ernest about Alice's condition; her brother was in total disbelief and just started shouting out loud.

"William, you have got to calm down. Alice does not know that she is dying and you cannot let her know either. You have got to go upstairs and sit with her and show her what a wonderful daughter she has," said Elizabeth, as the tears flowed down her face.

"How can I do that when I know she is dying?" asked William.

"You just have to," said Elizabeth.

William dried his eyes and then carried his new baby upstairs. He then sat down beside Alice and smiled at her.

"We have a daughter," said William.

"Yes, I know. I said I wanted a daughter this time and God has given us one," smiled Alice.

William gently laid the baby on Alice so she could touch her daughter, then Elizabeth and Ernest came into the room.

"Congratulations, she is beautiful," said Ernest.

Ernest then left the room so that Elizabeth and William could be alone with Alice for a while.

"What are you going to call her?" asked Elizabeth.

"Alice can choose her name," said William.

"What about Grace?" asked Alice.

"Yes, Grace it is," replied William.

"I think Alice should rest now," said Elizabeth.

William took baby Grace downstairs whilst Elizabeth stayed with Alice; then a few minutes later William came back into the room and sat with his wife. But Alice was so exhausted she gradually fell asleep.

Through the early evening Alice started to sweat and shake with a fever, so Elizabeth kept wiping her down to keep her comfortable.

"Where is my baby?" asked Alice.

"I'll just go and get her. You stay with Alice," said Elizabeth to her brother.

Elizabeth carried baby Grace upstairs and placed her in her mother's arms.

"She is beautiful, isn't she?" said Alice.

"Yes, she is, just like her mother," replied William.

Alice stroked her baby and kissed her head and then looked at William and smiled.

"Look after her," said Alice.

"We will both look after her," said William.

But Alice just closed her eyes and peacefully passed away.

"Alice! Alice!" shouted William.

"William, she has gone, she was just too weak," cried Elizabeth.

"She cannot be gone, she only just spoke to me," said William.

Elizabeth picked up Grace and carried her downstairs. She then saw Ernest sitting in a chair so she told him that Alice had died.

"I need your help to get William downstairs," said Elizabeth.

"I think we should give him a few minutes to be alone with her first," said Ernest.

"Yes, alright," said Elizabeth.

Elizabeth stood holding baby Grace in her arms, whilst her brother William sat upstairs with his wife crying bitterly.

Suddenly there was a knock at the door.

"I'll get it," said Ernest.

A few seconds later Elizabeth and William's parents walked into the room and they saw Elizabeth holding the baby.

"What did Alice have?" asked Elizabeth's mother.

"A girl, her name is Grace," replied Elizabeth.

"Our first granddaughter," said Elizabeth's father.

Suddenly William entered the room and when he saw his parents he burst into tears.

"What is it, son?" asked his father.

"It is Alice, she is dead!" he told his parents.

"What?" asked Elizabeth's mother.

"Alice had complications during the birth and she was just too weak to survive it," cried Elizabeth.

Elizabeth's parents were stunned by the news and did not know what to say or do to help comfort their son.

"Shall I go and see Emily and explain to her what has happened?" asked Ernest.

"Oh yes, would you? Could you also get me a change of clothes as I shall be staying here with William tonight," said Elizabeth.

"Yes, of course," said Ernest.

"What am I going to do without her?" asked William.

"Everything will be alright, William. You have two beautiful children now and they need your love," said his mother.

"Oh my God, I have just realised Benjamin is in boarding school and does not know anything," said William.

"Leave it with me, I'll contact the school and have Benjamin sent home," said Elizabeth.

"But how am I going to cope with two young children? I cannot afford to give up work," said William.

"We will work something out," Elizabeth told him.

"Did Alice get the chance to see her baby?" asked Elizabeth's mother.

"Yes, she did and she was so thrilled because she wanted a daughter this time," replied Elizabeth.

"But she will not be here to enjoy her, will she?" said William.

Elizabeth and her parents did not say anything, they just all looked at each other not knowing what to say.

That night Elizabeth stayed with her brother but he hardly said a word. The next day Emily opened the factory whilst Elizabeth's mother looked after Lizzie once more and Elizabeth stayed with her brother William to help out with his newborn daughter, Grace.

"We are going to have to sort out an arrangement as to who is going to look after Grace whilst you are at work," said Elizabeth.

"I cannot expect mother to do it as she has enough to do," said William.

"I know. I think the best solution is for Emily to give up her job at the factory so that she can look after Lizzie and Grace," said Elizabeth.

"Do you think she will do that?" asked William.

"I do not think that she has much choice. With Alice gone there is no one to look after Lizzie anymore whilst Emily is at work and if Emily has to give up work to look after her own child I do not think one more is going to make a lot of difference," said Elizabeth.

"But how will she get any money?" asked William.

"I will make sure that she is provided for," replied Elizabeth.

"But you know what Emily is like; she will not take money from you if she has not earned it," said William.

"Then I shall employ her as my housekeeper, then she will be earning her keep," said Elizabeth.

"I do not know what I would do without you, Elizabeth," said William.

"Just remember I have been in your situation before, so I know what you are going through," Elizabeth told him.

"I do not know how you survived because I cannot imagine my future without Alice," said William.

"It does get easier with time, but that does not mean you will ever stop caring because you won't," said Elizabeth.

Everything that had happened over the past few days made Elizabeth think of Edward even more.

"You do not have to stay here with me tonight, Elizabeth, I will be alright on my own," said William.

"You will not," said Elizabeth.

"But you have been here too long already, and just think of poor Emily, she has not seen you for two days now," said William.

"Oh, I forgot about Emily. She must be extremely upset because she got on really well with Alice," said Elizabeth.

"Has anyone informed her about Alice?" asked William.

"Yes, Ernest went to see her," replied Elizabeth.

"Well, I think you should stay with her tonight," said William.

"Emily will be fine, it is you I am worried about," said Elizabeth.

"But I just need to be on my own," William told her.

"Alright, I shall go and see Emily later and stay with her tonight, but only if you let Ernest stay here with you," said Elizabeth.

"Yes, alright. It will probably do me good to have Ernest here actually," said William.

"I will go and see him before I go home," said Elizabeth.

"Thank you for everything that you have done. I really appreciate it," said William.

"I will be back here tomorrow. I shall just get one of the ladies in the factory to help Emily out until I return," said Elizabeth.

That night Elizabeth sat talking with Emily and they both broke down in tears. They absolutely adored Alice as if she were their own sister and they were both deeply saddened by her death.

"Emily, you do realise that now that Alice is gone there is no one to look after Lizzie whilst you are at work," said Elizabeth.

"Yes, I know, I have already thought of that," replied Emily.

"Well, my mother said she will continue to look after Lizzie at the moment because you are helping me out at the factory, but as soon as I return you will have to look after Lizzie by yourself. But to save you losing your money I would like to employ you as a nanny to Grace and as my housekeeper," said Elizabeth.

"Yes, alright, I will do that," said Emily.

"You mean you do not mind?" asked Elizabeth.

"Well, Lizzie is my child and as Alice helped me out before, so the least I can do is look after Grace," said Emily.

"I am so pleased you said that because I was a bit worried about telling you that you would have to leave the factory," said Elizabeth.

"I really don't mind, honest I don't and, besides everyone needs help once in a while, I should know that more than anyone," said Emily.

Ernest stayed the night with William and they both sat drinking until the early hours of the morning, but as William was not used to drinking he got drunk rather quickly, so Ernest had to look after baby Grace that night.

The next day Elizabeth went to see her brother quite early in the morning, but he was still in bed suffering from a hangover.

"I trusted you to look after William. That did not mean getting him drunk," said Elizabeth.

"He was perfectly alright with me, Elizabeth, in fact, by him having some alcohol it took his mind off things," said Ernest.

"Do not even try and talk your way out of this, Ernest, you are totally irresponsible," said Elizabeth.

"How can you say that? I even took the day off from work today to look after Grace," said Ernest.

"Well, that is your fault because if you had not got William drunk he would have been perfectly capable of looking after Grace himself," said Elizabeth.

"Alright I am sorry. But at least I got William smiling again, surely that counts for something," said Ernest.

"Ooooh, you men make me so mad," said Elizabeth.

Ernest just sat in the chair and started to laugh; he thought it was quite amusing watching Elizabeth get angry.

"Will you stop laughing at me, Ernest, it is not funny," said Elizabeth.

"Sorry," he said as he smiled.

"You can stay at your parents house tonight. I will stay here and look after William," said Elizabeth.

"Oh, don't be like that. Besides William has already agreed to come over to my house tonight for a few drinks," said Ernest.

"No, he is not!" said Elizabeth.

"I am only joking with you, but I got you going, didn't I?" he laughed.

Even Elizabeth had to laugh at him and it made her realise that Ernest was the right person to get William out of his depressed state.

"Why don't you bring William over to my house tonight, then we can all have a night together. I think it will do William good to get him out of this house for a while," said Elizabeth.

"What about Benjamin? Do not forget he is due home today," said Ernest.

"Oh yes, I forgot. Well perhaps it will do him good to come to my house as well. After all, he needs his family around him now," said Elizabeth.

"Alright, I will ask William later when he feels better," smiled Ernest.

"Yes, well do not get any ideas about giving William any alcohol tonight, will you?" said Elizabeth.

"After the amount he drank last night I do not think he will want anymore this evening," laughed Ernest.

Elizabeth just looked at him and raised her eyebrows, as if to say you fool.

When Benjamin arrived home later that day William told him the sad news about his mother and Benjamin just broke down in tears. He seemed to get over his mother's death quicker than William had expected, but that was only because he had a new baby sister which gave him something to occupy himself.

"Benjamin has not left Grace alone all evening," said Elizabeth.

"Yes, I know. But at least he has not blamed her for the death of his mother, because that was what I was worried about," said William.

"Oh, I think Benjamin is old enough to understand that it was not Grace's fault. You only have to look at him to see that he adores her," said Elizabeth.

A few days later was the day of Alice's funeral. It was the day Elizabeth had been dreading, because it brought everything back to her about Edward. Elizabeth stood next to her brother throughout the service and whilst at the graveside, but after it was over William asked Elizabeth to meet him back at the house as he wanted to say a few words to Alice alone.

"It was a lovely service, wasn't it?" said Elizabeth's mother.

"Yes, it was. I think we did Alice proud," replied Elizabeth.

When everyone had left after the wake William decided that he wanted to spend the night on his own with his children.

"Are you sure you are going to be alright?" asked Elizabeth.

"Yes, I am positive. I just need some time alone with my children," said William.

Ernest stayed with Elizabeth and Emily for a while and they sat talking about Alice together. But Lizzie was quite restless that night because she had just started teething, so Emily decided to go up to bed with her.

"Are you alright, Elizabeth?" asked Ernest.

"Yes, I am now. I am just glad the funeral is over because I could not stop thinking about Edward and the tragic way he died," said Elizabeth.

"I know you still love him, Elizabeth, and I know you always will, but I hope one day you will find a place in your heart for me. I know I have not mentioned anything since my Aunt Ellen's party, but I do still love you, Elizabeth," said Ernest.

"Why do you always have to spoil everything by telling me that? I tell you that I love Edward and then you tell me that you love me. Why?" asked Elizabeth.

"Because it is true, I do love you," replied Ernest.

"No you don't, you just think you do," said Elizabeth.

"I think I know my own feelings for you. Am I that bad that you cannot love me back?" asked Ernest.

Elizabeth did not know what to say; she just stared at Ernest and stayed silent.

"I think I have my answer then," he told her.

Ernest then walked out of the door without even saying goodbye. Elizabeth suddenly realised that she had really upset him, but she had not done it intentionally. She then sat back down in a chair and burst out crying. Elizabeth knew she had not only lost Ernest but she had also lost his friendship as well.

The next day Elizabeth went to see her brother and his children and then later that day she paid Ernest a visit at the Lockwoods' house, only to be told that he had gone away for a while. Elizabeth felt quite sick as she knew that he had only gone away because of her, but she had not meant to hurt him; all she was trying to do was tell him how she still felt about Edward.

Elizabeth felt quite down over the next few days and even Emily had noticed a change in her behaviour, but she put it down to the fact that Elizabeth was missing Alice.

Ernest went away for a couple of weeks but even when he returned back to Yorkshire he did not contact Elizabeth; he thought that it was best he stayed away.

"Are you coming to the fete tomorrow?" asked Emily.

"I doubt it," replied Elizabeth.

"Why not?" asked Emily.

"Because I would prefer to stay home," replied Elizabeth.

"What is wrong with you? You have been really grumpy these past few weeks," said Emily.

"I just do not want to go to the fete, that's all," replied Elizabeth.

"Oh come on, William and I are going. We have even made some cakes and jam to sell on one of the stools," said Emily.

"I just said I do not want to go, didn't I?" shouted Elizabeth.

"I know why you are being like this. It is because Ernest has not been here for a while, isn't it?" asked Emily.

"I don't know what you are talking about," said Elizabeth.

"Oh, I think you do. You know you like Ernest but you are too afraid to show your feelings. Well, if you want to lose him altogether, then you are going the right way about it," Emily told her.

"Why does everyone keep going on about Ernest all the time?" asked Elizabeth.

"Because you are being such a fool towards him. You know he really likes you and I know for a fact that you like him, so do something about it and stop messing him about," said Emily getting rather angry.

"Why don't you mind your own business," shouted Elizabeth.

"Fine I will. You just sit here on your own sulking over him, but just remember you will lose out in the end if you are not careful," said Emily.

Emily then picked up Lizzie, took her upstairs and went to bed, whilst Elizabeth sat down on her own thinking about what Emily had just said to her.

The next day William came around early in the morning as he and Emily were going to the fete together.

"Are you ready?" he asked.

"Yes, I am just coming," replied Emily.

"Aren't you coming to the fete?" asked William.

"No," replied Elizabeth.

"Elizabeth is sulking because she has not seen Ernest," said Emily.

"Oh be quiet," Elizabeth told her.

"Come on, William, let's go. Enjoy your day on your own Elizabeth," said Emily rather sarcastically.

Elizabeth did not answer her but she knew deep down that Emily was right; she was missing Ernest and that was why she was so irritable. A short time later Elizabeth decided to get ready and go to the fete after all. She put on a pretty frock, put a bow in her hair and took a slow walk down there. When she arrived the place was packed with people. There were also lots of different stalls selling things and lots of games to play as well. Elizabeth looked around and saw Emily and William selling their cakes and jam, but she did not go over to them as she did not want Emily being rude to her again. Elizabeth watched as some small children giggled as they threw hoops over the hoopla to win a prize and it made her think of her son Adam.

"Roll up, roll up, and win a prize," shouted one gentleman.

Elizabeth just smiled and walked by.

"Aren't you going to have a go?" asked a voice.

Elizabeth looked around and standing behind her was Ernest.

"Hello," said Elizabeth.

"Well, aren't you going to have a go on the hoopla?" asked Ernest again.

"Perhaps later," she replied.

"How are?" asked Ernest.

"I am fine, thank you. What about you?" she asked.

"I am very well, thank you," he replied.

"I did call at your house a month or so ago but I was told you had gone away for a while," said Elizabeth.

"Yes, I went to London for a few weeks to see my brother Joseph," said Ernest.

"But if you only went for a few weeks, why haven't you been to see me?" asked Elizabeth.

"I did not see the point as you have made it very clear that you are not interested in me," replied Ernest.

"But I thought we were still friends," said Elizabeth.

"We are. But it is sometimes hard for me when I see you because of how I feel about you, and knowing you do not feel the same just hurts me, so I thought it best that I stay away," said Ernest.

"But I have really missed you and I do still want you to visit me," said Elizabeth.

"I have also missed you very much and it has been extremely hard for me to stay away because I really did want to see you," said Ernest.

"I have been rather horrible to you, haven't I?" said Elizabeth.

"I do not think you have been horrible to me. You are just confused about your feelings, that's all," said Ernest.

"Emily and I had an argument about you yesterday," said Elizabeth.

"Why?" asked Ernest.

"She told me I am being grumpy because I have not seen you and she said I am a fool if I do not do something about it," said Elizabeth.

"Have you been grumpy lately?" asked Ernest.

"Yes, very grumpy," smiled Elizabeth. "And Emily was right, it was because I had not seen you," she told him.

"Elizabeth, a lot has happened to you in the past and I understand how you still feel about Edward, But couldn't we just start again and see how things go?" he asked.

"Is that what you really want?" asked Elizabeth.

"You know it is. But we can take things slowly as I know you do not want to rush into another relationship. All I am asking is for a chance to show you how I feel and maybe one day you will feel the same," said Ernest.

"Alright, but I need to tell you something first," said Elizabeth.

"What is it?" asked Ernest.

"Let's go and sit down first and then I can tell you," said Elizabeth.

Ernest went and bought them both a cup of tea each, then they found a seat to sit down on.

"I have to be honest with you, Ernest, I do have feelings for you and I always have, but I feel confused as if I am doing something wrong," said Elizabeth.

"You mean you feel as though you are letting Edward down because you have feelings for me," said Ernest.

"Yes, I do," replied Elizabeth.

"Edward made you really happy, didn't he?" asked Ernest.

"Yes, he did," replied Elizabeth.

"That was because he wanted you to be happy and if he could come back now he would tell you he still wants you to be happy. You already said yourself that you have been grumpy because you have not seen me for a while. Well it is about time you thought of yourself instead of everyone else and gave me a chance to make you happy," said Ernest.

"Do you think I am being silly because of the way that I feel?" asked Elizabeth.

"No, of course not. I understand completely how you feel, after all you spent a good many years with Edward and you obviously married him because you loved him, but you cannot just give up your life for someone that is no longer here," said Ernest.

"You are not angry with me anymore. Are you?" asked Elizabeth.

"I was never really angry with you in the first place, just a little disappointed, that's all," replied Ernest.

"This was all down to Emily. She shouted at me and told me what a fool I was being and it made me think," said Elizabeth.

"I just wish you had told me all this before. You have got to stop thinking so much and talk to me more often," smiled Ernest.

"Yes, I know and in future I will, I promise," said Elizabeth.

Ernest picked up Elizabeth's hand and kissed it. He then looked at her and smiled.

"We shall take one day at a time," he told her.

"Yes, alright," said Elizabeth.

"Come on, I'll buy you a toffee apple," said Ernest, as he grabbed Elizabeth's arm.

Elizabeth and Ernest walked around the fete together and they both seemed extremely happy, especially as they had sorted out their differences and been completely honest with one another.

"Shall we have a go on the tombola?" asked Elizabeth.

"Yes," said Ernest.

Ernest picked out some numbers but he did not win a prize, but Elizabeth managed to win a bottle of red wine.

"Lucky you," he told her.

They then had a go on a coconut shy but Elizabeth missed every time and, even though Ernest managed to hit a coconut, it was not good enough to win him a prize.

"My luck is just not in today," said Ernest.

"Oh, is that so? Then why am I standing here next to you?" laughed Elizabeth.

"Oh well, when you put it like that, I have to admit my luck is definitely in today. I must be the luckiest man around," smiled Ernest.

"Of course you are," said Elizabeth jokingly.

"Oh look, there is Emily and William over there. Let's go and see them," said Ernest.

Elizabeth reluctantly walked towards Emily and William, but when Emily saw Elizabeth with Ernest she did not argue with her, she gave her a friendly smile instead.

"Is everything alright between you two now?" asked Emily.

"Stop being so nosey," replied Elizabeth.

"Things could not be better," whispered Ernest with a smile.

Once Ernest had said that to Emily she just screamed out loud with delight.

"You mean you and Elizabeth are courting now?" asked Emily.

"Emily, be quiet. Ernest and I are just seeing how things go that's all. We are taking one day at a time," said Elizabeth.

"Oh, I see," said Emily smiling.

As Elizabeth stood talking with her brother William, Emily looked at Ernest and gave him the thumbs up, just to say good for you. Ernest looked back at her with a huge smile upon his face and Emily was really pleased for them both. A few minutes later Elizabeth and Ernest had another look around the fete and had a few more goes on the games that were there.

"Elizabeth, would you like to have dinner with me this evening? Only I have the house to myself as my parents have gone away to visit my brother in London," said Ernest.

"I would love to thank you. It is a bit funny that you have not long come back from your brother's and now your parent's have gone there to see him. Perhaps they are trying to tell you something," laughed Elizabeth.

"I think perhaps they have got fed up seeing me moaning about, as I have been quite miserable recently since I have not been able to see you," said Ernest.

"Well you do not have to be miserable anymore because hopefully we will be seeing a lot more of each other," said Elizabeth.

"You can count on it," smiled Ernest.

"Oh look, there are my parents over there. We had better go and speak to them," said Elizabeth.

"Hello, are you enjoying yourselves?" asked Elizabeth's mother.

"Yes, we are having a lovely time, thank you," replied Elizabeth.

"We have just seen Emily and William on their stall, they seem to be enjoying themselves as well," said Elizabeth's father.

"Yes, I am glad Emily is getting William out a bit more. They seem to be getting on really well," said Elizabeth.

"Well, they have got things in common, after all they are both on their own with children," said Elizabeth's mother.

"Perhaps one evening I should invite them around for dinner," said Ernest.

"Yes, that would be nice," said Elizabeth.

"That would do William the world of good and I do not mind looking after the children for them. They are no trouble and they have been as good as gold for me today," said Elizabeth's mother as she looked at Lizzie and baby Grace.

"I am having dinner with Ernest this evening and I shall be taking my bottle of red wine I won earlier," smiled Elizabeth.

"I also won a bottle of wine earlier as well. You can have that one as your father and I are not a great lover of red wine," said Elizabeth's mother.

"Oh, thank you. Now we have two bottles to share over dinner," said Elizabeth.

"You can have the wine as I do not care for it much either," said Ernest.

"Oh I don't mind, more for me," she laughed.

Later that day Elizabeth went home to get washed and changed and then she arrived at Ernest's house at about 7.30pm.

"Come in, Elizabeth, make yourself at home," Ernest told her.

"Ummmm, something smells nice," said Elizabeth.

"That's the chicken. You do like chicken I take it?" asked Ernest.

"Yes, of course I do," replied Elizabeth.

Ernest poured Elizabeth a glass of red wine and they both sat talking for a while until dinner was ready.

"Ummm, this dinner is delicious," said Elizabeth, as she tucked into it.

"What about the red wine?" asked Ernest.

"It is very nice," replied Elizabeth.

"Yes, I thought perhaps you liked it. You have drunk over half a bottle already," he laughed.

"It is a good thing I have another bottle then, isn't it?" smiled Elizabeth.

"I can see I am going to have to carry you home later," said Ernest.

"No, you won't. I am perfectly fine," said Elizabeth.

"You will not be fine once you have drunk your second bottle," laughed Ernest.

"We shall see," said Elizabeth smiling.

After they had both finished their dinner Elizabeth poured herself another glass of red wine.

"Shall we go into the other room?" asked Ernest.

"Yes," said Elizabeth, as she picked up her drink.

Elizabeth sat next to Ernest on the settee and started to snuggle up to him.

"Are you alright, Elizabeth?" asked Ernest.

"Which Ernest is asking me? Because I can see two of you," said Elizabeth, as she burst into fits of laughter.

"I think you have had quite enough to drink for tonight," said Ernest.

He then took the second bottle of wine away from her, although there was not much left inside the bottle anyway.

"Come closer to me, Ernest, I cannot see you properly," said Elizabeth.

"Yes, you can, I am sitting right next to you," he told her.

"Just come a bit closer," said Elizabeth.

Ernest moved just a tiny bit closer to Elizabeth but then she suddenly threw her arms around him and tried to kiss him. Ernest held Elizabeth back as he knew it was probably not what she really wanted and he did not want to do anything that they might regret.

"Don't you want to kiss me?" asked Elizabeth.

"Yes, but not like this. You have had too much to drink and should go home," said Ernest.

"But I want to stay here with you," said Elizabeth.

"Lie down and I will sit with you until you are asleep," said Ernest.

"You will not leave me, will you?" she asked.

"No, I promise I will not leave you," replied Ernest.

"I do not want you to ever leave me again. I want to spend the rest of my life with you," said Elizabeth.

Ernest smiled to himself as he had never seen Elizabeth like this before, but at least this time she was saying nice things to him which pleased him. After a few minutes had passed Elizabeth had fallen asleep, so Ernest covered her with a blanket and then he also retired to bed.

The next morning Ernest woke Elizabeth as he had a cup of tea for her, but she did not want to get up.

"Oh my head, I do not feel at all well," said Elizabeth.

"There is a cup of tea here for you; drink it up and then I shall walk you home," said Ernest.

Elizabeth suddenly opened her eyes and looked around the room.

"Where am I?" she asked.

"You are at my parents' house. Remember? You had a bit too much to drink last night and you fell asleep down here," said Ernest.

"Oh, please tell me I did not do anything to embarrass myself," said Elizabeth.

"Well, apart from throwing your arms around my neck, then trying to kiss me and then telling me you wanted to spend the rest of your life with me, no you did not embarrass yourself," laughed Ernest.

"Oh! I did not do all that, did I?" she asked.

"I am afraid so," replied Ernest.

"I am so sorry. I am never going to drink wine ever again," said Elizabeth.

"The reason I have woken you so early is because you usually meet your family at church today," said Ernest.

"Oh, I cannot go to church today, I do not feel well enough," said Elizabeth.

"Well in that case, you might as well go back to sleep and I shall take you home later," said Ernest.

Thank you," mumbled Elizabeth.

Ernest stood back and started laughing to himself; he thought Elizabeth looked quite funny and what made him laugh even more was the fact that she was usually quite a responsible person, but even she obviously had her moments of acting the fool.

Later that day Ernest walked Elizabeth home and when Emily saw them together she started to ask them questions about where they had been all night.

"Elizabeth had a bit too much to drink last night and she ended up falling asleep on the settee," said Ernest.

"That's a good excuse," laughed Emily.

"Honestly, I am telling you the truth," said Ernest.

"Yes he is. You have only got to look at my eyes to see I am not my usual self," said Elizabeth.

"Alright, I believe you," said Emily.

Ernest did not stay too long as Elizabeth was still very tired and wanted to go to back to sleep.

"I will not come around this evening as I know you are tired, but I will call around tomorrow evening to see you," said Ernest.

"Yes, alright. I think I shall have an early night tonight," she told him.

Elizabeth had a good night's sleep that night and she woke the next morning feeling a lot better.

"I will not be in tonight when you get home from work because William has invited me to his house for dinner and he has also said that I can stay the night in his spare room, rather than take Lizzie home in the cold later tonight," said Emily.

"Alright, I hope you have a nice time and I shall probably see you tomorrow," said Elizabeth as she left for work.

Later that evening Ernest called around to see how Elizabeth was feeling.

"I feel much better, thank you," she told him.

"You were rather funny the other night, but it does not hurt to let your hair down once in a while," said Ernest.

"I don't know about letting my hair down. The way my head felt when I woke up yesterday was as though it had been taken off and stitched back on," said Elizabeth.

"I did warn you not to drink so much," laughed Ernest.

"And what with Emily, I am sure she does not believe I fell asleep on the settee," said Elizabeth.

"Of course she does, she was just teasing you," said Ernest.

"Talking of Emily, where is she tonight?" asked Ernest.

"She is having dinner at my brother's house and I think she is staying there tonight in his spare room," replied Elizabeth.

"What about you, have you eaten?" asked Ernest.

"Yes, I had something earlier," replied Elizabeth.

"Perhaps you would like a drink then, some red wine perhaps?" laughed Ernest.

"That is not even the slightest bit funny," smiled Elizabeth.

Ernest stayed talking with Elizabeth for the rest of the evening and it gave them time to talk to each other about how they both felt about one another.

"I had better be going in a minute as it is getting quite late," said Ernest.

"Yes alright, but before you go can I just ask you something?" said Elizabeth.

"Yes. What is it?" asked Ernest.

"Did I really embarrass myself the other night?" asked Elizabeth.

"No, not really," replied Ernest.

"But did I really throw my arms around you and try and kiss you?" asked Elizabeth.

"Yes, you did," smiled Ernest.

"What did you do?" asked Elizabeth.

"I held you back and told you to lie down and go to sleep because you looked tired," replied Ernest.

"Why didn't you kiss me back?" asked Elizabeth.

"Because it might not have been what you really wanted and I certainly would not have taken advantage of you in the state that you were in," replied Ernest.

"But I am not drunk now," said Elizabeth.

Ernest did not say anything he just looked at her.

"Well, are you going to kiss me or not?" asked Elizabeth.

Ernest smiled and then leaned towards Elizabeth and kissed her on her lips, but as they both stopped kissing Elizabeth moved closer to Ernest and kissed him again.

"I think I had better get going now," said Ernest, as he stood up.

Elizabeth walked to the door with him and they hugged each other, then Ernest kissed Elizabeth once more. They then both looked at each other and smiled; then Elizabeth put her hands up to Ernest's face and started to kiss him again.

"Elizabeth, I think I ought to be going now," said Ernest.

"But I do not want you to go," said Elizabeth.

"I have to," said Ernest.

"Why?" she asked.

"You know why," replied Ernest.

Elizabeth then took Ernest's hand and pulled him towards the stairs, but as she took her first step up the stairs Ernest stopped her.

"Are you sure this is what you really want?" he asked.

"Yes, I am sure," replied Elizabeth.

Elizabeth started walking up the stairs again still holding Ernest's hand, but as she got to the bedroom Ernest stopped her again.

"I do not think this is a good idea," he told her.

Elizabeth did not answer him, she just continued to walk into the bedroom and Ernest followed her. Once in the bedroom Elizabeth turned and shut the door and she walked towards Ernest and stood in front of him. Ernest put his hands up to Elizabeth's face and kissed her; he then picked her up and carried her over to the bed and gently laid her down.

"Are you alright, Elizabeth?" he asked.

"Just a bit nervous," she replied.

"So am I," said Ernest.

Ernest then laid beside Elizabeth and kissed her again and slowly started to undress her and a few minutes later he started to make love to her.

The next morning when Elizabeth awoke she leaned over and kissed Ernest on his lips.

"Good morning," he said to her.

"Did you enjoy last night?" asked Elizabeth.

"It was the best night of my life," replied Ernest.

CHAPTER SIXTEEN

As Emily had now left the factory to look after her daughter and also William's daughter Grace, Elizabeth had to find someone to take over Emily's position at work. So she appointed Katie Brown as she was one of her best workers.

One day whilst Elizabeth was in her office sorting out the paperwork, Katie Brown came in to tell her that there were two ladies waiting to look at the clothes designs.

"Can you send them in for me," said Elizabeth.

A few minutes later the two ladies came walking into Elizabeth's office and when Elizabeth saw them she almost had the shock of her life.

"Hello, Elizabeth. Do you remember me? I am Mrs Thornton. I was at Ellen's dinner party a while ago and it was then that you told me about the clothes that you make," she told Elizabeth.

"Oh yes, I remember," said Elizabeth.

"This is my daughter, Rosemary; she asked to come along with me," said Mrs Thornton.

"Hello, it is very nice to meet you," said Rosemary, as she put out her arm to shake Elizabeth's hand.

"I'll just go and get my designs to show you," said Elizabeth, as she totally ignored Rosemary.

The two ladies looked at each design and they both chose an outfit which they liked.

"I'll just get one of my ladies to have you measured," said Elizabeth.

After the two ladies were measured Elizabeth wrote their orders and measurements in her order book.

"Your clothes should be ready within a few weeks," said Elizabeth.

"Thank you, dear," said Mrs Thornton.

The ladies then left the premises and Elizabeth sat down in her chair feeling rather shaky and nervous, but she was also relieved because Rosemary had not remembered her. Later that evening before Elizabeth went home she went to see Ernest at his parents' house.

"I need to speak to you urgently," she told him.

"What is it?" asked Ernest.

"Mrs Thornton came to the factory today with her daughter, Rosemary," said Elizabeth.

"Did Rosemary say anything to you?" asked Ernest.

"No, not really. But I did get rather nervous," replied Elizabeth.

"Rosemary has probably forgotten all about you after all these years so stop worrying," said Ernest.

"I cannot help but worry, she did do some awful things to me, you know," said Elizabeth.

"But that was a long time ago, I am sure everything will be just fine," Ernest told her.

"I hope you're right only they are due to come back to the factory in a few weeks once their outfits are ready," said Elizabeth.

"I am sure you are worrying over nothing," said Ernest.

He then gave Elizabeth a hug and kiss and she looked up at him and gave him a slight smile.

"Just relax, everything will be alright," he told her.

Elizabeth went home after speaking with Ernest but she still could not get Rosemary out of her head.

"Is everything alright, Elizabeth?" asked Emily.

"Yes, I am just tired. I had a hard day at work," replied Elizabeth.

"Why don't you have some time off. You certainly deserve it," said Emily.

"Yes, perhaps I will. I might take one day off this week and go shopping," said Elizabeth. "Would you like to come with me?" she asked Emily.

"I would love to but I am far too busy looking after Lizzie and Grace," replied Emily.

A few days later Elizabeth took the day off from work and went out shopping for some new shoes. Elizabeth went into a number of shops but did not see anything that she liked, so before she looked in anymore shops she decided to go to a tea room for something to eat and drink. Whilst she was sitting quietly drinking her tea she was approached by someone.

"Hello, do you remember me? I came to your factory the other day to order some clothes," said the voice.

Elizabeth could not believe it when she saw that Rosemary was standing right next to her.

"Yes, I remember," replied Elizabeth.

"Do I know you? Only you look very familiar," asked Rosemary.

"No, I do not think so," replied Elizabeth.

"Are you sure?" asked Rosemary once again.

"I just said no, didn't I?" replied Elizabeth rather rudely.

Elizabeth then stood up and walked out of the tea room and she was absolutely shaking.

Oh *my God, she does recognise me*, thought Elizabeth.

Elizabeth did not stay out much longer as she did not want to bump into Rosemary again; she thought she might start trouble with her.

"Did you have a nice day out shopping?" asked Emily.

"Yes, thank you," replied Elizabeth.

But Elizabeth was not telling the truth as she did not want to burden Emily with her problems. But she was still extremely worried about what Rosemary might do to her if she did realise who she is.

When Elizabeth spoke to Ernest about Rosemary he once again told her that she was worrying over nothing. But a week later Rosemary came to the factory with her mother to see if their clothes were finished.

"I am sorry but no, they are not ready yet. I did tell you that they would take a few weeks and it has only been just over a week since we started making them," said Elizabeth.

"Oh not to worry, we shall come back in about a week," said Mrs Thornton.

Rosemary just stood quietly staring at Elizabeth, which made her feel very uncomfortable.

"I am sure I do know you," said Rosemary.

"I do not think so. Now if you'll excuse me I have work to do," said Elizabeth.

Elizabeth sat in her office and put her hands up to her face as she was getting rather stressed over the whole Rosemary situation. As the day went on Elizabeth tried to continue with her work as best she could, but she still could not get Rosemary out of her head. As the end of the day arrived Elizabeth was quite relieved to be finally going home. She saw all of her staff out, then had a tidy up and a while later she left the factory to make her way home.

"Elizabeth," called a voice.

Elizabeth looked around and saw Ernest standing waiting for her.

"What are you doing here?" she asked.

"I finished work early today so I thought I would meet you," he replied.

Elizabeth was extremely pleased to see him and she gave him a kiss and they both walked back to Elizabeth's house together.

"Would you like to stay for dinner tonight?" asked Elizabeth.

"Yes, alright, but only if it is no trouble," said Ernest.

"I have had my dinner, but I have left yours in the pan; it only needs to be heated up," said Emily.

"Is there enough for Ernest?" asked Elizabeth.

"Yes, there is plenty for you both," replied Emily.

Emily then grabbed her coat and got Grace ready to take back to William.

"You can leave Lizzie here with me if you like whilst you take Grace home," said Elizabeth.

"No, I had better take her with me as William said I could stay the night at his house, and I do not want to let him down because I think he likes a bit of company," replied Emily.

"You two seem to be getting along nicely," said Ernest.

"Yes, we are. We really enjoy each other's company," said Emily.

Elizabeth and Ernest had their dinner and then sat down together for the evening.

"What is wrong, Elizabeth? I can sense something is troubling you," asked Ernest.

"Oh, it is just all this business with Rosemary. It is getting to me quite a bit," replied Elizabeth.

"You worry too much," said Ernest.

Ernest then put his arm around Elizabeth and kissed her and she felt safe as she sat with him holding her.

"How do you feel about having an early night?" he asked.

"That depends how tired you are," replied Elizabeth.

"I am never tired when I am with you, so do not expect me to go straight to sleep," he laughed.

"In that case I would love an early night," she told him with a huge smile upon her face.

The next morning Elizabeth and Ernest left the house together and he walked Elizabeth to work before leaving her to go to his own job.

"I shall see you this evening," said Ernest as he kissed her goodbye.

Just as Elizabeth was unlocking the factory she saw a shadow move beside her, so she looked around and standing near her was Rosemary.

"I have finally realised who you are. You are that little slave girl that used to work for the Lockwoods, aren't you?" asked Rosemary.

"Just leave me alone," said Elizabeth.

"Why should I do that? After all, you have annoyed me," said Rosemary.

"What are you talking about?" asked Elizabeth.

"You are with the man I love. I saw you walking with him last night and he walked you to work this morning," said Rosemary.

"What I do is none of your business. And how can you say that I am with the man that you love? You had an affair behind his back," said Elizabeth.

"Only because Ernest would not satisfy my needs, he wanted to wait until we were married," said Rosemary.

"I really do not care. All I know is that Ernest loves me and I love him, so you had just better leave us alone," said Elizabeth.

"I know you are having relations with Ernest because I followed you both to your house last night, but do not think for one minute he will stay with you. Why would he? After all, you are just a slave girl, he is not really interested in you, he just wants you because you lay on your back for him," said Rosemary.

"I do not care what you think. I know Ernest loves me and he always will," said Elizabeth.

"You do not want Ernest, you only want his money. I suppose he set you up with this business, didn't he?" said Rosemary.

"That is where you are wrong. I have built this business up myself through working hard, not that you would understand what hard work is," said Elizabeth.

"How dare you speak to me like that, you little tramp!" shouted Rosemary.

"You can say what you like about me, it does not bother me anymore. All you are is a very unhappy lady and that is where we differ," said Elizabeth. "Now get out of my way, I have work to do," she told Rosemary.

Rosemary was left fuming with the way Elizabeth had spoken to her. Elizabeth walked inside her factory and had to quickly sit down. Her heart was racing through being so frightened, but she was not going to let Rosemary know that she feared her.

Elizabeth sat in her office for most of the day, but she could not concentrate at all on her work.

Later that evening Elizabeth waited for Ernest to arrive and when he did she told him about Rosemary and the horrible things she had said to her.

"Perhaps I should go and speak with her because I am not going to have her keep upsetting you like this," said Ernest.

"No, it might make things worse," said Elizabeth.

"Well I will see her, if you want me to," said Ernest.

"Thank you, but this is something I have to deal with myself, otherwise she will know I am scared and then she will never leave me alone," said Elizabeth.

"Alright, but I am here if you need me," said Ernest.

Over the next few days Elizabeth did not see anything of Rosemary, but that still did not stop her from thinking about her, or from her being slightly on edge. But as the weekend came Elizabeth had something to occupy her; the christening of Emily's daughter, Lizzie, was being held at the local church and Elizabeth was looking forward to becoming her godmother.

"Lizzie looks absolutely beautiful in her christening gown," said Elizabeth.

"Yes, she does. I just hope the day goes well for her," said Emily.

"I am sure it will. Ernest should be here soon. I know he is looking forward to becoming Lizzie's godfather," said Elizabeth.

As Ernest left his parents' house to make his way to Elizabeth's for the christening, he was suddenly stopped by Rosemary.

"Hello, Ernest. I have not seen you for a long time," said Rosemary.

"What do you want?" asked Ernest rather abruptly.

"That is no way to speak to the lady that you were once engaged to," said Rosemary.

"I have nothing to say to you," Ernest told her.

"Well, I have rather a lot to say to you. What on earth do you think you are doing with that slave girl? You are totally humiliating yourself," said Rosemary.

"If you are referring to Elizabeth, then let me tell you something, I am extremely happy with her and if anyone has humiliated me it was you. You were the one that had an affair behind my back," said Ernest.

"I know what I did was wrong, but I never stopped loving you. It was you that made me do it because you would never come near me, but you go near that slave girl. How do you think that makes me feel?" asked Rosemary.

"I do not care how you feel, you mean nothing to me," said Ernest.

"You know you do not mean that. I know you still love me," said Rosemary.

"Just go back to your drunken husband, I am sure he will satisfy your needs," shouted Ernest.

Ernest then walked away but when he arrived at Elizabeth's house he did not mention anything to her, as he did not want to spoil her day.

"Ernest is here," said Elizabeth.

"Look at Lizzie, doesn't she look adorable?" said Emily.

"Yes, she does," replied Ernest. "I have a little something for her," he told Emily.

Ernest gave Emily a box and inside it was a locket for her daughter bought as a christening gift.

"It is beautiful, thank you so much," said Emily.

"Shall we go to the church now?" asked Elizabeth.

"Yes," replied Emily.

As the christening took place it brought back memories for Elizabeth from when her son Adam was christened and she smiled to herself as she thought of Edward holding their son in his arms. After the christening had taken place everyone went back to Elizabeth's house for something to eat and drink.

"It went really well today, didn't it?" said Elizabeth.

"Yes it did. I do not think I have seen Emily smile so much in one day," said Ernest.

"I do not think it is just the christening that has made Emily smile. Look at her and William, they have not taken their eyes off of each other all day," smiled Elizabeth.

"It is good to see they are getting along so well," said Ernest.

"Yes, it is. William has been through a lot with losing Alice and having to cope with a new baby and Emily also deserves a bit of happiness after all she has been through, what with bringing up Lizzie on her own and everything," said Elizabeth.

"Things seem to be working out perfectly well for all of us," smiled Ernest.

Elizabeth and Ernest sat outside for a while and then Ernest had to leave as he had some paperwork to sort out for his court case the next day.

"I shall see you tomorrow," said Ernest.

"Yes, alright," replied Elizabeth.

"Cheer up," said Ernest.

"Sorry. I was just thinking about work. Rosemary and her mother's clothes should be finished this week and I am dreading having to see them. Well, not Mrs Thornton so much as Rosemary," said Elizabeth.

"I doubt if Rosemary will say anything horrible to you whilst her mother is present; she does it in a cunning way when no one is around," said Ernest.

"Yes, I know," said Elizabeth.

"If you are that worried about seeing them get one of your staff to deal with them, after all that is what you are paying their wages for," said Ernest.

"Yes, I think I might just do that," said Elizabeth.

So that is exactly what Elizabeth did. The day Mrs Thornton and her daughter Rosemary were due into the factory, Elizabeth let one of her staff show them both their finished clothes and they paid their account without Elizabeth having to set eyes upon them.

"Goodbye, Mrs Thomas," said Katie Brown as she left the factory to go home.

"Goodbye and thank you for all of your help today," said Elizabeth.

Elizabeth quickly tided up and then sat down for a few minutes in her office as she just wanted to collect her thoughts.

"Were you to scared to face me earlier today?" said Rosemary as she walked into the office.

"Get out!" shouted Elizabeth.

"I asked you a question so answer me, slave girl!" shouted Rosemary.

"I am not scared of you or anyone else," replied Elizabeth.

"Well you should be, because I have something very special planned for you," said Rosemary.

"Why don't you just leave me alone? I have not done anything to you," said Elizabeth.

"Yes, you have. I remember when I fell into the little stream and you left me there without even helping me out," said Rosemary.

"You did that yourself and why should I have helped you out after you hit me with your riding crop for no reason," said Elizabeth.

"That is not the only reason why I am going to get you back; you have also taken the man I love and I know you have only done this to spite me," said Rosemary.

"You really are mad if you think that," said Elizabeth.

"Oh, you think I am mad, do you? Well, you just wait and see when I am really mad, you will not know what has hit you," said Rosemary. "Sleep well tonight because I know I will," she told Elizabeth, as she left the office with a grin on her face.

Oh my God, how much more have I got to take? thought Elizabeth, as she sat and cried.

That evening Elizabeth told Ernest what Rosemary had said to her and he was absolutely furious to think that she was being threatened yet again by Rosemary.

"Do you think I should inform the police?" asked Elizabeth.

"I do not think there is much they can do because Rosemary has not actually harmed you," replied Ernest.

"But she hit me years ago and her brother tried to rape me," said Elizabeth.

"But you did not report it years ago and now that her brother is dead there is no proof," said Ernest.

"Well, what am I supposed to do? Just sit back and wait for her to do something to me," said Elizabeth.

"I do not think she will do anything, I think she is just trying to frighten you," said Ernest.

"Well, she is certainly succeeding," said Elizabeth.

When Ernest left Elizabeth's house Rosemary was watching him from behind a tree, but he did not know that she was there.

"Ernest," she called.

Ernest looked around and saw Rosemary standing close by and she looked awful.

"Please help me, Ernest, my husband has been beating me again," said Rosemary.

"Why should I help you? After the way you treated Elizabeth today," said Ernest.

"What are you talking about? I have not even seen Elizabeth today," said Rosemary.

"Do not lie to me. Elizabeth is in a terrible state because of you," said Ernest.

"I am not lying to you. I have not seen her today. I have been at home getting beaten by my husband, just look at my face," said Rosemary.

Rosemary had scratches all down her face and Ernest could see that she had been crying.

"Why are you telling me all of this? You married the man so just get on with it," said Ernest.

"I cannot go back to him, he will end up killing me. Please help me, Ernest, I am begging you. You know you still have feelings for me and I am sure you would not want to see anything happen to me," said Rosemary.

"If you are that worried about your husband then go to the police," Ernest told her.

"That will not do any good because once they leave he will hit me again for contacting them," said Rosemary.

"What do you expect me to do?" asked Ernest.

"You could at least let me stay at your house, then I will be safe," said Rosemary.

"Do you really think that my parents would let you stay at their house after what you did with their gardener?" asked Ernest.

"I did not mean I wanted to stay at their house. I was hoping you would let me stay in your little cottage that you let out," said Rosemary.

"I do not think so," replied Ernest.

"Please, I am desperate. I will make it worth your while. I will even do it with you now, if you want," said Rosemary as she started to unbutton her dress.

Ernest rushed towards her and tried to stop her from taking her clothes off.

"Where is your self-respect?" he asked her.

"Come on, Ernest, you know you want to do it. Surely you must have wondered what it would be like," said Rosemary.

"The only thing I ever wonder about is what on earth I ever saw in you," said Ernest.

"Fine, be like that, you are the one missing out," shouted Rosemary.

"I am not missing out on anything. I have everything I need with Elizabeth," said Ernest.

"You will be sorry you ever said that to me," said Rosemary.

"No, you will be sorry if you ever go near Elizabeth again," shouted Ernest.

"Do not think for one minute I wanted you anyway. My husband did not beat me, I put these scratches on my face myself and I put perfume in my eyes to make it look like I have been crying. All I wanted was to stay at your house so that I could tell Elizabeth we are having an affair and then she would not have wanted you and neither would have I," said Rosemary.

"It is such a shame that your plan did not work after all," said Ernest.

"Oh do not worry, I never really expected it to work. But I do have another bigger and better plan in store for both you and Elizabeth, so you had better just watch out," said Rosemary.

"Just stay away from us or you will be sorry," shouted Ernest.

"No, I won't. You and that slave girl of yours are the ones who are going to be sorry," said Rosemary, as she walked away laughing.

Ernest was furious by what Rosemary had said to him and he now understood why Elizabeth was so frightened, as he had never seen Rosemary behave like this before.

Over the next few weeks everything seemed to get back to normal; no one had heard from Rosemary and Ernest was hoping that she was now going to leave them alone. But one night whilst Elizabeth and Ernest were in bed something was thrown through one of the windows.

"I have a good idea who was responsible for this," said Ernest.

"Surely the police must be able to do something," said Elizabeth.

"How can we prove it was her?" said Ernest.

"I am just glad that Emily is at William's house. Imagine if that glass had gone all over Lizzie," said Elizabeth.

"Don't worry, I am going to pay Rosemary a little visit and stop this nonsense once and for all," said Ernest.

"What right now?" asked Elizabeth.

"Yes, because this has got to stop," he said.

"You will be careful though, won't you?" said Elizabeth.

"Of course I will. I won't be long," said Ernest, as he gave Elizabeth a kiss.

When Ernest arrived at Rosemary's house he banged on the door as hard as he could and within seconds Rosemary answered it.

"Why did you throw something through Elizabeth's window?" he shouted.

"I have not been anywhere near her house tonight," replied Rosemary.

"I never said it happened tonight. Did I? I know it was you Rosemary because it is almost 3.30 in the morning and you still have your clothes on," said Ernest.

"Would you like me to take them off for you?" laughed Rosemary.

"Do not get clever with me. I am warning you one last time, stay away from Elizabeth and I," shouted Ernest.

"Or you will do what?" asked Rosemary.

Ernest suddenly pinned Rosemary up against the door by her throat, until she went quite red in her face.

"I have never hurt a lady before, but my God, Rosemary, you are pushing me into doing something I might regret," said Ernest.

Ernest then took his hands off of Rosemary and she looked quite shocked and frightened by how he had reacted towards her.

"This had better be the end of your games, or it will be the end for you," Ernest told her.

He then stormed off in a temper and made his way back to Elizabeth's house.

Elizabeth and Ernest never heard from Rosemary again and they were quite relieved that she had finally got the message to stay right away from them both and leave them in peace.

"Ernest, get up. Emily will be home from William's house soon and if she finds you here it will be so embarrassing for us both," said Elizabeth one morning.

"Just give me a few more minutes, it is my day off today, after all," said Ernest.

"No, Emily will be home soon," said Elizabeth.

"Alright, I'll get up now," said Ernest.

But he had no intention of getting up, he just grabbed hold of Elizabeth and pulled her down on the bed with him.

"Ernest, stop it!" screamed Elizabeth.

"Give me a kiss and I will let you go," said Ernest.

"Only if you promise to get up now," said Elizabeth.

"Yes, I promise," smiled Ernest.

Elizabeth then leaned forward and gave Ernest a kiss, so he climbed out of bed and got dressed and they both went downstairs together for breakfast.

"Good morning to you both. I won't ask what you two have been up to," laughed Emily.

"I was just getting my coat as Elizabeth hung it up in her room," said Ernest.

"Of course she did," said Emily sarcastically.

"I think I had better go now," said Ernest.

"Aren't you going to have your breakfast first? Only I can see that the table is laid for two people," laughed Emily.

"I think Elizabeth was waiting for you to come home, which is why the table is laid for two people," said Ernest looking embarrassed.

"Stop telling fibs. Elizabeth knows I always have breakfast at William's house when I stay there the night," giggled Emily.

Ernest quickly sat down at the table as he knew it was a waste of time trying to convince Emily that nothing improper was going on; he knew that she was not the fool everyone thought she was.

"Don't look so embarrassed, Ernest. William and I are also sharing the same room now. And why shouldn't we? We are all adults," said Emily.

"Emily, I am surprised at you," said Elizabeth, trying to keep a straight face.

"Oh shut up. It is about time we all had some fun," laughed Emily.

With that they all started to laugh and Ernest almost choked on his cup of tea.

"What are you doing today?" Elizabeth asked Ernest.

"I have not planned to do anything apart from be with the lady that I love," he told her.

"Shall we go horse riding together later?" asked Elizabeth.

"Yes, alright," said Ernest.

"Don't worry about me. I shall just sit here on my own, all lonely," said Emily.

"Oh, sorry, Emily I did not think," said Elizabeth.

"Ha, ha, fooled you. I am going out with William today so you do not have to worry about me," laughed Emily.

"I am really pleased for you both," said Elizabeth.

Later that day Elizabeth and Ernest saddled up their horses and rode off together. They rode to the same place where they had had a picnic once before.

"I'll race you to the big oak again," said Ernest.

"Well, you will not win this time because I have had a lot of practice since," laughed Elizabeth.

"We shall see," said Ernest smiling at her.

Ernest let Elizabeth start the race first to give her a chance, but he still caught up with her and beat her.

"You'll never be as good as me," he laughed.

"Oh be quiet," said Elizabeth.

After they had both raced across the fields together a few times they dismounted from their horses and sat down on the grass for a while.

"If only every day was like this," said Elizabeth.

"Yes, if only," said Ernest.

As they sat together Elizabeth had an idea.

"Shall we go down to the little stream? I have not been down there for ages," said Elizabeth.

"Yes, alright. I have got some bread with me so we will be able to feed the ducks," said Ernest.

Once they got to the little stream they stood and fed the ducks and watched as the ducklings followed their mother. Then they started to laugh as one duckling had trouble getting up on to the embankment.

"Oh look, they are so beautiful," said Elizabeth, smiling at them.

Suddenly they both looked around as they heard horses galloping towards them, but Elizabeth started to get quite worried as she saw it was Rosemary and her husband George Todd. Both Rosemary and her husband pulled up their horses and dismounted and they started to walk towards Elizabeth and Ernest.

"This is the man that attacked me," shouted Rosemary as she pointed to Ernest.

"What are you talking about?" asked Ernest.

Rosemary's husband hardly let Ernest say a word; he just punched him hard in his face and knocked him to the ground.

"What are you doing?" shouted Elizabeth as she ran over to help Ernest.

"Get out of my way!" shouted George Todd.

"No, she is lying," said Elizabeth.

Rosemary's husband picked up Elizabeth and threw her out of the way, he then pushed Ernest again and started kicking him in his stomach and face.

"Stop it! Stop it!" shouted Elizabeth.

Elizabeth tried to get in between Ernest and George Todd, but Rosemary grabbed hold of her and held her back.

"Leave him alone, he has not done anything," screamed Elizabeth.

"Take a look at my clothes, they are ruined because of him he tried to rape me," said Rosemary.

"You are lying and you know it," shouted Elizabeth.

George Todd did not even give Ernest a chance to get back on his feet, he just kept kicking him until he was unconscious.

"Please stop, you are going to kill him!" shouted Elizabeth.

"I intend to kill him for what he has done," shouted George Todd.

"But he has not done anything. Why won't you believe me?" said Elizabeth.

"Are you calling my wife a liar?" asked George Todd.

"Yes, I am," replied Elizabeth.

"How can you stand there and say that? When you were encouraging him to do it to me," said Rosemary.

"You are totally mad," Elizabeth told her.

"You mean she told him to rape you?" asked George Todd.

"Yes, she did. She has hated me for years," replied Rosemary.

George Todd then walked over towards Elizabeth and hit her hard in her face, whilst Rosemary stood watching with a sickly grin upon her face.

"That will teach you," laughed Rosemary.

"Just tell him the truth," cried Elizabeth.

"It was awful, he pushed me to the floor and this bitch held me down whilst he tried to rip off my dress. It was just lucky for me that I managed to struggle free or else he would have actually raped me," cried Rosemary.

"You are a liar!" shouted Elizabeth.

"Do not listen to her, she is only trying to get herself out of trouble, probably because she has not got her lover to protect her anymore," said Rosemary.

George Todd sat down for a few minutes and pulled out a bottle of whisky and started to drink it. Rosemary then let go of Elizabeth and sat down with her husband, whilst Elizabeth ran over to Ernest to see how badly hurt he was.

"You have got to help him, he is seriously hurt," cried Elizabeth.

"Tie her hands behind her back and then tie her lover's hands up as well," said George Todd.

Rosemary ran over to Elizabeth and grabbed her hands behind her back and she pushed her to the ground and sat on her whilst she tied her hands up. She then pulled Elizabeth over towards her husband whilst she then tied up Ernest's hands behind his back.

"What are you going to do with them?" asked Rosemary.

"I am going to take them to that derelict barn over there and then I will decide what to do next," replied George.

He then grabbed hold of Elizabeth and pulled her into the barn. He then untied her hands and retied them around a wooden post that stood inside the barn, so that her hands were still tied up behind her back. He then went back outside and carried Ernest into the barn and just threw him on the ground.

"Go and tie their horses up outside," he told Rosemary.

"Perhaps I should do to you what your lover did to my wife," said George Todd.

"Neither of us did anything," said Elizabeth.

George Todd suddenly lost his temper and threw his empty bottle of whisky close to Elizabeth. Then Rosemary came back inside the barn and just stood and smirked at her.

"What are you going to do with them?" asked Rosemary.

"Just let me think, woman," he told her.

He then opened another bottle of whisky and started pouring it down his throat and by this time he was quite drunk.

"You are not going to let them get away with attempted rape, are you?" asked Rosemary.

"No, of course not," replied George.

"Then do something instead of just standing there drinking," shouted Rosemary.

By this time Ernest started to come round and as he opened his eyes he looked straight at Elizabeth and could see that she was tied up to a post. He felt quite frustrated because he could not do anything as he hands were also tied up behind his back and he felt quite sick as Elizabeth looked so frightened.

"Let her go she has not done anything wrong," shouted Ernest.

"You are not in any position to tell us what to do!" shouted Rosemary.

She then walked towards Ernest and kicked him in his stomach, whilst her husband just stood and watched.

George Todd then drank the last drop of whisky that was in his bottle and he threw it close to Elizabeth once again, missing her by inches. Elizabeth screamed as it frightened her and this made Rosemary laugh.

"Did I frighten you?" asked George.

He then ran his fingers through Elizabeth's hair and leaned towards her breathing his whisky breath all over her. Elizabeth felt sickened as he stroked her face, so trying to protect herself she brought her foot up and kicked him in his private parts.

"You little bitch!" shouted Rosemary as she slapped Elizabeth's face.

Rosemary's husband was on the floor rolling around in agony, but once he was back on his feet he walked towards Elizabeth again and stood on top of her feet, so that she could not kick out at him again. He then held her head up and started to kiss her, so Elizabeth spat in his face.

"That was not a very nice thing to do," said George.

"You kissing me is not very nice; the smell from you is disgusting," said Elizabeth.

"Perhaps this will feel nice," said George as he slowly moved his hand up Elizabeth's dress.

"Leave her alone!" shouted Ernest.

"Be quiet and watch. You never know, you might actually learn something," said Rosemary.

George Todd then started to unzip his trousers and it was then Elizabeth started to scream for help, so George tore a piece of her dress and shoved it in her mouth to silence her.

"Go on, rape her, make her suffer!" said Rosemary.

"You will hang for this," said Ernest.

George Todd suddenly hesitated for a moment and looked at Rosemary.

"Well don't just stand there, do it!" shouted Rosemary.

Suddenly Rosemary ripped at Elizabeth's dress tearing it from the top downwards and Elizabeth just stood there with her undergarment covering her breasts.

"This is wrong. Elizabeth and I did not do anything to Rosemary, she is making the whole thing up because I rejected her advances a few weeks ago," said Ernest.

"Is this true?" asked her husband.

"Don't be so ridiculous. Why would I want him?" asked Rosemary.

"You wanted me a few years ago. Didn't you, Rosemary? We were due to get married until I caught you romping with my parents' gardener," said Ernest.

"Is this true?" asked George.

"Of course not, he is lying," replied Rosemary.

"It is true. Rosemary has never forgiven me for turning her down so soon before our wedding," said Ernest.

"What has this lady got to do with all of this?" asked George.

"Rosemary has always been jealous of her. Even when Rosemary and I were courting she used to bully Elizabeth," replied Ernest.

"Just shut up, Ernest. My husband does not believe a word you are saying!" shouted Rosemary.

"I also found it hard to believe when Elizabeth first confided in me about the awful things you did to her years ago, like when you locked her in the drawing room and encouraged your brother to rape her. Remember, Rosemary, what you did?" said Ernest.

"She deserved it after not helping me out of the little stream when I fell in," replied Rosemary.

"Elizabeth did not deserve that, she is the kindest person I have ever met," said Ernest.

"So you did tell your brother to rape her, didn't you?" asked her husband. "Just like you are trying to get me to rape her now," he said.

"I promise you I did not do anything to Rosemary and neither did Elizabeth," said Ernest.

"I believe you," said George. "It is over Rosemary. Untie the lady and Ernest, I am going home," he told her.

"You are not going anywhere!" said Rosemary as she pulled out a handgun.

"Rosemary, don't be stupid!" shouted Ernest.

Rosemary's husband George just stared at her and looked at the gun that was aimed at him.

"Put the gun down, Rosemary. You do not want to be arrested for murder, do you?" asked George.

"It was not meant to be like this. It has all gone wrong, hasn't it?" said Rosemary as she started to cry.

"No, it has not. Now just put the gun down," said George.

"Listen to your husband, he is right you know," said Ernest.

"Who asked you to speak? If it was not for you and that slave girl none of this would have happened and I would not be in this mess," she told Ernest. "Look at her. I have never hated anyone like I hate her!" shouted Rosemary.

"You have got to let them go now," said her husband.

"Why is everyone telling me what to do? I have the gun so you will all do as I say. Now finish her off or I will shoot you," she told her husband.

"No, it is over and I am going home," replied George.

Rosemary's husband then turned and started to slowly walk out of the barn.

"Come back!" shouted Rosemary.

But George would not listen to her he just carried on walking so Rosemary shot him in the back.

"No!" shouted Ernest.

"You can be quiet as well," shouted Rosemary.

She then aimed the gun at Ernest and shot him as well. Elizabeth could not make a sound as she still had the piece of dress inside her mouth, but she saw what had happened and just stood there and cried.

Rosemary then threw down the gun after realising what she had done and she started to panic. She then ran outside to get on her horse, but she suddenly saw a lot of horse dung on the ground. She then picked it up and walked back inside the barn and rubbed it into Elizabeth's face and hair. Rosemary went back outside and washed her hands in the little stream and then came back for her gun. But before she left the barn again she hit Elizabeth in the face with the gun and knocked her unconscious. Elizabeth slid down the post and fell on to her bottom with her legs straddled apart. Rosemary then trod on Elizabeth's legs as hard as she could and then walked out of the barn. She then untied the horses and frightened them away, all but her own horse which she used as her escape. Rosemary rode away on her horse leaving her husband and Ernest lying in a pool of blood and Elizabeth tied up and unconscious on the ground.

CHAPTER SEVENTEEN

When Elizabeth regained consciousness she could see that Ernest was losing a lot of blood, but she could not do anything to help as she was tied up herself. She could not even call for help as she still had a piece of her dress inside her mouth. After a while Ernest started to regain consciousness but he could hardly speak as he was so weak through loss of blood. He lay on the ground shivering as his temperature had started to drop.

When Emily and William returned home they thought it very strange that Midnight was loose in the garden.

"Elizabeth, are you home?" called Emily. "That is strange. Elizabeth does not seem to be home," said Emily.

"There must be something wrong. I know for a fact Elizabeth would never go out without putting Midnight back inside the stable first," said William.

"What do you think has happened?" asked Emily.

"I don't know. But I think I should go and look for her," said William.

William mounted Midnight and went looking for his sister, but he rode around for ages without any success of finding her.

"Elizabeth, where are you?" called William.

William rode on a little further but he still could not find Elizabeth and he started to get quite concerned.

"Elizabeth, can you hear me?" shouted William.

But there was still no answer. Then William came to the little stream so he let Midnight have a drink and it was then that he heard a horse neigh. When he looked towards where the horse was he saw Ernest's horse, Admiral, standing outside a barn, so he quickly ran over to the barn. William then made his way inside the barn and he was horrified at what he saw.

"Oh my goodness!" he said, as he untied Elizabeth. "Are you alright?" he asked.

William took the piece of material out from Elizabeth's mouth and she looked at him and wept.

"I think my legs are broken," she said. "But do not worry about me; go and see if Ernest is alright as he has been shot," said Elizabeth.

William untied Ernest's arms and carried him to his horse; he then looked at Rosemary's husband but he was already dead, so William left him where he was. He then carried Elizabeth and put her on her horse, but she screamed as she was moved as her legs were extremely painful. William then managed to get Elizabeth and Ernest home rather quickly.

As William arrived, Emily heard the horses so she quickly ran out of the house to see if William had found them.

"Go and fetch a doctor as quickly as possible," said William.

He then carried Elizabeth upstairs and then came back outside to get Ernest.

When the doctor arrived he examined Ernest first as he had been shot and had lost a lot of blood. The doctor managed to remove the bullet from his shoulder but he was worried because Ernest had been left for so long.

"Ernest is extremely lucky that the bullet hit his shoulder, but I need you to keep him warm as he will probably get delirious and get very feverish," said the doctor.

"He will be alright though, won't he?" asked William.

"We will just have to wait and see how he copes within the next twenty-four hours, but I cannot promise anything as he has lost a lot of blood," replied the doctor.

The doctor then examined Elizabeth and was with her for quite some time. Then he went and spoke with William.

"Your sister has got a rather large bump on her head where she was hit, but it is not life threatening. My main concern is her legs. One of her legs is broken in two places, but the other leg is not only broken, I think it might be severely damaged and I am not certain whether she will ever walk again," said the doctor.

"But you are a doctor, surely you must know whether Elizabeth will be able to walk again?" said William.

"It is too early to say at this stage. But I have cleaned and bandaged them up as best I can and I have also given them both something to ease their pain," said the doctor.

"William, the police are here to speak to Elizabeth," said Emily.

"I shall call back again tomorrow," said the doctor.

The police were shown to Elizabeth's room and she told them exactly what had happened, even from the time when she worked at the Lockwoods.

"We will put a search out for this woman but we will probably not be able to do anything until the morning as it is getting rather dark now. But do not worry, we will catch her," said the police officer.

"Thank you," said Elizabeth.

"We shall be in touch soon," said the police officer.

Emily saw the police out and then went upstairs to see Elizabeth, as she had not had chance to speak with her yet.

"How are you feeling?" she asked.

"Oh, Emily, I am just so glad to be home, that awful woman has got so much to answer for," said Elizabeth.

"It will be alright, Elizabeth. The police will soon find her and she will be punished for her crimes," said Emily.

"But it will never be alright. The doctor has already told me I might never walk again," said Elizabeth.

"Of course you will. You are a born fighter and if you are determined to walk again then you will," Emily told her.

"What about Ernest? Is he alright?" asked Elizabeth.

"Yes, he is going to be fine. The doctor has removed the bullet from his shoulder, and he is still very weak, but I am sure he will make a complete recovery," said Emily.

"Where is William?" asked Elizabeth.

"He has gone to tell your parents what has happened and he is also going to let Mr and Mrs Lockwood know about Ernest," replied Emily.

"I cannot believe anyone could be as cruel as Rosemary is. I have never done anything to her to make her hate me this much," said Elizabeth.

"I do not think it is just you. I think Rosemary had a grudge against everyone, including her own husband," said Emily.

"Will you let Katie Brown know what has happened? I will need her to take over at the factory until I am well enough to return," said Elizabeth.

"Of course I will, so don't start worrying yourself about work, you need to rest," said Emily.

"I feel so tired," said Elizabeth.

"I am not surprised after what you have been through. Is there anything you need? As I am going leave you to get some rest," said Emily.

"No, thank you, I just need to sleep," replied Elizabeth.

Emily left the room and went to see how Ernest was feeling, but he now had a fever and was burning up. Emily went and got a bowl of water and washed him down and as she came downstairs William walked into the house with his parents.

"How is Elizabeth?" asked her mother.

"She is doing fine but she is very sleepy," replied Emily.

"I think it best we do not disturb her then," said Elizabeth's father.

"What about Ernest? Is he going to be alright?" asked Elizabeth's mother.

"I cannot really say. He has had the bullet removed but he now has a fever. Only time will tell us the outcome," replied Emily.

"I have informed Mr and Mrs Lockwood about Ernest's condition and they will be here soon," said William.

"Shall I make some tea for everyone?" asked Emily.

"That would be lovely, dear, thank you," replied Elizabeth's mother.

A few minutes later the Lockwoods arrived and they rushed into the house looking extremely worried.

"Hello, Emily. Could we possibly see Ernest for a few minutes?" asked Mrs Lockwood.

"Of course you can. Come with me, I will show you which room he is in," replied Emily.

Mr and Mrs Lockwood followed Emily upstairs and they had the shock of their lives when they saw their son.

"Oh my goodness! He looks terrible," said Mrs Lockwood.

"He does have a fever at the moment which is why he looks so ill, but I am sure he will be alright," said Emily.

"I do hope you are right, my dear," said Mrs Lockwood.

"How is Elizabeth?" asked Mr Lockwood.

"She has two broken legs but one of them is quite badly damaged and the doctor has said that he does not know if she will ever be able to walk again. I am just praying that he is wrong though," said Emily.

"Oh that awful woman Rosemary ought to be shot herself for what she has done and if I get my hands on her I will do it myself," said Mrs Lockwood.

"I can understand how you feel, but our main priority is to make sure Elizabeth and Ernest get well soon," said Emily.

"Yes, of course. I am so sorry for my sudden outburst, but that woman makes me so angry. She has been nothing but trouble all of her life," said Mrs Lockwood.

"I think we should leave Ernest to rest now. Come downstairs with me and I will make you some tea," said Emily.

After everyone had drank their tea they took it in turns to see Elizabeth. When she first saw her parents, Elizabeth just broke down in tears and her mother also wept when she saw how swollen her daughter's head was from being hit with the gun.

"That woman could have killed you. I hope when they find her they string her up," said Elizabeth's father.

"I hope they find her soon as well, because I do not think I can rest until she is caught," said Elizabeth.

"You look tired, dear, we will go now but we will call in again tomorrow to see how you are," said Elizabeth's mother.

"Yes, alright," said Elizabeth, as she fell back to sleep.

Elizabeth's brother William decided to stay the night at his sister's house, as he was afraid that Rosemary might return. Emily and William took it in turns to look after Elizabeth and Ernest, whilst Elizabeth's parents kindly agreed to look after Lizzie and baby Grace.

Ernest was very restless throughout the night and had to be watched constantly just in case he fell out of bed.

The next day the police arrived at Elizabeth's house early in the morning. They still had not found Rosemary but a huge search was on around the town and they even had help from many of the local people.

The doctor also called again and he was very pleased with Ernest's progress. His fever had now broken and he was also conscious.

"How are you feeling?" asked the doctor.

"Very thirsty," replied Ernest.

"Could you please get some water for Ernest to drink, but make sure he drinks it slowly," he told Emily.

Elizabeth also felt a lot better although she was still suffering from a lot of pain in her legs.

"I will give you something for the pain, but your legs will hurt for quite some time yet," said the doctor.

Elizabeth felt quite helpless as she could hardly move and she hated the indignity caused when Emily had to wash her down.

"Ernest is feeling a lot better today. He has drunk plenty of water and eaten some soup that I made. Would you like some?" asked Emily.

"No, thank you, I am not hungry," replied Elizabeth.

"But you have to eat as you need to build your strength up," said Emily.

"I just told you I am not hungry, didn't I?" said Elizabeth.

"Alright, I will leave you to rest," Emily told her.

When Emily left the room Elizabeth began to weep; her legs were hurting her very much and she had started to get quite depressed as she felt like her life was over.

Emily came back to check on her a short time later and she could see that Elizabeth had been crying.

"Are you alright?" asked Emily.

"Yes, I just have a bit of pain in my legs, that is all," replied Elizabeth.

Elizabeth did not tell Emily that she was afraid that she might never walk again, or the fact that she felt as though her life was over.

"I am just going to see how Ernest is, but if you need me just give me a call," said Emily.

Elizabeth laid in her bed and kept thinking about the previous day when Rosemary and her husband had attacked her and every time she closed her eyes all she could see was Rosemary's face laughing at her.

291

Over the next few days Ernest was able to sit up in bed and he felt a lot better than he had done a few days before, but Elizabeth just felt the same. She could not move her legs and was starting to get very frustrated with herself.

"William has gone out to see your parents, but if you need anything I will be downstairs so just give me a call," said Emily.

"You look worn out," said Elizabeth.

"I am a bit tired but I will be alright," said Emily.

Elizabeth fell asleep but was woken by someone leaning over her. It was Rosemary who had somehow got into Elizabeth's house without Emily seeing her.

"What are you doing here?" asked Elizabeth as she started to shake with fear.

"I am here to finish the job I set out to do. If I am going to hang for murder then I might as well kill you as well," replied Rosemary.

"My brother and my friend will come upstairs in a moment, so you had better go quickly or they will contact the police and you will be arrested," said Elizabeth.

"I saw your brother leave the house a while ago and, as for your friend, she will not be much help to you, as she is asleep downstairs in a chair," said Rosemary.

"What are you going to do to me? Shoot me?" asked Elizabeth.

"No, I am not going to shoot you as the gun will make too much noise. I think suffocating you will be a much better way of seeing you die," replied Rosemary.

"I think you had better leave before I scream the place down," shouted Elizabeth.

"Please do not threaten me," said Rosemary.

She then grabbed hold of Elizabeth's hair and pulled her head back. Elizabeth gave a slight squeal so Rosemary put her other hand over Elizabeth's mouth to stop her making a sound.

"You had better stay quiet or else I will really make you suffer," said Rosemary.

Rosemary then let go of Elizabeth and got out her handgun and aimed it at Elizabeth's head.

"If you shoot me you will wake up my friend Emily and then you will never get away with murder!" said Elizabeth.

"Why don't you just let me go and then you can just walk out of here without anyone ever knowing that you were here," Elizabeth told her.

"I will never be free because there are police everywhere looking for me and it is all your fault!" shouted Rosemary.

Ernest who was in the next room could hear what was being said and although he was very weak he still managed to get out of bed and creep downstairs.

"Emily, wake up," said Ernest.

He then put his hand over Emily's mouth so that she could not speak loudly.

"Rosemary is upstairs in Elizabeth's bedroom. You have to go and get the police right away, but warn them that she is armed," said Ernest.

"She must have got in through the back door as it is not locked," said Emily.

"Yes, I know. Please go now, Emily, as we do not have much time!" said Ernest.

"What are you going to do?" asked Emily.

"Do not worry about me, just do as I ask and leave the door slightly open so that the police can get in," he told her.

Emily carefully opened the door trying not to make a sound; she then ran outside to get the police, whilst Ernest crept back upstairs. Ernest could see Rosemary pacing up and down the room as the door was slightly ajar; she still had the gun in her hand and she was waving it around. Ernest picked up an oil lamp that was on the landing table, he then slowly opened the bedroom door as Rosemary was facing the opposite way and he suddenly leapt into the bedroom and threw the lamp at her. The lamp hit Rosemary on her head and knocked her to the floor and as she fell she dropped the gun so Ernest quickly picked it up.

"You bastard, you will not get away with this!" shouted Rosemary.

"Get up off of the floor," said Ernest.

Rosemary stood up and saw that Ernest had his arm in a sling as he had been shot, so she threw herself at him and elbowed him right in his wound. Ernest was hurting badly but he still kept hold of the gun and aimed it at her.

"Sit down in that chair," he told her.

"Do not start ordering me about, Ernest, it really does not suit you," said Rosemary.

"Shut up and sit down!" shouted Ernest.

"Why should I? You are not going to shoot me, you are too much of a coward," said Rosemary.

"I said sit down!" shouted Ernest.

Rosemary could see by the look on Ernest's face that he was extremely angry, so she walked towards the chair, but just as she was about to sit down the police came running upstairs and into the bedroom. Ernest turned to look at them which gave Rosemary an opportunity to try and get away. She pushed Ernest so hard he almost fell over and he dropped the gun, so Rosemary quickly picked it up and aimed it at the policemen.

"Put the gun down!" one of the policemen told her.

"Be quiet and let me think," said Rosemary.

"It is over, Rosemary, you might just as well give yourself up before anyone else gets hurt," said Ernest.

"Get over there with the others," she told him.

Ernest moved towards the door and stood beside the policemen. Rosemary still aimed the gun at them all so they did not dare move. She then pushed the chair towards the window and stood on it so that she could climb on to the window ledge and she pushed the window wide open.

"Come down from there before you fall," said the policeman.

"Just stay back or I will jump," Rosemary told them all.

"Please just give me the gun and then come down," said the policeman.

"Do you really think I am stupid enough to come down from here just so you can arrest me?" said Rosemary.

"Would you prefer to jump from a window then?" asked Ernest.

"You can go to hell. This is your fault anyway!" shouted Rosemary.

Rosemary then looked at Elizabeth and started to laugh hysterically, but Elizabeth did not say a word, she was too frightened at what she might do next. Suddenly as everyone stood watching her make a complete fool of herself, one policeman rushed towards Rosemary, but she fired a shot into the room and everyone had to dive for cover. Rosemary was not sure if she had shot anyone or not, but she still started to panic. She then looked around at everyone and she knew she had no way of escaping; so she moved forward on the window ledge and before a policeman could stop her she jumped to her death.

Ernest walked towards Elizabeth and he sat on the edge of her bed and she just put her arms around him and held him really tightly.

"It is over now, Rosemary cannot hurt you anymore," said Ernest.

"I was so frightened," said Elizabeth as she began to cry.

"I know, so was I," said Ernest.

"I will have to take statements from you both," said the policeman.

"Yes, of course. Can you just give us a few minutes first?" asked Ernest.

"Yes, certainly," replied the policeman.

Elizabeth lay in bed shaking through shock and Ernest tried to calm her down as much as he could.

"Where is Emily?" asked Elizabeth.

"I think she is making some tea for everyone," replied Ernest.

"How are you feeling, Mrs Thomas?" asked a policeman.

"I feel relieved that it is all finally over," replied Elizabeth.

"Yes and you can at least get back to normal now," said the policeman.

"I don't know how you can say that. Just take a good look at me. I am never going to be normal again!" cried Elizabeth.

"Calm down, Elizabeth, he did not mean it like that," said Ernest.

"Then he should think before he speaks," Elizabeth told him.

Ernest just looked at the policeman and did not know what to say to him and the policeman looked very embarrassed.

"Tea is ready downstairs," said Emily. "Would you like a cup?" she asked Elizabeth.

"No, I just want to be left alone," replied Elizabeth rather rudely.

Ernest went back to bed and the doctor came to look at his wound again, as Rosemary had elbowed him very hard in his shoulder. The doctor told him that his wound was fine and healing nicely, but he was badly bruised where he had been hit by Rosemary.

A while later Elizabeth's brother William returned and when he found out what had happened he was shocked and also angry because he had not been there to protect his sister.

"I am so sorry, Elizabeth. I should have been here for you," said William.

"It was not your fault. You were not to know that Rosemary was going to come here," said Elizabeth.

"But if anything had happened to you I would never have been able to forgive myself," said William.

"At least it is all over now. I just want to forget about it," said Elizabeth.

Once Ernest was well enough he went back to his parents' house and a few weeks later he was back at work. Elizabeth was given a wheelchair to get about in and once her bandages were removed she had a nurse visit her every day.

"Soon you will be able to get out of that wheelchair and start learning to walk again," said the nurse.

"I doubt that very much," said Elizabeth.

"Of course you will," Emily told her.

"How would you know? It is not your legs that are broken," said Elizabeth.

"I am only trying to help," said Emily.

"Well, I do not need anyone's help. So why don't you all just leave me alone!" shouted Elizabeth.

"Take no notice, Emily. Elizabeth is feeling very low at the moment, which is understandable after what she has been through," said the nurse.

"But she does not have to take her anger out on me. I have not done anything wrong," said Emily.

"You are the closest person to her, so therefore you are bound to take the brunt of her anger," said the nurse.

A short time later Ernest arrived, but Elizabeth was in no mood to socialise with anyone.

"Hello, Elizabeth. How are you feeling?" asked Ernest.

"Well, I have not been running around all day if that is what you think," replied Elizabeth.

Ernest looked at Emily and she just raised her eyebrows at him and Ernest did not know what to say.

"Would you like me to make some tea?" asked Emily.

"Well you do not expect me to get up and make it, do you?" said Elizabeth.

"Why are you being like this? Emily is only trying to help," said Ernest.

"All the help in the world is not going to make me walk again, is it?" said Elizabeth.

"Will you stop feeling sorry for yourself because in a few weeks you will be up walking again," said the nurse.

"Do not patronise me. I know for a fact that I am never going to walk again. So why are you all giving me false hope?" asked Elizabeth.

"You will never know until you try," said the nurse.

"You try sitting in this chair all day and see how it feels," shouted Elizabeth.

"I am not going to argue with you, Elizabeth, I am here to help you. But if you are ever going to walk again you have to be determined and stop blaming everyone else," said the nurse.

"But it is not my fault I am like this," said Elizabeth.

"It is not your friend's fault either," said the nurse.

"The nurse is right, Elizabeth, you should listen to what she is telling you," said Ernest.

"What would you know?" asked Elizabeth.

"I know you are being very pig-headed and blaming everyone else for what has happened and it is totally unfair," said Ernest.

"Well if anyone is to blame for this it is you. I warned you what Rosemary was like and you would not listen, you even told me not to go to the police," said Elizabeth.

"But I did not realise she would go this far," said Ernest.

"It is a bit late to say that now!" she shouted.

"I think I had better be going," said Ernest, looking quite down in the dumps.

"Yes, go on, just walk away. That is more than I can do, isn't it?" said Elizabeth.

Ernest walked out of the house feeling quite humiliated by Elizabeth's sudden outburst and he was almost in tears.

"How could you speak to Ernest like that? It is not his fault what Rosemary did to you. All Ernest has ever done is love you," said Emily.

"Well perhaps I do not feel the same about him anymore, after all, I warned him what Rosemary was capable of and he just did not listen to me," said Elizabeth.

"You really have changed. Do you know that if you are not careful you are going to lose everyone that has ever cared about you," said Emily.

"Good, I do not need anyone," said Elizabeth.

"We shall see," said Emily, getting rather angry.

Ernest did not visit Elizabeth for a while, but he did see her brother William to ask how she was doing.

"Elizabeth is being very difficult with everyone at the moment, but I can understand how she feels. It must be terrible for her not knowing whether or not she will ever be able to walk again," said William.

"I just wish I could talk to her, but she does not seem to want to know me anymore," said Ernest.

"She just needs a bit of time. I am sure everything will turn out fine in the end," said William.

"I hope you are right," said Ernest.

One morning Emily put the breakfast on the table but Elizabeth refused to eat it.

"What is wrong with it?" asked Emily.

"Nothing. I just do not want you waiting on me that is all. If I want some breakfast I shall make it myself," said Elizabeth.

"Fine, do it yourself in future," shouted Emily.

Elizabeth sat in her chair and stared at the wall. She did not even acknowledge William when he arrived at her house with Grace.

"I do not know what has got into Elizabeth lately; she is behaving like a spoilt child," said Emily.

"I think we are all going to have to be a bit patient with her. We should stop fussing around her so much. Let her do things for herself a bit more, that way she might feel a little bit better in herself," said William.

"Yes, perhaps you are right," said Emily.

After William left for work Emily tidied up the house, but she hardly spoke to Elizabeth for the rest of the day. Emily went upstairs to put clean bedding on the beds, but whilst she was upstairs she heard Elizabeth scream, so she quickly came running down to see what was wrong.

"I have spilt boiling water over my arm!" cried Elizabeth.

"What were you trying to do?" asked Emily.

"I was trying to make a pot of tea," replied Elizabeth.

Emily looked at Elizabeth's arm and bandaged it up; she then made Elizabeth a pot of tea herself.

"Next time you want a cup of tea ask me and I will make it," Emily told her.

"But I need to do things for myself," said Elizabeth.

"You are still weak and you have not got the use of your legs yet. So how can you expect to do anything?" said Emily.

"I know that, you do not have to keep reminding me," said Elizabeth, as she began to cry.

"Oh, Elizabeth, please don't cry, I did not mean to get angry with you," said Emily.

"I am just so scared that I might not ever walk again," said Elizabeth.

"I know you are. But you have got to think positive," said Emily.

Later that evening Ernest decided to visit Elizabeth as he had not seen her for a while and he was hoping that she was in a better mood than when he last saw her.

"Hello, Emily. How is Elizabeth?" asked Ernest.

"Still very moody I'm afraid," she replied.

"Hello, Elizabeth, I have brought you some flowers," said Ernest.

"Why? I am not dead yet, even though I look it stuck in this chair all day," said Elizabeth.

Ernest looked at Emily and she whispered to him.

"I did warn you," she told him.

"I shall leave the flowers here; if you do not want them you can throw them away," said Ernest.

Ernest then walked towards the door and Emily followed him.

"Do not take it too seriously. I think Elizabeth is worrying about whether she will ever walk again and she is snapping at everyone," said Emily.

"Nevertheless, I think it will be best if I do not come around anymore, well not until Elizabeth asks me to," said Ernest.

Ernest once again felt very humiliated because of Elizabeth and Emily was not too pleased with her either.

"If you are not careful you are going to lose Ernest altogether. Is that what you really want?" asked Emily.

"I do not know what you are talking about," replied Elizabeth.

"Yes, you do. Ernest brought those flowers here for you and you did not even have the decency to say thank you to him; all you did was insult him," said Elizabeth.

Elizabeth did not answer Emily, she just sat in her chair and ignored her.

When William arrived to collect Grace, Emily told him about Elizabeth's behaviour towards Ernest, but William told her to let Elizabeth get on with it.

"But I could tell that she has really upset him," said Emily.

"Do not worry, I shall call in to see Ernest before I go home," said William.

After William had left, Emily cooked the dinner, but when she put it on the table Elizabeth refused to eat it.

"Why don't you want it?" asked Emily.

"I am not hungry," replied Elizabeth.

"But you need to eat something to keep your strength up and do not forget the nurse will be here tomorrow to help you start walking again," said Emily.

"I do not know why she is bothering. All I am going to be doing is learning to walk with crutches," said Elizabeth.

"But that is just the beginning; before you know it you will be walking on your own. Now come and eat your dinner," Emily told her.

"I just said I did not want it, now stop fussing and leave me alone!" shouted Elizabeth.

"Fine, I will," said Emily.

Emily then went upstairs and packed some clothes, she then picked up Lizzie walked out of the door and made her way to William's house, leaving Elizabeth on her own.

Elizabeth managed to wheel herself over to the settee; she then lifted herself out of the wheelchair and fell asleep on the settee.

The next morning William came to see Elizabeth to make sure that she was alright, but she told him to leave as she did not need anyone. William did not argue with his sister as he knew she was just being stubborn and he did not want to make the situation worse, so he just left her to be on her own.

A short time later the nurse arrived. She gave Elizabeth some crutches and helped her out of her wheelchair, but Elizabeth's legs were still very painful.

"Take your time, dear," said the nurse.

"It hurts," cried Elizabeth.

"It will hurt for a while, but the more you use your legs the easier it will get," said the nurse.

Elizabeth held on to her crutches and slightly moved one of her legs, but the other leg seemed to drag behind.

"Just take things slowly, Elizabeth, you are doing very well," said the nurse.

The nurse called in to see Elizabeth every day and Elizabeth was actually pleased with the company, as she had not seen anyone for quite a few days since she and Emily had fallen out.

But a few days later out of the blue Emily arrived at Elizabeth's house. She was interested to know how Elizabeth was getting on with the use of her crutches.

"Elizabeth is doing marvellously well," said the nurse.

"If you had not run off to stay at William's house, you would have known how well I was doing," said Elizabeth.

"If you had not been so rude and pig-headed, I would not have gone to William's house in the first place," said Emily.

"Ladies, ladies, please stop arguing. Elizabeth has a lot of work to do and does not need all of these interruptions," said the nurse.

"Perhaps I should just go back to William's house then," said Emily.

"Yes, do that," Elizabeth told her.

Elizabeth knew deep down that she was in the wrong, but she just needed to take out her frustration on someone.

After Emily had left Elizabeth started to cry; she realised how cruel she was being and to her best friend of all people.

"Now, now, wipe those tears. We have got a lot of work to do over the next few months and I am not going to have you feeling sorry for yourself. I am going to get you walking again, if it is the last thing I do," said the nurse.

Elizabeth looked up at the nurse and smiled.

"Do not just stand there, get moving," the nurse told her.

As Emily was almost at William's house she saw Ernest.

"Hello. Where are you going?" she asked.

"I was just going to see Elizabeth as I have some time off this morning. I thought perhaps things might have calmed down a bit," said Ernest.

"Well, I hate to tell you this but things have got a lot worse. Elizabeth is just unbearable to be around," said Emily.

"Oh I see. Perhaps I should just stay away then," said Ernest.

"I would if I were you," said Emily. "I am just on my way to William's house. Would you like to share a pot of tea with me?" asked Emily.

"I would love to," replied Ernest.

After the nurse had left Elizabeth's house Elizabeth started to feel quite lonely and she kept looking out of the window to see if anyone was about. After a while she kept looking at the clock as she knew William should have finished work by now, but she got bored with waiting for him and in the end she fell asleep.

As the next week passed Elizabeth had still not seen anyone apart from the nurse and she was beginning to regret all that she had said to her friends. But the nurse had informed Emily of Elizabeth's progress and it was she that had suggested that they stay away for a while, as she wanted to make Elizabeth realise that she did need her friends after all.

When the nurse arrived a few days later Elizabeth was sitting in her chair crying.

"Now what is all this for?" asked the nurse.

"I miss my friend Emily and my brother. I did not mean to say all those things to them, but I just get so angry at times," said Elizabeth.

"I know. I can understand how you feel, I see people in your condition all the time. Some people cope really well and others don't," said the nurse.

"I suppose I am one of those people that doesn't cope well," laughed Elizabeth.

"Yes, I suppose you are," said the nurse smiling. "Come on, let's see what you can do today," she told Elizabeth.

Elizabeth stood up with the help from the nurse and then she used her crutches to slowly walk by herself.

"You are doing extremely well. You are getting much more confident, which is a good thing," said the nurse.

"I feel a lot better in myself now," said Elizabeth.

"Good," said the nurse.

The nurse stayed with Elizabeth for quite a few more hours and as she left she saw Ernest standing outside.

"If you have come to see Elizabeth she is inside the house, not out here," said the nurse smiling at him.

"I was just wondering whether or not to go and see her," said Ernest.

"I would. I think she will be pleased to see you. She has calmed down a lot since she has been walking with her crutches," said the nurse.

"She is not going to bite my head off, is she?" asked Ernest.

"No, I don't think so," replied the nurse.

Ernest knocked at the door and then walked into the house and when Elizabeth saw who it was she was extremely pleased to see him.

"How are you?" asked Ernest.

"Very well, thank you. I am walking better now that I have my crutches to help me and the nurse has been absolutely wonderful," said Elizabeth.

"I am really pleased for you and I have missed you," said Ernest.

"I have missed everyone," said Elizabeth smiling.

"My brother Joseph and his wife have been here visiting my parents. He looks very well. He was shocked when I told

303

him about what Rosemary did to us and he has said that you are welcome to go and stay at his house in London if you need a break away," said Ernest.

"Oh that is nice of him," said Elizabeth.

"He has asked me to go as well so you will not have to travel on your own," said Ernest.

"I don't know, I will have to think about it," said Elizabeth.

"Well, the offer is there if you change your mind," said Ernest.

"It's not that I don't want to go, it's just that I have the nurse in every day to help me walk and I need to keep it up," said Elizabeth.

"Well, I am sure that if you do your exercises every day, the nurse will not mind if you take some time away," said Ernest.

"I suppose not. I will speak with her first to see what she says," said Elizabeth.

"I saw Emily and William earlier today," said Ernest.

"How are they?" asked Elizabeth.

"They are fine but I think they are missing you," he told her.

"I have been rather horrible, haven't I?" said Elizabeth.

"Yes, I hate to admit it but you have," replied Ernest.

"Do you think they will ever forgive me?" asked Elizabeth.

"Oh I am sure they will. I will speak to them later and let them know that you did not bite my head off this time," laughed Ernest.

"Would you like a cup of tea?" asked Elizabeth.

"Ummm, yes please," replied Ernest.

"You had better go and make it then," laughed Elizabeth.

"And there was I thinking you were getting about a lot better," said Ernest.

"I cannot hold my crutches and tip boiling water into a teapot," she told him.

"I suppose I had better do it then, before I die of thirst," smiled Ernest.

Elizabeth just looked at him and started giggling.

The next morning William came to see Elizabeth before going to work, but before entering the room he put he head around the door and smiled at her.

"Is it safe to come in?" he asked her.

"Yes, of course it is. I am really pleased to see you," said Elizabeth.

"Ernest said that you are a lot happier. It is good to see the old Elizabeth back with us again," said William.

"I am so sorry for the way I have been behaving recently," said Elizabeth.

"It does not matter anymore. All I care about is seeing you happy," said William.

"Is Emily going to speak to me again?" asked Elizabeth.

"Yes, of course she is. She told me that she is coming to see you later today, so please be nice to her," said William.

"I will," Elizabeth told him.

William did not stay very long at Elizabeth's house because he had to go to work, but before he left he reminded Elizabeth to watch her manners in front of Emily.

"I will behave, I promise," said Elizabeth.

A while later the nurse arrived to help Elizabeth with her exercises.

"You look a lot happier today," said the nurse.

"Yes, I am. I had a long talk with Ernest last night and my brother came to see me earlier. I think they now understand why I have been so miserable lately. But now I am getting around a bit better on my crutches I feel a lot happier," said Elizabeth.

"Good, that is what I like to hear. Now let's get you up so you can show me what you are capable of doing," said the nurse.

"I am still finding it quite difficult to put pressure on my right leg," said Elizabeth.

"You will for a while, but that should get much better in time," said the nurse.

Elizabeth took a few steps and then stopped for a rest, but as she started to walk again she did not realise that Emily had come into her house and was watching her.

"Well done!" said Emily as she clapped her hands.

Elizabeth looked at her and smiled.

"Elizabeth is doing remarkably well, isn't she?" asked the nurse.

"Yes, she is. I never would have thought you were walking already," said Emily.

"Do not give Elizabeth all the praise. I have also given her a lot of encouragement," smiled the nurse.

"It is true. If it was not for the nurse I would still be sitting on my backside," laughed Elizabeth.

"Well, do not stand there talking; we have got a lot of work to do," said the nurse.

"She is very bossy, isn't she?" laughed Elizabeth.

"I heard that," said the nurse.

Elizabeth and Emily looked at each other and just burst into fits of laughter.

Later that evening Emily cooked a dinner and invited William and Ernest to join them and they all had a lovely evening together.

CHAPTER EIGHTEEN

A few weeks later Elizabeth decided to go to London with Ernest to visit his brother Joseph, but before she left the nurse told Elizabeth that she had to keep doing her exercises.

"The more you practise the better you will get. I know it seems like a long process but you have to persevere because it is not just going to happen overnight," said the nurse.

"Don't worry, I will make sure Elizabeth practises her walking," said Ernest.

When they arrived in London Elizabeth was really pleased to see all the wonderful sights again and it had not changed at all since she had left.

As they arrived at Joseph's house he came out to greet them, then Ernest carried Elizabeth into the house whilst Joseph took their luggage inside.

"It is really nice to see you again, Elizabeth. I hope you will enjoy your stay with us," said Joseph.

"I am sure I will; thank you for inviting me," said Elizabeth.

Ernest brought Elizabeth's wheelchair into the house and helped Elizabeth into it.

"Would you like some tea? Or something a bit stronger?" asked Joseph's wife.

"Tea will be fine, thank you," replied Elizabeth.

"How are you feeling now?" asked Joseph.

"It has been quite a struggle but I am determined to one day walk without my crutches," replied Elizabeth.

"It is good that you are thinking so positively," said Joseph.

"It must have been a terrible ordeal for you, but you seem to be coping very well," said Joseph's wife.

"I did not cope very well at first as Ernest will tell you, but then I realised how horrible I was being to the people that cared for me and I knew I had to change," said Elizabeth.

"Yes, you were rather horrible to me, but I found it in my heart to forgive you," said Ernest.

"Ernest has told me that you design your own clothes," said Joseph's wife.

"Yes, I do," replied Elizabeth.

"Perhaps I can have a look at them the next time I am in Yorkshire," said Joseph's wife.

"Yes, of course, I would be more than willing to show you them," said Elizabeth.

"Do you still paint at all?" asked Joseph.

"I have not painted for a while as I have been concentrating on my dressmaking business, but painting will always be my first love," replied Elizabeth.

A short time later Ernest carried Elizabeth upstairs so that she could wash and change for dinner. Once dinner was over they all sat and watched Joseph playing the piano.

"Joseph plays very well, doesn't he?" said Elizabeth.

"I can play better than him," smiled Ernest.

"I did not know you could play the piano," said Elizabeth.

"I am full of surprises, aren't I?" he laughed.

Ernest then sat next to his brother and they played the piano together. They started off playing slowly and gradually got faster and faster, until they fell about laughing.

"That is enough for me," said Joseph looking exhausted.

"You are getting old, that is your trouble," laughed Ernest.

"Yes, I think I must be," said Joseph smiling.

Ernest then looked at Elizabeth and sat down near her.

"Are you alright?" he asked.

"I am a bit tired after that long journey," replied Elizabeth.

"Would you like me to carry you upstairs?" he asked.

"Yes, please," she replied.

"It was quite an enjoyable evening, wasn't it?" said Ernest.

"Yes it was. Your brother and his wife have made me feel very welcome in their home," said Elizabeth.

The next morning after breakfast Elizabeth and Ernest spent the day looking around London. Ernest walked for miles whilst Elizabeth sat in her wheelchair being pushed by him.

"Shall we go and get something to eat and drink?" asked Ernest.

"Yes, alright, I am rather hungry," replied Elizabeth.

"I just want to sit down as my feet are aching," he laughed.

"Where are we going to go after we have finished our tea?" asked Elizabeth.

"I thought perhaps we should go back to my brother's house as you still have your exercises to do," replied Ernest.

"Oh, do I have to do them today?" asked Elizabeth.

"Yes, you do. Remember what the nurse told you? The more you practise the better you will get," said Ernest.

"Yes I know," said Elizabeth sarcastically.

When they got back home Ernest gave Elizabeth her crutches and helped her up on her feet and she started to walk very slowly, but she suddenly went quite red in her face as she saw Joseph standing in the doorway watching her.

"Sorry, I did not mean to embarrass you. You are doing extremely well, you should be very proud of yourself," said Joseph.

He then left the room so that Elizabeth could continue with her exercises without being interrupted.

That evening Joseph and his wife invited Elizabeth and Ernest out with them to watch a show. Elizabeth was not keen on the idea as she felt embarrassed in case people stared at her because she was in a wheelchair, but they all persuaded her to change her mind and she eventually went out with them.

As they arrived at the theatre Ernest carried Elizabeth to a seat as she did not want to be seen sitting in the wheelchair.

After a few minutes had past Elizabeth heard someone call to her and when she looked around she noticed a man and lady who she knew as she had painted for once before.

"Hello, how are you both?" asked Elizabeth.

"We are very well, thank you," replied the lady.

"Would you like to join us for a drink?" asked Elizabeth.

"That would be lovely, thank you," replied the gentleman.

Elizabeth introduced the couple to Ernest and they all sat down together and had a drink.

"We had better go to our seats in a minute as the show is about to start," said Joseph.

They all left their drinks on the table and made their way inside the theatre and Ernest lifted Elizabeth in his arms and carried her to her seat and it was then that the man and woman started to look at her quite strangely.

"Why were you carrying, Mrs Thomas?" asked the gentleman.

Ernest looked at Elizabeth and could see that she felt uncomfortable and this was one reason why she had not wanted to go to the theatre in the first place.

"I had a accident a while ago and I have lost the use of my legs, but hopefully I will be able to walk again one day," replied Elizabeth.

"Oh I see," said the gentleman.

"You poor dear, that must have been terrible for you," said the lady.

"It was at first but I am used to it now," said Elizabeth.

"But you used to be so agile, it must be so upsetting for you having to be carried around like a baby," said the lady.

"It is really not a problem," said Elizabeth.

Ernest could see that Elizabeth was getting rather agitated as the lady and gentleman would not let the subject drop.

"I do not think I could be as brave as you, my dear, I would be devastated if I could not walk again," said the lady.

"Well, hopefully one day I will be able to walk again," said Elizabeth.

Elizabeth looked at Ernest and raised her eyebrows, as if to say I wish they would be quiet.

"Are you alright?" asked Ernest.

"No, not really. I would prefer it if you took me back to Joseph's house," said Elizabeth.

"Yes, of course," said Ernest, as he lifted her in his arms.

"Where are you going? If you do not hurry up you will miss the beginning of the show," said the gentleman.

"Leave Mrs Thomas alone; she cannot hurry up because she cannot walk," said the lady.

"I am so sorry," said the gentleman.

"If you must know Ernest is taking me to the toilet and then he will have to wipe my bottom because as you keep telling me I cannot use my legs," said Elizabeth.

"Oh I say!" said the lady looking rather shocked.

Ernest continued to carry Elizabeth out of the theatre and once they were outside he burst out laughing.

"You really told them, didn't you" he laughed.

"I also told you I did not want to come here tonight because I knew this would happen, but you would not listen to me. In fact, you never listen to me," said Elizabeth.

"I'm sorry," said Ernest.

"Just take me back to your brother's house," Elizabeth told him.

As they travelled home by carriage Elizabeth did not say a word to Ernest; all she kept thinking about were the lady and the gentleman and how insensitive they were. Then Elizabeth thought about herself for a few minutes and she also thought about Ernest and how all of this was affecting their relationship and it was then that she made a decision.

"Would you like a drink?" asked Ernest when they arrived home.

"No, thank you, I would like to go up to bed," replied Elizabeth.

"But it is still early," said Ernest.

"See, you never listen to what I want," Elizabeth told him.

"Alright, I'll take you to bed, if that is what you want," said Ernest.

Ernest carried Elizabeth upstairs and gently laid her down on the bed and then he sat beside her on the edge of the bed.

"I am sorry about tonight. In future I will listen to you and I will do what you ask," said Ernest.

"Ernest, there is no future for us," said Elizabeth.

"Of course there is. Why are you saying that?" asked Ernest.

"Because I want to be on my own," replied Elizabeth.

"You do not mean that, Elizabeth, I know you don't," said Ernest.

"Yes, I do," she told him.

"But I love you and I know you love me," said Ernest.

"How can you love me? Just take a good look at me," said Elizabeth.

"I do love you, you know I do," said Ernest.

"But I have changed. I am not the person you fell in love with," said Elizabeth.

"Just because you cannot walk does not mean I do not love you," said Ernest.

"Well perhaps I do not love you anymore," said Elizabeth.

"That is not true, is it?" he asked.

"Yes, it is. I do not love you anymore and I would like you to take me home tomorrow," said Elizabeth.

"Elizabeth, please don't do this, you cannot mean what you are saying," said Ernest.

"Well I do. I want to go home tomorrow and then I want you to leave me alone," said Elizabeth.

"Fine, if that is what you want then so be it!" said Ernest.

Ernest then walked out of the room and went downstairs; he then poured himself a large brandy and sat in a chair and sobbed. Elizabeth lay on her bed and could hear Ernest crying and it made her cry to think she had hurt him so badly. All Elizabeth wanted was for Ernest to be happy and she thought that it could never happen if she stayed with him, as she felt that she was a burden to him.

The next day Ernest made an excuse to his brother that Elizabeth was homesick. He did not tell his brother the real reason why they were going home, as he felt bad enough as it was without everyone else knowing his business.

When they arrived at Elizabeth's house Emily came running outside as she thought there was something wrong.

"Why are you back so soon?" asked Emily.

"You will have to ask Elizabeth that, seeing as she knows all the answers," replied Ernest.

Ernest carried Elizabeth into the house whilst Emily helped with the luggage.

"Elizabeth, please give me another chance that is all I ask," said Ernest.

"I'm sorry, I can't, it's over," Elizabeth told him.

Emily suddenly walked in with the luggage so Ernest left without even saying goodbye to anyone.

"Why is Ernest in such a mood? And why are you back so soon?" asked Emily.

"I do not want to talk about it," replied Elizabeth.

"What have you done, Elizabeth?" asked Emily.

"Just leave me alone," she told Emily.

"Fine, I will go and see Ernest then. He will tell me what is going on," said Emily.

"No, I do not want you to go and see him," said Elizabeth.

"Then tell me what is going on," said Emily.

"I have told Ernest it is over between us, I do not love him anymore," said Elizabeth.

"You have done what? Why? You know as well as I do that you still love him," said Emily.

"No, I do not," said Elizabeth.

"I really don't understand you. How could you do that to him?" asked Emily.

"Just leave me alone!" said Elizabeth as she began to cry.

"Fine, I will. I will go and see how Ernest is, after all, he does have feelings, unlike some people I know!" shouted Emily.

When Emily left the house to go and see Ernest, Elizabeth cried and cried. She did not mean to hurt him; she thought by ending their relationship it would give him a chance to find someone that he did not have to look after all the time.

All Elizabeth wanted was for Ernest to be happy and she did not think she could make him happy in her condition.

When Emily finally returned home she was furious with Elizabeth for what she had done to Ernest.

"All you do is think about yourself, you do not care about Ernest's feelings. He is at home right now sobbing his heart out and his mother is trying to console him," shouted Emily.

"It is for the best," said Elizabeth.

"Why is it?" asked Emily.

"It just is," replied Elizabeth.

"You are so selfish, it is a wonder you have any friends left," said Emily.

Elizabeth understood why Emily was so angry with her, but she still felt that she had done the right thing by letting Ernest go, even if it meant that she lost the man she loved.

Over the next few weeks Elizabeth had not heard from Ernest at all. She was missing him terribly though, but she thought that in time the loneliness would go.

"You do not seem your usual self today. Are you still missing that young man of yours?" asked the nurse.

"Yes, I miss him very much," replied Elizabeth.

"Well, tell him that," said the nurse.

"I can't," said Elizabeth.

"Why ever not?" asked the nurse.

"I ended our relationship because I did not want to be a burden to him," said Elizabeth.

"You poor dear, Ernest loves you and you love him, you should be together," said the nurse.

"But I cannot expect him to waste his life on me, I might never walk again," said Elizabeth.

"Well, I am going to make sure that you do!" said the nurse.

"If only it were that easy," said Elizabeth.

"Nothing in life is easy, but if you work hard enough you can achieve anything," the nurse told her.

Elizabeth practised her walking every day with the help from the nurse, but as each day passed Elizabeth started to get very down. She got fed up sitting indoors every day and she started to get bored, depressed and very lonely.

"What is wrong with Elizabeth? She looks so unhappy," asked William one day.

"I think she is missing Ernest, not that she will admit it though," replied Emily.

"Perhaps I should take her out for a while and speak to her," said William.

"I have tried talking to her but she does not seem to want to listen," said Emily.

"I cannot understand why she told Ernest it was over between them. I know for a fact she thought the world of him," said William.

"Perhaps she led us all to believe she thought the world of him. If she did think anything of him she would not have treated him in that way," said Emily.

"I know Elizabeth. I think she is hiding something from us. Elizabeth would have never treated Ernest badly without a good reason. I have only ever known Elizabeth to be kind to people, she always goes out of her way to give people help if they need it," said William.

"Well it is poor Ernest I feel sorry for, not Elizabeth," said Emily.

"I think you are being too hard on her, there has got to be a reasonable explanation for all of this," said William.

"Then go and talk to her if you think it will help," said Emily.

William sat down with his sister and asked her if she would like to go to the park with him for a while. Elizabeth was thrilled at the idea as she just wanted to get out of the house.

"I'll make some sandwiches for us to take," said William.

"Yes, alright," said Elizabeth.

William pushed Elizabeth in her wheelchair and when they arrived at the park he found a bench to sit on, which was by a small pond.

"It is lovely here, isn't it?" said Elizabeth.

"Yes, it is," replied William.

They sat together watching the ducks and swans and Elizabeth threw some bread for them to eat. Then suddenly some pigeons flew down near Elizabeth, so she gave them some bread as well.

"Are you alright, Elizabeth?" asked William.

"Yes, I am fine, thank you," she replied.

"I mean are you alright in yourself? It's just that you have been looking so sad lately and I do not like seeing you like that," said William.

"I have had a lot on my mind lately what with learning to walk again and trying to keep my business going," said Elizabeth.

"There is something that you are not telling me, isn't there?" asked William.

"No, of course not," replied Elizabeth.

"I know you better than anyone and I can see that you are missing Ernest. Why did you tell him you did not love him anymore? Because I know you do still love him," said William.

"There is no fooling you, is there?" smiled Elizabeth.

"No, there is not. Now answer my question," William told her.

"You are right, I do still love Ernest, but I want him to be happy. How can he ever be happy if he is with someone that cannot walk?" said Elizabeth.

"Is that what this is all about? Ernest loves you for the person that you are. If he did not want to be with you he would have walked away long ago, but because he cares so much about you he stayed with you," said William.

"But I will be a burden to him," said Elizabeth.

"Look how well you are walking with your crutches, you could not do that a few months ago. Every day is a day nearer to you getting better," said William.

"I just think Ernest will be happier finding someone else, someone that can run around and have some fun with him," said Elizabeth.

"Well he is not having much fun at the moment because all he thinks about is you and you are exactly the same; you are miserable without him," said William.

"It is for the best," said Elizabeth.

"No, you are wrong. The best thing would be if you both got back together and actually talked to each other about how you feel," said William.

"I do not think that Ernest will speak to me now anyway," said Elizabeth.

"Yes, he would if you explained to him how you feel," said William.

"I don't know," said Elizabeth.

"Just think about it, that is all I am asking," said William.

"You will not tell Emily about our conversation, will you?" said Elizabeth.

"Of course not, it will be our secret," replied William.

"I do not want you to say anything to Ernest either," said Elizabeth.

"I will not say anything to anyone. It is now down to you to decide what you want to do," said William.

"Can you take me for a wander around the park now?" asked Elizabeth.

"Yes, of course," replied William.

As William pushed Elizabeth through the park, she looked around and started to think about all the wonderful things that she was missing through being stuck indoors everyday.

"It is so nice to be here today, I am starting to get rather fed up being in the house all of the time," said Elizabeth.

"Well, why don't you start painting again?" said William.

"I never thought of that, what a good idea," said Elizabeth.

"You could do your exercises in the morning and then get the nurse to take you out so you can do your paintings and then I could come and collect you when I finish work," said William.

"Yes, I think I shall do that and then I will not get so bored," smiled Elizabeth.

Elizabeth had still not decided what to do about Ernest, so William did not mention him to her anymore. William had already had his say and now it was down to her to make the decision.

Elizabeth started painting the following week and she felt good to be out in the fresh air once more. She also still kept up with her exercises and was now able to walk around the house with just her crutches, but if she went on long distances she still had to use her wheelchair.

One day whilst Elizabeth was painting she saw Ernest walking by, so she called to him. Ernest looked across at her, but when he realised it was Elizabeth he carried on walking and totally ignored her. Elizabeth was devastated and she now knew that she had lost him for good and she thought that there was no point in even trying to explain her feelings to him anymore.

As the months past Elizabeth started to get on with her life without Ernest, although she never forgot him.

Elizabeth's son Adam, had now come home from boarding school for Christmas and Elizabeth started to get very excited as she decorated the Christmas tree.

"Oh, the tree looks lovely, Elizabeth," said Emily.

"Can I put the presents under the tree now?" asked Adam.

"Yes, of course, but after you have done that it is time for bed, as we have got to be up early for church in the morning," said Elizabeth.

"Yes, alright," replied Adam, rather reluctantly.

Elizabeth followed Adam upstairs but she had to hold on to the stair rail for support, as that was the easiest way for her. She then tucked her son into bed and gave him a kiss goodnight.

"You always look happy when Christmas is almost here, but I can sense that deep inside you are sad," said Adam.

"Of course I'm not," said Elizabeth.

"Mother, I know you and I know that you are sad. Is it because you are missing Ernest?" he asked.

"Yes, I do miss him very much," replied Elizabeth.

"Do you still love him?" asked Adam.

"Yes I do, but that does not mean that I do not still love your father," said Elizabeth.

"I know that. But if you still love Ernest then tell him because I want you to be happy," said Adam.

"It is not as easy as that. I do not think that Ernest wants to speak to me anymore, so it is best that I leave things just the way they are," said Elizabeth.

"But you should try and speak to him because I know deep down you two are meant to be together," said Adam.

"You are so young and yet so grown up at times," smiled Elizabeth.

"Next time you see Ernest go and speak to him. Do it for me," said Adam.

Elizabeth did not answer her son; she just gave him another kiss and left the room.

The next morning everyone got ready to go to church and Elizabeth sat in her wheelchair waiting for her brother to arrive. William pushed Elizabeth to the church as it was too far for her to walk with her crutches and Adam walked along beside her. As Elizabeth entered the church she saw Ernest sitting a few rows in front of her, but as he looked around and saw Elizabeth he suddenly walked out of the church.

"Quick, Mother, go and speak to him!" said Adam.

Elizabeth turned her wheelchair around and wheeled herself out of the church, but as she got to the door the brake locked and the wheelchair would not move.

"Ernest, wait!" called Elizabeth.

But Ernest was in no mood to speak to her.

"Ernest, please wait!" she shouted.

But Ernest just continued to walk away from her.

Elizabeth then lifted herself out of the wheelchair and called to him once more.

"Ernest, please wait, I love you!" she shouted.

Ernest suddenly stopped and looked around and he was shocked to see Elizabeth standing up by herself. Elizabeth then tried to walk towards him, but she only took about three steps and then fell to the ground. Ernest came rushing towards her to help her up and she threw her arms around him.

"I love you, I have always loved you, so please don't go," said Elizabeth.

"Do you realise you have just walked a few steps by yourself?" said Ernest.

"Yes, I know. It is surprising what you can do when you are in love," said Elizabeth.

"Why did you tell me that you did not love me anymore?" he asked.

"I felt like I was a burden to you and I did not want you to ruin your life by staying with me," replied Elizabeth.

"My life can only be ruined if you are not in it," said Ernest.

"I am so sorry, I never meant to hurt you. I love you so much," cried Elizabeth.

"Oh, Elizabeth, you mean everything to me. Without you I am nothing," said Ernest.

"I feel the same," she told him.

"Come on, let's get you back inside the church and do not think for one minute I am going to let you go again because I am not," smiled Ernest.

"I hope not," said Elizabeth, as they kissed.

When they arrived back at Elizabeth's house everyone was thrilled that Elizabeth and Ernest were back together again and they all had a celebration drink.

"See I told you that you were meant to be together, didn't I?" said Adam.

"Yes, you did, and you were right," said Elizabeth.

"Would you like to come here for Christmas dinner?" Emily asked Ernest.

"I don't know. It is up to Elizabeth really," he replied.

"Of course you can come here, you are more than welcome," said Elizabeth.

"Say yes, Ernest. William will be here as well," said Emily.

"Alright, the answer is yes," said Ernest.

On Christmas Day everyone opened their presents, but Elizabeth had something rather special for her son Adam.

"I was asked to give you this when you were old enough to appreciate it and I think that time has come," said Elizabeth, as she gave her son a box.

"What is it?" asked Adam.

"Open it and you will see. It belonged to your father and he wanted you to have it," said Elizabeth.

"It's a pocket watch," smiled Adam.

"Please treasure it as your father did," Elizabeth told him.

"Oh I will," said Adam.

"I have something for you as well, Ernest," said Elizabeth.

Elizabeth then gave Ernest a painting and when he unwrapped it he just stood and smiled.

"It is beautiful," said Ernest.

Elizabeth had given Ernest a painting of the big oak tree, the one they used to race each other to when they went out horse riding together.

"Now I have something for you," said Ernest as he gave Elizabeth a present.

Elizabeth also smiled when she opened her present, as Ernest had bought her a pair of new shoes.

"I want to see you walking in those very soon," he told her.

"Thank you, they are lovely," said Elizabeth smiling.

"It is good to see you smile. I have missed your smiling face," said Ernest.

After everyone had opened their presents they all sat down for Christmas dinner and later that afternoon Elizabeth's parents joined them for a Christmas drink.

"Oh, before I forget, my parents have invited you all to their New Year's Eve party," said Ernest.

"Oh how lovely," said Elizabeth's mother.

Elizabeth had one of the best Christmases ever that year and it was certainly one to remember.

"Elizabeth, are you ready yet? Ernest will be here soon to take you to his parents' house," said Emily.

"I am almost ready," she replied.

"I am going around William's house to see if he is ready. I will see you at the party," said Emily.

"Yes, alright," said Elizabeth.

A short time later Ernest arrived to take Elizabeth to the Lockwoods New Year's Eve party.

"Shall we have a drink here before we leave?" asked Ernest.

"Yes, alright," replied Elizabeth.

After they had drunk a couple of drinks Elizabeth and Ernest made their way to the Lockwoods house, but when they arrived the house was all dark and quiet.

"That's funny, there does not seem to be anyone here," said Ernest.

"Are you sure that your parents are having the party here and not somewhere else?" asked Elizabeth.

"I assumed it was being held here," replied Ernest.

"Let's have a look inside," said Elizabeth.

Ernest went inside first and Elizabeth followed him, but there was no one around.

"I think I heard something in the dining room," said Ernest.

Elizabeth held on to her crutches and followed Ernest to the dining room and as he opened the door there was an almighty cheer from everyone. Elizabeth looked surprised and shocked as the room was full of people.

"This is to congratulate you for being so brave and having the courage to persevere to walk again," said Mrs Lockwood.

"I don't know what to say. Did you know about this Ernest?" asked Elizabeth.

"Of course I did," he replied with a smile.

"Oh look, there are some of my old clients from London and my Aunt Beth is also here. How did you know how to get in touch with everyone?" asked Elizabeth.

"It was not hard. Do not forget Emily knew a lot of your clients whilst she lived in London with you," said Ernest.

"Oh, Emily, I might have known," laughed Elizabeth.

"Hello, Elizabeth. It is a nice surprise, isn't it?" asked Emily.

"It is a lovely surprise," said Elizabeth.

Elizabeth walked around on her crutches thanking everyone for making the evening so special for her, but as she was enjoying herself so much she did not realise the time.

"It is one minute until midnight," said Ernest.

As the clock chimed twelve everyone celebrated the New Year in and they all kissed and hugged one another.

"I can feel that this is going to be a really happy year for all of us," said Elizabeth.

"I think so as well, but there is one thing that could make me even happier," said Ernest.

"What is it?" asked Elizabeth.

"I would be a lot happier if you would say yes you will be my wife," said Ernest.

Elizabeth stood next to Ernest with a huge smile upon her face.

"Yes, yes, I will marry you," she told him.

"Now I am happier than I have ever been," said Ernest as he kissed her.

CHAPTER NINETEEN

Elizabeth and Ernest decided to get married in the spring and they married on 16th March.

Elizabeth looked stunning in her wedding gown and she could not wait to show it off to Ernest.

Elizabeth arrived with her father at the church and he helped her out of the carriage.

"Would you like me to hold your bouquet for you? As you will not be able to hold that whilst holding your crutches," asked her father.

"Yes, please," replied Elizabeth.

Elizabeth and her father walked towards the church and as they got to the door the organist started to play the wedding march tune, but Elizabeth suddenly stopped and looked at her father.

"What is it?" he asked.

Elizabeth took away her crutches and leaned them up against the door frame, she then took the bouquet from her father and held it in her hand. Then she put her arm in her father's arm and they slowly walked up the aisle together. Everyone looked around as Elizabeth made her way towards Ernest and when Ernest saw her walking up the aisle by herself his eyes just filled up with tears. Elizabeth had come a long way since being beaten up by Rosemary and Ernest was so proud of her; and although it was hard for her, Elizabeth was determined to walk to Ernest on her wedding day.

After they were married Ernest carried Elizabeth from the church and they then had their photographs taken. Elizabeth then picked up her crutches and told Ernest she needed five minutes by herself. She then walked around to the church cemetery and found her brother's grave.

"Such a lot has happened since you passed away, but I still think about you often. I wish you had been here with me today, I am so happy I could cry. I know you are looking down upon me and I hope wherever you are you are happy. If you see Edward please tell him I do still love him and I always will and give him two kisses for me, one from me and one from his son Adam and just remember I love you all," said Elizabeth.

Elizabeth then laid her bouquet on to her brother's grave. As Elizabeth was about to walk away she suddenly felt a cold breeze go through her and then she saw a vision of Edward standing in front of her. Edward smiled at her and then disappeared and it was then that Elizabeth knew that Edward had given her his blessing.

Elizabeth then walked back to Ernest and he kissed his new bride.

"Congratulations," shouted Emily.

Suddenly a little girl ran into Elizabeth and almost knocked her over, so her mother quickly ran after her and grabbed her hand.

"You must be more careful, Shirley," her mother told her.

"That's an unusual name," said Elizabeth.

"It is rather nice though, isn't it?" said Ernest.

"Yes, it is," replied Elizabeth.

"Perhaps we could call our firstborn daughter Shirley" laughed Ernest.

"Yes, perhaps we can," smiled Elizabeth.